PAY DIRT

ALSO BY SARA PARETSKY

PAY DIRT

A V.I. WARSHAWSKI NOVEL

SARA PARETSKY

WM

WILLIAM MORROW

An Imprint of HarperCollinsPublishers

PAY DIRT. Copyright © 2024 by Sara Paretsky. All rights reserved. Printed in the United States of America. No part of this book may be used or reproduced in any manner whatsoever without written permission except in the case of brief quotations embodied in critical articles and reviews. For information, address HarperCollins Publishers, 195 Broadway, New York, NY 10007.

HarperCollins books may be purchased for educational, business, or sales promotional use. For information, please email the Special Markets Department at SPsales@harpercollins.com.

FIRST EDITION

Designed by Michele Cameron

Library of Congress Cataloging-in-Publication Data has been applied for.

ISBN 978-0-06-301093-2

24 25 26 27 28 LBC 5 4 3 2 1

for Eve, part of my beating heart

PAY DIRT

1

NIGHTMARE

GUNSHOT. WHEN YOU hear it, you know it's not a backfire, not an M-80. Sprint up the stairs. Peter shoves past me into the room. I grab his arm. "You can't go in there blind. You don't know who's shooting, who they're shooting at."

He shoves me aside and plunges into the room.

A second shot, a third. Screams. I follow him in.

Blood, brain, bone. I slip in them. The air, acrid, thick with smoke. I can't see who's alive, who's injured, who has weapons. Stumble on Peter lying across Taylor's body, bellowing, "No! No!"

The cry woke me. I was weeping. I reached for the lamp switch, hand finding empty air. I was in a strange place, alone. Panic hit me. Taylor's mother had kidnapped me, I'd been jumped in a Chicago alley, I was in a KGB prison. I tried leaping out of bed, but the sheets were knotted around me like a mummy's tapes and I landed on the floor.

And finally remembered I was in Kansas. Lawrence. Not in a dump in Chicago's Uptown where Taylor Constanza had been murdered by their father. Taylor had died five months ago, but the nightmares wouldn't release their grip on me.

It was my own thrashing that had knotted up the sheets. I extricated myself, remade the bed. My sleep shirt was soaked through with sweat. I took it off, washed myself off in the B and B's small bathroom, put on a T-shirt. It was only three in the morning. I tried to go back to sleep.

I'd driven down to Lawrence to see Angela Creedy join an elite group of basketball players who'd broken the three-thousand-point lifetime scoring marker. She was a star on Northwestern University's team, a star attracting international attention. She was also a housemate of Bernardine Fouchard, Bernie to me, who was a hockey player and my sort of goddaughter.

Angela and her Northwestern Wildcats had beaten the hometown Jayhawks in last night's game, but it had been close, exciting to watch. Dozens of girls in Kansas regalia had crowded around Angela when she left the visitors' dressing room, thrusting their programs at her.

She'd squatted with easy grace to their head-level and signed their programs, chatting in a way that left the girls starstruck. When the crowd thinned, she joined me and Bernie in the hall, along with their other roommates. Angela and Bernie were close, so I'd grown close to her as well. The three other women I knew only in passing.

Angela embraced me. "Vic, I know it wasn't easy for you to come, but thank you! It means so much to have you here, especially since my mom couldn't make it. We're going downtown to celebrate. Come along, won't you, please?"

Angela's mother was a nurse in Shreveport. Her rare days off were spent caring for her own aging mother, and soaking her swollen feet in a eucalyptus bath.

"Yes, Vic, you should come," Bernie said. "We are going to a place called the Lion's Heart. Everyone on the team will be there."

"Thanks, babe, but the night belongs to Angela and your friends. I'll find some tamer form of entertainment."

Bernie Fouchard grabbed my arm as I moved away from the group. "Vic, you cannot go back to your room alone. When you are alone, you—" She flung her hands up, trying to think in English, but gave it up. "*Broies du noir*! You must be with other people."

I could guess the meaning. My smile tightened. "Bernie, don't pretend to know what I need or not. I'll be happier alone than in a noisy bar with drunk students."

She put both hands on my arm. "Vic, I only want you to be well, not to insult you!"

I pulled away, roughly. "You persuaded me to join you in Kansas. I'm glad I came, glad I got to see Angela in triumph, but that's my limit. Join your friends, have a good time, but not so riotous you can't be safe on the road tomorrow. Text me when you get back to Evanston."

She looked at me for a long moment, her expression disconsolate, but she finally joined the group around Angela. I had an impulse to cross over to her to apologize, but they left before I acted.

I'd driven to Lawrence by myself, needing privacy from the high-octane energy of five NCAA athletes, needing privacy most of all from Bernie's insistent hammering at me: when you fall, when you're injured, you get back on the ice *immédiatement!* She'd pressured me into coming down to watch Angela, which was probably a good thing, but she couldn't stop at one good thing. She relied on me as an example of women's strength; she needed me to be who I was last September, not who I'd become since Peter's and my Incident.

Peter Sanson was an archaeologist and director of a famed institute at the University of Chicago. He was my lover, and I was in love with him, which had not happened to me in many years. This made the Incident harder to overcome.

Taylor Constanza had been one of his second-year students. Taylor disappeared the week the fall term began. The parents were frantic, threatening to sue the university for dereliction of fiduciary responsibility and threatening Peter in more ominous language. Taylor was a trans femme who'd been on a month-long dig with Peter and five other students in August. The parents were claiming Peter had coerced their son into a sex change to fulfill his sexual fantasies.

It was a sickening scenario. When the police came up empty, I agreed to look. Sadly enough, Taylor had been easy to find. They were sheltering with other runaways in an Uptown firetrap. Taylor pleaded with me to keep the location secret; they were frightened of their parents, who'd reacted violently when they came out after the August dig.

I'd promised, but Peter felt he needed to let the school and the parents know that Taylor was safe but needed time away from both. The parents were furious with me and with the university, which in turn pressured both Peter and me to reveal the address. When we wouldn't, the parents hired another detective who easily followed the same trail as me. This second investigator ignored Taylor's plea for safety.

The next day I got a terrified text from the student. Their father had shown up, with a gun. By the time an ambulance arrived, father and child were both dead.

Afterward, Peter suffered in every way. One of the bullets had winged him. He needed multiple surgeries to recover from damage to his shoulder, and the pain was unrelenting.

He was also awash in guilt. Even though I'd told him the student was afraid of their parents, he'd felt he had to let Mrs. Constanza know I'd found her child. Peter had a high sense of responsibility to his students; he felt he'd let Taylor down badly. The university didn't make his life easier. Their lawyers deposed him along with everyone else on the August dig, hoping to prove Peter had never touched Taylor.

Peter knew he shouldn't blame me, but he did. If I hadn't been a detective, skilled at finding the hidden, he would have left matters to the university. He could have kept himself three removes from the carnage.

I knew I needed to cut him slack, but I'd been the one who stayed to comfort the other runaways in the apartment. I was the one who answered hours of cop questions at Area 2, while I still had bits of bone and brain on my clothes. I was also the one who spent hours on the phone with the dead student's mother. My own nerves were sheared to the root. I'd hung up on her, and ignored the university's demands that I make myself endlessly available to lawyers, both Mrs. Constanza's and the university's.

Peter and I wore each other out. We fought, made up, fought again. Peter had always been a steady person, not prone to furies. If we argued, he could almost maddeningly see my side as well as his own. Now it horrified him to see how easily he gave way to anger.

Finally, exhausted by his demons, he decamped to Malaga, Spain, where he was helping excavate a three-thousand-year-old Phoenician settlement on the shores of the Mediterranean. It was a relief for both of us when I dropped him off at O'Hare shortly before Christmas.

It was after he left that the nightmares began. Sometimes, like tonight, I'd re-enact the moment of Taylor's murder. Other times I'd have dreams about my mother. Gabriella had died of ovarian cancer when I was in my teens. I was an only child, born after numerous miscarriages. She was fierce in her love for me, but she pushed me also to be independent, to stand up for myself, not to settle for second best. Her loss left a hole that no other love ever completely filled.

Gabriella had been an immigrant in a neighborhood with many immigrants, but she'd also been a Jew in a neighborhood without them. The physical battles I'd fought on South Chicago's playgrounds, to defend her from the insults the local kids liked to chant, distressed both her and my father. Now, in my current nightmares, she was under attack and I was helpless to protect her.

After Taylor's murder, I started second-guessing my work decisions, forgot important meetings, left invoices unsent. I began retreating from my friends, taking long runs up the lakefront with the dogs, even avoiding my elderly downstairs neighbor. He was 1,000 percent in my court, but his constant fulminations against Peter wore on me. (*I thought he was better than those losers you usually bring around, but he's just as bad as that Murray Ryerson, only thinking of hisself.*)

It was Bernie Fouchard who forced open a crack in my shell, or rather, Bernie's mother, Arlette. Bernie herself had driven me to fury, with her badgering me on "getting back on the ice after a bad fall."

"People depend on you. Everyone is hurting in their lives, not only you, but only you can help people who are in trouble."

"I'm not a superhero and I'm not a robot. Trauma shatters me the way it does everyone. So take your platitudes and your naïveté back to the hockey arena."

She looked shocked and hurt, but she mercifully shut up and disappeared. In January, though, her mother flew to Chicago with the Canadiens. Her husband had been my cousin Boom-Boom's closest friend when the two of them played for the Blackhawks. Boom-Boom was Bernie's godfather, and when he died, he more or less bequeathed the godparenting to me.

Arlette Fouchard pushed past me into my apartment. "Bernardine has been telling me your troubles."

"Bernie thinks I'm made of titanium, not flesh and bone. She wants me to be something nonhuman. She and everyone else." Clients, friends, strangers who contacted me online, either wanting to know how to protect their trans children, or vilifying me for brainwashing a boy into thinking he was a girl, using language whose ferocity and obscenities were terrifying.

"Bernardine is not subtle or tactful," Arlette said, "but she understands you better than you are able to believe."

She moved into my kitchen and began washing the dishes I'd let stack up on the table and in the sink. I watched in irritation, but finally dug a clean towel from a drawer and dried the plates and put them away.

"Victoria, it's true that people depend on you, and that is a burden for you right now," she said when the last pot was scrubbed shiny. "I'm not here to persuade you otherwise. You witnessed something beyond bearing, a man murdering his own child. It is—is—*accablant*—something that can make the strongest person deranged.

"I'm here to speak to *you*. Not for your clients or your friends, but concerning what you need for your own nurture. If you don't have money, you need to work, *n'est-ce pas*? But if detecting work no longer nourishes you, then find new work. You need to stay in motion, though, unless you wish to become an opera heroine, some Juliette or Aida, locked in a tomb and dying out of martyrdom."

With the dishes done, she made tea, which I normally drink only when I'm sick. But I was sick, sick of myself, of the vileness and violence that surrounded me.

We took tea into my living room and sat on the couch, not speaking much. At length, she said, "Victoria, I only ask this of you: to be less harsh. With yourself, *bien sûr*, but with others as well. Most of us have been spared the horrors you saw, but these times are hard for everyone. The insults against you on social media, they are dreadful, but most people mean well, including my daughter. If she is *maladroite*, it is not out of malice. We all have seen too much of death, too much of anger from the strain of this Covid, from the strain of war and other violences, from the hastening of the death we all must face. Try not to be so severe."

She waited a moment for my response, but I couldn't give her one. She went into the kitchen again and put together an omelet, which she brought out to me in the living room. She left when I started eating. I took the dirty dishes back to the kitchen. It seemed wrong to put them in the scrubbed and shining sink, so I washed them.

The next day I began picking up the pieces of my practice. I still felt fragile, as if I were an uncooked egg whose shell might shatter at any moment, but Arlette was right: staying in motion created a rhythm that was in and of itself healing. I put to one side the question of whether I wished to continue to be an investigator and returned to work.

In February, when Bernie urged me to witness Angela's moment of glory, I was still feeling rocky, but I'd regained enough balance that I'd felt able to join her in Kansas.

2

CHANGING THE CLIMATE

THE FEBRUARY EVENING had turned cold during the game and the wind had picked up. When I left the field house, a gust pushed air back into my lungs. I bent down, choking, and was almost knocked over by a group of excited girls coming out behind me.

"She signed my program, too. *Love, Angela*," one was saying.

"It's not like she's in love with you, Rina—that's what she put on all our programs," another said scornfully.

"I think she was trying to say she loved all you girls for wanting to be your best in the world," an adult suggested.

I moved out of their way, smiling a little over the exchange, when a man running full tilt toward the field house barreled into me.

"Whoa," I cried. "Plenty of room here for everyone."

He ignored me but pelted on to where the girls were standing. He grabbed one by the arm and yanked her from the group.

"You're not to come near my daughter. Not ever!" He bellowed at the adult so loudly I could hear him above the wind and the sound of the cars exiting the lot.

I turned, dumbfounded. The girl he'd grabbed was the one who'd sighed so happily over Angela's signature. She started to cry now, silently, the wind crystallizing the tears on her lashes. I couldn't hear the response from the adult with the group. I trotted back into earshot.

"You've been suspended without pay, Perec." The man was still shouting. "That means you don't come near any children in my school district."

"You don't own the county, Santich, even if you did get your school board to suspend me. Ruthie's mom asked me to bring the girls, since she tested positive."

"Cady Perec?" I blurted, astonished by the interchange. "It's V.I. Warshawski." We'd met when I came down to Lawrence on a case a few years earlier.

"I don't care if you're Wyatt Earp's ghost," the man bellowed at me. "I'm talking to Perec, so mind your own business."

"You almost knocked me down, you·were so eager to make your daughter cry, so you are my business," I said.

Santich surprised me by looking down at his daughter. When he saw her tears, he put an arm around her and said in a soft voice, "I'm sorry, honey, sorry to get you upset. I'm just trying to protect you."

Just as quickly, he resumed his attack on Cady. "As for Lela Abernathy, if she thought you could be trusted with her daughter, I'll have a few words with her and Keith. I'll give the rest of you girls a ride home."

The girls pressed closer to Cady, who said, "Their parents are coming for them, Santich, just like you came for Rina, so don't get your undies in a bundle."

Several people had stopped to watch. Santich glared at Cady, me, at the onlookers, while his daughter turned her back on the other girls, perhaps embarrassed by her father. At that moment, one of the mothers arrived. A ripple of relief flowed through the group as she thanked Cady for chaperoning the outing.

"Was it wonderful?" she added to the girls. "I heard on the radio that the player from Chicago broke a record."

"She was awesome, Mom," her daughter said, but without enthusiasm: Santich had drained the excitement from the group.

In another few minutes the rest of the parents arrived, leaving only one girl with Cady. Santich told her he'd drive her home.

She looked at him stonily. "My mom wants Ms. Perec to take me home."

He put out a hand for her, but dropped it when he saw me and the other bystanders watching. He scowled, but shepherded his own daughter away.

"What was that about?" I asked. I didn't know Cady well, but molestation seemed out of character. Besides, if she'd been accused of molesting a student, what parent would trust their daughter with her?

"He and I had a policy disagreement," she said tightly. "I need to get Ruthie home."

She and Ruthie were headed into the parking lot when we heard another bellow from Santich. He was next to a Kia SUV with its doors open, but he'd seized someone by the shoulders and was roaring at him. The second man shook himself free.

Not your business, I reminded myself, but I walked over to them anyway. Two of the bystanders who'd been watching Santich with Cady tagged after me.

"Damn you, Garrity! Defacing my property and right out in public!"

"I wasn't defacing it, asshole. I was improving it. You should thank me."

Garrity was a thin man with a halo of wild hair. He was wearing an old army parka, unzipped to show a faded sweatshirt with the ubiquitous Jayhawk on the front.

"I'm calling the cops," Santich snarled. "You're going to be in front of a judge first thing tomorrow."

A squad car pulled up, but not from the city police; it had the university's seal on the door. The driver got out.

"What's going on here, folks?" he said. His southwestern twang was so thick I could barely make out the words, but that's the time-honored response of a cop to a family dispute.

"I want him ticketed," Santich said. "Vandalizing property."

"What'd you do this time, Trig?" the patrolman asked.

"Like I said to his royal heinie here, I was improving the look of his gas guzzler. Or at least, I was helping him let the world know he's aware of what he's doing."

Santich pointed to the back of the car. I followed the patrolman around and saw that Garrity had put a bumper sticker on, one of the

ones urban guerillas used to tag SUVs twenty years ago: I'M CHANG-
ING THE CLIMATE: ASK ME HOW.

"Just the fact you think I'm desecrating your guzzler tells me you
know you're destroying the planet," Garrity said. "Case closed."

Santich demanded that the patrolman arrest Garrity or at least
ticket him for defacing property.

"Daddy, please," Rina cried from the back of the SUV. "Can't
we go home? I'm freezing, and Mom texted, she wants to know where
we are."

"Yes, why don't you take your little girl home, Mr. Santich?" the
campus cop said. "Tomorrow if you still want to press charges, we'll
write him up, but let's all sleep on it. You, too, Trig. And get out of
this parking lot before I ticket you for vagrancy."

"Where were you when Lord Santich here was harassing Cady
Perec?" Garrity demanded. "It's okay for him to attack her in front
of a bunch of kids, but it's against the law for me to confront him?
That is justice in America, plain and simple, before you wrap it up in a
pretty package of Constitutional rights that only the rich get to have.
No wonder you got Perec fired, Santich: you're afraid she'll teach
your kid to think."

Santich lunged at him, trying to punch him, but the patrolman
grabbed his arm. "Not saying Trig doesn't deserve it, but you get on
home. You don't want your kid to see me writing you up for assault."

"What?" Trig cried. "He owns the county, so I deserve to get hit
by his platinum arm, but you make sure he goes home safe and sound?"

The patrolman's lips tightened. "Trig, you get off the university's
property in five or you'll be in a holding cell for the night."

Trig hunched down into the parka, scowling as fiercely as Santich,
but he shambled off in the direction of the campus. Santich climbed
into his Kia and roared out of the lot with a great squealing of rubber.

"That seems like a long-standing feud," I said to the campus cop.
"What was the business about Cady Perec?"

"If you don't know, it's not my job to tell you." The patrolman
got back in his car. He shut the door but didn't move until Trig was
off the premises. The remaining onlookers took off, leaving me alone
in the parking lot with my Mustang.

3

ON YOUR MARK

T HE PLACE I'D found to stay in was built into the side of a hill, so that the back was underground. The front, which had its own entrance, was glassed in.

When I got back, I sat by the picture window facing down to the town and searched online for news about Cady Perec. A local paper, the *Douglas County Herald*, had covered her troubles. When I'd been here before, Cady had taught social studies in one of the Lawrence schools, but she'd moved to a new consolidated school in Yancy, northwest of town.

Cady had come under fire for her segment on Douglas County in the 1850s and '60s. She'd put together a curriculum where kids acted out arguments over slavery, built a replica of the kind of shanties where Free State homesteaders lived, even tried to survive for a week on the meager rations the Free Staters scrounged.

Yancy parents had gotten riled up over a part of the curriculum dealing with the Delaware Nation, who had helped the Free Staters during the Civil War. It was hard to tell what had gone amiss from the *Herald*'s sketchy reports, but I read an account of a fiery school board meeting, where the board had voted to suspend Cady pending a full inquiry into her teaching methods.

The next week, a woman named Clarina Coffin had started picketing the school and writing rambling letters to the *Herald* about Indigenous rights. Trig Garrity had picketed with her. For the first few days, university students joined them, demanding that the full history of Indigenous people and of Black settlers in Kansas be told. And then parents showed up, shouting that they didn't want their kids indoctrinated with critical race theory.

Oh, and the chair of the school board was Brett Santich. Bad blood all the way round.

This was old news, or oldish, since it had happened last fall, shortly after the start of the school year. I didn't see any more recent news about Cady, but Trig's name popped up quite a few times, shouting at county or commission meetings on a variety of issues, or picketing construction sites. He seemed to have moved on from Cady Perec's woes, but a later story, really just a paragraph, announced that Yancy had suspended her without pay for the remainder of the year, with her contract terminated effective the following June.

I got ready for bed but didn't draw the curtains. I lay watching the lights twinkling around the town, every now and then punctuated by police strobes. Maybe it was Bernie and her friends, lighting up the town, hammering home the visitors' victory. Or maybe it was Trig Garrity. He was furious with Santich, the man with the platinum arm, and was breaking windows in downtown Lawrence to let off steam.

I slipped into sleep, thinking of the happy girls whose mood Santich had broken. Maybe that was why my demon dream woke me at three. It was a long time before I fell asleep again, but it wasn't really sleep, just that gritty state one step below wakefulness.

My phone jolted me fully awake at six. I was hoping for Peter, but the screen told me it was Bernie Fouchard. I let it go to voicemail, but as I was drifting off again, she called a second time, and then a third.

"Okay, Bernie, you woke me. Where's the fire?"

"It is not a fire, Vic, but Sabrina. We can't find Sabrina."

My brain was muzzy from sleeplessness. "Sabrina?" I echoed.

"Vic, please! Sabrina! You know her, my housemate, she plays soccer, you saw her only last night, you must remember her!"

I did remember, now that Bernie had goaded me. Sabrina was a soccer forward, apparently a leading scorer in the Big Ten conference. At the restaurant where I'd met Bernie and her friends for supper before the game, Sabrina had looked thin, almost to the point of anorexia, with a waxy pallor. I'd had trouble imagining her breaking through an opposing line to score.

"Sabrina isn't here. Did she say she was coming to see me?"

"She has said nothing because no one has seen her since last night." Bernie was shouting, her voice pitched high from fear. "Hear what I am saying! We don't know where she is."

"Wasn't she staying with you at that motel?"

"She was supposed to, but Amber says she never came to bed. We must leave for Chicago now. We must be back by five—Angela and I have practice, we all are past due with essays."

"Send Sabrina a text and tell her you have to leave without her."

"Of course we have done this! That is not the point."

I put my phone down and lay flat. I knew what the point was. I didn't want to hear it. Bernie continued for a minute, so loud I could make out her demand that I search for Sabrina. Finally the phone went silent.

I longed for sleep, that clean cool rest that knits the ravelled sleave of care, not the febrile state I'd been in before the phone rang. I lay still, trying to breathe, but I couldn't let go of fear, the fear that if I got involved, Sabrina would end up dead. I would be covered in blood and bone. All my friends would turn against me, but not as harshly as I would turn against myself.

I watched the eastern sky turn light, watched a sickly sun rise over the Kansas River Valley. I was going to drive back to Chicago later today myself. I had planned a run and a cortado at the Decadent Hippo before setting out, but when I tried to put on my sweats, my legs felt too heavy to lift. I tried to do some warmups, but I kept stopping mid leg lift or arm lift, unable to coordinate my movements.

I shuffled into a shower that my landlady had built in an old closet. I could pick up coffee and something to eat on my way out of town. When I came back into the room, wrapped only in a towel, my landlady was there. Norma Something. I'd corresponded with her about the room but couldn't remember her surname.

She apologized brusquely for showing up unannounced. "I'm on my way to work. A young woman is upstairs. She says she's your niece and she needs to see you. I didn't want to let her in without checking first—"

"Vic!" Bernie burst in behind her. "Vic, please! You have to help us."

"Of course I do," I said brittlely. "No consideration about my own obligations, let alone my state of my mind or state of dress, should come ahead of what you need."

"Oh, Vic, don't. Don't talk in that mean way. I can't stay on down here, and anyway, I don't have any idea how to start looking for Sabrina, but you would." Bernie wasn't a person who cried often, and when she realized she was crying, she brushed the tears away with an angry hand.

"Who is missing?" Norma asked.

I was still clutching the towel around my breasts. I put my T-shirt back on while Bernie explained Sabrina to my landlady. "She is a soccer player, for Northwestern University—we are all athletes in different sports. Sabrina rode with us from Chicago to watch our friend Angela Creedy play basketball. Now she is not in her room, she is not answering her phone. We have to drive back today, now, *enfin,* and where is she?"

"You don't think she hooked up with someone?" Norma asked drily.

The obvious explanation. I was so unraveled by the death of Peter's student I couldn't think simply anymore.

"Maybe," Bernie said doubtfully. "Of course, it is possible. In fact, Angela says she saw Sabrina at the bar with three boys. No one in our group saw her leave, but if she went with them—!"

She turned back to me, wringing her hands in anguish. "Oh, Vic, please! Can't you wait until afternoon to leave? At least can you call the police to see if someone found her? Perhaps these boys—Rohypnol or something even worse—she is so—so *faible*—"

"I'll check with the hospital, just in case," my landlady said. "I'm on the nursing staff there. What's your friend's name? Her date of birth?

"Sabrina Granev. I don't know her birthday."

Bernie watched anxiously, moving from foot to foot, while my landlady phoned. "Norma Rolfson here. I'm running a few minutes late but I need to check whether there was an overnight admission."

She spelled out Sabrina's last name, but shook her head at Bernie when she finished. "I have to run, but Ms. Warshawski, if you need to stay on, I don't have any other bookings for a few days. Let me know."

She left the way she'd come, through the door that led to her basement and her garage. Bernie was looking at me pleadingly.

"Bernie, do you know what you're asking of me? To try to find a missing student?" My throat felt as though something large, a basketball perhaps, was lodged in it. I could barely get the words out.

She blinked back more tears. "I'm sorry, Vic. *Maman* told me not to ask it of you, but I'm so used to you being calm, figuring out what to do when there is a problem, and if you don't know what to do, how can I know?"

I sat down heavily, hands over my eyes.

Bernie came over to me, shoulders drooping. "I am sorry, Vic. I see—*Maman* is right. You are a wounded eagle, she said, and that is the truth. We must leave now, but I will report Sabrina missing to the soccer coach when we get home."

A car had been honking in front of Norma's house for several minutes. "Amber and Chantel are waiting for me. It is necessary that I go."

I made myself look at her. Her face was pinched and pale with distress.

I wrapped the towel around my waist and got up to put an arm across her shoulders. "Okay, babe. I'll see if she was picked up on a disorderly, but police don't consider a person who's been gone only overnight as missing. Do you know Sabrina's parents' names? Where they live?"

"Sabrina, she is not truly part of our group. She only came to live in our house in October when we were looking for a fifth person to help with the rent, so I don't know her well. Also, soon after that, she broke her ankle. Her mother came, *bien sûr*, but Mme. Granev stayed in a hotel, so really, we spoke only to say, hello, yes, we can bring you coffee. She was always on her phone, her computer, except when she was pushing Sabrina to work on her rehab.

"Everyone in our house, we are all serious athletes, and Sabrina was, too. She toured with a national youth team, she is already scouted by different clubs, and so at first she was working hard, but something went wrong with the joint. The harder she worked the worse the bone got. That was when she started acting so differently.

"We hoped the mother would notice at Christmas, but after the winter vacation, it was even worse. Sabrina stayed in her room all the time. We tried to talk to her and she became angry. Angrier. So why she decided to come to Kansas with us—I don't know."

The car honking became more insistent, and then someone rang the upstairs bell. Bernie blinked at me nervously.

"I must run, I am sorry. As to where the parents are, that I'm not sure. The West, I know that. Colorado? Maybe New Mexico?"

"Ask the others if anyone knows where her parents live. I'll try to reach them. And I'll call Angela, see if she can describe the boys at the bar."

"I—thank you, Vic. I will ask the others. Angela, she's on the team bus, but Chantel or Amber, they may know where to find the parents." She hugged me convulsively and darted through the outside door to the street.

4

GET SET

AFTER SHE LEFT, I collapsed onto the bed. My body felt as though someone had laid an iron weight on me, pushing my belly button into my spine. I lay without moving, not sleeping, not thinking. Maybe this was how a caterpillar felt inside a cocoon. No ticking clock, no responsibilities, floating to music only nature could hear.

After a time, something in me shifted and my mind went reluctantly to the missing student. Missing, not dead, not shot. Arlette Fouchard had told her daughter I was a wounded eagle. That was grandiose. I was just wounded, along with most of the planet these days.

The papers are full of reports of people walking away from work, but most people keep going to their jobs. Something keeps them going, even if the job feels like drudgery. Before Covid, maybe it was workplace camaraderie, or family responsibilities. Now, with disease, political upheaval, economic uncertainty, it was hard to keep going.

Personally, I was tired of responsibility. I hadn't become a private eye to take on the weight of other people's worries but for the excitement of uncovering what lay behind a given crime. Even more, I got pleasure from those times I could make justice happen.

My dad had been a cop. After law school I'd been with the public defender for three years, handling street crime, so I didn't have dewy-eyed notions of law and order. While I was defending inarticulate street youth, trying to get them not to plead their lives away, it made me crazy that the big offenders, the ones who damaged hundreds or thousands of lives, walked off whistling a happy tune and pocketing a few billion more dollars. I chose detective work to try to take some of the air out of those whistles.

The challenges were greater today than when I started because the deck had been stacked ever more heavily on the whistlers' side. That meant I either should quit completely, or become smarter and wilier than when I started.

Smarter and wilier. That required at a minimum that I get out of bed, get my head back in the game. I rummaged in my overnight bag for a pair of clean jeans and a long-sleeved knit top. As I dressed, I could still feel the weight on my chest, but it receded to a small point under my heart. I could almost ignore it, and focus instead on what I knew of Sabrina Granev.

Bernie had said Sabrina was something of an outsider to the group of women who shared the Evanston house. They were all athletes, all attending university on athletic scholarships, but in different sports. While they often cheered each other's home games, they didn't have the time to go to away games. Last night had been an exception: they all wanted to see Angela's big moment in the spotlight.

At dinner with the women before last night's game, I hadn't tried to join the conversation, which was in a kind of code, young people speaking in fragments, punctuating their comments with bursts of laughter or cries of "No way!"

The dinner party had strained my endurance. The young women's exuberance made me feel invisible, made me want to walk away. Only my affection for Bernie kept me at the table. I'd noticed Sabrina Granev because, like me, she seemed listless, forcing herself to take part in jokes, but toying with her meal.

Depression over her ankle, I'd thought last night. It would be natural enough for her to envy her healthy housemates while she remained on the bench.

She'd been restless, twitching, during the meal. Drugs. I hadn't thought it consciously, but of course that was Bernie's worry—not that Sabrina had hooked up for sex but that she'd been desperate for drugs. Bernie and the other roommates were protecting Sabrina, but they knew she was using.

I texted my landlady to say I would be staying an extra night. I texted my dog walking service in Chicago, asking them to put in another day with Mitch and Peppy. I called Mr. Contreras, my down-stairs neighbor in Chicago. He keeps close tabs on my comings and goings—closer, since last fall's debacle—but he's in his nineties and not able to take the dogs for long walks these days.

He loves me, but he dotes on Bernie; he was vehement in his ap-plause that I was going to help her.

"I don't want to help her," I growled. "I want to take the dogs and sit on a warm beach where the only thing I have to find is a dry towel when I get out of the ocean."

"Don't go talking like that, doll. You wouldn't be happy with yourself if you left little Bernie in the lurch, you know that."

I hung up before I started a longer whine about how it was my turn to get looked after. "No one is going to shoot Sabrina," I told my face in the mirror. "She will not bleed out in your arms. You will find her because you are a clever detective."

I tried to figure out where to start my search. In Chicago, I have friends in the police who could tell me if someone had been brought in overnight. I was a stranger here, not someone with contacts who might tell me where a young woman seeking—what? oxy? fentanyl?—might have gone. Still, the police department was the logical place to start.

I drove down to the Decadent Hippo for my coffee, which they make the way I like. I drove the two miles to the cop shop. They'd moved since the last time I was here, to a shiny new building on the town's expanding west side. At the information counter, I produced some ID, including my PI license, and asked if Sabrina Granev was in their system.

The woman behind the counter checked her database. Sabrina hadn't been booked, at least not under her own name.

"Do you have any Jane Does?"

The woman looked at her screen and gave a little snort of laugh-ter. "Just one, who can't be your missing gal. Aside from the fact that everyone in town knows who he is."

"Trig Garrity?" I suggested.

She put both hands on the countertop. "What game are you playing, Ms. Chicago Detective?"

"Sorry. Not a game, a wild guess. He went after someone in the field house parking lot last night. University security broke it up, but I wondered if he'd been angry enough to attack the other guy later."

She gave me the old cop look: *I've been spun a lot of lines, and I know when I'm hearing one.* I looked back steadily: *I am an honest loyal citizen who speaks nothing but the truth.*

"If you're here for Garrity, his bail hearing will be at eleven in Judge Bhagavatula's courtroom. If you're really here about a missing student, what does she look like?"

"About five-eight, thin enough to see through, white with dull skin, lots of brown hair pulled into a ponytail, or at least it was the last time I saw her."

The woman didn't write any of this down. Maybe she'd been trying to trip me up—if I couldn't manufacture a description quickly I wasn't here on legitimate business. Instead, she repeated my landlady's suggestion, that Sabrina had hooked up with someone and wasn't answering her phone.

"I don't know this young woman well," I said. "I'm the godmother to one of the friends she rode down with, but I was wondering more about whether she'd hooked up with drugs rather than sex. If an outsider is looking to buy here, where would they go?"

The woman picked up a file folder and slapped the counter with it. "Is that what you were really hoping to find? A place to score? If that's what you need, you're on your own, Chicago."

I knew a sergeant in the Lawrence force, a man named Deke Everard whom I'd met when I was here before. He wasn't in, the woman said. I didn't believe her, but I didn't have a way of challenging her.

Back in my car, I stayed in the police lot while I called Angela. The team bus was noisy, but earbuds let us carry on a conversation.

"Bernie told me she'd talked you into looking for Sabrina. I'm sorry, Vic—sorry she pressured you when you're so—well, vulnerable. I love her, but sometimes she's such a giant mosquito the only appropriate answer is to swat her."

Laughing at the image made me feel a bit better. "She told me you saw Sabrina at the bar with three white guys. What did they look like?"

"They were strutting. The kind of boys we stayed as far from as possible when I was in high school. They like to get you in trouble and then laugh at you while you try to dig your way out. And just because a woman is white, like Sabrina, isn't any protection from guys like that. I called over to Sabrina to come back to our table, and one of the boys said, 'You her nanny?'"

I sucked in a breath, involuntary.

"Yes." Angela's voice was as dry as the dust on my windshield. "Sabrina said, 'She's our star. I'm just one of her planets.' So I walked away. I didn't look back at them. Maybe Sabrina left with them. Probably she left with them, but I didn't want to know. She has a way of making me not want to be my sister's keeper."

"I hear that," I said. "I couldn't help thinking drugs when I saw her twitching at our pregame supper last night. Your strutting boys may have offered her oxy or fent."

"Could be," Angela agreed.

"Can you describe any of them more than that they were cocky?"

"You mean, like, did one have a Proud Boy tattoo on his neck? The bar was full, I wanted to recapture my mood. I didn't try to memorize their faces. One had a lot of curly dark hair, that's the only detail I remember. And they were wearing Tom Brady's sportswear line—that's why I figured they were rich."

I thanked her. "Forget the boys, forget Sabrina, go back to your well-deserved high. See you soon in the Big Garlic."

"Big Garlic?" she echoed.

"You know, New York is the Big Apple. In fifth grade we were taught that Chicago was named for some kind of wild garlic. Why not?"

That made her laugh in turn. "Got it, Vic. Thank you for—well, everything."

Back in the old downtown, I parked in a free city lot. What an incredible luxury—free parking in the central business district. Did these people have any idea how lucky they were?

I figured there were some things I could look up in the library. On my way there, I walked past too many rough sleepers in shop doorways, still wrapped in blankets or sleeping bags as the town came to life.

My route took me past the Meadowlark, a bakery cum sandwich shop. Since the Incident, I never seemed to be hungry, but I hadn't had breakfast. A sourdough roll with espresso would do. The espresso was thin and bitter, but I made myself eat the whole roll.

I signed up for one of the computers on the library's lower level and went into the law enforcement databases to read incident reports for both the town and the county. I covered the most recent six months, looking for drug busts. I found several. I opened a map app in another window and looked up the locations. There'd been one in a newer part of town to the southeast, but most were in the parts of the county with the sparsest population. I noted the coordinates, although if the cops had busted a place, they'd have shut it down.

I also came on suicide reports. The numbers seemed high for a county this size. Like the drug busts, most had happened in the remote parts of the county, but some were on the college campus. That conjured a fresh worry about Sabrina Granev. Far from healing, her ankle had deteriorated. A young woman who'd been an international star six months ago, using opioids (perhaps), she could be seriously at risk.

Bernie hadn't gotten back to me with information about Sabrina's family, but I found them in one of my subscription databases. Her parents lived in a suburb of Albuquerque. Both had been athletes—her father a budding footballer in Zagreb when the Serbian civil war prompted his own parents to emigrate to the States. Her mother had also been a soccer star. The pair met at the University of New Mexico. Sabrina was their only child.

I found photographs of Sabrina easily enough—Instagram, Tik-Tok, Facebook—all showing a bright-faced athletic young person, not the gray, drained woman at last night's dinner table.

I went outside to call the parents. Both phones sent me to voicemail. The message I left—who I was, where I was, Sabrina's phone wasn't answering—sounded thin.

I walked back to the lot where I'd left my car, shoulders hunched, mood somber. This wasn't the first time Bernie Fouchard had talked me into doing something that wore me out.

5

(DIS)ORDER IN THE COURT

THE LOCAL COPS hadn't been helpful, but the university had its own force, as I'd learned last night. I phoned instead of trying to go in person. I was a worried aunt who'd come down from Chicago for last night's game. The officer on duty checked their incident reports for the past twenty-four hours. They'd picked up three drunks and one assault victim, but they could identify her. She wasn't Sabrina.

I hung up, unsure what to do next. It was eleven o'clock. The woman at the police information counter had said that was when Trig Garrity was having his bond hearing. It was a long shot, but there would be cops in court. Depending on why Trig had been arrested, Deke Everard himself might be present. If not, maybe an officer on active patrol would be willing to smuggle a message to the sergeant.

The county courts were in an old stone building a short walk from the Hippo. By the time I'd gone through security and found Judge Bhagavatula's courtroom, it was a quarter past the hour, but the judge was hearing enough cases that Garrity was still in the courtroom. Even though I'd only seen him under a streetlight, his wild hair and dirty parka stood out.

Three uniformed officers were sitting in the front row, all male. I couldn't tell from behind if any of them was the sergeant. A small number of spectators was sprinkled among the benches.

Two people were called ahead of Trig, one for attacking a man with a broken beer bottle, the other for attacking a grain silo with a backhoe. The backhoe earned a higher bond than the beer bottle. One drunk more or less was negligible, but this was farm country, and the backhoer was destroying the livelihood of many farmers.

A woman in the front row had a cell phone trained on the bench. Illinois doesn't allow journalists to record court proceedings, but Kansas apparently did.

The backhoer's attorney tried to plead some mitigating circumstances, namely the plaintiff had stolen his client's backhoe and the client had come to take it back. The judge deplored that argument and sent him away with a fifty-thousand-dollar bond. The woman with the cell phonee scribbled a note.

"Irwin Garrity," the clerk read. "Charged with violating a peace bond by willfully invading the property at"—he rattled off a set of coordinates—"with the intent to damage said property. How do you plead?"

The woman with the cell phone trained her device on Garrity, who stayed seated. The lawyer who'd been arguing for the backhoer scurried to his side and began a whispered argument with him.

"Irwin Garrity, if you don't come forward, I'm going to hold you in contempt and give you a fine as big as your head of hair," the judge said.

"I do not answer to the name Irwin."

"That's what's on your driver's license," the district attorney said.

"I told the low-paid flunkey who arrested me to use 'Trig,' which is the name I've used for thirty years."

"Then you should change it legally," the DA said.

The judge rubbed his forehead, eyes shut. "Mr. Garrity, will you approach the bench and tell us how you plead?"

Garrity got to his feet and stepped forward with a world-weary sigh. "Not guilty. No matter what the billionaire's flunkeys say."

"No editorials, Mr. Garrity," Bhagavatula said.

The DA explained that Garrity had been on a piece of private land. Someone had seen him nailing a sign to a tree inside the property, and had called the sheriff.

The deputy who'd made the arrest wasn't in the courtroom. The judge asked what was on the sign.

The DA looked at his tablet. "'Murderer! Destroying life for profit.'"

"No direct threats were made against the person or property of the owners, is that correct?"

"No, Your Honor, but the defendant was on private land that he's been bonded to stay away from."

"Why can't you come out and call it Brett Santich's land? Is his name too sacred to say out loud in court?"

"Mr. Santich's name isn't on the complaint," the judge said. "Sheriff's deputy Hanover wrote the ticket in response to a call from the night watchman at Kirmek Construction."

"Typical bullshit," Trig said. "All those layers between Santich and the public he's working to poison."

"You're not helping your case by flinging around slanderous comments," the judge said.

Trig started to argue that truth was a defense against slander, but the judge silenced him. "Mr. Garrity, you were here five months ago for disrupting a planning commission meeting. You were in front of me three months ago for harassing administrators at the Yancy Consolidated School. Six weeks ago you allegedly violated NO TRESPASS signs at the Wakarusa coal plant. What else do you do with your time besides create a public nuisance?"

"I'm a watchdog. This county and this town require a great deal of watching, because every time I blink, some rich, powerful person is taking steps to destroy free speech, or the air we breathe, or the river where we get our drinking water."

Bhagavatula thumbed through some papers that his clerk handed to him, along with a whispered comment. The judge looked back at Trig. "If you were serious about watchdogging, Mr. Garrity, you would start with basic research. Brett Santich doesn't own that land."

"Because he sold it to some equally brazen billionaire."

"Because he sold it to a brazen billionaire, *Your Honor*," Bhagavatula said. "This land had three mortgages on it. The owner sold it six years ago to a trust administered by the Pioneer State Bank and Trust."

Garrity looked goggle-eyed at the judge.

"Since the arresting officer isn't here, I'm dismissing the charges.

However, although you call yourself a watchdog, you do not get to decide what the law is in Douglas County or the State of Kansas. The next time you're in front of me I'm going to lock you up for sixty days for the good of the community."

Garrity made a sweeping bow, a parody of a costume drama courtier. "The king's justice is an avatar for the king's person."

He walked backward down the central aisle.

"Lucas, if you can't control your client, I'm going to fine you, too," Bhagavatula growled.

The defense lawyer grabbed Garrity's shoulder. He turned him around and frog-marched him to the exit. The woman with the cell phone followed.

"I will not defend you the next time they pick you up," the lawyer hissed as he opened the door. "You deliberately break the law. Then you turn the courtroom into a circus. I won't support a defendant whose only goal is to mock the law."

"Pity Martin Luther King didn't have you for a lawyer," Garrity said. "Or John Lewis. All that law-breaking over a piddling thing like the vote. Or in my case, a piddling thing like destruction of the planet."

The lawyer looked murderous but didn't try to prolong the battle. When the door shut again, the judge called a ten-minute recess.

We all rose. I left as the defense attorney said to the DA, "I wish Bhagavatula would lock him up. I'm tired of trying to defend assholes who don't want a defense."

I remembered that feeling well from my days with the Cook County public defender, but I still felt some sympathy for Trig.

The three cops went into the hallway. I followed, hoping to interest them either in Sabrina's disappearance, or getting a message from me to Deke Everard. They weren't rude, but they weren't willing to help, either.

Farther down the hallway, the journalist with the cell phone was interviewing Garrity. I went to a quiet corner at the opposite end to check my messages. Sabrina's parents hadn't gotten back to me. I tried them again, as well as Sabrina, but all three still went to voicemail. I did have a text from Bernie—she'd come up with the name of a friend of Sabrina's.

I reached Bernie while her group was taking a lunch break in Des Moines. "We texted this friend, Darla Browder her name is. She plays for Iowa, but she and Sabrina have been besties since their first soccer camp," Bernie reported, "Darla hasn't heard from Sabrina since before we left Evanston."

I took the friend's name and number and sent her a text, explaining who I was, before phoning. Darla took my call. She was worried about Sabrina, but she couldn't tell me much.

"Angela Creedy said Sabrina was talking to three guys at a bar," I said.

"Probably they were hitting on her," Darla said. "She's beautiful, with a lot of charisma. At least, before her injury she was always the center of attention. Not showing off, just a vibe she radiates. Used to radiate. She's not into guys, but they always glom on to her. Now she's pretty depressed. It's been hard for her to be on the bench with her ankle, so she's acting different in a lot of ways."

"Different how? Would she be medicating herself?"

"Medicating? Oh . . . You mean, is she taking drugs, besides Tylenol or something? She's an athlete, she knows better, she knows that's how you ruin yourself."

Phone interrogations are frustrating. You can't see the person's face or what they're doing with their hands, and the transmission flattens a lot of the emotion out of the conversation. I couldn't tell if Sabrina was doing drugs and Darla didn't know about it, or if she knew and was protecting her friend.

I pushed, but gently. I couldn't alienate her if I needed her help down the road. Instead I asked her to text me some photos.

"I want to start showing her picture to people, and all I have is her team photo, and some murky selfies her roommates took last night."

I gave her my number and tried to figure out what else I could or should do. Lunch, maybe, and return to the library to work on projects for my own clients. I was walking slowly along Massachusetts Street, hunched down in my coat, when the young woman from the courtroom appeared next to me.

"Hi. I'm Zoë Cruickshank with the *Douglas County Herald*. I saw you at Trig's hearing just now." She was very young, probably not thirty, and pulsing with energy.

I introduced myself. "That was a very theatrical event. I used to be a public defender in Chicago, and our most dramatic moments usually came from the bench."

She laughed, revealing crooked lower teeth. "That bow Trig gave on his way out? I figure he must have practiced for a month to make sure he didn't fall over. Fortunately, I got it on video so I can post it to the *Herald*'s web page. Is that why you were in court? To compare Kansas justice to Chicago?"

She had her phone out, ready to record me.

"Why do you want to talk to me?" I said.

"I'm the entire news desk for the *Herald* and I'm trying to turn Trig's court appearance into a story. It's hard to make news about him anymore, since he's always protesting something, and he's often in court for stuff like violating a peace bond. If you're an old friend, it would give me another angle."

"What was the 'murderer' placard about? Is Santich operating an abortion clinic?"

"Good grief, no. Santich's family owned all this land going back about a hundred years. He sold it, like the judge said. I haven't been able to burrow behind the Pioneer State's trust to get the actual owner's name, but they're building a giant resort on top of Yancy Hill. They've cut down a lot of old-growth trees, and Trig is trying to rouse opposition, but he fights so many wars no one listens to him anymore. He can't even get the Students for Environmental Justice to work with him. If you don't know Trig, why did you come to court?"

"People do, you know. Cold February day, it's free entertainment."

"What, you really were comparing Kansas and Illinois courts?"

I relented. "Deke Everard is an acquaintance of mine. Do you know him? Sergeant with the LKPD. They wouldn't let me try to reach him at the station, but I'm hoping he might help me in a search for a missing Chicago-area athlete, a young woman who came down to watch last night's game. I saw Trig mixing it up with Brett Santich in the field house parking lot after the game. When I learned Trig was going to be in court today, I was hoping Everard might be present, or at least that one of the officers there could get a message to him. The LKPD isn't interested, but Everard might help me for old times' sake."

"Missing student?" Zoë's dark eyes gleamed. A real story. "What's her name?"

The more information I could spread around, the better my chance of finding Sabrina. I gave Zoë what I knew, including the pictures Darla Browder had texted. Most were selfies of the two of them—under an umbrella on a beach, playing volleyball in the sand, hugging after a soccer match.

In the photos, Sabrina did radiate a vitality more attractive than conventional beauty. They were a pointed and poignant contrast to the sallow young woman I'd seen last night. I AirDropped them to Zoë so that she could put them on the *Herald*'s web page.

Zoë still wanted to interview me. I assured her I didn't have a story to tell, but I went with her to the *Herald* office. They were in one of the old buildings along the river, where rents were cheap because the owners didn't put any money into maintenance.

The lock was loose, and she had to work the key around for a bit until the tumblers engaged. She led me down an unlit hall to her office.

"This whole building used to belong to us." She sighed. "We had printing presses in the basement, and a big editorial and reporting staff. Now it's just me, a guy who covers sports, and an editor who doubles as an ad manager. Most days, they don't even come in, but I like to work here. I like to feel I'm part of a real newspaper, even if we don't set type for it."

It felt colder inside her office than on the street, even when she turned on an arthritic space heater. She questioned me about Trig's confrontation with Santich last night, and then she wanted a detailed rundown on Sabrina.

I told her the little I knew, omitting my suspicion about opioids. Before I left, I asked her about Cady Perec.

"I met her along with Sergeant Everard when I was here two years ago. Cady was at the game last night. Right before Trig had his blowup with Brett Santich, Santich attacked Cady. I read—I guess it must have been your piece, right?—in the local paper, but it didn't seem to justify Santich's rage."

Zoë preened a little over my finding her work, but said, "That was Trig, too. He and this woman who sometimes protests with him, they started picketing the Yancy school after Cady was suspended.

See, Cady was reprimanded for pushing critical race theory on to un-suspecting students, but the hearing was to decide whether she should be punished in some bigger way. Of course, I wrote it up—it was news—which was how Trig heard about it."

I told her I'd read the story in the *Herald*'s online version.

Zoë grinned again. "The online version is all there is anymore. I loved covering Cady's troubles—so much action. They even picked up my story on Kansas City's TV stations. Trig and Clarina Coffin, they carried signs comparing Santich to Stalin: toe the party line or be sent to the gulag. And Trig has a bullhorn, so he was bellowing through that. It was during the day, school was in session, and Santich went nuts.

"Cady's been a respected teacher for seven or eight years, first at a junior high here in Lawrence, and then out in Yancy, plus her grandmother knows everyone in town, including the people on all the different school boards, even the one out in Yancy. The board probably wouldn't have fired Cady, would have stopped at a repri-mand, if Trig hadn't gotten them so angry. One of the families who fought with Cady when she was a social studies teacher here in the town came to the meeting and said some ugly stuff. That added to everyone's hysteria."

"I guess that explains why no one wants to join Trig in his fights. That, and the little bombshell the judge dropped. Did you talk to Trig about that in your postcourt interview?"

Zoë made a wry face. "He felt a little bit ashamed. It never oc-curred to him to ask about who owned the land, and really, Brett sold it to a hedge fund, something anonymous, years ago.

"See, until they actually started bulldozing the top of Yancy Hill, Brett kept farming the land. The top, it was woodland, with natural springs, which made the next level down the hill ideal for crops. If anyone even thought about it, they must have assumed Brett had got-ten the land back. Now it turns out he was leasing the farmland from the Trust owners until they started building, which was only a few months ago. Brett still owns a little patch at the bottom of the hill, with a few buildings on it."

I got to my feet. "You seem to know everything in this county. If I wanted something like fentanyl, where would I go?"

"Fentanyl? You don't want anything like that. Leave it alone. It's super-bad stuff."

I didn't say anything.

"You do look thin," Zoë said. "Get yourself into rehab, but don't go looking for drugs like that here."

"What—Douglas County is so pure you don't have dealers?"

"We have way too many dealers. They are a creepy bunch."

I nodded: dealers are always creepy, whether they're in the city or the country. It seemed like a good time to leave, before she connected the drugs to my questions about Sabrina.

6

BLOOD ON THE PIZZA

I **WALKED ALONG THE** river, kicking at rocks on the path. The water was slate colored, reflecting the dirty gray clouds overhead. An eagle was perched on a dead tree on a sandbank. I stopped and watched until it swooped down and pulled up a fish.

Maybe that's what I needed—not a live fish, but lunch, something to augment the sourdough roll I'd eaten at nine. Massachusetts, the town's main street, was packed with eateries, offering almost any kind of food you might want, from pizza to Asian or South American or Greek. Nothing sounded appealing.

I caught sight of myself in the store window. My jeans were hanging loose around my hips, and my cheekbones were pronounced. Not as extreme as Sabrina's gray pallor and downy anorectic face, but thin enough to make Zoë Cruickshank think I had a habit to feed. If Peter saw me now, would he be repelled, or moved by pity?

Queen Margherita's Pizza Palace stood across the street, next to a diner advertising Vietnamese, Thai, and Chinese food. Pizza seemed a safer bet. I bought two slices and took them outside to one of the benches the city placed on its main street.

When I opened the box, the tomato sauce looked like congealing blood. My stomach heaved, and I started to my feet, looking for a trash can, then saw myself again in the storefront. I could not continue like this.

In my years as an investigator, I've seen the bodies of other brutally murdered people. It's never easy, but with Taylor's slaying I felt as if my skin had become a sausage casing, holding not my own inner self, but all the bone and blood and brain I've witnessed over the decades.

It was the times, the times of pandemic, the times of fake news, endless wars, assaults on our government, assaults on thought. The times they aren't so much a-changin' as grinding us into sand.

I looked at the pizza for a long moment, then made myself eat a slice. One bite at a time, slowly, chewing, eyes shut so I didn't see the red sauce. I'd bought a bottle of water and I drank half to wash down the pizza.

"This tastes like tomato and olives, it does not taste like blood. The water tastes clean."

I said it out loud and a man in a nearby doorway looked up. He had a scraggly beard and matted brownish hair that stuck out from under a moth-eaten ski cap.

"Blood? You got a mouth full of blood? Like this here?" He poked the roof of his mouth open with one grimy finger so that I could see all the holes where he used to have teeth.

His face was as crusted as his finger. For a moment I thought I wouldn't be able to keep the pizza down. I forced myself to study him clinically. The teeth that remained were black, and the gums were full of lesions. Meth, maybe, or heroin.

"Something like that," I agreed. "I've been covered in too much blood lately. You?"

He rolled up his pant leg, and I could see the blood trails where he'd been injecting himself sloppily. "You got these?"

"Not for public consumption," I said primly.

"Public consumption. That's a good one. But there you are, consuming pizza in public while starving people are bleeding into the sidewalk all around you."

I squatted on the sidewalk near him and handed him the box. He took the second slice, inspected it for a second, then folded it in half and ate it in one long noisy mouthful.

"Yep. These here are definitely tomatoes, not blood." He eyed me hopefully. "You got any more food you're scared of? Can of Pepsi?"

"Right now I'm mostly scared I won't be able to find me any oxy before the end of the day. Or trams, I'd settle for a tab if I had to."

"Don't look at me." He backed away, anger and fear chasing each other across his face. "Just because I'm on the street doesn't mean I'm an addict or nothing."

"Of course not! But I bet you see and hear a lot out here on the street. Someone told me I could find a connection at the Lion's Heart, but I don't know who to ask for."

"You a cop?"

"I am not a cop. I came down here for the basketball game and I can't get back to Chicago until tomorrow. I have to get something to tide me over. Soon!"

"Oh. You're an athlete. I get it."

"So who do I ask for at the Liony place? Or is there somewhere else better?"

"You give me fifty bucks. That'll buy me food for a week."

Or drugs for a day, but I kept that unhappy thought to myself. "How about twenty."

"How about you do your own research?"

When we compromised on twenty-five, he laughed, showing his rotting gums. "You want drugs, you got to be connected to a network. You got to know what bars the dealers go to, what bars the cops go to, see? Last night maybe they was at the Lion, tonight, maybe at the Boat Yard or Peewee's Palace. You're from out of town, so you don't have connections."

"You're right," I said, voice humble. "I don't have connections, which is why I'm talking to you. One of my team scored oxy at the Liony place last night. She said she was talking to three white boys, who looked like frat boys, but she knows I want to get in line ahead of her, so maybe she was lying. Maybe she really found a heavy from Kansas City."

My friend sucked on his toothless gums. "Don't know. Rumor is some frat boys deal for fun, or maybe to pay for their rides. I see 'em cruising sometimes in one of those fancy Jeeps. One might have a Porsche. Three white boys having a good time, could be from the Omicron fraternity."

I got to my feet, forgetting to move like a desperate addict. My friend said, "You are a cop!"

I pulled up my hoodie and the sweatshirt under it. "No wire," I said. "I'm not a cop."

"You better not be. I find you ratted me, I'll come up to Chicago and break your face in so you can get all the blood in your food you want."

"That's scary," I agreed.

I went back to my car and tried Sabrina and her parents again, but still had no answer. I tried the LKPD again, but Deke Everard also wasn't available.

I went over to the Lion's Heart. This was a student bar, decorated with plastic Jayhawks, ceramic Jayhawks, Jayhawk jerseys, and this year's men's basketball schedule. It was an ill-lit space in a half-basement, with a story above it that was connected by an interior staircase. It might be a perfect place for a dealer to hand out wares, but in midafternoon, the only customers were older, nursing a beer or a shot. I sat at the far end of the bar, next to the cash register, where the stink of stale beer was strong enough to make me feel drunk.

The bartender was wiping glasses in the time-honored fashion of bartenders everywhere. The cloth looked surprisingly clean.

"What'll it be?"

Close up, I saw he was wearing a blue sweatshirt with the ubiquitous Jayhawk on the front.

"Help, I hope." I laid my phone on the bar, with a twenty underneath and showed him Sabrina.

"She's disappeared. The last time anyone saw her was late last night when three frat boys were talking to her here at the bar. Were you on duty?"

"Duty? I was working. Didn't know that included being on duty for coeds who drink too much and get themselves into trouble."

"People tell me the frat boys are dealing here in the bar."

"People will tell you anything." He pushed the twenty toward me. "If you're looking to score, go someplace else. Lion's Heart is clean."

A thickset man came over from a table in the back of the room. "Trouble here, Joey?"

"No trouble," I said. "I'm just trying to find the boys who went off with my niece last night. She was here celebrating with friends from Chicago, and the last they saw of her, she was at your bar with three white guys."

"There were probably three dozen white guys here last night and maybe another ten or twelve Black. If your niece hooked up with someone, that was something she did on her own, not something my bar would arrange or condone. Anything else?"

"They came in a Porsche," I said, wondering how reliable my rough sleeper's narrative was.

"They could have come in a helicopter, but they wouldn't have driven it inside the bar, so that doesn't ID them for me. You talk to the cops, file a missing person, don't come bothering me."

From the way he was looking at me, I suspected that he knew more, but I couldn't think of a way to get him to reveal it. I left the bar, panicking at my inability to come up with a coherent way to look for Sabrina.

My rough sleeper's story was thin, but it was the only story I had. Would a college fraternity really be able to run a drug operation without the campus cops and all their friends and neighbors noticing? It was hard to believe, even harder when I drove up the hill to the university campus.

The sun was starting to set, and gold light glinted on the limestone buildings. A warm and friendly place, where you'd be glad to send your child. They would be safe here. No one would be peddling tabs or powders.

The Omicron Delta Beta house was on the northwest edge of the campus. It was a well-maintained brick building with mullioned windows and fake Tudor beams across the front, set in carefully planted and groomed grounds. I wandered around the perimeter until I found the parking garage.

I'd thought my homeless friend had thrown in Porsches to make his story more colorful. There actually were two Porsches, an older Carrera with Kansas plates, and a new silver Boxster 718 from Virginia. An assortment of muscle cars, including a newer version of my own Mustang, and a good half dozen Jeeps.

I photographed the plates on the Jeeps and the Porsches.

"What the fuck do you think you're doing?" It was a young man in chinos and a yellow cashmere sweater. Sockless loafers despite the February wind.

"Admiring the wheels," I said. I hadn't heard him approach. Not good.

"Admire them somewhere else. This is private property, off limits without an invitation."

"I'd love an invitation," I said. "I hear some boys were cruising around the Lion's Heart last night, offering people something more special than craft beer. Friends of yours?"

A ghost of a smirk twisted the left corner of his mouth. "Lion's Heart is where nickel girls can move up to dime. You look like about two cents. Maybe just one."

"And where's the bank where you move those nickels around?" I asked.

"You could be funny," he said, "but you're trying too hard."

I walked around the Carrera. Mud was caked in the hubcaps and had splattered the fenders.

"Your bank must be in the country. This car isn't happy crawling around the mud."

The smirk became more pronounced. "Could be. Now get out of the garage. Unless you'd like to leave on a stretcher."

I studied him up and down, pretty sure I could take him, even as out of shape as I was. Wondering what I would gain if I did so.

I gave a mock salute. "Got it, frat boy. See you at Salamis."

"Is that where old worn-out ho's drink?" He drawled his words to make sure I knew how offensive they were.

I clicked my tongue on my teeth. "Oh, little boy, you'd better start spending some of your mommy's money on your classes. Salamis, where the Greeks wiped out a Persian force more than twice their size. You should try to pick up a little knowledge to tide you over when the drug money runs out."

"You're not just old and ugly, you're crazy," the boy said.

"Crazy is unpredictable, more dangerous than sane. Better go to your psych classes as well, to be on the safe side." I sauntered out of the garage, not looking at him but bracing myself in case he jumped me. In a way I was sad he didn't—I would have enjoyed showing him what an older woman could do to a punk.

Back in my own muscle car, I couldn't say the visit was wasted. The punk's smirk suggested that he could be one of the boys Sabrina had been talking to at the Lion's Heart last night.

Trouble was, I still had no idea where she might be. The countryside around the town was vast. If that mud-spattered Carrera had ferried Sabrina to an abandoned house out in the country, I'd need a Persian-size army of my own to hunt for her.

I looked up the other two bars my rough sleeper had mentioned. The Boat Yard was on the north side of the river, Peewee's Palace on the south, where the university and most of the town were located. I tried the Palace first.

As at the Lion's Heart, the Palace held a handful of older drinkers, male and female, at a grimy bar. They stared ahead, as if the foggy mirror behind the bottles could show them something happier than their own thoughts.

The bartender, who was as apathetic as his clientele, was unmoved by my missing niece who'd last been seen with three college boys. Even when I showed him the picture of her glowing with health on a beach, he hunched a heavy shoulder and said coeds were always getting in over their heads, not his problem. Anyway, rich boys with expensive cars went to Kansas City or St. Louis to drink.

The Boat Yard was a different story. They were doing a lively business, mostly early supper for families with small children, along with long-haul truckers coming off the nearby interstate exit. It didn't seem like a probable drug haven, but you never know.

Two waitresses, both brisk, middle-aged, exuding a kind of maternal cheer with their customers, were racing from kitchen to tables. I had to wait ten minutes before I could speak to anyone.

The bartender turned out to be the Boat Yard's owner. He was sure no one ever came around selling drugs, or seducing young women. Certainly no one in a Porsche. Lawrence wasn't that kind of town.

He turned back to a couple at the end of the bar, old friends, apparently, who were laughing at some long story he was telling.

I left, feeling helpless and useless. Night was closing in, but the highway lights and all the little bars and shops north of the river made the stars invisible.

I had my hand on the Mustang door when someone behind me called out, "Miss! Miss? Don't go just yet."

I turned to see one of the waitresses in her pink-striped dress, not even a sweater against the night chill. She had her hands rolled up in her apron.

"Greg doesn't want to admit anything could go wrong in this place, but I've seen those boys you're talking about. They don't cruise here often, we're more family and truckers, but—" She looked over her shoulder, to see if anyone was listening.

I moved up next to her, close enough to read the name HOLLY on the plastic tag pinned to her dress.

"It's my sister," Holly breathed. "We fight about this all the time, but she cleans a house out west of town, on Yancy. She knows as well as me that they're holding drug parties there, but she says she never sees anyone using. She gets a message to have everything set up—glasses, napkins, fresh towels in the toilets. They leave a hundred dollars for her on the kitchen table and she does the whole downstairs, comes back the next day to clean it all up. Sometimes there's all this puke, they should pay her double, but really, she shouldn't work there at all."

"I'm a stranger here," I said. "Yancy?"

"It's a hill just outside town, farms, woods. Right now they're doing construction on top. Anyways, there's an old brick house on East 1450 Road. I don't know whose land it's on, but it's been abandoned a long time. Sometimes I drive past, wondering what mess Ivy's got herself into, and I see a fancy sports car there. Couldn't tell you the make."

I thanked her effusively. She waved off the twenty the Lion's Heart bartender had rejected and trotted back into the restaurant.

7

THREE CROWS MEANS A SUMMONS

YANCY. THE NAME kept cropping up, first in Bhagavatula's courtroom, then at the school whose board fired Cady Perec for corrupting the children of Douglas County. Finally, it was the site of a house where a woman named Ivy cleaned up after drug parties. Three crows means a summons. That must mean I was destined to go to Yancy.

It had been cold in Chicago when I left, so I'd worn my heavy winter jacket. I needed clothes that allowed for quick movement over country terrain. In an outlet mall behind the Boat Yard, I bought a thick hoodie, navy with the inevitable Jayhawk over the heart, and fleece leggings. Socks, since the pair I was traveling in was dirty enough to make my toes itch. A cheap pair of trail shoes. A flashlight so I wouldn't drain my phone battery.

Bernie had texted while I was shopping. Back in my car, I called her, hoping Sabrina had surfaced on her own.

"No, Vic, it is not so. We are now home with no word from her, and her phone is still turned off."

I told her I hadn't had any luck, either. "I have one slim lead. If it doesn't pan out, I'll be coming home tomorrow."

I'd been afraid she might start hectoring me, but she agreed in an unusually sober, un-Bernie-like way. She was sharing her worry over Sabrina's possible opioid use when my phone told me I had an incoming call from Valerie Granev. I switched to her immediately.

"Ms. Granev! This is V.I. Warshawski. Have you heard from your daughter? I haven't—"

"Ms. Warshawski? Have you found her? What happened to her? I should never have let her go to Kansas with her friends. But she sounded better—"

She was frantic, almost incoherent. I was finally able to interject a few words.

"Sabrina went with her friends to a bar here in Lawrence. The last they saw of her she was talking to some boys there. Did she text you, let you know what she was planning?"

"I knew those other girls wouldn't take care of her," Valerie cried. "I've been in a high-security meeting all day, we couldn't access our phones, this is my first chance to call you. I'm on my way to the airport. I'll be getting to Lawrence about one in the morning. Tell me where to meet you, or can you meet my plane? What do you know?"

"Very little, I'm afraid. I may have found at least one of the boys Sabrina was talking to, but I don't have any leverage here."

"She wouldn't go off with strange boys, not without a good reason. But if she was abducted—"

"Abducted?" The horror stories of young women held captive flashed across my mind.

"My work," Valerie was saying. "Someone—the Russians and Chinese want this technology—someone could work for them, hold Sabrina for ransom. You have to stop looking. A hundred thousand things could go wrong if you find her and they feel cornered."

"Has someone approached you, Ms. Granev? Someone demanding ransom? Have you talked to the FBI?"

She didn't answer, just wailed, "I wish I knew what—who to trust—anyway, I'm on a plane, I'll be there as soon as I can, but don't do anything until you see me."

The connection went. What kind of investigator are you, V.I., that you didn't dig deep enough to learn what kind of powerhouse job Valerie Granev held?

I started my car, turned on the heater. My eyelids felt heavy, my brain full of cotton.

I couldn't let the lassitude of the last few months encase me again. I turned on the overhead light and looked up Valerie Granev. She headed the electronic engineering unit for the aeronautics division of Tulloh Industries. Access to her research on avionics was blocked. Access to her research reports was blocked. Even if I could access her work, I wouldn't understand it; I wouldn't know if a foreign power would want it badly enough to kidnap her daughter.

Maybe the FBI should be involved. I thought Sabrina had been looking for drugs. In fact, if she was addicted, it would be easy for someone to abduct her—she would go with anyone promising her access. Trouble was, I couldn't see the Bureau listening to me. Missing student whom I barely knew? They'd be all over Bernie and her friends as well as me, and would be unlikely to start a serious search for Sabrina.

I took a look at Valerie's husband to see if he was also some kind of engineering wizard. Ramir Granev had apparently embraced the great Southwest with gusto. He worked for a sports equipment store but when I called the store, the manager told me Ramir was on a weeklong trek in the Sangre de Cristo mountains with a group of teen skiers. No cell phone coverage there.

"He takes kids wilderness camping all year round," the manager said.

"There's a family crisis," I said. "Has his wife been in touch?"

"What kind of crisis?" the manager tried to sound concerned but came across as eager.

"Ms. Granev was pretty rattled," I said. "She seems to think their daughter is at risk. She didn't give me details but I thought her husband should know."

Ramir was reachable only by sat phone, but the manager assured me Valerie would know that. "She probably got him some souped-up phone that can make calls to Venus in an emergency. Even if she called him, it would take Ram eight or more hours to hike out to where they left the vehicles. But Ram would be the first to say, let Valerie take care of a crisis, unless it's like a rescue mission in the mountains, where he definitely knows what to do."

I blinked at the flow of information, although it did offer an insight into the Granevs' relationship. I asked how I could call into Ramir Granev's sat phone. I couldn't, as it turned out, unless I had a device that would transform my cell phone into a satellite phone.

By the time the store manager finished telling me everything he knew about phones, which was a lot, the February night had shut down completely. Despite running the heater, the damp cold was seeping through the windows.

Stay here and freeze, feeling sorry for myself, so Lotty and Mr. Contreras could erect a tombstone with SHE DROWNED IN SELF-PITY on it. Or get moving.

I found the card Zoë Cruickshank had given me and called her cell phone. "I have some news for you. Have your sources already told you that my missing college student has a high-powered mom? No? Valerie Granev, she's a significant electronics person for Tulloh Industries. She's afraid Sabrina was kidnapped to force her mom to reveal national secrets."

"How do you know? Is the FBI involved? Where can I find the mom?"

"She's flying in from Albuquerque. She begged me to stop looking for her daughter because she worries my search could get Sabrina killed. The hell of it is I don't know if Valerie has reason to suspect kidnapping, or it's her way of denying her daughter might be in other kinds of trouble."

Of course Zoë had a thousand questions, including what secrets Valerie had access to.

"All her work is blocked off by security fences. Even if I had the skill to climb over them, I wouldn't understand her work. I barely understand what 'avionics' means. She could be sitting on an entire Vesuvius of inventions for the air force. If you do run across any Bureau types, write your story up and publish before they slap an injunction on you. They can suppress the story if you run it, but once it's on the Web it won't disappear completely."

"Do you think Sabrina was kidnapped?"

"I don't know," I said. "She could be anywhere in the world right now. Even if she's still here in Douglas County, it would take an army to go through every possible hiding place. I don't know," I repeated.

Valerie's and Bernie's calls had sidetracked me before I'd written down the address that the waitress had given me. I shut my eyes, slow breaths, going into track, my old physics professor used to call it. As if Professor Wright were whispering in my ear, the address came to me: E. 1450 Road.

My map app showed a single road on the hilly outcropping that was Yancy. The satellite view showed cultivated land on the hill's lower reaches, pockmarked by sections of woodland. East 1450 Road was easy to spot. There was only one building on it that could be the house the waitress had mentioned.

I needed to rest. I'd been on the go since early this morning, with another stint looming. Back in my room, I set the timer on my phone for ninety minutes and fell heavily into sleep. Before the timer rang, my landlady came in and shook me awake. She turned on the bedside lamp, and I blinked up at her.

"You told me I could stay another night. Didn't you get the message that I'd be here?"

"I'm sorry, Ms. Warshawski, it's not about that, but someone is here from the FBI."

"FBI?" I repeated.

A man came in behind my landlady. He flashed a credential that glinted gold in the lamplight. "Cornell Stamoran, FBI."

I sat up. I was naked except for a T-shirt, which seemed to be my dress code for greeting visitors. "Have you found Sabrina?"

Stamoran looked away from my crotch. Good. I had some privacy.

"I need you to answer some questions about her," he said.

I went into the bathroom and soaked a facecloth in hot water, rubbed my face and eyes. Cornell Stamoran stayed in the doorway, perhaps to make sure I didn't have Sabrina hidden in the shower. I ostentatiously wrapped my torso in a towel, took my time combing my hair. Stamoran followed me back into the sleeping room and watched as I put on my new fleece leggings, clean socks, sweatshirt, hoodie.

"Tell me about Sabrina," I said.

He shook his head. "We need answers to some questions before we decide what action to take."

I waited.

"How much research did you do into the Granev family before you started looking for Sabrina?"

This was the entrance to a hall of mirrors, where they tried to prove I had done something with Sabrina Granev in order to get a reward or a ransom or something from her parents.

"I didn't have a chance to study your credentials," I said. "Let me make sure you're really with the Bureau."

Nurse Norma the landlady had stayed in the room, standing behind Cornell near the exit to the street. She nodded approvingly.

The agent's mouth tightened, but he pulled out his badge again. I took it from him and studied it. He was from the Bureau. Or it was a good AI forgery.

"How much did you know about the Granev family when you started your search for Sabrina?" he prodded.

I took my phone out and turned on the recording app. "This is V.I. Warshawski, making a statement to Cornell Stamoran from the FBI about Sabrina Granev." I gave the date and time.

"Sabrina Granev drove to Kansas with three of her housemates to watch a fifth friend play basketball on Sunday evening. Sabrina's housemates came to me Monday morning, concerned because she had not returned to their motel Sunday night. They asked me to delay my return to Chicago to look for her. I found her parents' phone numbers online and kept phoning them, as well as Sabrina, until I connected with Valerie Granev, who told me she was afraid her daughter had been kidnapped. She was frantic, as any parent would be, and it was painful to tell her I'd made no progress in finding her daughter. Beyond those bare facts, I know nothing about Ms. Granev. I know nothing about her family."

Stamoran ignored my speech. "You have a reputation for impulsive, even violent action, to achieve your goals."

I said nothing.

"You made a major mistake looking for a student in Chicago last October."

I studied my fingernails to keep from damaging Agent Stamoran in a violent impulsive act.

"It's been suggested that you hid Sabrina yourself, hoping you could find her and erase the mistake you made in the winter."

I pressed the play button on my phone, and my statement repeated itself in the small room.

"You say you knew nothing about the Granev family. How much do you know about Valerie Granev's work?"

"I know nothing about her work."

"You know she works for Tulloh Industries."

"I learned from Ms. Valerie Granev that she worked for Tulloh. I did not know that before we spoke."

"You deny that you abducted Sabrina Granev in order to collect a large ransom from Tulloh Industries?"

"I don't understand the question," I said.

He repeated it, raising his voice. I repeated my answer. He tried shouting the question. I stopped trying to answer.

Stamoran finally gave up and asked something more sensible. "You said you made no progress in looking for her. What steps did you take?"

"I checked with the Lawrence police, to see if she'd been picked up overnight. I tried to file a missing persons report, but the police told me Sabrina had not been missing long enough to qualify. I gave her picture to the local newspaper and asked them to run it online so that anyone who'd seen her could get in touch with me. My landlady checked with the hospital in case she'd been in an accident."

Norma said, "That's right. I'm a nurse at the Lawrence hospital. I was leaving for work when the young women came over to consult Ms. Warshawski because they were worried about their friend. The young woman hadn't been admitted, either to the main hospital or the university's."

"I think you know where the girl is," Stamoran said, "but just in case you're telling the truth, back off from your search. You could jeopardize her life. Got it?"

"Got it," I said, wondering what he thought I was agreeing to.

Stamoran finally left, without him arresting me or me slugging him.

When Norma had seen him out of her house, she came back and studied my face, looking troubled. "You didn't abduct her, did you?"

I gave a tired smile. "I did not abduct her. Her mother apparently does something high-powered with aviation electronics, and thinks someone could kidnap Sabrina and ask for her mom's secret research as ransom. I guess that's why the Bureau got involved, but if they really thought Russia or China had snatched Sabrina, they would have sent a sharper guy than this Stamoran to investigate."

Norma smiled. "When you put it like that, I can't disagree. Can you tell me what happened to the student the agent was talking about? The one where things went wrong?"

I gave her an outline of the Incident.

Norma nodded thoughtfully. "What went wrong wasn't because you did anything, but because the parents were unbalanced. Is that affecting your judgment? Are you afraid if you tell the parents where Sabrina is they might, well, react in the same way?"

"You're right. It's why I didn't want to start looking in the first place. But now that I'm looking, I have one lead on a place where I might find Sabrina. I think she might have a serious opioid problem, and I've learned about a house out in the country that hosts drug parties. I want to drive out there. This FBI agent might be watching your house to see what I'm doing. Would you be willing to drive my car into the next street and let me leave through your upstairs door?"

Norma's eyes widened. She studied my face for a long minute, then held out her hand for the keys.

8

THIS OLD HOUSE

THE ROAD TO Yancy was a two-lane job with ditches on either side and no shoulder. When I left the town limits, I drove by a cluster of new houses at the base of the hill. A sign pointed to the turnoff for the Yancy Consolidated School. After I passed that subdevelopment, I was shrouded in dark. The county had installed streetlamps at the crossroads, but these were a quarter mile apart. I stuck to the middle of the road to avoid the ditches.

My headlights picked up patches of mist rising from the land. An occasional fox or raccoon sauntered across the road. If the Omicron frat boys were selling product, I couldn't believe they'd chosen this isolated terrain.

When my GPS told me I'd reached my destination, I couldn't see anything but trees and bracken. I thought at first my aerial map must be out-of-date, but after a moment I spotted a rutted muddy drive leading into the overgrowth. My headlights glinted on windowpanes at the end of the drive.

I backed away, reluctant to park there. You couldn't see the house from the road, and I didn't want to risk parking in the muddy cul-de-sac.

Beyond the house, the road curved past a plowed field. I found a farm track about a quarter mile away and bounced the Mustang along it until I came to the shelter of a tree.

If I'd had a chance to scout the terrain in daylight, I might have risked walking cross-country so I could come at the house from the back, but I had to stick to the road. I pulled the hoodie well forward over my head.

The walk along the dark road was more unnerving than a Chicago alleyway at night. I used the flashlight to keep out of the ditches, but this made me visible and vulnerable. Bushes grew wild on the far side of the ditches. Anyone could have been lurking there.

A car passed me, the first I'd seen since turning onto 1450 Road. The driver turned on their brights, blinding me. I hugged the edge of the tarmac until they'd passed.

When I reached the turnoff to the house, I saw that the drive had been covered in gravel, although the damp ground meant that the cars that used it had gouged tracks into it. There had been a lot of traffic, and a lot of it was recent. Perhaps this was where the Porsche hubcaps had become caked in mud.

I worked my way to the house without the flash, tripping over potholes and tufts of grass, but managing to stay on my feet. The drive ended in a small turning circle near the house's back door. Risking the flash again, I could see more signs of recent traffic. Very recent, judging by the freshness of the mud under the gravel. Had an Omicron party been in progress? Had the frat boys sent everyone home so they could lie in wait for me?

The house was brick, the soft rose-colored clay that's stood up to the weather for a long time. It needed remortaring, but there weren't any broken windows.

Hugging the side of the house, in case anyone was watching from the windows, I made a circuit, stumbling on bottles and machine pieces that had been dumped in the tall grasses in the back. No lights seeped around the window blinds. No vehicles stood between the house and the encroaching woodland behind.

I returned to the side entrance. The door was heavy, with a new lock. When I tried the handle, it opened silently. A new door with well-oiled hinges. In a movie that's the sign that the heroine is about to be violently attacked if she goes inside.

I opened the door just wide enough to slip through. Pointed my flash at the checkerboard linoleum on the floor. An enameled table in the middle of the room was covered with half-empty boxes of carryout food. There were bottles of designer vodka and gin on a sideboard, beer, melting ice in a large chest, stacks of plastic glasses. There'd definitely been a party underway, one that had been abandoned in a hurry.

The kitchen was cold, but I could feel a bit of warmth in the radiator. The pipes wouldn't freeze and burst.

I moved resolutely toward the interior of the house, through three small rooms that held cushions and balance balls along with a few old-fashioned chairs and a settee. Beer bottles and half-drunk glasses were scattered around the floor. Ivy would earn her hundred dollars when she next came to clean.

The third room must have been the house's formal room when it was built; it had a fireplace, and an archway that opened on a small hallway, with a front door that special visitors would use, and a stairway to an upper floor.

I shone my flash on the front door. And saw a bundle wedged against it.

A cold sweat drenched me. I dropped the flashlight and couldn't see where it landed. Pulled my phone from my hip pocket, but I was shivering with cold and had trouble swiping it open.

I pulled the hoodie sleeve down over my hand, rubbed some circulation into my fingers, turned on the flashlight app.

I knelt and prodded the bundle, gingerly at first, but when I couldn't feel flesh or bone I pushed my hand down onto it. I sat back on my heels. An empty tartan blanket, not a dead soccer player. My heart settled down, and I found my flashlight in the corner by the door.

I was getting to my feet when I heard a whimper. I stood still. Heard the sound again. Not my own wheezing breath or a night creature. Someone was in the house, on the upper floor.

The staircase was steep, the risers so narrow that the heels of my trail shoes hung over the edges. The stairs ended at a small circular landing. Three doors opened onto it, two open, one shut. The two open rooms both held a couple of bare mattresses. You could come up here to sleep off your drugs, I guess, or have sex.

I paused at the door of the third room. Heard the whimper. Flung the door open, burst into the room.

My flashlight picked out a figure wrapped around itself so tightly that it looked like a ball. Brown hair visible between the knees.

"Sabrina Granev? Your mother is worried and the FBI is looking for you. Let's get you out of here."

She didn't hear me, but kept whimpering, rocking herself. I knelt beside her, trying to talk her into responding, but she kept herself tucked into a tight ball. I tried to pull her hands away from her shoulders so that I could lift her. She was clenching her muscles so hard that I was panting in earnest by the time I had prized her arms and legs apart. I put my hands under her armpits and dragged her, lifeguard fashion, to the stairs.

She screamed in terror, words that I couldn't make out, and began kicking and thrashing, jerking me around in a circle. I dropped her arms, and she scuttled back to the room.

I called her name in the low, firm voice that lifeguards are supposed to use with frenzied victims. She screamed louder.

I did a two-finger whistle, loud, I was the coach. She stopped screaming. I whistled again.

"You cannot stay in this house, Granev. I am here to take you away. Get to your feet. Now!" I used the sternest voice I had, coach unhappy with a lackluster team effort, ten laps around the track.

"I am Coach Warshawski. You need to do exactly what I tell you. Do you understand? Say, 'yes, Coach!'"

After a moment, she said, "Yes, Coach," in a trembling voice.

"Come to me and take my hand." I turned on the flashlight on my phone and shone it on my face and hand, then pointed it at her. She stumbled forward, grabbed my hand.

I led her down the steep staircase, moving step to step on my butt in case she started thrashing again.

When we reached the bottom, Sabrina was shaking so violently I could barely hold her. She clung to me but didn't fight me. I marched her through the rooms to the kitchen door. She was icy after her long hours in the underheated house, but she apparently still had enough remnants of an athlete's physique to keep going.

When we were outside, I took off my heavy hoodie and wrapped it around her. Athlete's physique or not, she was too depleted to walk back to my car. I was trying to figure out the warmest, safest place to park her when strobe lights split the night. A trio of squad cars turned up the drive. They squealed to a halt with a great spraying of what was left of the gravel.

The lead car turned on its spotlight. A voice bellowed through a bullhorn. "Let the girl go and no one will get hurt."

9

ACADEMIC EXERCISES

I SPENT A LONG night with Lawrence's finest, along with deputies from the sheriff's office. FBI Agent Stamoran had apparently been monitoring the police frequency, because he showed up with a subordinate. There was the usual jurisdictional squabble you get anytime the feds step in, but everyone had the same basic question: What had I been doing in the abandoned house?

We were meeting in the LKPD's big conference room, but the number of LEOs meant that Agent Stamoran was forced to stand. He and I were the only two wearing masks, which did not turn us into BFFs.

"Just be glad we knew to go to that house," Stamoran said to me. "Otherwise you could be facing a murder charge if the Granev girl had died."

"Since I had nothing to do with the young *woman* being in that house, there is no possible way a murder or any other charge of grievous harm could be made. How did you know to drive out there?"

"A neighbor reported suspicious activity," Stamoran said.

"Oh, my," I said. "That's the kind of session we're going to have? Where you disrespect me so blatantly that you don't pretend to make up a credible lie?"

"What is that supposed to mean?" Stamoran asked.

"There are no neighbors closer than a quarter mile away. Unless someone was flying drones over the place, I don't know what activity they could have seen."

"We all know you've been struggling since that student you were looking for killed himself," Stamoran said. "We know you have a tendency for violence. We figure you could have drugged Sabrina Granev and hidden her so you could find her and look like a hero."

I felt a wave of vertigo, dug my nails into my palms to steady myself. And felt something viscous in my right palm. Blood. Not now, don't do this, not when you need your wits, don't go seeing blood. My left hand was clean. I shut my eyes, looked again. Real blood, someone else's. Sabrina's?

"Well?" Stamoran bawled. "Nothing to say? I guess we can all agree that's how it went down."

The whole room was staring at me, not my hand, which they couldn't see. Jackals, wanting to bite and be done with it.

"How it went down?" I made myself smile at him, my evil smile. "That's a TV cop cliché, a fallback for the times when you don't know how to think. You're referring to a tragedy, about which you know so little that I know you didn't get your information from the Bureau or the Chicago Police Department. Maybe someone gave you a Classic Comics version to save you reading the big words."

My eyes swept the room. A few people were hiding smiles at my insult: the agent hadn't made himself popular. "Agent Stamoran is talking about a tragedy in Chicago last fall. A student was murdered. The horrible details are a matter of record: the student, a young trans woman, was murdered by their father and the death is considered infanticide: a child murdered by its parent."

The junior LEOs shifted uncomfortably in their seats. One of the county deputies cleared his throat and asked why I'd gone out to the house on Yancy Hill tonight—the Dundee place, he called it.

"Sabrina Granev's friends were worried that she had an opioid problem after her injury. I talked to street people who told me college kids were dealing in the area bars. I made a tour of downtown bars. Someone told me about the house—they didn't tell me it was called the Dundee place. I didn't know Sabrina would be there. It was the only lead I had, so I followed it."

"You should have reported that to us!" a town cop said.

"I ordered you to stop looking," Stamoran said to me, and then turned a dull mahogany as he realized how stupid that made him look.

"I tried talking to the Lawrence department this morning—I guess by now that was yesterday morning—and your team dismissed me, treating me like an addict looking for a score."

More uncomfortable shifting among the troops. I eyed them sardonically, before continuing my report.

"I'd tried reaching Sabrina's parents all day yesterday, and finally connected with her mother. As you can imagine, Valerie Granev was frantic. She didn't want to believe her daughter would be using drugs—no parent wants to face that. She said what Stamoran here repeated, that she feared her daughter had been kidnapped. Ms. Granev apparently works on sensitive projects for the DOD. She worried that someone could use her daughter as leverage to pry out national secrets.

"If she was right, I didn't want to get in the FBI's way, but I didn't think looking at a possible drug house would cross national security lines. And, in fact, there was plenty of evidence of drug use at the Dundee house. And Sabrina Granev was, in fact, there, in the grip of a pretty horrifying drug overdose."

That caused a general outcry and a new volley of questions: the identity of the dealers, the identity of whoever told me about the Dundee place, and, from Stamoran, an accusation about my role in getting Sabrina out to the house.

"You're recording this session," I said. "Play my remarks back. They explain everything I did and why."

As I spoke, Zoë Cruickshank, the young reporter with the *Douglas County Herald,* burst into the room. When she saw me, she forced her way through the mob of LEOs to my side.

"Oh, no! I got here after you finished your statement. Did you record it? Can I copy it from your phone? I heard on my scanner that someone found a body in the old Dundee place. Was it that student you were looking for?"

"Who let her in?" a Lawrence cop groaned.

"You know me, Deke, I can track you to the ends of the county if you're part of a story. Chicago—how'd you know the old Dundee place was a drug house? Pretty smart work for a stranger in town."

Deke Everard. The sergeant I'd tried to reach yesterday. In the chaos, both in the room and in my head, I hadn't recognized him.

Everyone seemed to know Cruickshank, all but the two feds. Deke and his team treated her like an annoying kid sister, someone whose questions made them laugh but not take seriously. In the middle of their chaffing, a young cop raised a timid hand.

"Uh, Deke, uh, Sarge—I put out a request to Uber and Lyft to see if someone drove Sabrina Granev out there Sunday night. I just got a message from the Uber driver who took her to Yancy. He says he picked her up outside the Lion's Heart just before midnight. She was alone."

"Did she die out in the drug house?" Zoë demanded.

"No," I said. "She was alive when I found her. I think they took her to your local hospital. Was she wounded? Bleeding?"

Sergeant Everard shook his head. "Not that I know. We don't have all the details yet, but the EMTs said she was suffering from hypothermia and an OD."

At that, Agent Stamoran seemed to think his expertise was needed elsewhere. He packed up his subordinate and left, without even looking at me.

"He was so sure the Granev girl had been kidnapped, he'd already taken over the chief's conference room as a federal incident room," Deke explained to the rest of us. "Meanwhile, Warshawski, let's have the name of the bartender who sent you to the Dundee place. It's okay if you use big words with me—I move my lips when I read them to make sure I get them right."

His team laughed—with him, with me. Stamoran had rubbed them all the wrong way. I decided not to remind him that Sabrina was a woman, not a girl—they were on my side, at least for the moment. Don't spoil it.

"People kept telling me that a group of frat boys from the Omicron Delta Beta house were dealing. Then someone in the parking lot at the Boat Yard told me she thought there were wild parties out at the Dundee place. That didn't seem like a big enough tip to bother you with, but, as I said, it was the only lead I had."

I hoped by positioning Holly in the parking lot, she would sound like a customer. I didn't want to put her and her sister in police sights. Even though I knew they both should be questioned, I was feeling protective, as if they were friends or clients.

Deke started handing out assignments, who was to follow up at the Boat Yard, who was to go around to other bars to see if the dealers could be identified, who was to go to the Omicron house to see what they could find.

Zoë turned to me. "I want an exclusive, Chicago. Tell me what happened tonight."

"It's not very interesting: I went into what I now know is the Dundee house, heard Sabrina crying on the floor above me, and walked up and found her."

"Details." She held her phone under my nose.

"Not at three in the morning," I said.

"And not when she needs to talk to the LKPD." Deke moved between Zoë's phone and me.

He beckoned to a young officer to accompany us into the cubicle that served as his office. He asked for more details about anything I'd noticed at the Dundee house, and anything I'd seen in the Omicron garage.

We went through a few more routine questions and then Deke asked about the blood on my hand. He'd been watching me more closely than I'd realized, which was a discomforting thought.

"It's why I wondered if Sabrina had been wounded. Getting her out of that room and down the stairs was a—it was an intense physical experience. There's blood on my leggings, too."

He got up and looked at my hand and legs. "You know, Warshawski, you should get an HIV test. Drug house, blood, and that stuff hadn't congealed when you landed in it. I'll pass the word on to the county that they'd better have a hazmat team when they go through the place." He made a note.

I got up to leave but asked if Valerie Granev had made it into town.

"Yes. She was actually at the station with the chief when the call came in that you'd found her daughter. She was hot to get out to the Dundee place, but the chief persuaded her to meet the ambulance crew at the hospital. She's probably still there. I don't know why the fed was throwing his muscle around. It was like he'd hoped the girl had been kidnapped so he could strut his stuff. You made him look bad by finding she was a druggie.

"That kid you found in Chicago—the one whose father murdered them in front of you—most cops never have to witness that kind of horror show. Sorry Stamoran rubbed your face in it."

"It keeps haunting me, way more than any other violent crime I've witnessed. I keep seeing blood everywhere."

"Maybe because we're so awash in blood these days," Deke said drily. "When are you heading back?"

"Tomorrow. When I wake up. Do you have someone who could drive me to my B and B? I was hustled into town in a squad car and my Mustang is out on 1450 Road somewhere."

Zoë Cruickshank had been hovering outside his door. When she offered to drive me, the sergeant said, "Give the lady a chance to sleep, Cruickshank. I'll take her home."

Interlude I
GERTRUDE AND CADY

GERTRUDE PEREC WAS at the computer in the alcove she used as an office when Cady came down to the kitchen. Gertrude was sitting with shoulders that would do a marine proud, but she managed to stiffen them farther at her granddaughter's footsteps.

"Nine A.M., missy. You planning to spend the rest of your life sulking over losing that job?"

"I'm not allowed to be depressed? To mourn my career?" Cady spoke to the steel spine.

"I expect better from you than feel-good jargon. Depressed. Mourning your career. Even when I lost your mother, and the grief felt like a saw cutting my body in half, I didn't lie in bed feeling sorry for myself."

Cady shut her eyes. She thought she might scream if her grandmother bragged once again about her stoic commitment to duty.

"Open your eyes when I'm speaking to you, missy."

Cady's face must be reflected in the computer screen. Or Gertrude was a seer. That was entirely possible.

"If you want to fight the firing, go to your union representative, or get your own lawyer. If you want to turn a page and move forward in your life, start figuring out what your next step is. But don't droop like a willow tree—it's hard on the people around you and does you no good in the bargain."

Cady took half a grapefruit from the refrigerator and moved to the breakfast nook without speaking. When five minutes passed in silence, Gertrude said, "Pat Everard was at breakfast this morning."

Cady grunted. The breakfast was a midweek ritual among the most enthusiastic members of Riverside Congregational's women's group. Pat Everard ran the group with Gram, so it wasn't news that she was at the breakfast.

"That Chicago detective is back in town."

"I know," Cady said. She was texting, but she looked up from her phone. "I saw her after the game Sunday."

"You didn't mention that. I never liked that woman."

"I know, Gram. It's why I didn't tell you." Cady looked at her screen and ate another section of grapefruit.

"Cold, I thought. Arrogant, even if she knows her business. As she did in this case—she found that missing student—in time to save her life, Deke told Pat."

"That's good." Cady paused. "Brett Santich was in the parking lot when I was leaving the game. He as good as called me a pedophile."

"Sticks and stones, Miss Cady," Gertrude said sharply. "And you know it's rude to text while I'm talking to you."

"The tongue has no bones, but it's strong enough to break them," Cady said. "Trig Garrity got into a fight, practically a physical one, with Brett over the land on Yancy. Everyone who was still in the parking lot stopped to watch—that's when I saw the detective."

"Trig would fight a dead rabbit if he thought it looked at him sideways. I don't like the deal Brett did over the land, either. Once he sold it, he lost control over it, but that was years ago, not yesterday. There's no point to screaming about it now, the way Trig does. The land means something to me, something personal, which it never did to him. Apparently not to Brett, either."

Gram's family had owned the land when the town was being built in the 1860s, but they'd had to sell during the Great Depression of the 1930s. It hadn't been in her family for close to a century, but she still acted as though she had a stake in it.

"I guess Brett got overextended when he built that little subdivision on Yancy," Gertrude added. "He mortgaged just about everything, from what Pat and I could make out, when he applied for planning permission. And then he did a deal with that Topeka bank."

For Gertrude, doing business with an out-of-town bank was like doing a deal with the devil, even if the out-of-town was only twenty-five miles away.

Gertrude gave a snort of bitter laughter and added, "If Trig Garrity didn't make me see red, white, and blue, I'd have joined in his protest. Anyway, it was out there on Yancy land where that missing student turned up. The Dundee place, that old brick house on the south side of the hill."

"Is that who owned the land at the bottom of the hill? Dundees? Were they cousins or something I never heard of?"

"When my mother was a girl, when the family still owned the land, they leased it to a tenant farmer. Schapen, I think, but definitely not Dundee or even Santich. Santiches rented it out during the 1960s, the hippie craze, you know, when all the long-haired kids wanted to lie around in the country pretending to raise their own food but smoking pot. Whoever Dundee was predated all that history."

"Gee, Gram, if you don't know, the Dundees probably never existed."

Gertrude narrowed her eyes—was it a joke or a criticism? Cady liked to accuse her of getting overinvolved in local people's lives.

She sidestepped the issue. "Pat Everard said the place was being used as a drug house, but no one knew, either in the sheriff's office or the city."

"Oh, please, Gram! If V.I. Warshawski discovered it after being in town twenty-four hours, the cops must have known about it. Not to mention Brett himself. He's just trying to avoid legal liability. The students' parents could sue him for operating a dangerous business, so he's trying to pretend he doesn't know. Ditto for the police, even if Aunt Pat's your oldest friend and Deke is the best-looking single guy in town."

Cady put her grapefruit skin in the compost bin and the spoon and bowl in the sink. She was leaving the room, but turned back to kiss Gertrude on the head.

"I'm okay, Gram. I just need to sort out where I go from here. I am tired of parents screaming at me because their baby got an F for not doing any work, or because I want their kids to think in bigger ways about the big world around them. Maybe I'll join Trig on the barricades, screaming at Santich until he admits he's a jerk."

10

ROPE BRIDGE

SHOWERED WHEN I got back to my room, Lady Macbeth scrubbing blood from my hands. I hoped the hot water would relax me, but when I slid beneath the comforter, I couldn't sleep. Every time I turned over I seemed to feel Sabrina's bones, sharp, too close to her skin, poking into my breasts.

Bernie phoned at seven, just as I'd managed to drop off. I had texted her when I got to my room, to let her know Sabrina was safe, but I'd forgotten to silence my phone. Bernie wanted to know where I'd found Sabrina and how.

My first impulse—hang up—I put aside. Talk to her now, get it done.

"The guys Angela saw her talking to in the bar must have given her the address of the house where I found her."

"Ah, Vic, I knew you would make it happen, almost like magic."

"It wasn't magic, Bernie, it was luck, luck plus following the only trail I could turn up."

"Even so, I am grateful, Angela is also. Thank you for doing what was painful. Now maybe the Granevs will take Sabrina out of school and send her to a clinic. Living with her has made us all *stressées*. She is depressed, not eating, us guessing she is using while the parents and coaches act as if she had flu, an illness she will recover from swiftly."

"You and Angela had a difficult fall trying to support her," I said. "Did you talk to your own coaches about her behavior?"

"We were afraid maybe we would be responsible for her losing her scholarship," Bernie said. "Anyway, now can you see that you are wrong to let doubts devour you? You are still the brilliant problem solver."

My stomach twisted. "You know those rope bridges you see in movies? The ones that connect two inaccessible mountain peaks? In the movies the ropes are fraying. The hero makes it across seconds before the last strand breaks. That's me, Bernie. The last strand is fraying."

"But, Vic, I don't see this at all. In one day you discover a drug house, you recover a person close to death. You should feel as high as angels. You proved you are still a great detective. This is what you needed."

I hung up before my anger overcame me and I began shouting at Bernie: *I don't need this, more blood, used needles, I need to sit by a stream on a sunny day with a cool drink, listening to birds and not thinking of anything.*

I lay back down, trying to take those deep breaths that fitness mavens say are key to relaxation, but I couldn't relax back into sleep. I finally gave up on it. Got up, tried to move my tired muscles into some stretches, bathed my gritty eyes in hot water. Sergeant Everard had asked me to stay in town another day in case there were follow-up questions, but I planned to leave as soon as possible.

The cleanest clothes I had right now were the ones I'd worn when I drove down on Sunday. They were clean only relative to the soiled hoodie and trail shoes I'd bought yesterday. I took those and the bloodstained leggings out to Nurse Norma's garbage can. Maybe the dirt could be cleaned off, but not the memory of Sabrina Granev gibbering on the floor.

When I was packed, and had put my used linens in Nurse Norma's washing machine, I phoned Sabrina's mother. The call went to voicemail. I left a message, saying I was glad I'd found Sabrina in time but would like an update on her condition. I sent a text to Nurse Norma, thanking her for helping me evade possible surveillance last night. You may have seen the news that I found the missing student in a drug house northwest of town.

Zoë Cruickshank phoned as I was starting to summon an Uber to take me to my car. "Chicago! I need my exclusive."

Her energy was as nerve-jarring as Bernie's. "I can't tell you anything more than you can learn from the police," I said.

"You're wrong, Chicago: they won't talk to me, not even Deke. Please—this is my big chance!"

"Addiction up close and personal is your big chance?" My voice was harsh.

"I didn't mean it like that," she muttered. "You have an important career, you're a success, but I'm getting by on part-time jobs because the paper can only pay me twelve thousand a year. If I can cover an important story then I could get more freelance work."

Put like that—twenty-five years old or so, ambitious but with bleak prospects—she didn't need me stomping on her dreams. I said if she'd drive me out to my car, I'd tell her what I could.

She was at the curb in ten minutes. One big attraction to Lawrence: you could get anywhere fast. On the way out to 1450 Road, Zoë had her phone on the dash, recording our conversation. I repeated what I'd told the cops last night.

"I was surprised that no one was there when I arrived," I said. "The tire tracks and empties made it look as though they'd had a big crowd, but it wasn't even midnight when I showed up. The amount of debris in the house, and the number of tire tracks stirring up the driveway, there must have been a good-size crowd."

By the time I finished answering Zoë's questions, we'd reached the bend in the road where the Dundee house stood. Zoë stopped at the mouth of the driveway. "That's Trig Garrity's car up there."

She turned in and pulled up behind a battered van. It was hard to tell what the original color might have been. The rear bumper was plastered with stickers advocating to save the earth, whales, and democracy, and to overturn *Citizens United* and *Hobby Lobby*.

Zoë got out and dashed up to the house. Trig, still in his faded army parka, was at the kitchen door. He seemed about to knock out a pane of glass with a rock when we arrived.

"I know it's a fucking crime scene, Cruickshank. It's a crime that the whole county puts up with this house and what goes on in it. I pointed that out to Prince Santich, but he said it wasn't his problem."

"At the police station, they called it the Dundee house," I said. "Does it actually belong to Santich?"

Trig glared at me. "Who are you? Some hotshot lawyer?"

"She's a hotshot detective from Chicago," Zoë said. "She found Sabrina Granev in this house last night when the police and even the FBI didn't know where to look."

"Local pigs couldn't find a cornfield if they drove into it." Trig spat. "They're all in bed with Santich. Yes, your moneyness, no, your moneyness, tell me how low to stoop, your moneyness."

"That's so not fair!" Zoë cried. "Deke Everard is a good cop and so is—"

"Everard's arrested me five times on Brett Sant-snitch's say-so. And then Brett started after Cady, because she was speaking truth to power. And now he's going after Clarina Coffin for the crime of supporting my work."

I didn't want to hear Trig rant about his work as the county watch-dog, so I repeated my question about whether the Dundee house belonged to Santich.

"The Dundees aren't around to defend it so Santich probably stole it from them," Trig said.

He swung his arm back to smash the glass door pane, but I grabbed his wrist and pulled his hand down.

"Why do you want to go to prison?" I asked.

"What—you come all the way from Chicago to arrest me?"

"I'm a private investigator. No arrest powers."

"Private, public, pigs both."

I let go of his wrist. "Go ahead. I can see why your PD is tired of trying to defend you."

"Trig, don't be an asshole," Zoë said. "You know if the sheriff or Chief McDowell find out the house has been broken into, they'll want to talk to you. Vic is smart; you should pay attention to her."

"Tell me something, then, Ms. Smart-from-Chicago."

"Can't tell you anything," I said. "You know it all already. However, if I were investigating, I'd wonder what use you were making of this house. Did you store stuff here, figuring the dealers and users wouldn't bother about it? Posters and bullhorns, or something bigger, more worrying if a sheriff's deputy found it?"

He gave a bark of something like a laugh. "You are so far off base you're not even playing the right game."

He stomped over to his van and took off. The doors rattled and the tires were balding, but the engine ran quietly, and he didn't leave an exhaust trail.

I looked after him. "In court Monday, the judge said Santich didn't own the land, that some corporation did."

"I went over to the recorder's office," Zoë said. "The little bit of the property Brett hung on to includes this house. He still owns and farms that field"—she pointed toward where I'd parked my car—"but he lives over in that subdivision around Yancy School. He raised the money to build it, but then he got slammed in the downturn and had to sell the houses to some hedge fund. Back in the 1930s the Santiches were super rich. Gertrude Perec's family couldn't hang on to the farm- land they owned here on Yancy, so they sold to Santiches, I think to Brett's grandfather. Anyway, it must be unlucky land because who- ever owns it can't afford to keep it."

She laughed. "Maybe I'll do a little paragraph on how it's un- lucky to own land on Yancy—can the new resort going up break the curse?"

"If Brett is bankrupt, why is Trig so hot against him?"

Zoë shrugged. "Maybe it's like Judge Bhagavatula said, Trig didn't do his homework. Anyway, Brett's family are like so many farmers around here, they can't compete with the big corporate farms in the west of the state, and so they scramble to hang on to their land. Only Brett lost most of his with some unlucky investments. It's a shame, really, that Trig doesn't understand the odds farm families are fighting. They could use some support."

"What about the Dundees? Are they another local family?"

Zoë shook her head. "I never heard of them. Not that that means anything—I didn't grow up here and so all these family connections, they're something I have to learn as I go along. I've been working for the *Herald* for two years now and I'm hoping it will lead to better things—which this drug story could make happen."

Her face brightened, and she put a hand on my arm. "Why don't you stay and find out what's been going on in this house, and who the Dundees are. I could report the investigation as it unfolds, like a docudrama!"

"And your twelve thousand a year would cover paying for my

time and expertise? I charge by the hour, plus expenses, which in this case would include moving my household to Kansas. Why don't you investigate and do a daily podcast on your progress? That would get you a big audience and a new career direction."

"It would be better with two people," she wheedled.

My face must have looked ominous—she hastily moved away to take pictures of the outside of the house. While I was waiting on her, I got a call from someone named Jenna Ettenberg who said she was the Granev family's attorney.

"Valerie Granev wants to talk to you. She's staying with her daughter at the local hospital; if you could meet her there it would be a help. Text her when you get to the lobby."

11

TAKE ME TO THE LIMIT

VALERIE GRANEV'S FACE belonged in a funhouse mirror. She'd started the day yesterday with makeup, but her foundation had caked and cracked. She had mascara smears under her eyes, accentuating her look of unbearable grief.

"How is Sabrina doing?" I asked.

"Not too well." She swallowed, looked away. "When we got to the hospital, she was screaming, having frightening hallucinations. She said monsters were waiting outside the window, she begged me to make them go away.

"I—I was useless, I thought if we went to the window she would see—but the nurses explained it was hallucinations from cold and dehydration and"—she flinched—"whatever drugs she'd taken. At least when they put in the IVs she calmed down. They let me sleep with her and at seven she woke up and screamed 'they're still there, they're still there, make them go away.' I told her that Daddy had gotten rid of them and she went back to sleep, but right before you got here she started seeing them again."

She squeezed her eyes shut. "I've been so—negligent. I saw at Christmas that she wasn't well. Ram—my husband—we're an athletic family. For New Year's, we always go to a place in Utah to ski. Sabrina couldn't ski—this year—her broken ankle wasn't healing—she was in a lot of pain. She was already too thin, not eating, not working at her rehab."

Granev kneaded her fingers. "I pushed her to take her rehab seriously. She—she was ranked among the top twenty young U.S. soccer players before the ankle break. Twenty Under Twenty. She's competitive and ambitious."

A sob caught up with her.

"She was. That's my nature, and she has it, too. But at Christmas she was apathetic, didn't seem to care, and all I did was scold her.

"I flew to Chicago at Thanksgiving and saw she wasn't making an effort with her rehab. I lectured her but didn't really pay attention—I was under a deadline, as if killing more Russians was more worth my time than my own daughter."

Her mouth twisted in a spasm of self-loathing. "Instead, I tried getting her housemates to push her to do her rehab, but of course they couldn't. It wasn't fair to them. I—I didn't want to see the problem."

I nodded, not speaking.

"The young Black woman Sabrina lives with—the basketball star—she tried to tell me when I came back with Sabrina after the winter break, and all I did was tell Sabrina to follow—what's her name? Angela? Angela's training schedule and she'd be back on her feet. How cold was that? The truth is, I was annoyed with Sabrina for not taking her career as seriously as Angela takes hers. I didn't want to know she was struggling with these damned drugs.

"And now—we don't know how much damage she has. Brain, body—will she walk properly, let alone play, or have a family—" The enormity of her daughter's losses crashed in on her, and she began to weep in earnest.

A hospital staffer stopped near us, looking down in concern. *Water?* I mouthed. She nodded and came back in a moment with a bottle and a cup.

"Were you able to reach your husband?" I asked. "I gather he's up in the mountains away from normal phone service."

"Yes, wilderness camping is his great love and he longs to run year-round programs, and get the resources for less-able children. We used to go camping in the Uinta Mountains when Sabrina was little, but then my career got more demanding, and when Sabrina was a teen she wanted to spend spring break at soccer camps or with her friends. I—I used to argue with Ram that he didn't care about her future, and he said I cared enough for two, so he turned his attention to the youth programs he works with."

She rubbed her eyes, further smearing the mascara.

"Ram is hiking down from the camp, but with the kids and equipment it will take hours and then—anyway, as soon as it's safe to move Sabrina, we're getting her to a rehab clinic that works with—with addicts, so there's no point him coming here. Although maybe if Ram shows up he can persuade her that Daddy got rid of her monsters."

She went over her failures like an accountant with a spreadsheet, her coldness, her imperceptiveness, her absorption in her avionics career. "I loved being one of the 'Forty Under Forty STEM Women to Look Out For.'" Her voice cracked. "And when Sabrina was one of Twenty Under Twenty, I was so proud, like these numbers mean something more than paying attention to your own child."

She was crying in earnest. I let her cry, found more water and a box of tissues.

She finally wound down and looked at me. "I know I owe her life to you, the police told me that, but how—how did you know where to find her?"

"I didn't," I said. "I'm a stranger in this town. When I asked questions of likely people, the house where I found her was the only thing close to a lead I turned up. I wasn't expecting to find your daughter, but I thought if there was a party going on, I'd get leads on other places to look for someone trying to score—trying to find meds. The FBI agent ordered me to stop looking, in case she'd been kidnapped, but I thought finding leads to dealers wouldn't interfere with a kidnapping investigation."

"Agent Stamoran thinks you got her to go out there. He said you need to look like a hero after making a big mistake with a different college student last fall."

"Yes, he made that slanderous and outrageous statement in the police station last night. I don't know why he felt he needed to discredit me, but he is, in fact, wrong."

"He says you can't prove you didn't take Sabrina out there." She didn't sound accusatory, more anguished and uncertain.

"You can't prove a negative, Ms. Granev." Big lies, small lies, all circulating on the net, destroying life after life. The sheer tawdriness of life today made the whole world appear gray.

I summoned what I hoped was a reassuring tone. "Even though we disagree on my role in what happened to Sabrina, your FBI agent should be able to track down the dealers who sold drugs to her. The Bureau has the resources for that kind of work."

She gave a little headshake. "He's not my agent. I don't know who called the Bureau about Sabrina's disappearance. It wasn't me, but anyone who heard me on the phone with you or with Ram—I was so distraught I wasn't careful where I spoke."

She pressed the heel of her hand against her forehead. "I can't finish a coherent thought today. Agent Stamoran—maybe old Mr. Tulloh called the Bureau. If he heard about Sabrina—everyone jostles for space close to the head man—anyone could have told him. When you're a billionaire, you know everyone wants to do you favors, even the FBI, so maybe that's why they sent Stamoran over from the Topeka office."

She produced a smile to keep from crying again. "I saw Stamoran this morning. He says since Sabrina wasn't kidnapped, the Bureau doesn't have jurisdiction to track down dealers, that it's the business of the local police. I know I should care more, get on some soapbox and demand they protect other people's children, but that doesn't matter to me."

"Don't add that to the list of other things you're beating yourself up over," I said. "You have one job right now, looking after your daughter. The local cops are good; they'll follow up."

"There's one thing I wanted to ask you." She looked up at me again. Her mascara had turned into black stalactites, reaching from her eyes to her jaw.

"I know Sabrina is hallucinating when she's screaming about the monsters coming to the window, but what if she really saw something last night? If it's someone who could come after her—I—she doesn't seem to remember anything else. I'm asking you—you did what no one else could, finding Sabrina. I want you to find out what she really saw when she was in that house."

"No!" My response was involuntary. She winced, and I tried to soften my answer—my home was in Chicago, my clients as well as my elderly neighbor needed me, I was here without clothes or even my computer.

"Today and tomorrow," she said. "I can pay whatever your fee is, send it by Zelle to your bank. The FBI and the police, they won't pay attention. You could go out to that place and see—I don't know what a detective can see."

I started to say "no" more forcefully, and then I thought of the blanket by the front door, with blood on it still fresh last night at midnight. A party had been interrupted, everyone but Sabrina had fled. She'd been screaming when she saw me, nonsense syllables I'd thought at the time, but maybe she'd thought I was one of her monsters.

It hadn't occurred to me last night, but I'd gone into a house where a party had been at full swing not too much earlier, and yet I hadn't seen any cars leaving as I walked to the house from the farm track where I'd parked. The blood on the blanket was just starting to congeal. That meant someone had been dripping blood less than fifteen minutes before my arrival.

I pulled up one of my contracts on the app I'd created for my business. Valerie filled it out and signed it, including her private cell phone number, and sent me four thousand dollars without blinking.

12

MONSTERS

PARKED IN THE same place I'd used before and walked down the road to the Dundee house. The day was dull, with snow threatening. The wind had risen, stirring dust devils in the plowed field on the south side of the road.

Despite the cold air, I moved slowly up the drive, trying to see if anyone had driven here after Zoë and I left this morning. I was hoping to find signs of the Omicron boys' Porsche. The county hadn't sent a crime scene unit in yet; the fraternity crew might have come to collect leftover product, but I didn't see any signs of them.

The kitchen door was unlocked. Trig apparently hadn't tried the handle but had gone straight for a rock. He wanted to go inside, but when I suggested he was hiding something in the house he'd been scornful: I was so far off base I wasn't even playing the right game.

What was the right game? Drugs? The protests he was running with the woman named Clarina? Or had Cady Perec's firing felt personal to him?

I waited for a moment inside the kitchen door, ready to run if anyone tried to jump me, but the house felt empty.

The kitchen looked worse in daylight. When I turned on a light, roaches skittered away from the cartons of food. I could see more drug detritus—not needles, but the foil wraps and test-tube bottles that tabs and powders come in. Ivy hadn't shown for her cleanup gig. Or she'd come, not seen her pay, and left again.

I stood still, listening for a creaking floorboard, stifled cough, but didn't hear anything except the wind rattling the windows. I moved past the downstairs rooms into the front hall.

The blanket was gone. Someone had returned for it. Someone could be in here now, silent as a grave, waiting for me.

"Don't go there, V.I." I said out loud. "Keep your head."

I climbed the stairs to the upper floor, stomping loudly on the narrow risers. At the top, I hugged the wall, making myself as small a target as possible, but no one appeared, no one shot at me.

I checked the three small bedrooms, found a bathroom tucked into what had been a closet, saw nothing.

The window in the room where I'd found Sabrina overlooked the woods behind the house. If she'd seen monsters, they would have come across the fields or through the woods. Maybe deer or some other animal that her drug-riddled brain had turned into something from a horror film.

Back in the kitchen, I saw another door that I'd overlooked before. The cellar. I found a string attached to a naked bulb that swung above my head like a noose.

Another steep narrow staircase. No handrail. In movies, you yell at the heroine not to go down those stairs. I wasn't a heroine, though, but something less dazzling, an exhausted detective far from home.

I almost missed the woman. She was propped against the wall under the stairs. Her head had flopped to one side, but her eyes were open, irises cloudy. She was wearing a down coat that someone had stuffed her into, unskillfully, one arm in, one showing where her clothes had been ripped away from her body.

I didn't touch her, but bent over her. Bra unhooked, pants pulled away from her hips. Her feet were bare.

The blood on last night's blanket had come from the back of her head. Someone had smashed it, hard, probably more than once. Blood and bone chips had fallen onto the coat's collar.

"*Poverina*," I whispered, blinking back tears. "Who hated you this much?"

13

WHOSE WOODS THESE ARE

YOU HAVE SERIOUS explaining to do." Deke Everard's voice was raw with fatigue. He probably hadn't been to bed at all since dropping me at Norma's place in the predawn.

"What would you like me to explain?"

"What you really know about the Dundee house. You conveniently uncovered two crimes there in"—he looked at his wrist—"just about twelve hours. Don't bat your eyes and tell me you never heard of the place before."

"I'm not an eye batter, Sergeant, but I never heard of the place before last night."

He smacked the tabletop. "Don't give me that crap. The DA is looking into what we can charge you with. Obstruction, concealing a crime for starters. Just so you know, that fed has shown up again, making more noises about kidnapping."

We were in an interrogation room at the LKPD headquarters. The building was new, so new that the interrogation rooms didn't yet smell of blood, sweat, and tears.

"Who was the woman whose body I found?" I asked.

"Clarina Coffin. Tell me what you know about her."

"Nothing," I said. Zoë had told me about Clarina Coffin's role in getting Cady Perec fired, but you don't do yourself any favors by rambling on to the cops.

Deke demanded that I tell him what I was doing at the Dundee place this morning.

"You know I didn't put Ms. Coffin's body in that basement," I said. "Nor did I hit her over the head hard enough to kill her."

"You had blood on you last night," he said. "Where did it come from?"

"A blanket by the front door. I was terrified Sabrina Granev's body might be inside, but when I unrolled it, nothing was there."

"And you didn't think to report it?"

"I mentioned the blood to you, but in the stress of finding Sabrina, I forgot about the blanket." I kept my voice steady. Don't push on a cop who's already close to the edge. "There'd been a party going on, which apparently broke up abruptly. You surely noticed all the booze and foil wraps and so on, right? No cars when I got to the house last night. But if I'd thought about the bloody blanket at all, I'd have guessed a fight among the partygoers. You find out who set up the party? Was it the Omicron boys?"

All the time I was talking, I knew I should keep my mouth shut. I could hear how a DA would spin this in court: *The defendant had a bloody blanket in her possession. The defendant was at the crime scene off and on during twelve hours when a woman was murdered and a second woman close to death from an overdose.* I had always told my clients, *Don't talk if you don't have a lawyer with you and even then, don't talk.* Yet here I was, saying way more than I should.

"You disappeared after the emergency crew showed," Deke said. "Where did you go?"

"I gave a statement to the first responders. And then I went to my car. I was badly shaken. The woman's dead body was hard enough, but the way her clothes had been ripped—the violence—the violation—"

I'd sat in the Mustang's passenger seat, my knees pulled to my chin in a little Sabrina-like ball. I probably would have screamed like Sabrina if someone had tried to pry me out of my car.

In the months after the Incident in Chicago, I'd consulted a trauma specialist. She'd suggested a technique—arms crossed over the chest, tapping side to side in a heart-like rhythm, chanting something. This morning I tried "You are safe/You will survive." After a time I was able to uncoil myself, drink some water. I dozed for almost an hour.

By the time I woke and drove back to the Dundee house, the emergency responders had left. I tried calling Valerie, to let her know that her daughter's monsters had brought a woman's body into the house. The call went to voicemail.

I stood irresolutely in the drive, the dust and sleet stinging my face. I tried to work out a timeline for the monsters. How had they avoided the party and me both last night?

The blood had been fresh when I went to the house last night, but since there'd been no cars, I thought it likely that the body had been carried through the woods. I went into the undergrowth north of the house. Not directly in the line of sight from Sabrina's window, but parallel to it.

The bushes and trees immediately behind the house hadn't been tended to for years. It was easy to see breaks in the branches, but the ground was still hard in mid-February, not holding footprints. About ten yards beyond the thickest undergrowth, I found a trail, overgrown but a definite path up the hill. I followed it, my running shoes slipping in the rotting leaves.

A little farther along, I came upon the remains of a chimney, the kind they used to build up the sides of houses when the fireplace was the main heat source. When I squatted to study the area, I could see a dimple in the ground where the foundation had been laid.

The trail, or what was left of it, continued upward through woods that hadn't been pruned for so long that dead trees blocked the trail in places. I found ruins from three other buildings, including an old well with a rusted cover bolted over it. Some kind of little community had tried to make a go of it here, but only the Dundee house had survived.

I finally came to a fence, with a worn sign proclaiming PRIVATE PRO . . . TRESPASSERS WILL . . . It was as if Piglet from Winnie-the-Pooh had set up house nearby. I looked around and was unnerved to see an actual owl, a big tawny creature who watched me with amused contempt: *You're no match for the countryside, detective. Go back to Chicago where you belong.*

The TRESPASSERS WILL sign had pulled the wire away from the

fence post. I stepped on it, pushing it to the ground, and walked on. The land was flattening out, and the area had been clear-cut. I came to a more formidable fence, a new Cyclone number that also was signposted, this time spelling out the prosecution that awaited trespassers (the full extent of the law! Be afraid!).

It was cold on the hilltop. A steady wind was blowing from Chicago. I put up my arms, begging the wind to pull me aloft, fly me home. Nothing happened.

Zoë had said that someone was building a resort up here, maybe some apartment buildings as well. The hilltop had been leveled. In the middle of it was a slab of concrete, perhaps a hundred yards square, with the pipe sticking up from the edges, showing where electrics and plumbing fittings would go.

Industrial lampposts dotted the perimeter, providing cones of light that gave a sense of the size of the project. A road led into the site on the side of the plowed field farthest from me. Trucks were beetling up and down, stirring up clouds of dust.

The south side, where I was standing, held the trailers that served as offices. One was labeled KIRMEK CONSTRUCTION, PROJECT MANAGER. The other was for the project architect and engineer.

When I'd watched Trig's court appearance last week, the judge had said it was a night manager at Kirmek who had filed the trespassing complaint against Trig. This was where he'd been protesting the destruction of old-growth trees.

I wandered over to the western edge of the open field, where outsize machinery was standing near some equipment sheds. These were what you'd need for building something big—bulldozer, giant steam shovel, drilling rig, blazoned with the letter *K* in a circle. They'd installed the tower for a pylon, but hadn't yet built the cage, nor laid any cable as far as I could tell.

On the north side of the giant concrete slab, stack of poles, like outsize Lincoln Logs, lay on the ground next to a piling hammer. I guessed a second pylon would go up there. It would be more challenging to build pylons on the slope, but the essential equipment seemed to be in place.

I didn't see anything that looked like the foundations for hotels or shops. There was one small structure built from cement blocks that looked more permanent than the trailers.

I headed toward that, eyes on the ground, hoping to find something, a fragment of cloth, something that would show the dead woman had been carried over the fence last night. I didn't see anything, but as I reached the cement blocks I heard shouting.

On the far side of the building, two men were in an angry confrontation. The wind was too strong to carry their words, but they were poking each other with index fingers when they weren't balling their hands into fists. One had a hard hat on; the other, bareheaded, looked like the man Trig Garrity had been baiting in the field house parking lot the other night.

"Mr. Santich!"

The pair had been so wrapped in their fight they hadn't seen me approach.

"Who the fuck are you and how did you get here?" the hard hat roared.

"I'm a detective. I'm detecting how a dead woman's body ended up in the Dundee house."

"You can be an astronaut looking for the moon, but you don't do it on this land. It's posted. Clearly. Private Property."

The hard hat hadn't registered my words, but Santich had.

"What are you talking about? A dead woman? What—that Chicago girl who went missing?"

"You're not keeping up, Mr. Santich. The Chicago *woman* isn't dead, she's in the hospital recovering from a drug overdose. Haven't the police talked to you about drug parties happening in your house?"

I paused, but he didn't say anything.

"No, what I found was the body of an older woman, recently dead, in your basement."

"I live on the other side of the hill," he muttered.

"The Dundee house doesn't belong to you? I thought that bit of land it sits on was still yours."

"Yes, it's my land, but the house—no one's lived there for years."

"Someone rents it from you? To use for entertainment?" I prodded.

"I don't have time to look after the house. It's historic, it can't be torn down, but if someone's been in it, no one's told me. You seen activity down there?" he asked the hard hat.

"I don't have time to go crawling around all those trees down below. My responsibility stops at the fence, which *you* have trespassed." On the last phrase, he turned to lean over me, making sure I saw the handle of a large-caliber something in a shoulder holster underneath his bomber jacket.

I didn't move, although he was close enough that I could have counted his nose hairs if I'd wanted to.

He stepped back. "Let's see your badge."

"No badge," I said. "I'm private, not public."

"What, are you part of that asshole Urine's harassment brigade?"

"Asshole Urine?" I repeated.

"Don't play dumb with me, bitch. I didn't just fall off a turnip truck."

"No, indeed," I agreed. "You damaged your brain years ago."

He reddened and reflexively put a hand on his gun grips.

"Off the land, now," he roared.

I saluted and turned around. My shoulders itched, worrying about a bullet, but I refused to look back or to move fast.

I wished I knew what he and Santich had been arguing about. Santich hadn't known about the dead woman, I was pretty sure of that, but maybe the hard hat did. And who was the asshole Urine with a harassment brigade? Or was he saying, the asshole's urine?

Asshole Urine. Of course. In court yesterday, Judge Bhagavatula had called him Irwin, and Trig had reacted. It was the kind of ugly nickname bullies would have slapped on him in third grade. No wonder he wanted to be called Trig.

But who was on Trig's harassment brigade? The dead woman? She'd meet him at the Dundee house during the day—there was no risk of any drug parties at noon—and they'd map out strategy? Had he been there this morning because he had a meeting scheduled with Clarina Coffin?

The woodland near the fence had held the usual dreary litter of modern life—Styrofoam, chip bags, bottles—but between the hilltop and the clearing around the Dundee house, the woods were clean. I hoped Santich could hang on to the land so there'd be a little refuge from trash. Was that what made Trig so angry with Santich? He knew the guy was planning a secret deal for these woods?

Close to the wellhead by the remaining chimney stack, I saw a scrap of paper. Litter after all. I picked it up, hoping for some revelation, but it was just a few lines torn from a larger document. Someone had been disappointed or angry and torn it up.

> through the grapevine that
> eries about Kansas his
> like to be first in line to
> dy to reveal your work to
> lunch in our offices in Westbro

I was going to drop it back on the trail, but I stuck it in my pocket. It might be a clue, although to what it was impossible to say.

14

INSECURITY BLANKET

WHEN I FINALLY made it back into town, I tried again to reach Valerie. I left a second message, saying it was possible Sabrina's monsters had been real people carrying a dying woman through the woods into the house.

Clarina had been wrapped in a blanket. I pictured Sabrina at the top of the steep stairs, watching the men maneuver Clarina through the house to the basement. It's not easy to carry a dead person. The blanket flipped open, Sabrina saw the face. She hadn't cried out—if she had she would have been killed herself. The sight cut the last strand tethering Sabrina to the world around her. I couldn't prove it, but it was a workable scenario.

When I called Norma to extend my stay yet again, she said, "You can have one more night, but I have a couple arriving tomorrow evening who've booked the suite for a week. I hope you can go home tomorrow so that you're not left hanging."

I hoped so, too.

I had two messages from Deke Everard, three from Zoë. *Chicago, I told you we needed to team up. Did you know Clarina was dead when we were at the house this morning? Call me!*

Deke wanted me at the LKPD headquarters on the double. I bought yet another pair of clean jeans, went back to Norma's to wash the woods out of my hair, and got to the cop shop only ninety minutes after Deke's second text.

I told him what I'd been doing, although I left out the part where I was huddling in my car on the brink of a meltdown. I suggested they look at Santich's finances to see if he was making money from drugs at the Dundee house. I asked if he knew what the relationship was between Santich and the construction on top of Yancy.

"You're sounding like Trig, wanting to blame Santich for all the problems in the world. Santich grew up here, everyone knows him. He sells insurance to support his family. He's well-respected in the town, even if he went a bit overboard with Cady."

"Sergeant," I said, "the house is on land that he still owns. It isn't blaming him for the evils of the world to ask why he's letting someone hold drug parties there. He claims he doesn't know about them, but that is hard to believe."

"Santich lives on the other side of Yancy," Deke objected. "The Omicron Delts, or some group like them, probably took advantage of an empty house where the owner wouldn't see their activity."

"I went up the hill a little bit ago to see if I could find any trace of Sabrina's monsters," I said. "I came on Santich arguing, quite fiercely, with someone on the construction site."

"That isn't proof that Santich murdered the Coffin woman, or hid her in the Dundee house."

"Convenient," I said. "It's always the Dundee house, never the Santich house."

"It's how things are in this county," Deke said. "People called Larkin have lived in my family's old home for fifty years, but folks still call it the Everard place. You find something that proved Santich murdered the Coffin woman?"

His jeering tone made me reluctant to share, but I showed him the scrap of paper I'd found in the woods.

"This could be anything from anyone," he said, impatient. "It doesn't have any connection to the Coffin woman's death, or to activities at the Dundee place."

"One thing you can see is that the paper is fresh," I said sharply. "It hasn't been lying about in the woods long enough for the paper to start disintegrating."

"Yeah, maybe." He made a sour face but put it in an evidence bag. "I still think it's irrelevant. I'm not spending time and resources on maybes. Stamoran and the DA, Frank Karas, are breathing down my neck, wanting proof that you were responsible for bringing both Sabrina whosis and Clarina to the Dundee house. Don't make it hard for me to stand up for you!"

"Not that I'm not grateful for your support, but all I'm guilty of is stumbling on a dead woman and a nearly dead young woman. I was here two years ago. You saw me working, you know who I am and how I do what I do. Why would you think I'd suddenly become a deranged drug dealer and killer?"

Deke ran his hands through his hair. "Two years ago you hadn't witnessed a man killing his son."

"Daughter," I snapped. "Taylor was denied their rightful identity in life; don't take it away from them in this interrogation room. Their murder makes me weep, even now, but it did not change my own rightful identity. I've said everything you're going to hear from me, and I've said way too much. From now on, you'll speak to my lawyer."

I got up and swept from the room. And ran into Zoë in the lobby.

"Chicago!" Zoë cried. "Didn't you get my messages? How did you find Clarina?"

"Old-fashioned legwork," I said. "The sergeant can tell you everything you want to know—he has my story plus all the forensic evidence they've gathered so far. And you know who Clarina is, or at least what she was doing in Lawrence, which I don't."

"Before you turn the LKPD into your private conference room, how did you get back here, Cruickshank?" Deke said.

"Us reporters have to cultivate contacts." She grinned saucily at him.

"I don't have anything for you. The chief will make a statement to the press later today. Now, off you go." He spoke in the indulgent tones of a big brother with a sister whom he liked to tease.

"People are saying that Clarina was assaulted," Zoë said.

"She was murdered," Deke said more seriously. "We don't have forensic evidence back yet, so I can't tell you more than that. Was she sexually assaulted? I don't know. Her body was taken to the Kansas City lab for a postmortem. We'll release results when we know them.

"The only hopeful thing I can tell you, not for publication until we have an official report." He paused to make sure Zoë understood that. "Her clothes had been torn from her body, but she was dead, or close to death, when that happened, our own CSI says—something about how blood pooled around the garments."

He pushed Zoë toward the exit. While she flung more questions at him, I made good my escape. I did not want to dwell on the dead woman's abused body.

Zoë caught up with me in the parking lot, where she repeated the question from her text: Had I known Clarina was in the Dundee house when we'd been there this morning?

I assured her I did not, and got into my car to call my lawyer. Freeman Carter had already read about my finding Sabrina: anytime one of his clients appears in the news he gets an alert. I told him about my potential legal troubles, both with the FBI agent and with the Lawrence cops. He promised to find a good criminal defense lawyer in the area.

"Don't insert yourself into an investigation that belongs to the Kansas crews," he said.

"I'm not inserting myself; I'm being shoved into it. They want to make me an interested party, if not a guilty one, because I was lucky enough to find a student who was overdosing, and then unlucky enough to find a dead body."

I talked Freeman through what was going on, gave him the local DA's name, as well as Deke Everard's.

Murray Ryerson had called, indignant that a tiny local publication knew what I was doing before he did. Mr. Contreras wanted to know if I was safe. Lotty sent love. Three of my clients wanted to know if I was hotdogging in Kansas at their expense. Valerie Granev was still not answering her phone.

Zoë was still waiting expectantly next to my car. I rolled down my window. "Zoë, I need to go to the hospital. I'll catch up with you after that."

At the ICU entrance, I explained to the charge nurse that I had important information for Valerie that might help her deal with her daughter's fears.

"I am an investigator," I explained when the nurse hesitated. "Ms. Granev hired me this morning hoping I could find out what

Sabrina might have witnessed in the drug house where I found her late Monday night."

The charge nurse pointed me toward a waiting area and said she would check with Ms. Granev. Two families were also in the waiting area, the children sprawled on the floor playing with crayons or tablets, but everyone spoke in a soft murmur.

The chairs were cushioned and deep, covered in soft colors, purples and greens, and the walls were hung with photos of prairie grasses and rivers. A circulating waterfall created enough background noise to make private conversations possible. I leaned back in one of the chairs.

Valerie woke me about twenty minutes later. She'd had a chance to shower and change. With fresh makeup, a severe white shirt and blazer, she looked like an important corporate player, not a terrified mother.

"Ms. Warshawski, I was beside myself when I talked to you earlier. I sent you off on a wild goose chase without thinking, or taking time to consult my husband. I have to apologize. We have good news about Sabrina."

"That's great." I was dopey from my brief sleep, but Valerie's manner meant I needed to be alert. "You're able to get some answers from her? How she came to be at that house, and what she saw there?"

Valerie's poise faltered briefly, but she produced a tight smile. "Not that great. She's far from out of the woods. But there's a rehab facility in Florida that's considered one of the best in the nation for people with, well, with damage like my daughter's. We—Ram and I—we learned about an hour ago that they have space for Sabrina. She'll be medevacked out there today. I'm taking care of all the paperwork now.

"As I said, I owe you an apology for sending you off looking for—for—"

"Monsters," I supplied, before she could come up with a euphemism. "When I went back to the house, I found the dead body of a woman. I wondered if Sabrina had seen her killers. She might have watched them from a window, or seen them at the bottom of the stairs. The killers had wrapped—"

"Enough!" Valerie put up her hands, shielding herself from unpleasant information. "I just explained to you that I hired you without thinking it through or talking it over with my team. We can't subject Sabrina to any kind of interrogation. I must ask you to stop. Send me an itemized account of your expenses; if they exceed the retainer I paid you, we'll take care of it. If there's an overpayment, consider it a goodwill offering for your time."

She turned on her heel—a highly polished boot—and retreated.

"The helicopter will be here in about forty-five minutes, and there is a lot of paperwork to complete," the nurse said. "Families in crisis are often abrupt with other people. Try not to take it person-ally."

"I'm taking it professionally," I said, "which means I'm baffled by what she's afraid I'll tell her. The people who treat Sabrina should know that there's a reality to her monster fears. You heard what I just said to Sabrina's mother? Can you make a note on Sabrina's chart?

"There was a dead woman in the basement of the house where I found Sabrina. It's possible she saw the woman being carried to the house. That's a lot for a sober person to process, but the nightmares will haunt Sabrina more if no one knows they're grounded in reality."

The nurse backed away from me. Perhaps I sounded overwrought, talking about bodies in basements. I invoked Nurse Norma's name, which got this woman to add my name and phone number to Sabrina's chart—but with no explanation of who I was or what my connection to her was.

While I'd been talking to Valerie, my car had sent a message to my phone. Someone had opened the door, someone had opened the trunk.

Zoë was waiting for me in the lobby, but I ran past her to the parking lot. The trunk was shut, but the driver's door was unlocked. I used my remote to pop the trunk, standing well back in case of ex-plosives. When no fire erupted, I went to look inside. A dirty tartan blanket had been dumped there, on top of my own overnight bag.

Interlude II
GERTRUDE AND CADY

CLARINA'S DEATH

SUPPOSE SOMEONE TOLD you Clarina Coffin is dead," Gertrude said over supper.

"Yes," Cady agreed. "Zoë Cruickshank called. She wanted a comment. I suppose she wanted me to shout, *She had it coming,* or some crap like that."

"That young woman is a menace, prying into everyone's lives. But that doesn't mean I want to hear you use that kind of language at the dinner table. Or anywhere else, for that matter."

"Zoë works hard in a dying field. I don't have a problem with that." Cady cut the beans on her plate in half, and then halved them again. Gertrude tried not to watch as she sliced them into smaller pieces without eating them.

"Anyway, I didn't wish Clarina ill, at least not in that way. I wished her to mind her own business, instead of trying to design my lesson plans for me, but I didn't wish any of the school board, not even Brett Santich, to die for the way they treated me."

Gertrude put down her knife and fork. "I thought, from what Pat said, she was found dead of an overdose."

"Zoë says Deke told her she was hit over the head. Probably she was left to die in the basement out there. Zoë says—rats—"

She took her plate of uneaten food and scraped it into the compost bin.

Gertrude's voice didn't soften, but she pleaded with Cady to eat something. "Even ice cream."

Cady went to her grandmother and kissed her forehead. "You are worried, aren't you, Gram, if you're offering me dessert when I haven't eaten my dinner."

She brought a carton of butter pecan and two bowls to the table. Gertrude hadn't eaten much of her meal, either, but she put her plate to one side and filled both bowls.

"Did Zoë have other information?" Gertrude asked after a moment.

"You mean, something else Deke wouldn't have told Aunt Pat?"

"I wondered if the police talked to the Chicago detective. After all, she was in that house looking for the missing student."

"V.I. Warshawski is the person who found the body, and according to Zoë, Deke's been questioning her hard. She found the student with the overdose, she found Clarina, and then she found a blanket in her car that maybe was used by Clarina's killers. Zoë apparently was bird-dogging her all day."

Cady grimaced. "Zoë's like a terrier, you know. She sees our little crime wave as her ticket to the big time. If she hears that Clarina annoyed the Riverside women's group, she'll come around questioning you."

"Clarina annoyed us because she acted as though she knew more about Lawrence history than people who've lived here their whole lives, and their grandparents before them," Gertrude said. "She pretended she knew our deepest secrets, as if a bunch of middle-aged women running a food bank and a homeless shelter have deep secrets."

She paused. "When you get old, your sleep is light. Footsteps, doors shutting, they wake you."

Cady was loading the dishwasher, but she stood up to face her grandmother. "Do they, now? And can you tell if the noisy walker was in the house, watching the garage, or coming from the outside?"

The two women stared at each other. Before either spoke again, the front doorbell rang. Cady switched on the porch light and looked through the glass.

"It's Deke Everard with another man," she called to her grandmother. "What on earth do they want this time of night?"

15

MR. WATSON, COME HERE!

LAWRENCE COPS HAD impounded my Mustang. They hadn't arrested me, but they were moving closer. They'd told me I couldn't leave town until they'd done a complete inspection of my car. When I asked how long it would take, Deke Everard said, "As long as it takes."

Since Zoë had been present when I found the blanket, she followed me back to the cop shop, where they kept me until well past dark. By the time we finished, Zoë had left: an overturned semi had sent chickens all over the road. I was grateful to the chickens. The last thing I needed was Zoë peppering me on top of the LKPD interrogation.

Lawrence had a free bus service, I learned from the officer on desk duty. She handed me a printed schedule and instructed me on how to find the closest stop. Waiting at the bus stop, anonymous in the dark, I asked myself the same questions the cops had pounded me with.

Why had someone chosen my car to plant the blanket—assuming this was the blanket I'd stumbled on in the Dundee house Monday night? Deke kept asking me that, and of course I didn't know.

"Maybe because they figure you're putting me in the frame," I said. "You won't look further if you have a suspect." I stopped on the brink of adding: "time-honored cop behavior."

My car had been alone in a field near the Dundee house; it was distinctive, a red Mustang with Illinois plates. Anyone who'd spotted it there would have recognized it in the hospital parking lot.

"Maybe the Omicron boys are behind this. They'd feel it was payback for touring their garage to ask about their drug business Monday afternoon."

"Are you accusing a fraternity of murdering Clarina Coffin?" Deke asked.

"I'm not accusing anyone of anything. I'm trying to understand why my car was picked as an evidence-dumping ground."

We went around the same questions so many times I felt I'd been on a whirligig by the time they gave me a statement to sign, along with an admonition not to leave the area.

Waiting for the bus, I kept asking myself the questions the cops had dwelt on. I had explained to Deke and the LKPD major who joined him for the interrogation about Granev hiring and then firing me in rapid order. I gave them her private phone number so they could verify it with her, but they didn't seem to think Valerie Granev was relevant to the story. The question still remained, though: Why had she pushed me away after begging me to find the source of Sabrina's monsters?

The bus was almost empty when I got on, but it picked up students along the way. I kept an eye on the street signs to make sure I didn't miss my stop, but it wasn't until we were a few blocks east of Westbrooke Circle that the name struck me.

"Lunch in our offices in Westbro"—the scrap of paper I'd found in the woods had read. I got off at the next stop and walked back up the street to explore the circle.

The circle was small; the one significant building on the land belonged to the University of Kansas press.

Someone had been invited to lunch at the press and had torn up the invitation. A piece had landed in the woods behind the Dundee House.

Zoë said Clarina Coffin had thought of herself as an expert on Kansas history, and that she'd upended Cady Perec's teaching career over Cady's approach to teaching Kansas history. Maybe Coffin had been a serious historian; perhaps the university press wanted to publish her work.

While I waited for another bus, I thought about texting the suggestion to Deke, but cops look with heightened suspicion at anyone who tries to help them find clues, even a trained investigator. Maybe especially a trained investigator. Keep it to yourself, Warshawski. Solve this murder, make them look like hamburger past its shelf date.

The bus decanted me a few blocks from Nurse Norma's home on the hillside near the university. My long day had worn me out. I took off my shoes, thinking I'd lie down for ten minutes, and woke up an hour later.

I got up feeling stiff and dirty and stood under Norma's shower for ten minutes, washing cop grime and Dundee house dirt out of my mind. I couldn't answer any questions about Valerie Granev's behavior, but I could search for information on Clarina Coffin.

After burrowing through my subscription databases, which harvest far too many personal secrets, I began to think Clarina was a myth, some kind of 3D figure created by artificial intelligence. There wasn't a single record about her before she showed up in Lawrence some two years ago, and even here I could find only wisps of information.

If she had a phone, it wasn't registered in her name. Whether she was renting or owning, she was either paying cash or paying under a different name. I found a Kansas suffragist named Clarina Nicholls, but I didn't discover any descendants named Coffin.

I couldn't even find photos of her on the *Douglas County Herald* website, beyond the blurry shots Zoë had taken of her picketing the Yancy school. Trig was with her, recognizable with his halo of graying curls, but there were other people, carrying signs proclaiming, BLACK LIVES MATTER, NO CRT IN OUR SCHOOLS, OUR HISTORY IS YOUR HISTORY, NATIVE NATIONS WERE HERE BEFORE THE *MAYFLOWER*, and no one's face showed up clearly.

I sent what I had to Murray—he has access to sources that I don't—and added "I'll call tomorrow. Cops have me talked out tonight."

I walked into the town to find some supper. I felt lonely, desolate, and over a meal in a quiet café I sent a long message to Peter.

Everyone thinks I'm unstable because of Taylor's death. I suppose
I am in some ways. I find myself crying or forgetting to eat. But
I am not kidnapping college students, or bringing them to the
point of death to salvage my honor.

I hope you're having an easier time in Malaga. I miss you. xxxVI

WHEN I WALKED back up the street to Norma's place, Cady Perec got
out of a car in front of the house.

"Vic. I'm sorry to show up unannounced. I need to talk to someone, someone besides Gram and Zoë, I mean, and you know how
the police work. Deke Everard—I've been knowing him since I was
born, but he came around and interviewed me like he thought I'd
killed Clarina."

"Did you?" I asked.

"Vic! Please, I need help."

I gritted my teeth but let her in. She produced a bottle of white
wine. I found some glasses in the kitchenette.

"Did he say why he was talking to you?" I asked.

"I guess because her wild talking got me fired. He wonders if I'm
bearing a grudge so intense I'd kill to get my job back."

"Tell me about the firing, or about her. Clarina isn't in any of my
databases. Did she ever talk about where she came from?"

Cady shook her head. "She wasn't the kind of person I wanted to
know. She came to the women's group at Riverside Congregational—
the church Gram and I belong to—a few times, but I'm not active in
the group. She rubbed a lot of the women the wrong way, Gram says,
because she pretended she wanted to pick their brains on local history,
but really what she wanted was to show how much more she knew
than everyone else. Gram's words."

I'd met Gertrude Perec when I was here two years ago. She had
not hidden her displeasure with me for involving myself in her and
Cady's affairs. I tried to imagine her hitting Clarina over the head for
the crime of showing off. People have killed for many strange reasons,
but it was hard to picture.

"What about when Clarina picketed your school? Did she get in touch then?"

Cady's lips were tight with anger. "She certainly did. I'd been asked to take a few days' leave while the board looked at my curriculum. Of course that pissed me off, the board second-guessing a teacher with my experience, but I thought we could sort it out. Then Zoë called wanting my comment on Clarina and Trig picketing. I drove over to the school, and there they were, with kids from the university campus. I begged Trig and Clarina to stop.

"That was what did me in: someone photographed me talking to Clarina, and parents claimed I was joining in the picket. I tried to explain, but you can't prove a negative. When Zoë talked to Clarina during the picket, Clarina claimed I was privately happy to have her there but couldn't say so publicly. I wanted to—" She cut herself short.

"Slug her?" I suggested.

She turned crimson. "Something like that."

"Did you try to talk to her again?"

"No. My union rep advised me not to, and so did Gram—it was clear Clarina would twist anything I said the wrong way."

"What about before the suspension and picketing and so on, when she wanted to get involved with your syllabus?" I asked.

"I don't know how she learned about my lesson plan, but she started wanting to be part of it. She thought she knew a ton about Kansas history, Civil War stuff, what happened to the Kansa and Delaware nations after the war, all kinds of stuff. She'd say she could prove what she was talking about, but when I asked her to show me, she wouldn't or couldn't."

The lesson plan had been called "We All Have a Kansas History." Students were going to write essays on their own family's history in the state—where they came from, why and when they landed here. Cady had also planned segments on the state's geological and ecological history, with help not just from the school's science teachers, but also from graduate students at the University of Kansas, whose main campus was in Lawrence. She also had someone from Haskell, the local Indian Nations University, lined up to speak.

"Clarina called my class 'woke lite,'" Cady said with a brittle smile. "I was certainly going to cover the way both the national government and local European settlers forced Native Americans first to come here from farther north and east, and then after the Civil War, pushed them into Oklahoma, but that was just a piece of the lesson plan.

"Clarina lectured me about my reading list. Did I know what the first governor did to the Delaware nation after the war? Did I know about recent murders of Native Americans in the county? Did I know this, did I know that. She told me I should start the syllabus with an acknowledgment that we in Lawrence were occupying lands that had been the historic home of the Delaware and the Kansa nations, and that our own ancestors had forcibly removed these original inhabitants from their land."

Cady gulped down her wine and poured herself a second glass. "I wouldn't talk to her after that first phone call, but she wrote a letter to the *Herald*, saying my class was a perfect chance for students at Yancy to learn the true history of the land they lived on. 'The land their families stole' was how she put it, and that my lesson plan should be required throughout the state. So then some of the parents got angry, because I was woke, and teaching critical race theory, if they even knew what that is. I was called in front of the board. Clarina and Trig declared themselves my champions, and then I got fired. Suspended without pay, technically."

"I can't find a phone number for Clarina. How did she call you?"

Cady looked blank. "On the phone. What do you mean?"

"Sorry—if she had cell or land service in her name, it should show up somewhere. When she called, did her name appear on your screen, or 'unknown caller'?"

Cady squinted, trying to look into the past. "'Unknown caller,' I guess, but she did leave a number for me to call back. Only I didn't keep it because I didn't want to talk to her."

I returned to the controversy that had landed Cady in trouble. I hadn't seen Clarina's letter when I looked for her in the *Herald* archives, but Cady pulled it up for me. It was long, the kind of essay-cum-harangue that everyone grinding an ax writes these days.

Clarina included a lot of history, including dates and atrocities, and ended her letter by declaiming that "everyone here does have a

Kansas history. We all have some of that blood on our hands, and it's time our children learned to see it."

"Had she written a book about all this?" I asked.

"A book?" Cady echoed. "I never thought her ideas were organized or coherent enough for a book. Why?"

"Grasping at straws," I said, "or scraps of paper. I found a fragment near the Dundee house suggesting a meeting at the university press. It's such a small fragment, it doesn't include any names. I just wondered if it could have been sent to Clarina."

Cady's mouth twisted in bitterness. "I couldn't stand it if she turned out really to be an expert on Kansas history! I know she's dead, but honestly! All that stuff she put in her letters, it got the parents riled up against me. The police seem to think it's a motive for me killing her, and if there's a book—it will look like I tried to shut her up before she could make all her ideas public."

She picked at her cuticles. Blood pooled around her forefinger.

"Deke came with a Major Somebody in the department. Because Gram used to be his Sunday school teacher, he couldn't question either of us himself, he just babysat while the major interrogated us separately. When he was talking to me, the major said no one could seriously think Gram killed anyone, but he says, if she did, it was to support me. He *encouraged* me to say what reason she'd have to protect me."

She saw the blood and wiped her finger on her jeans. "Vic, could I hire you? To investigate Clarina's death?"

I was startled. "The cops suspect me, Cady. They've impounded my car."

She ignored that. "They say Gram went out to the Dundee house, like at three in the morning, after you found Sabrina and all the emergency responders were back in town. First she got on her high horse, denied it, but someone sent in an anonymous photo.

"So then Gram said, she got a message, phone message, saying one of her friends was having car trouble out there. And when she got to the Dundee house, there was no sign of Lela Abernathy, but Trig was there; he'd gotten a message about something different, something about Brett Santich, or at least he claims that was what it was.

"Gram and Trig waited for an hour and then they left. She says." She squeezed her bloody finger, so hard I thought she might break it.

"Vic, the two of us living together all these years—since I was born—we hide our secrets. It's how we can live together and have some privacy. We know not to poke each other's secret spots. But—we both heard each other in the night, coming and going."

"And you came and went?" I asked.

"I have trouble sleeping these days. Since I got fired. I went for a walk, down to the river. When I got home, the garage door was open. Gram's car wasn't there. I wondered if someone had stolen it, but when I went to her room to tell her, she wasn't in bed. I waited for her to come home, listened to her on the stairs, then went up myself. We heard each other, but we didn't talk about it."

"You told the cops?"

Cady shook her head, face unhappy. "I guess the reason they didn't arrest Gram is they can't prove she was inside the Dundee house."

"Also, they suspect me. And probably Trig," I said drily.

"But they took all our coats," Cady said. "They want to test them to see if there's any trace of Clarina's blood on them. Please say you'll help. I can't pay what you probably usually ask, but Zoë told me you need a place to stay after tonight. We have an apartment over our garage. You could use it rent-free instead of a fee."

"If they don't have any evidence linking you or your grandmother to the murder, the two of you should be able to ride it out," I added.

"Please!" Cady cried. "Maybe in a big city you can 'ride out' an accusation like that, but a town the size of Lawrence, where everyone who counts has known you since your first day of preschool? And then, people are saying if Gram killed Clarina it was to punish her for destroying my career. I'll never get a teaching job while that kind of accusation is floating around. Maybe not even after we prove we're innocent—nothing disappears from the internet, after all."

I knew all too well how unforgiving internet stories were, even for someone who lives in a large city.

"Your grandmother can't stand me," I reminded Cady. "How are you going to persuade her to let me live over the garage?"

"She's worried. I told her I was going to invite you and she said, 'Sip with the devil, make sure you have a long spoon.'"

"So I'm the devil now? Lines up with a lot of my trolls' posts, except their language is earthier."

"Sorry, Vic," she said in a small voice. "But if you have to stay here anyway, I could really use your help."

I felt a sinking in my middle. Was this how Alexander Graham Bell's assistant felt when he got the world's first phone call? *Mr. Watson, come here, I want you, no matter what is going on in your own life?*

I wanted to be the prima donna for once, the person who got to say, I need you, and my minions dropped whatever they were doing to race to my side. Instead, I pulled up my app, got Cady to sign a contract and pay me a hundred dollars as a token fee. We also agreed on a modest rent. I explained that if I found evidence condemning her or Gertrude, living rent-free would make it hard to share anything I found with the police.

"There's nothing for you to find," she insisted.

"Including proof of your middle-of-the-night walk along the river in the freezing air?" I said.

"You don't have the right to ask—"

"Cady, that's going to be the problem. The only way to get answers is to ask questions. If my questions touch you on the raw that much, then I'm giving back your retainer and erasing the contract."

She bit her lip, fortunately not hard enough to draw blood. "I didn't kill Clarina. Neither did Gram. I'll try to answer your questions, but when they are offensive, I—well, I'm offended."

She walked out of the room, leaving the bottle of wine behind.

16

NEW LIFE IN OLD METAL

THE NEXT MORNING, the thin February sun was just warm enough that I could sit outside the Decadent Hippo, nursing a cortado. Zoë Cruickshank bounced up the street.

"This is going to be great, Chicago, you working with me to solve Douglas County's crime wave. And you're staying with another prime suspect, so I can cover the whole story with one interview."

"How did you know I'm going to be at the Perecs'?" I asked.

She grinned. "Gertrude Perec told me."

"*Gertrude* Perec?"

"Yep, her and me, we're BFF's." Zoë laughed. "Actually, she looks at me like I'm a piece of fish a cat dug out of a dumpster, but I talked to her because I needed to know how her interview with the police went. I went to a meeting of Bring Lawrence Home—it's an organization trying to find housing for Lawrence's homeless population.

"Of course, Gertrude is on the board—she runs just about every important civic organization in the county. Her and Pat Everard. Anyway, she couldn't throw me out of the meeting, since they want the coverage. I made sure to walk inside at the same time as her, even though I had to lurk in the lobby for ten minutes. She was pissed that I'd caught her in public where she couldn't hang up on me. She wouldn't tell me anything about the police interview, but she did say if I wanted to know anything about the investigation I should talk to you, since Cady was letting you snoop around the house."

"Those her exact words?"

"Not exactly," Zoë admitted. "She said since I was Lawrence's self-appointed busybody, I'd find out sooner or later that Cady had invited you to move in. She called you that 'interfering know-it-all from Chicago,' and said you and I would make the perfect couple."

Zoë's teeth flashed white in her dark face. "Of course, I took that as a great compliment. Gertrude said she couldn't have both you and me nosing into her personal business, but I thought, that is exactly what we need. You go over for dinner tonight and tell me what she says and how she says it."

"That sounds like tons of fun for everyone," I said. "Me at the Perec dinner table isn't likely to happen—especially since the last time I was in Kansas, she sprayed Lysol on me whenever I passed her house."

Zoë laughed again. "But you must know why the police interviewed her. I mean, if Cady invited you to stay with them, she must be scared about what they're finding out about Gertrude."

"I don't think those Perec women frighten easily. Tell me more about Clarina. I haven't turned up the faintest whiff on where she came from. How about you?"

Zoë shook her head. "No one I've talked to even knows when she arrived in town. All I can say is, she definitely is not from here, or people would know about her.

"About two years ago, not long after I graduated and joined the *Herald,* she started showing up at local history meetings, correcting mistakes she thought people made in their presentations. She did research in the university archives, and people say they saw her over in Topeka at the Kansas Origins Museum, but after one meeting, where she was correcting this history professor!—can you believe that?—I asked her what she'd published.

"She got all huffy: she wasn't giving away her hard work for free to a small-town paper. But, you know, to me that was saying she'd never really written anything."

"Where did she live? She must have given some kind of personal information to a Realtor if she was renting or buying."

Zoë shook her head. "You'd think, but she sublet a trailer in a mobile home park south of town, and the manager of the park doesn't know anything about her, except that she was a good tenant. She didn't have to give a credit history because she's subletting. The manager says Clarina pays—paid—the rent on time, didn't keep pets or smoke or play loud music or fire her gun at cockroaches."

"She has—had—a gun?"

Zoë hunched a shoulder. "That was on the list of things bad tenants do, according to the manager. Not guns, we're four-square for unregulated weapons here in Kansas, but shooting cockroaches. It sounds made up, but the woman said it happened. 'Not that we want roaches in our park, but there are easier ways to deal with them than shooting out the doors and windows.'"

"Clarina paid the manager herself? Cash?"

"Gosh, I didn't ask. Is it important?"

"A check or credit card would give you an entrée into her financial records, and maybe a way to find her personal history."

"See—we're already better as a team. I wouldn't have thought of that, but it would have been harder for you to find where she sublet."

Her phone beeped. "Fire over in North Lawrence. I should go look at it."

She got to her feet but was reluctant to leave, asking me more questions about what I planned to do, and whether I thought Gertrude or Cady were guilty.

"Of course not. Cady is my client, and my clients are never guilty."

Zoë finally left, trying to make me promise to see her tonight to tell her what I'd uncovered. I agreed to a phone chat, since that was the only way I could get her to give me the name of the trailer park where Clarina had lived: Prairie View.

Clarina had been an ardent amateur historian who never published anything. That scrap of paper I'd found with the address (probably) of the University Press could have been addressed to Clarina, or to someone who knew Clarina. Of course, as Deke had said, it most likely had nothing at all to do with her murder.

I needed a car if I was going to be here any length of time. And if I had to stay here for days, or even weeks, I needed to get back to Chicago to move my office down here. I called Deke for an update on my car. They'd get to it when they got to it, was the essence of his response.

I looked up car leasing. The $4,100 my Kansas clients had paid me so far would not cover a long-term car rental as well as living expenses.

I walked across the bridge to the north side of town. I'd thought about Uber, but I didn't want a computer trail of my moves.

I spotted the billboard, newly painted, as soon as I crossed the train tracks on the far side of the bridge. LOU & ED: BREATHING NEW LIFE INTO OLD METAL. I breathed a sigh of relief: they'd survived the pandemic.

When I reached the scrapyard, I saw they'd put up a high fence since I was last here, but otherwise, the place looked the same—rusted car fenders and plowshares, rebar, and a lot of machinery I couldn't identify.

I had to press a button for admittance, but when I said my name over the intercom, the gates swung open. One of the men was on the concrete apron in front of the shop building, working with a welding torch. He didn't stop, but his partner came out of the building. Lou Arata, I saw when he walked over.

"We heard you were in town. Wondered if you'd remember us," he said.

"I'll never forget you and Ed or what I owe you," I said.

"Saw all the ruckus on TV about you and that student, volleyball player, was she?"

"Soccer."

"Thought for sure you'd stop by."

"I'm sorry," I said. "I wasn't expecting to stay in town. I wasn't expecting to end up under a police microscope. It has me rattled, more than it should, maybe."

Lou looked at me more closely. "You are rattled. You lost weight. You haven't taken up dieting, have you?"

"Never. I—it's been a stressful winter. I'm getting better, but having the FBI blame me for finding a student who could have died hasn't helped get my balance back. There was another student in Chicago—" I broke off.

"Read about that," Lou said. "Not your fault, but you got caught in the middle, didn't you. This gal, this soccer player, local cops don't really buy that *federale*'s line, do they?"

"I hope not, but yesterday, I found a dead woman in the drug house basement."

Lou grunted. "You are definitely a whiz as a magician, but maybe you need to tone down your act—say, rabbits and hats instead of bodies and basements."

"It's hard to attract an audience these days unless you have shock value," I said.

"Give you credit, you've got that and more where it came from. Law think you put the woman down there?"

"I'm in the top four people of interest, maybe top two now: someone planted a blanket in my trunk that may be tied to the dead woman. I know they're looking at Cady Perec and her grandmother—Cady's a schoolteacher who might have lost her job because of the murder victim's interference."

"Yes, read about Cady's troubles for trying to teach some indigestible version of Kansas history," Lou said. "Can't believe Five-O would go after the grandmother. She's in charge of the town, or big chunks of it. Anyone arresting her would find themselves out of a job."

"That's why I'm leading the pack of suspects," I said. "The shortest distance to the nearest powerless person makes the problem go away."

"You want us to hide you here at the yard?" Lou asked.

His words were bantering, but his tone was serious. He knew I'd come for a favor, and he was bracing himself for the ask.

"They've impounded my car. I was hoping you had a working wreck here I might rent."

Lou led us over to Ed, who nodded, finished the join he was working on, and turned off the fire. "Bad penny turned up, Ed. She needs help."

The men looked at each other, stepped back a few paces and began talking in low voices. After half an hour, and a couple of phone calls, the men came back to me.

"Got a Toyota you can use. We're looking after it for the owner while he's laid up. He says you can borrow it. You pay the insurance plus a hundred twenty a week."

"Just so you know, I'm not supposed to leave the jurisdiction," I said. "I have to drive back to Chicago, to collect clothes and computer files and all those things. If I get stopped, I guess the cops could seize that car, too. Your guy okay with that?"

Ed curled a lip. "What with drones and all that surveillance, seems like a jurisdiction covers a lot of ground these days. Keep to the speed limit. Don't run any red lights. Don't drink and drive."

"And bring the princess back with you. You need the company," Lou added. He meant Peppy.

"He thinks he's going to persuade you to trade her highness for a tractor," Ed said.

The Toyota was at their home, some ten miles farther out in the country. Ed went back to his welding while Lou drove me out to pick up the car.

When I first met them, I thought they were brothers, they looked so much alike, same height, same square jaws, same gray-green eyes in their coffee-colored faces. It was later that I realized they were a couple. No rings, but each with a tattoo: TIL DEATH on Ed's right forearm; US DO PART on Lou's left.

They'd changed their names, too: Ed Lyndes became Ed Arata Lyndes and Lou became Lou Lyndes Arata.

If Peter ever got back to me, if we ever got back together, how would he feel about becoming Peter Warshawski Sanson?

Lou pulled up in front of the house and turned off the engine. "The dead woman, Coffin, she came to talk to us a year or so back."

"What did she want?"

"She was looking for old diaries or letters, any kind of family papers we had. She said she was talking to all the 'people of color,' she called us, in the county, hoping to do a proper history of Black folks in Kansas."

"She say anything about what she was writing? I mean, a book, or some articles, or a podcast?"

Lou shook his head. "I didn't pay that much attention. Something about her seemed a little off-kilter, if you know what I mean. Ed and I, we talked it over with some of the neighbors. One Black woman over at the university, she thought it was an opportunity to get more complete Black history out in the world, but the prof ain't from here, so she didn't have the kind of documents the Clarina woman was looking for."

"Was Clarina Black?" I asked. "I haven't seen a clear photo of her."

"Ed and I thought she was a wannabe, thought maybe she wanted to produce a history to prove she was."

He got out of the truck. I followed him behind the barn, where they'd parked the Toyota. It was exactly the car I needed—beige, a couple of dings on the fenders, but in good working order. Lou handed me the Toyota keys. I gave him seven twenties—a week's rental plus the insurance.

"You get in over your head, and you don't call me and Ed, that will be the crime we won't forgive or forget, you hear? And fuck's sake, Warshawski, start eating. That skinny white-girl look is never attractive, least of all on you."

"Got it," I said, a lump in my throat. I'd been needing a true ally down here.

17

NEW LIFE IN OLD DETECTIVES

THE ROUTE BACK into town led past the Boat Yard. I pulled into their lot. Ten A.M., business was light. Greg, the bartending owner, was talking with a couple of truckers standing at the counter drinking coffee.

Holly was setting up tables for lunch. She looked up when I came in and frowned, worried.

"Am I too late for breakfast?" I asked. "A short stack?"

She nodded and went to the kitchen window to put in the order, bringing a thermos of coffee on her way back to me. She poured without asking if I wanted it.

"I saw where you found your missing girl out in that house on Yancy."

"I did," I agreed. "I didn't feed you to the police, if you're worried about that. Or your sister, but I wondered if she showed up yesterday morning to clean the place."

She shook her head. "I was scared about that when I saw the news, but she said someone told her to stay away."

"Who?" I asked.

She hunched a shoulder.

"I'd like to talk to her," I said, "see what she can tell me about who's running those parties."

"Please don't," Holly begged. "She needs the money."

"No one's going to be doing anything in that house for quite some time," I said. "It's a major crime scene, and anyway, now that the sheriff knows someone's selling drugs there, they'll shut it down."

"But she could be arrested as an accessory or something, if the police learn she knew drugs were being used there and didn't report it."

A ding from the kitchen window called her to pick up my order. She set the plate in front of me, said, "Anything else?" and left the tab on the table. She stayed well away from me—when I got up to pay, she went into the kitchen, leaving me to settle the bill with Greg.

"You weren't harassing Holly, were you"—he held my credit card close to his face—"V.I. Warshki?"

I shook my head. "I was looking for someone I thought she might know, that's all."

He eyed me narrowly. "Not that I don't appreciate your business, but if it means upsetting my team, maybe you should eat somewhere else."

I smiled, signed the slip, average tip so I didn't look guilty. "Your team is lucky to have you in their corner."

The truckers followed me out, watched me get into the Camry before climbing back into their rigs. Holly was lucky to have a protective boss. Greg was lucky to have loyal customers. I was lucky for some reason. I just couldn't put my finger on it at the moment.

The strip mall where I'd bought my change of clothes yesterday was right behind the Boat Yard, but I thought it prudent to leave the parking lot. My overnight bag had been in the Mustang's trunk. The police hadn't let me take it with me, which meant I had to buy yet more jeans, socks, toothbrush, change of underwear.

Murray called while I was clothes shopping to say he'd also come up blank on Clarina. "Maybe the Coffin woman was a Chinese or Iranian spy, with such a deeply buried backstory she didn't know herself who she was."

I gave him a full interview while sitting in the Camry, including all the details of finding Clarina, and finding the blanket in my trunk.

Before he hung up, Murray said casually, "Sabrina's plight seems to have had some positive fallout. Some anonymous angel gave her father a hundred grand to build a youth camp in the mountains."

"Any hints on the ID?" I asked.

"No one's using their trumpet yet."

I hadn't bothered looking at the Granevs or the Perecs on my different news feeds. I squinted now at the screen, the gray day making it hard to read.

It was an Albuquerque story picked up on the national wires because my rescue of Sabrina had made the national news. "If this happened before one week ago, I am dancing up the mountain, so happy to have money for my youth camp," Ramir Granev said. "Now? Now I am grateful, very grateful, but my own child, my own heart, lies between life and death. My heart is sliced in two: joy, sorrow."

"You still there?" Murray demanded.

"Just catching up on the story. Ramir seems like a good guy," I said. "His wife is more puzzling. I was looking to see if she's mentioned anywhere. After unraveling on me and persuading me to go look for monsters at the drug house where I found her child, she told me we were done. They'd gotten a spot for Sabrina at some exclusive Florida facility. She was medevacked out yesterday afternoon."

Murray whistled. "Private clinic? Could run over fifty K for a month. Maybe Ram will have to leverage his gift for youth camping or whatever it is."

"Valerie is a higher-up in Tulloh Industries' aeronautics division. The Granevs probably have gold-plated insurance and cash in the bank, too. The part that bothers me is that at the moment I found a likely source of her daughter's terrified screams, Valerie axed me. I'm wondering if it was under pressure from the FBI."

"Why? Jurisdictional jealousy?"

"Yesterday morning, when she was sharing her fears and so on, Valerie said it was Tulloh who got the Bureau involved. She seemed uncomfortable with the agent, guy named Stamoran. Stamoran acts as though he wants to print and book me but doesn't have enough evidence. The LKPD is also gunning for me, so I'm supposed to stay here and wait for the DA to decide whether to charge me with being an outsider in Lawrence's power structure. It didn't move the local sergeant to know I'm here without a computer or clothes or toothpaste, so I'm driving up tomorrow to collect what I need for a week or two down here."

"Oh, boy. Warshawski, the fugitive from justice. This is going to be my story when they pick you up, not that Kansas newbie's."

"The Kansas newbie gets twelve thousand a year to do real journalism. She's making an amazing job of it, so don't try to push her to the margins. Anyway, can you let Sal know I'm coming? I'll call Lotty and Mr. Contreras. We can have a good old-fashioned get-together at the Glow before I head south again."

When we finished, I saw I had a message from my lawyer, Freeman Carter. He'd found a criminal lawyer in Kansas City for me, a woman named Faye Mitchell who'd been in law school with one of Freeman's associates. She'd be expecting a call from me. I didn't tell Freeman I was planning a quick trip north, or that I wouldn't call Mitchell until I was back in Lawrence. I wasn't really fleeing the jurisdiction, but better to ask forgiveness, and so on.

I called my Chicago clients to assure them their affairs were uppermost in my mind. Yes, I knew I'd been in the news over a murder and a drug house; I'd be in Kansas for a week sorting things out but I would be taking care of everything they needed from me, not to worry.

I looked at myself in the rearview mirror. Dark circles under the eyes, cheekbones still too gaunt. I am a chronic overachiever, I chanted. I can free myself of suspicion, find Coffin's murder, solve the drug-use problem of Douglas County, and run my business. *Come on, V.I.,* I adjured myself. *Breathe new life into old detectives.*

My final call was to Mr. Contreras. He was ecstatic that I was coming home, even for a day. He didn't want me taking Peppy, but he understood, doll, he understood she'd look after me. After forty-five minutes, I gently disengaged myself so that I could move into the Perec garage.

I apologized to Cady for being late—I'd said I would be there an hour earlier.

She shrugged. "I wasn't doing much. Gram is on me to stop moping around feeling sorry for myself, so I'm tutoring in the library's after-school program, but I still need to pull my socks up and get marching, Gram says. Apply for jobs, rethink my career goals, all the stuff that self-help books tell you marks the difference between success and failure."

"I always wonder about those books," I said. "They seem to me to be a form of fantasy fiction. 'In my dream world I was an Olympic diver who became the person who brokered peace in Sudan. In my real life I'm a checkout clerk in a grocery store.' Maybe with artificial intelligence coming to dominate us, we won't be able to tell the difference, but for now, keep doing what you're doing."

She laughed and showed me where to park. She escorted me up the stairs, which ran outside the garage, mercifully on the far side from the house so that Gertrude couldn't monitor my comings and goings.

It was a small space, but one with plenty of light. The furniture seemed to be leftovers from generations of Gertrude's family: a bureau with a marble top and an old streaked mirror, a rocking chair, a narrow couch with crocodiles carved into the arms and legs. A bookcase next to the narrow bed held a selection of mysteries and Kansas history books.

Cady had clearly scrubbed it down in my honor, and had even put a bunch of flowers in the middle of the table.

"Gram built this place when my mom was pregnant with me, hoping she would stay here, only of course she died when I was a few months old." Cady offered this in a matter-of-fact voice, repeating a story she'd been told many times.

She watched while I put away my few belongings. "Have you learned anything about Clarina?"

"So far, only that no one knows anything about her, except for her obsession with Kansas history. I have to stay here until I clear my name, but I'm going to drive up to Chicago tomorrow to get my computer and clothes and so on. I'll be bringing my dog back with me, so let me know if I need to look for a different place."

She assured me the dog would be fine as long as she was housebroken. She seemed eager for a longer tête-a-tête, but I told her I had to start investigating or I'd be in Gertrude's garage until Memorial Day.

As I drove off, I saw her in the rearview mirror, shoulders slumped when she thought I was no longer watching her.

I made my way around the town on side streets that turned into county roads, checking for company. Lawrence was well supplied with traffic cams; I expect Deke could track me online if he knew about the Camry, but at least for now no one was following me.

The Prairie View Mobile Home Park where Clarina had lived

was between Yancy Hill and the town. If Clarina had been an energetic walker, she could have gotten to the Dundee house and the Yancy school on foot.

Some prairie remained for park residents to view, but the north side of the development faced a fertilizer plant, while the east backed onto a busy county road. The entrance, on the west side, listed the amenities: Wi-Fi, running water and electricity, a community room with a gym, and a park. The manager's home/office immediately inside the entrance was clearly marked.

I pulled into a parking space next to the office trailer. A pair of cement blocks served as a step up to a muddy stoop, but the doorframe was freshly painted. The manager's name was also freshly painted on a white plaque with a border of bright flowers: MIGNON TRAVERS.

She buzzed me in and called out, "To your right."

To my right was her home office, filled with green plants along with a television, a recliner, and a desk. Travers was in the recliner, playing a computer game on a tablet with fierce attention. She was a heavy woman, her dark hair scraped back into a bun that accentuated her round cheeks.

She didn't glance up from her screen. "You looking to rent or buy?"

"Neither. I'm a detective, I want to look at Clarina Coffin's place."

"Sheriff and city cops both have been through here already. Which one you with?" She looked up for a moment, eyes shrewd behind her dark heavy frames.

"I'm private. Coffin was a historian. I've been hired to look for her papers, to see if she has anything in shape to be published." I took my PI license from my wallet, but Mignon wasn't interested.

"Somebody already went through that place. God knows what they were looking for. Cops was plenty mad about it when they saw the damage, like I'm supposed to be a security guard or something. All I do is make sure trash on the *outside* of the homes is picked up, rent collected on time, nobody shooting guns inside the homes, even if they're the owners, 'cause we all live close together and between you, me, and that geranium over there, the walls are not that sturdy."

"Is it true someone was shooting at roaches?" I asked.

"*They* said, not me." Her thumbs were moving furiously.

"Even if someone went through Coffin's place already, I'd still like to see for myself."

"Got to earn your fee, I suppose." She flicked her eyes at the wall by the door. "Keys are hanging there. 1732 Squash Blossom Lane."

Duplicate keys for all the homes were hanging on a pegboard, addresses written on white disks in a neat hand. I found 1732 easily enough. Anyone could have found it if Travers ever left her recliner long enough for someone to pop in.

"I understand she sublet. Who was the owner?"

"You ever going to finish talking? I'm concentrating here. I have to answer back to the cops, but not to a private."

"I'll be gone so fast you won't know I was ever here," I said. "Just tell me who she rented from."

"A fund, like a bush. Not local, but who knows where they're located. They own about twenty of the units, and we only have but forty-eight."

"A hedge fund," I said, but she didn't answer. Hedge funds, Squash Blossoms, Mignon herself, a kind of plant. It was an effort to turn a spartan space into a garden. The hedge fund was probably not much help.

The homes themselves were trailers, some single wide, some double, set on a grid of streets around a rectangle of grass with playground equipment—I guess that was the park part of the community. I drove there and inspected the layout on my map app. Squash Blossom Lane was four streets down. I parked and walked over.

The homes were close together, close enough that if neighbors weren't mindful about their TV volume everyone on both sides could hear it. Even though it was the middle of the day, plenty of people were inside, devices loudly competing among country, rap, and soaps.

The February freeze and thaw had left the ground raw, but some dormant grasses were still there, along with a few spindly bushes. The streets were cleaner than in my neighborhood at home; Mignon did a good job of making sure people picked up their trash, or maybe Kansans were naturally tidier than Chicagoans.

1732 Squash Blossom was a single wide, which meant a single bedroom at one end, with a bathroom tucked in between that, and a kitchen-dining-living room at the end where the door was.

I studied the lock before I stuck the key in. It hadn't been jim-
mied, and the hinges were all straight. Whoever came in before me
either was skilled with a picklock or, more likely, picked up a key
while Mignon wasn't looking.

My predecessors in the search hadn't been interested in hiding
their presence. Every possession Clarina Coffin had owned had been
pulled from cupboards and drawers and dumped where the intruders
had stood when they examined it. I could hear them cursing, getting
angrier as they moved through the narrow space, because the destruction in the bedroom was worse than in the main room. The couch
had been upended and the cushions unzipped, but in the bedroom,
they'd slit open the mattress and the pillows.

Mignon, or the hedge fund, had turned the power off to the
trailer. It was dark and cold and my phone flash didn't give enough
light for a thorough inspection, but I wore down the battery poking
through the debris. I didn't find any personal papers, or even scholarly
papers. Of course, I was third in line. I was assuming her killers had
been the first—they'd killed her looking for something, and had been
furious when they couldn't find it. They or the cops would have impounded any digital devices.

The only personal items I found, if you could call them personal,
were three pictures. One was a black-and-white photo of a white
woman in the kind of dress I associated with Mary Todd Lincoln—a
tight bodice and full skirt. She was sitting with her hands folded in
her lap. The print was old and faded; the black of her dress had turned
a kind of sienna.

I would have thought the woman was wearing mourning, except
she seemed to have a wreath of flowers looped around the wings of
hair that covered her ears. She had a large brooch pinned to where
the collar met at her throat, and she was staring at the camera with
seeming defiance.

The vandals had broken the frame around the photo. A piece of
glass was embedded in the woman's skirt. I removed it, carefully, trying not to tear the paper itself.

The other two pictures had had the grainy, blurry quality that
comes from printing from microform or digitized files. One showed
a fight in progress, white against Black, apparently at a train station.

Pieces of broken furniture were scattered around, along with a few chickens and a calf.

The third picture showed the smoking remains of a building that had burned to the foundation. There were no people in the picture, and no label to tell me whether it had been a house or a business.

The flashlight had worn out my phone battery. I wrapped the pictures carefully inside a dish towel and went back into the cold day.

18

REBEL WITH TOO MANY CAUSES

TRIG GARRITY WAS the one person I could identify who'd spent time with Clarina. I was sure the cops had already been on him, but that might make him more willing to speak to an independent investigator.

Trig lived in the old part of town, in a tired house on Vermont Street, with cracked siding and gaps in the foundation that would make the place an easy mark for rodents. Dead plants sat stiffly in pots along the porch railing. A child's tricycle, missing a wheel, was upside down below them. Four mailboxes hung next to the front door.

I buzzed 2-E, Trig's apartment, several times, but didn't get an answer. A woman came out as I was heading back to my car. She wore a backpack and had her face stuck on her device while she scrolled through her screen.

"Excuse me," I repeated loudly when she didn't stop scrolling.

"Sorry," she said, drawing out the second syllable in annoyance.

"I'm sorry to interrupt you," I said. "But I'm looking for Trig."

"You one of the protesters? He's at work, but you can sign up at Kansans4Freedom."

"Where does he work?"

"Prairie State Recycling over in Eudora, last I heard, unless he was fired." She looked back at her screen, swore under her breath, and started down the street at a jog, the backpack thumping into her.

"You late somewhere? I'll give you a lift."

She thanked me effusively; she was a student, heading up the hill to class, which started in nine minutes. "I wasn't watching the time. Thank you, thank you. I've been late the last three classes and Prof. Rand is threatening to lower my grade."

"How long have you been living in the same building as Trig?" I asked as she shut the passenger door.

"Just this year. He's been in that house forever; he has the best apartment, the one with the sunroom overlooking the garden. Well, yard. It's mostly weeds and dirt, but, still, when the trees are in leaf it's pretty. Are you a protester?"

"Just an ordinary person with some questions about a murdered woman. She used to take part in some of his events."

"Oh! That woman someone found walled up in a basement!"

"Not walled up. But dead in a basement out in the country. Her name was Clarina Coffin. I'm trying to find out who she was and what brought her to Lawrence. Did you ever meet her?"

"She came around a few times when Trig was protesting at some school."

I started up the steep hill to the campus, the Toyota slow but not complaining.

"Do the police suspect Trig?" She was suddenly alert, a hostile undertone in her voice.

"I'm not with the police, so I don't know what they're thinking. Did she ever say anything about where she came from? People say she was exploring Lawrence history, but no one seems to know what her background was."

The young woman shook her head. "She never really talked to me, except to see if I'd come out to that school with her and Trig. He gets a bad rap—he's such a good-hearted person, caring about the planet, and all kinds of injustices, it's hard for him to understand why some of us don't have his time or energy for protests. When I first moved into the building I helped him paint some signs, but it all got to be too much. The stuff he protests, he's right about all these issues, so if the police or whoever are trying to stop him, it's because they're not paying attention."

We'd reached the campus security checkpoint. I couldn't drive past it without a permit, but my passenger gave me another brilliant smile, she was only four minutes away if she ran, and for sure I'd saved her life.

I pulled over on a side street and consulted my GPS for directions to Prairie State Recycling. Eudora was a town to the east, about eight miles in a direct line from where I was parked. I started down the hill. I was turning onto Fifteenth Street when I remembered Lou's admonition about skinny white girls.

I hadn't eaten much of the pancakes at the Boat Yard. I drove back into town, where I made myself eat a large bowl of chicken-noodle soup. It rested uneasily in my stomach, but I reminded myself of the Warshawski coat of arms: a dinner plate, with knife and fork rampant, and the motto *Never Skip a Meal, Always Clean Your Plate.*

Prairie State Recycling was easy to find. Signs told me where to park, in a lot around the side, away from heavy machinery and debris. Signs told me where to deposit my material. Another sign begged me to do a simple sort before I dropped off anything. IT SAVES WEAR AND TEAR ON OUR NERVES AND ON OUR MACHINES, AND LOWERS THE COST TO YOU!

The center itself was in a large, simply built shed, whose outer doors were raised so that conveyor belts could feed material into shipping containers outside.

A couple of people were emptying bags onto a belt. The light inside the shed was dim, but Trig's halo of wiry curls was easy to spot. He was facing the belt and moving items onto smaller belts, hand-sorting glass from different metals, tossing nonrecyclables into a bin at his feet. Prairie State Recycling's customers apparently ignored the signs and didn't do a simple sort themselves.

The din from the machinery and the clanging of bottles and metal on the belts was intense. Even if I'd wanted to interrupt Trig midtask, no one could have heard me over the racket.

A woman who'd been emptying bags onto the belt came over to me, lifting her earmuffs from her head.

"Can I help you?" she bellowed. "Are you a member?"

"I want to talk to Trig," I shouted back. "How long before he finishes?"

She looked at a giant clock on the wall. "You one of his marchers? He'll take a break in about ten minutes."

I went back to the Toyota, where I could block out the worst of the noise. GATES INTO THE YARD ARE SHUT PROMPTLY AT FOUR, a sign read. If I were a member, I could enter my code on the pad and leave my recyclables in the yard.

I was studying the sign when the woman came over to me and said Trig was taking a break. "No one can work the belts for more than thirty minutes at a stretch."

I agreed that the work looked both tedious and dangerous.

"It baffles me how people completely disregard our instructions and jumble everything together, but no one ever said life was supposed to be easy."

When I got back to the shed, the noise was down because the belts weren't running. Trig was leaning against the wall, scrolling through his phone. He'd put on the army parka I'd seen him wearing in the courthouse.

"Tina said you wanted to volunteer," he said when I introduced myself. "But she didn't say what you wanted to do. It's best if you go to the website."

"I'm sorry—all I told her was that I wanted to talk to you. I'm an investigator, trying to learn more about Clarina Coffin."

His expression soured. "Oh, yes. The private pig hanging around with Zoë. Every step I take, one of you jerks is writing me a ticket for moving my feet the wrong way."

"Mr. Garrity, I don't have ticket-writing powers. I'm interested in you only insofar as you can tell me anything about Clarina Coffin. Do you know her home was trashed? Someone was trying to find something there. If you have a whiff of an idea about what it could be, I'd love to hear about it."

He scowled. "Why do you care about Clarina?"

In time-honored pig fashion, I sidestepped the question. "Do you know her background, where she lived before she came to Lawrence? She talked to people like Cady Perec about her interest in history. I just searched the trailer she was renting. Whoever trashed her apartment took anything she might have written, including any computers she might have written on. Do you know what she wrote?"

He hunched a shoulder and muttered she'd never shown him her work.

"In the woods behind the Dundee house I found a fragment of a letter suggesting a lunch date at the University of Kansas press building. I wonder if it's a letter she received?"

"You really are a snooper, aren't you? Busy in her trailer, busy in the woods?"

Bhagavatula had a ton more patience than me—I would have locked him up months ago. I tried to keep my irritation from showing. "Did she mention a possible meeting with anyone at the press?"

"Not to me," he said after a pause, perhaps reluctant to admit she hadn't confided in him.

"Trig!" Tina called from the shed. "We're going to start up the line again."

He turned back toward the shed.

I put a hand on his arm. "Can we meet for coffee or a drink when you get off work so we can finish this conversation? I'll wait for you at the Decadent Hippo."

"What, so you can try to frame me? I know how the police work. If you can't pin Clarina's murder on me, you'll round up some Black or Native person to arrest, case closed, next!" He mimed a judge banging a gavel.

"On top of having no ticket-writing powers, I have no power to arrest anyone. You're in the top tier of people they're interested in because you keep showing up at the Dundee house."

"So do you, and for that matter, so does Queen Gertrude. I guess I should thank you—if the two of you hadn't gone out there, I'd be in a cell, for sure."

"Very likely," I agreed. "Judge Bhagavatula can't be the only person on the bench who you've pissed off. However, the sooner I can find out who actually killed her, the sooner I can return to Chicago and a vestige of normal life."

Tina called his name again, and he stomped off toward the shed.

"And stop it with the pig-naming," I called after him. "It's a worn-out cliché. You're clever enough to think of something new."

19
DREAMS OF GLORY

ONE OF THE junior editors, Kayla Huang, at the University Press remembered Clarina, not with enthusiasm. "Her murder is shocking, and I'm sorry for it, but she came around several times, maybe eighteen months or two years ago. I was the newbie, so they sent her to me. She thought she had a great memoir to tell, about her life in the context of her family's involvement in the abolitionist movement, but she didn't have anything in writing to show me. She had this whole file of clippings from the *New York Times* on memoirs that had been written by ghost writers, where the books had surprised their publishers by generating huge sales."

Huang took me into her office, a cubbyhole filled with books and manuscripts, some on the floor, some stacked on chairs. She let me read the correspondence between the press and Clarina, a series of increasingly angry letters from Clarina, accusing everyone in Lawrence of bigotry and a refusal to acknowledge true Kansas history.

When I showed Huang the photo I'd taken of the letter fragment, she frowned over it. "I can't tell if it came from our offices or not. There's no sign it was written on letterhead. I supposed if it was an invitation to meet in Westbrooke Circle, it would have meant to come here, but there's no way of telling. And you can't see who it was written to, either."

Huang took me back to the reception area. A redheaded woman

in a blue cleaner's smock was emptying the trash by the counter into a blue cart labeled RECYCLABLE PAPER AND CARDBOARD ONLY.

Huang asked the young man at the counter if Clarina had been in anytime in the last few weeks. "She might have thought someone had a lunch date with her."

He looked at the visitors log, but Clarina's name wasn't in it. "Bruce had a lunch here with Tracy Clark, and Nandar had one over at the faculty club with Lori Rader-Day. That's all for the past month, but I can get you a list for the rest of the year if you want."

"The paper was fresh," I said, "not stained by snow or dirt, so I don't think it would go back very far."

The woman taking care of the trash stood holding the empty container, waiting for us to get out of her way.

"I'll send out an email blast to everyone on staff asking if they saw or corresponded with Clarina in the last month," Huang said. "I'd be surprised—she might have refused to work with me, since I hadn't gotten her the contract she wanted, but they would have sent her to me first if she came around recently."

When I thanked her and left, I saw the woman with the trash still standing in the hall, staring after me.

I drove back to what the map app called "Old Lawrence," the part of town close to the river where the nineteenth-century pioneers had settled. Gertrude Perec lived in the tony section, big houses, big lots, trim and siding painted, streets and sidewalks well maintained. It was only a short walk east from her place to small houses that seemed to stay upright due to some anti-gravity device. The sidewalks there were brick, and buckling.

Everything in Old Lawrence, including the homes, the shops and the courts, was in a walkable area about a mile square. I parked the Toyota in front of a tumbledown house and walked back to the Perec garage. I couldn't hide from the cops indefinitely, but the longer it took them to connect me to the Camry, the easier it would be for me to slide out of town tomorrow.

When I'd dropped off my supplies, and eaten some cheese, I walked back into town. It was a transition hour at the Hippo, from coffee to cocktails. In the mornings only three or four people would sit at the big wood tables inside, but it was nearly five when I got there; the place was filling up.

The Hippo's signature cocktail was the River Bottom, a mix of bourbon, Aperol, and orange pulp. I don't usually drink this early in the day, and rarely cocktails, but I ordered a River Bottom and wedged myself into a spot behind the door. It was too cold to wait outside, but I wanted air on me, even if people claimed the pandemic was over.

While I waited, wondering if Trig would show, I did a sketchy search on my phone. Trig was forty-seven. He'd been a student at the University of Kansas but apparently had dropped out halfway through his third year. He'd left school, but he couldn't tear himself away from the town. There wasn't any record of a marriage or children.

I pay for information on things like arrest records. Trig had been picked up countless times for crimes against property—trespass, defacing storefronts—under his birth name, Irwin, but I couldn't find any history of violence. I don't have access to employment records unless people post their work history themselves, so I didn't know what jobs he'd held before Prairie State Recycling. The plant was eighteen years old, so even if he'd been there from the beginning, he must have been doing something before that. I also couldn't find a reason for his nickname.

I was about to close the search and do some paying work when a header caught my eye: GALLOPING GARRITY RUNS BACK HIS EIGHTEENTH INTERCEPTION FOR A TOUCHDOWN. Trig as a football player seemed improbable, but I opened the file.

Mark Garrity was the galloper, not Irwin. Mark had played for the University of Iowa, where he'd set numerous Big Ten and NCAA records. He'd gone on to a career as a defensive end with the Chiefs. The year Trig dropped out of school, Mark had been named defensive MVP in his conference. Dr. Freud could probably suggest a connection there.

The bio didn't mention Trig/Irwin, but both men came from Waterloo, Iowa. Both had parents named LeRoy and Patty. Mark, the football star, was the elder by five years.

I looked up Trig's site, Kansans4Freedom. As is true for every website these days, the first page was an invitation to donate time or money. Photos showed Trig in front of a belching smokestack, confronting a deputy in front of the Yancy school, nose to nose with an abortion foe outside a clinic, facing off with a group holding assault weapons. The sad thing was, he was alone in most of the pictures on his side of the protests.

"Can I get you another?" One of the waitstaff appeared in front of me. I'd been so absorbed in my reading I hadn't noticed that the crowd at the bar had grown to four-deep. I was occupying valuable real estate for someone nursing a single drink. In fact, I'd only taken a few swallows, but it was thick and sweet, not to my taste.

It had gotten to be six-thirty; it didn't seem likely Trig would show. I was edging around the table to get to the door when the young woman I'd met earlier at Trig's apartment appeared.

"It's you," she said, relieved.

"It is indeed," I agreed. "You made it to your class without your grade being docked?"

"By seventeen seconds." She grinned. "I was looking for you but couldn't see you in the crowd. Trig sent me. He hates this place, but he can talk to you at the apartment if you go over there."

I offered her a lift, but she was hooking up with friends. By the time I reached the street she'd disappeared into the mob at the bar, and someone else had grabbed my seat.

I'd hoped that Trig's apartment would be an oasis of tidy calm in his angry life, but when he undid the chain bolt, after studying me through the gap, I walked into a paper factory. Posters, posterboard, paints for writing on posterboard, covered an old sofa and part of the floor. News stories printed from the Web were taped to the wall with key paragraphs circled in red.

The furniture was old, the curtains threadbare, but he had a new-looking iMac on the corner table that served as his desk. The desk chair was a good ergonomic model. He swiveled it around to face me but didn't offer me a place to sit. I shifted some of the posters on the couch. He muttered under his breath about pigs thinking they had the right to mess with people's private belongings.

I pretended I hadn't heard. "Clarina Coffin was a modern-day miracle. She had no existence anywhere on the net before she showed up here."

I waited a beat, but he was watching me warily, not responding. He might be a loose cannon but this wasn't his first interrogation.

"I'm guessing Clarina Coffin was a fake identity. There was a suffragist named Clarina Nicholls who lived in Kansas in the nineteenth century. Clarina Coffin claimed to be deeply interested in local history, so I'm wondering if she named herself after that activist. There are thousands of people in the country with the 'Coffin' surname. Did your Clarina ever talk to you about how she chose her name?"

"She wasn't 'my' Clarina. Just someone who understood the importance of the issues facing our country."

"When did she start joining the protests?" I asked.

"What does this have to do with her death? You think Brett Santich murdered her to stop her picketing his school?" He sat up straighter, expression hopeful.

"I don't think anything because I don't have data," I said. "I'm hoping you can help with that. Was Cady Perec's suspension the first time Clarina joined you in one of your actions?"

"How can I trust you to keep what I say confidential?"

"You can't," I said. "It's a murder investigation. If you tell me something that connects to her killer, I'm bound to act on it. But if you tell me something about trespassing or throwing paintballs at a building, I'll keep it to myself."

"Yeah, that's about the level I'm good at," he said bitterly. "I thought I could make a difference in the world, but trespassing and throwing paintballs doesn't change anything."

He watched me for signs of ridicule, perhaps, or judgment, but I sat still, not speaking, keeping my face neutral.

"It's not a big secret. Clarina first came around last fall, when Santich and his lackeys suspended Cady Perec for trying to teach their children the truth about race and class in America. Zoë, the kid at the paper, wrote up the way the school board reacted to Cady's class on Kansas history. Clarina read the story. She said she'd been digging into Lawrence history and could shed some amazing light on hidden corners of it."

"What kinds of things did she think she could reveal?"

"Things like lynch mobs in Kansas, or the way the heroes of the abolitionist movement treated Indigenous people after the Civil

War. She offered to help Cady improve her reading list. The Perecs go around with their damned noses in the air, acting like they're the people who created this town, so of course Cady told Clarina she didn't need her help.

"Clarina wasn't the kind to take offense. When Santich took things with Cady to the next level and got his lapdog board to fire her, Clarina came out to picket with me."

Trig breathed heavily, his fury at Santich boiling to the surface again.

"Anyway, I told her about the Yancy project when she was working with me at the school. Brett Santich farmed that land on top of the mound, and suddenly he gives it over to some company that wants to put in a fancy resort. Like, all the rich people in Kansas City will invite their friends here for skiing or whatever rich people do, instead of going to Aspen.

"High-and-mighty Perec, she was head of the planning commission when the deal went through, she says it's a private concern, not run by local government. But when I ask why local government doesn't have responsibility for environmental impact or safety, but this private concern has, she tells me to raise the question with the right authorities. And when I do that, they tell me I don't have standing. So I picket, because it's all I can do. I'd been out there Tuesday mornings, because Tuesdays and Wednesdays are my days off from the recycling center.

"Santich, he got the sheriff to come around with some kind of injunction, but I fought that one—it's one of the few times that Judge Bhagavatula took my side. I'm moving, I've got a sign. Yes, I have a bullhorn, but the only people I'm disturbing are the creeps working the site."

When his bitter avalanche ended, I tried to bring the conversation back to Clarina, asking if she'd mentioned specific documents she'd thought Cady should use in her class.

Trig looked at me blankly. "I don't know. I don't know what she had, just that this was her life's work, research on displaced native people, that kind of thing."

"She tried to get the university press to publish her memoir, but she couldn't show them anything in writing. Still, someone tore her place apart, looking for something," I said. "You have any idea what that could have been?"

He shook his head.

"When did you last see Clarina?"

He thought it over, and finally decided it was the Thursday before she died. She'd joined him at the access road to the Yancy construction.

"She said it was probably the last time she'd be coming out to picket with me. I asked if she was leaving Lawrence, and she gave this kind of superior smile and said, maybe, if everything worked out the way she hoped."

I pushed a little, hoping he'd asked Clarina what she meant, where she was heading if she left town, but he said she did stuff like that all the time. "She'd throw out some crumb of information, see if she had your attention, then she'd act all mysterious and not say anything else. I appreciated her support, but I got fed up with her act."

"Why did you go out to the Dundee house Tuesday morning?" I asked. "Did you get a message from Clarina?"

He picked at his nails, finally said without looking up, "I have a scanner so I know where the cops or sheriff are going to be. I saw they were out at the Dundee place."

I turned that response over in my mind. "You knew the Dundee place was used for drug parties?"

He looked up at me, looked down again. "Not in so many words."

"You didn't go to parties out there?"

"You think I'm that stupid? Cops are on my ass twenty-four-seven and I tempt them by going to a drug house? Besides, I don't use anything. I hate that loss of control."

"Did you think Clarina would be at the house when you saw the police activity?"

"Not her. Someone I know," he muttered after another pause. "I worried whether they'd get caught in some kind of sweep. When I got there, the place was all shut down. I was going inside to look, then her majesty Queen Gertrude showed up."

"Was Sabrina Granev the person you were looking for?" I asked.

"Who? Oh, the missing college student. No. It was someone who shouldn't be there but won't stay away."

It was all he would say: he wasn't going to feed an innocent person to the cops.

"You must have been surprised when Gertrude Perec showed up."

"I was sure the cops had sent her. She's so tight with Everard's mom you'd think the two were doing a synchronized act—maybe looking down their noses in unison."

I hadn't expected that kind of mordant humor. He had depths, which meant I needed to watch my step around him.

"She had some story about looking for a friend, but she wouldn't say who, so I thought Everard's mother. Of course I didn't tell Gertrude why I was there, and I wasn't going to go inside as long as she was hanging around. I finally took off. Was Clarina—was she there then?"

"Yes," I said. "Dead, in the basement where I found her a few hours later."

Peter's student, on the floor with their face in pieces, blood and bone and the soft gray mass that had been their agonized mind, appeared before me. I dug my nails into my head. *You will not faint. You have never fainted and tonight will not be the first time.*

Trig was suddenly in front of me, forcing a glass of water into my hands. The glass was greasy, but I drank, anyway.

"You going to be okay?" he asked roughly.

I nodded. I would be okay. Maybe not tonight, but surely someday soon. I was exhausted but I still had some questions.

"The picture. The police have a picture of you and Perec outside the house. Who took it?"

He snorted. "If I knew that I'd be outside their house right now with a bullhorn. It's the only reason I'm telling you why I was there. Because of the picture. It wasn't photoshopped, I was there."

I got unsteadily to my feet and sidestepped the cardboard and paper on the floor. In the doorway I stopped to look at him again. He'd swiveled in his chair to face his computer.

The screen saver had come up, a boy with a mop of dark hair and a gap-toothed grin. A redhaired woman was bending over him, hands crossed over his chest. When Trig saw me looking at the picture, he pressed a key and his files came back up on the screen. He gave me a menacing look: I dare you to say anything about that picture.

I said nothing about the picture. I asked instead whether Clarina ever said anything about where she came from.

"I told you, no! No, every time you ask, so stop asking."

He started a routine rant about cops not caring about the truth, no matter whether they were public or private, but something about me, maybe the lingering anguish in my face, caught him up short.

"There was this one time. It was—I was telling her—I have a brother. Football star. Me, I was the skinny nerdy one, but not nerdy enough to be a genius and win prizes." His eyes squeezed shut from decades-old pain.

"At school, teachers and everyone thought I'd be another star, so when I couldn't even catch a ball I turned into a joke. The jocks liked to—never mind what they did. My brother, he was on TV every Saturday running back touchdowns for Iowa. To my parents, I was the world's biggest loser. When I was beaten up in school, my mother told me not to be a crybaby.

"Clarina, I told her about it one time. It was that jerk Santich, he was taunting me outside the school. Somehow he'd figured out who my brother was. His nickname, Galloping Garrity, so Santich, he said he'd get the police to tear-gas me and see—see if I could run as fast as Galloping Garrity."

He looked at me sideways, to see if I was going to join the mockery. "Clarina said, she came from a place where the town name meant everyone in school piled on, making fun of her for being chubby."

"The town name?" I echoed, bewildered. "What—was it some kind of Indigenous word for 'fat'?"

"She didn't say. I didn't pay enough attention, I guess."

I made my way out the door and down the linoleum stairs. Outside I walked to the end of the block and back, sucking in the cold air. Parents shoot their children, they bully their children, children bully each other. Was there no end to the grief we cause each other?

20

PISSING FOR JUSTICE

ALL NINE HOURS from Kansas to Chicago, I'd been thinking happily of reconnecting with Mr. Contreras and the dogs, followed by a peaceful night in my own bed. That happy fantasy was crashed by reality. When I reached home, Mr. Contreras was agitated, almost in tears: someone had come this morning and searched my apartment.

"They had a warrant, doll, I couldn't hardly stop them. I stuck with them, me and Mitch, to make sure they didn't steal nothing or maybe plant some drugs or something on you, but they was hardly civil."

The searchers had been with the FBI. My neighbor had studied their credentials. "Told them I was old, needed time to make sure they hadn't got those things out of a cereal box, and I wrote down their badge numbers, like you taught me, but I couldn't stop them. There was three of them, but one, he never showed me his badge, and the other two said he was an observer."

I asked if they'd let slip anything to say what they were looking for. They hadn't said anything, but they'd been searching through all my papers, including my mother's music, which I hold sacred. They hadn't been sloppy, exactly, but they hadn't used ordinary courtesy. I spent my first hour home inserting loose pages back in the proper folders. I even sprayed the collection with Lysol to get rid of federal cooties.

They'd also been to my office, my leasemate reported. They hadn't taken it apart, not like the searchers in Clarina's trailer, but as with Gabriella's music, they hadn't taken pains to hide their footsteps.

On Thursday, the home news got even more distressing. I'd cheered myself with a long run up the lakefront with the dogs, then stopped near Lotty Herschel's clinic. She took an hour away from duty to have coffee with me. After that, I'd seen Sal Barthele, who owns the Golden Glow in the South Loop, to catch up in private ahead of my upcoming night meeting there with Murray.

My happier frame of mind ended with my third slice of Mr. Contreras's French toast. That was when Bernie called.

"Vic, have you seen the news? I am so sorry, it is my fault they are saying these things about you!"

"Who is saying what things?" I asked.

"*Mon Dieu,* you haven't seen, then? It is the Lawrence *policier,* they arranged a press conference about this murder you found, and about Sabrina."

My neighbor has a tablet, which he mostly uses to keep in touch with his grandsons and his old buddies from his Machinists local. I found a video of Lawrence police chief Rowland McDowell's press conference.

McDowell and the county sheriff met reporters on a small plaza in front of the Douglas County Judicial Center. Cornell Stamoran, the FBI agent, was on the dais, along with a man who was identified as Frank Karas, the Douglas County DA. Deke Everard stood behind the chief and the sheriff.

The first questions had to do with Clarina Coffin: no one had come forward who claimed to be a relative, or know anything about her past, the chief said, so if anyone could help with that information, please call the number on the screen. They also posted a portrait, where they'd photoshopped out the blood and fixed up her matted hair.

Reporters asked about time of death, cause, weapon, suspects—all the usual. The chief said they didn't have any details to give yet.

A Wichita reporter asked about the drug house where both Sabrina and Clarina had been found. Another man, in a suit and tie, was next to Stamoran. He was never identified, but before the chief answered, the stranger stepped forward to murmur into his ear.

The sheriff nodded. "The owner of the property has promised to put better security in place. It's a historic house, dating back to the Civil War, and the owner is trying to get landmark status for it. He definitely doesn't want it used for drugs or murdered bodies"—a ripple of laughter at that.

Another person wanted to know about the Chicago detective who'd found both Sabrina and the dead woman.

"She's a person of interest," Chief McDowell said. "We've told her to stay in the jurisdiction until we're a hundred percent sure she's not responsible for either crime."

Zoë piped up. "The Chicago detective is V.I. Warshawski. She saved Sabrina Granev's life, Chief. Why does that make her a person of interest?"

I blew her a kiss while the chief waffled around.

Someone who identified himself as with the Kansas University newspaper said, "Warshawski apparently came on campus on Monday and accused Omicron Delta Beta members of selling drugs. Trevor Millay, he's the chapter president, said she was snooping around their garage. He thinks she was looking for drugs. Do you know if she's a user herself?"

The chief turned to Deke, who said, "We saw the post Millay made on the chapter's Instagram account. We don't believe Ms. Warshawski is a drug user, but we will take measures to make sure of that."

A red mist rose in front of my eyes. I looked up the Omicron account and their other social media. They'd picked up my photo from the Web and posted it over the caption: *Pretending to look for a missing student but really searching for drugs for herself?*

Trevor Millay was the name of the punk I'd seen in their garage on Monday. *"Don't cross a South Side street fighter, buster,"* I hissed, *"because I can make you sorry you ever drew breath."* I had just enough self-control not to post the threat on his feed.

"That's terrible, doll, terrible," Mr. Contreras said. "What can you do to shut him up?"

"I don't know," I said. "It's a lie, but these days, incredible lies spread faster than Canadian wildfires, and they're harder to extinguish. I'll check in with Freeman Carter, and the woman in Kansas City whom Freeman found to represent me, but if I find Clarina Coffin's killer, that should quiet some of the more obnoxious creeps."

"How you going to do that?" he fretted. "You don't have any friends down there, and if the cops are fixing to frame you—"

"I do have a couple of friends, but my big advantage is an open mind. The cops are looking at me and maybe two or three other people. I'm willing to look at everyone in Kansas as a suspect. After that, I'm going to nail that frat boy's hind end to his Porsche."

A good speech, but we all know how valuable talk is. My troubles hadn't exactly peaked, either. I had a voice message from Deke Everard.

"We knew you were staying in Gertrude Perec's garage, but when I went by to talk to you, Cady said you'd gone back to Chicago. You were told not to leave the jurisdiction. The DA is issuing a subpoena. Unless you are back in Lawrence by ten Monday morning to talk to Karas, we will send sheriff's deputies to bring you back."

I forwarded the message to Freeman, who phoned me at once.

"You are not my client who's the biggest pain in the ass, but you are in the top ten," he said. "There is no good 'why' in this scenario."

"Freeman, I struggle to keep on top of your bill. I cannot afford to set up a separate household and office in Kansas. I'm here to collect my computer, my files, my clothes, all those things. I'll be back in Kansas by tomorrow night. I'm even putting on my red Magli pumps to seal the deal."

"You're not convincing me," he said. "Someone could mail you all those things. Meanwhile, you're adding another buck-fifty to your outstanding balance with me. Shipping your home to Kansas wouldn't cost that much."

Shorthand for a thousand fifty. Which went up to twelve hundred when he phoned again half an hour later.

"Someone in Kansas hates you, Vic. The LKPD wants a urine sample to prove whether you're an opioid user. They've agreed to let the Chicago cops oversee it, but this isn't negotiable. They have a warrant, Chicago will honor it."

Opioids don't stay long in the bloodstream, but you can find a trace in urine up to four days after using them. It had been about eighty-four hours since I'd found Sabrina. If they thought I'd ingested something in the Dundee house, they would need the sample now.

Peeing for justice is humiliating, and humiliation makes me angry, but I drove over to the police lab on Harrison.

The Chicago cops sent a sergeant I knew, Lenora Pizzello, who arrived with the warrant. Pizzello and I had worked around each other several times in the past, sometimes cordially, even, but she never forgot her first loyalty was to the wide blue line.

While we waited for one of Freeman's female associates, who would be a witness for the accused, I tried to make conversation. "This seems like such an intimate moment, but so one-sided, only one of us getting naked. I could bring out a bottle, put on a record, so that you could get in the mood."

"I don't want to be here, Warshawski!" Pizzello's face was red. "This isn't my idea of police work. And I thought better of you than for you to be a user."

"Me, too, Pizzello, and I expect the lab to bear out our joint good opinion."

Freeman's female associate arrived, the two women watched me pee, both looking like stuffed owls to hide their embarrassment. I don't know how I looked, but I'm sure it wasn't happy. The lab tech sealed the specimen cup and dated and initialed it; Pizzello and Freeman's associate initialed underneath, also with the date.

"When I'm super famous, you'll be able to brag about this moment to your grandchildren," I said. "Like people who touched Elvis's dead body: I got to watch the astonishing private eye, V.I. Warshawski, pee into a cup."

"You're already famous," Pizzello said. "People from as far away as Schaumburg want to know why you aren't behind bars."

My clients were worried, too. The Millay kid's social media posts were getting a big play. Two of my accounts canceled during the afternoon. The other nine for whom I was doing active work all needed phone conversations that showed how assiduously I was handling their business.

"Oh, Bernie," I murmured as I packed my wardrobe, my toiletries, my computer, and Peppy's food and blanket. "You meant well, but I was so much better off sitting at home feeling sorry for myself."

21

THERE'S NO PLACE LIKE—WHEREVER

PEPPY AND I arrived in Lawrence late Saturday night. In between packing the files and clothes I'd need for a week out of town, I'd caught up with friends. My evening at the Golden Glow with Sal and Murray had been a great spirit reviver, but it made my lonely arrival in Lawrence feel more desolate.

The lights were off in the Perec house. I moved our things into the garage apartment as quietly as I could. Peppy was uneasy in the unfamiliar space, but when I took her for a walk in the park near the library, she relaxed. She'd been there with me two years ago. Dogs have some kind of mental scent library; she knew she was in a familiar space.

Sunday morning, I drove to a co-op grocery on the west side of town where I stocked up on enough basics to last a week. I hoped I wouldn't have to stay here any longer than that. I sent a text to Lou and Ed, letting them know the Camry and I had made the round-trip without an arrest, assault, or impoundment.

After unpacking, and parking some distance from Gertrude's, I took Peppy over to the river. The path led us past the Riverside Congregational Church, where Clarina had offended the women by acting as though she knew more about Lawrence than they did. The parking lot was full; I could hear a hymn trickle faintly through the stained glass windows.

As the dog and I walked the river path, I pondered again Cady's claim that she'd been down here early Tuesday morning when Clarina was being murdered. The path was well maintained and easy to walk in daylight, but tree roots and rocks would be hazards in the dark. Had she really been here? And if not here, had she been at the Dundee place, assisting her grandmother in moving Clarina's body into the basement?

Trig claimed he'd been at the Dundee house early Tuesday morning because he worried that a friend would be caught up in a police sweep. Trig was such a loner, I tried to imagine who he would care about enough to try to protect them.

I wondered about the boy in Trig's screen saver. Perhaps that was a nephew, the son of Galloping Garrity. If he was part of Trig's life, I could see him going out of his way to protect the child, but I couldn't see the rage in Trig that this murderer had exhibited. Even his flare-ups with Santich didn't rise to that level of fury.

The church was perched on top of a ravine, with a steep path down to the river. I let Peppy off her leash. She ran ahead of me, exploring the underbrush lining the river path, and even jumped into the water for a few minutes. The river must be cold this time of year, but so is Lake Michigan. She's a dog who likes the cold.

The path we were on ended at the boathouse for the university's rowing teams. A disused boat trailer was sinking into the mud at the back, but the building was locked up tight and, par for the Lawrence course, there wasn't any litter on the ground around it. If I managed to clear my name and find Clarina's killer, maybe I'd move here permanently.

By then, Peppy was so filthy I had to take her to a DIY dog wash before I could go back to the apartment. While I was drying her, Deke Everard texted me. He hoped I was back in the jurisdiction: Did I remember the DA was going to interview me first thing tomorrow?

Of course Zoë had sent several messages, panting for another meeting in our supposed collaboration.

I called Everard from the Hippo, where I'd become such a regular that they invited Peppy inside with me. My call went to voicemail, but I got a text from him almost instantly, asking for my location.

While I was waiting for him, a woman about my age, in skintight Lycra with her hair pulled into a ponytail, popped into the Hippo, asked if I was me, and handed me a subpoena. She bounced out the door, resuming her run. That would be a good gig: process server while training for a marathon. I photographed the subpoena and texted it to Faye Mitchell.

When Deke came into the Hippo, a couple of people greeted him by name, and the barista brought him a mug of black coffee.

"Your pee is clean," he said by way of greeting.

"Good to have my essential purity confirmed," I said.

"Your essence is not exactly pure. You're screwing around in an LKPD murder investigation, and that makes you look suspicious."

"Sergeant, I'm screwing around in your investigation because I'm a suspect and I don't want to be railroaded for a crime I didn't commit. I would be happily drinking espresso in my own home right this minute if your crew had searched the Dundee house from top to bottom after I found Sabrina."

His lips tightened and he looked away.

"The blanket that showed up in my car trunk was in the front hall at the Dundee House when I went inside. Which means most likely Clarina was already dead in the basement. I haven't been able to talk to Valerie Granev since she moved her daughter to some facility in Florida, but she told me Sabrina was screaming about seeing monsters. I don't have any subpoena powers but if a competent interrogator spoke to Sabrina, they might discover she'd seen the killers carry Clarina into the house."

He hadn't put milk or sugar in his coffee, but he stirred it around, so forcefully that some of it slopped onto the tabletop. "I won't argue about that with you. Hindsight is always perfect. But believe it or not, I'm trying to protect you—I don't think you killed Coffin any more than I believe Aunt Gertrude did. Or my mom, for that matter, but you and Aunt—and Gertrude both were at the crime scene the same night that Clarina died. The DA, the Bureau's guy Stamoran, and even the chief keep coming back to that point. The fact that Gertrude also showed up there is all that's keeping Karas from charging you and Trig."

"So Gertrude really was there? And Trig? Why?"

"That's the impossible part of the story," Deke said. "Trig refused at first to admit he'd gone there. When we showed him the picture of him by the back door with Gertrude, he claimed it was photoshopped. Finally, he said he got an anonymous call telling him he could catch Brett Santich selling drugs if he showed up without announcing himself. In fact, Trig's phone shows him *making* a call, to a pay phone—there are still a handful in Lawrence. But we don't have any evidence that he received any calls."

"What does Santich say about that?" I wondered if Trig had been lying to me, or to the cops, or maybe telling each of us a separate lie.

"Santich says he wouldn't invite Trig to leave a burning house, let alone out to his land at any hour of the day or night."

"What about Gertrude?" I asked.

"Gertrude says she had a message from one of the women in her book club, saying her car had broken down outside the Dundee place and could Gertrude come wait with her, since it was creepy out there at night."

"Can you verify that?"

"She did get a call just before three. From a burner. Someone wanted her in the frame. She rubs a lot of people the wrong way—she and her mother before her are steamrollers in this town, flattening opposition to their vision of Lawrence's future. If the killer resented her enough, he—or she, I guess—could have thought it would be a good joke to put her at the crime scene."

"In the same way they thought it was a good joke to leave the blanket in my car," I said, my voice very dry. "How are you coming with inspecting it? When can I have my ride back?"

"Our CSIs are being very thorough. Any misstep with any evidence now could endanger a prosecution when we finally make an arrest."

"And that's what you call trying to protect me? Trying to find any evidence against me in my car?"

"Don't be so damned touchy. How about, thanks, Deke, for making sure the prosecution can't try to prove we overlooked drugs or weapons or whatever? We did find traces of fentanyl in your trunk, but they seem to have come from the blanket. Our super extra care shows they weren't in your clothes, your carry-on bag, or in the interior."

Prosecution could take those traces of fentanyl and turn them into a drug habit, or worse, a drug dealership, so I didn't thank him. Instead I asked about the Omicron boys. "Any luck tracing drug sales to them?"

"The Omicron house is under the campus force's jurisdiction. Our patrol cars are doing sweeps of the bars, looking for action, but we can't search campus housing."

He got up. "Be very careful here, Warshawski. This isn't Chicago, where you have good friends on the force. A wrong step here, and you could be looking at some serious charges. Chicago's a big city and anonymity is easier than in a small place like Lawrence. You'll be surprised by how easy it is for us to find out if you're being—let's say, unorthodox."

I smiled at him. "I'm living above Gertrude Perec's garage. She and your mother are BFF's. Zoë Cruickshank is dogging my steps. So, no, I won't be surprised if you know what I'm doing before I've figured it out myself."

I reported the conversation in person to Faye Mitchell, the Kansas City lawyer Freeman had found for me. The Kansas men were playing basketball Sunday evening. Mitchell had a ticket. I learned that meant she had serious connections—it would be easier to see Taylor Swift live, she told me. She talked to me at the Perecs on her way to meeting friends for lunch.

Mitchell was in her forties, with auburn hair pulled up from her face by a couple of combs. She was dressed like everyone else on game day—in a Jayhawk sweatshirt—but she sported an impressive pair of high-heeled cowboy boots.

She made a face when she learned I'd already spoken to the police, or at least to a police officer, since getting back into town. "I know it won't be possible for me to be here with you every time you talk to the local LEOs, but keep it brief, and record everything. Deke Everard's a good cop, straight shooter, but the local DA is pushing on the LKPD to find enough evidence for an arrest, and you have that FBI agent hovering on the sidelines like a bad fairy at a christening."

I told her about Sabrina's monsters, and Valerie Granev's troubling behavior. "She said that she hadn't wanted to bring Stamoran into the search for Sabrina, that it was a decision of senior management."

Mitchell's carefully shaped eyebrows shot up. "Senior management at Tulloh Industries? Does that mean one of the family?"

"It's family owned?" I asked.

I should have looked them up when Valerie told me she worked for them. Another sign of slippage. Get your head in the game, Warshawski!

"Oh, yes," Mitchell said drily. "It's very much family owned, and the family in turn owns a big chunk of the state legislators in Kansas. If Matthew or his son Robert wanted the FBI involved, they'd have called the Bureau chief, who would have given them instant support."

"Valerie told me to lay off at the same time her husband got funding for a pet project of his," I said. "The gift for his outdoor wilderness center was anonymous, but I suppose the Tullohs could have been behind it. A bribe to persuade Valerie to ask me to lay off."

"Could be," Mitchell said. "It doesn't explain why the fed is trying to implicate you in a nonkidnapping, but it's a good point to follow." She looked at an outsize Breitling watch on her right wrist. "I have to run. See you here at nine tomorrow ahead of the depo. Rock Chalk!"

"Rock Chalk?" I was bewildered.

"That's how Kansas supporters ID ourselves. You've got to learn to think like a local if you want to beat them at their own game."

22

ROCK CHALK

WHEN SHE LEFT, I looked up the Tulloh family. Matthew Tulloh was close to eighty. He'd started his business life with three grain elevators his wife had inherited, and parlayed them into an international business with tentacles in a lot of different industries. Their headquarters were in a town called Salina in central Kansas, where they were close to the natural gas wells that made up a chunk of Tulloh Industries' business. They apparently didn't try to compete with Boeing or the other big plane manufacturers; their aviation division specialized in the kind of electronics and avionics work Valerie Granev did.

Since Tulloh Industries was privately held, it was hard to get an idea of how big they really were, but the business press said Matthew, his two sons, and his daughter each could count their personal wealth in eleven digits. Digits—I'd have to grow an extra finger just to count their money. What a disturbing image.

It was easy to see why the FBI would respond to a command from Tulloh to get involved in Sabrina's disappearance. It was impossible to see why the FBI would try to implicate me in a bogus kidnapping. If Matthew Tulloh was calling that tune, why?

I couldn't do anything about it, certainly not on a Sunday, but there were other tasks I'd overlooked, like the three photos I'd found in Clarina's trailer. They'd been ignored by the cops and the robbers, but they'd been important to Clarina.

I'd promised Lou and Ed I'd bring Peppy out to see them this afternoon. There was time for a stop at the Lawrence library, where I showed the pictures to the reference librarian.

"I'm hoping they can shed some light on who Clarina really was, where she came from, and maybe even on why she was killed."

The librarian's face clouded. "That was a terrible thing, her murder. She came in here a few times, but I sent her to the Origins Library in Topeka—Kansas Origins Museum and Library. They have a significant archive of papers and artifacts from the state's first fifty years, much bigger than our collection. These photos date to that time frame."

She wrote the museum's address and website on a scrap of paper. "Are you the woman who found Clarina? That must have been a terrible shock. You're a detective, aren't you? I hope you can find her killer."

It was pleasant to have a local greet me with a vote of confidence instead of a snarl. I thanked her and drove on out to the country with the dog. The afternoon was cold but sunny. Peppy had a glorious time chasing rabbits through Lou and Ed's fields, then persuading the men that I kept her on starvation rations.

When we got back into town, the crowds were growing for pre-game parties. Traffic was backed up, horns blaring. The fresh air on the hilltop farm had made me hungry. I climbed the stairs, picturing a bowl of pasta with the cheese I'd picked up at the local co-op grocer, but I knew as soon as I unlocked the door that something was wrong. It was the smell, hard to identify, but not there earlier. A faint whiff, a sweet tobacco, maybe, or even aftershave.

I turned on my cell flashlight and held it away from my body. Nothing moved. I stuck my left arm out and fumbled around until I found the light switch. No one was in the main room. I left the door open, stuck my phone in my hip pocket, moved around the space. No one behind the half-wall that separated the kitchen from the big room. Nothing in the bathroom. Nothing in the alcove for the bed.

Peppy pattered anxiously behind me.

I shut the outside door and locked it before inspecting the room in detail. Little things. The suitcase that I'd slid under the bed was visible, instead of tucked completely away. I opened it, felt in the lining. Nothing there. My computer wasn't where I'd left it. I opened it, inspected it to see if someone had put a physical tracer on it, ran my malware software. It seemed okay.

I flicked through the blind slats, wondering if the intruder had planted a bug. They're almost impossible to spot these days without special equipment, but I still tried to search. Strangers in your room, handling your things, it leaves you feeling vulnerable and even dirty.

The skin along the base of my skull prickled, but I finally put on water to boil for pasta. When I took the box from the shelf, though, I felt a revulsion—I couldn't eat food intruders might have touched. I threw out all the food I'd bought yesterday and tied up the garbage bag.

I pulled the bin out from under the sink to stuff in the bag. It was heavy. Much too heavy for cheap plastic. It took me a minute, but I finally realized it had a false bottom. I pried it open with a knife blade. Underneath was a piece of industrial plastic, wrapped a few times around something I couldn't make out through the layers.

I put on my cotton running gloves and lifted it out, gingerly, in case it was a something that exploded, but it felt like a piece of heavy tubing.

I found a paring knife in one of the drawers and slit open the wrapping. A pipe wrench about fifteen inches long. Made of a heavy steel but rusted at the business end. Not rust, steel like this doesn't rust. Blood. My gorge rose, blood in my room, on my hands.

"Stop!" I shouted.

The dog looked up at me, startled. I put a hand on her neck, felt her warmth through the glove. "Sorry, girl, sorry. Someone is messing with us, trying to mess with us, but they can't, they won't."

This was the weapon that had killed Clarina Coffin, or someone wanted the police to think it was. They'd planted it, they would call the cops and get them to find it. If I reported finding it they wouldn't believe it had been planted; with the blanket it would be enough to put me in a cell.

"And then what would happen to you, my beautiful one?" I murmured to Peppy, but I was already rewrapping the tool as I spoke.

I noticed the letter K embossed inside a raised circle at the holding end. It looked like the symbol you see on kosher food. This wrench is kosher for murder. The thought raised a bubble of hysterical laughter.

The dog was clinging to my legs, my fears oozing through my skin, worrying her. "It's okay, girl, we're okay," I tried to soothe myself as well as her.

I must not linger in the apartment, but I scrubbed out the bin under the bathroom shower and left it upside down to dry. I put the wrench inside a plastic garbage bag, then swept all the food I'd bought into a second one. I couldn't bear to eat anything the intruders would have touched.

The bathroom window opened on the Perecs' backyard. I leaned out and lowered the bags onto the bushes. I hated to leave Peppy alone in the apartment, especially since I'd caused her so much worry, but I didn't want her with me on this errand. I couldn't keep an eye on a dog and on traffic or possible tails.

I ran down the stairs and rang the Perecs' bell. Cady came to the door. "Vic! Do you need something?"

"Someone broke into the garage apartment while I was out today."

"Vic—no—that's terrible! Gram!" She shouted over her shoulder.

Gertrude appeared, the frown lines around her nose and mouth deeply grooved. "We're at dinner, Ms. Warshawski. If you have something you must discuss, come back tomorrow."

"Gram! Someone broke into the apartment today. We need to call the police. What did they take? Did they break down the door?"

"They either had a key or some good lock-picking equipment: I didn't see signs of forced entry. They didn't take anything, but they went through my things, my clothes, the food I'd bought. I'm wondering if you let someone in?"

"Why would I do that?" Gertrude bristled. "I'm not interested in anything you might own."

I smiled at her, my death-dealing smile. "Someone could have told you they were with the gas company, or inspecting for roaches or rats."

"I did not let anyone into the apartment. Now, if you'll excuse me, I'll return to my meal." Ramrod back, military-style U-turn, and she disappeared into the reaches of the house.

"I'm so sorry, Vic," Cady said. "But it's frightening. We've never had to worry about break-ins or vandals or anything. I'll call a lock-smith and get a new lock in the morning. If—I know Gram sounds fierce, but if you're afraid to spend the night alone up there, we do have a spare bedroom you could stay in until we get the locks replaced."

"I'd be more afraid of your grandmother putting an ax in my head if I was in the same house."

She smiled, but said she still thought I should call the police.

"They didn't take anything," I said. "Cops are too overworked to fingerprint an apartment because the resident says her stuff was moved around. For now, I'd like to leave through your garden."

Cady took me to the back door. "It's dark in the garden, though. Are you sure you want to leave this way?"

"I want to double back," I said, "see if anyone is watching your house."

The explanation alarmed her, but she shut the door. She'd parted the curtains covering the glass upper panel, peering at me in worry. I smiled, waved, crossed out of her sight line, and crept back to retrieve my garbage bags. When I had them, I went south, to a park a few blocks from the house. I didn't think anyone had followed me.

The park was a few blocks from the main downtown street where the pregame celebrations were growing in enough intensity to reach me here. Tip-off must be soon.

I didn't think anyone was watching me. I left the garbage bag with the food on a bench, but took the wrench with me. Tricky part. Disaster if someone stopped me now and found it on me, but I walked through the park to Sixth Street, one of the town's busiest arteries. Cars were parading up and down, horns blaring. A cop was furiously blowing a whistle at the intersection with the main north-south street, where most of the happy fans were ignoring the lights. I skulked along on the edge of the park, finally found a break in the flow, and slipped across.

On the north side of the street, the park led straight down to the river. This was the route Cady claimed to have taken to walk off her insomnia the night Clarina Coffin was murdered. A few streetlamps made it possible to keep the path in view. A few runners were out, a couple of cyclists, and, despite the weather, some heavily loving couples. Maybe Cady really had been here. Maybe someone else who couldn't sleep at 3:00 A.M. would remember seeing her.

Near the end of the path, I found the old boat trailer Peppy and I had spotted this morning. Fluid motion, no looking over the shoulder. I walked up to the trailer, thrust the bag well underneath it, walked farther up the path to another garbage can where I lost the gloves: if blood had leaked through the plastic wrapping, the gloves would give me away. I strolled back up the path and merged with the mob on Massachusetts.

23

HANDS-ON CARE

———————

BACK AT THE garage, I crept cautiously to the staircase but didn't see anyone watching, didn't find anyone on the steps. Peppy was lying just inside the door, trembling and whimpering.

I took her outside with me and sat on the top step, petting her, crooning Italian lullabies to her, until we were both calm again. We walked east, past the student bars, where people had crammed in to watch the game, and found a place with outdoor seating and heat lamps. I lingered there with the dog, sipping wine and feeding us both bits of risotto.

When we returned to the Perec place a few hours later, Deke Everard stepped out of an unmarked car across the street. Men were hanging around on street corners, hoping to talk to me. At least, one man was, even if he was a cop. Maybe I'd text that to Peter, see if it would rouse a current of jealousy that would make him call me.

"Wondered when you'd get back, Warshawski."

"Sergeant, that's so touching. What are there, a hundred thousand people in this town? And you keep track of us one by one to make sure we're safe? Chicago cops would never be so caring."

The streetlamps gave enough light that I could see him make a swatting gesture. "Aunt Ger—Ms. Perec—told me you'd gone out a couple of hours ago. She said you claimed someone had broken into the apartment over her garage."

"I claimed it because it happened."

"Where did you go when you left here?"

"Whoa, Sergeant. It's one thing to care about a single visitor to the town, especially on game night when you have thousands of visitors. It's quite another to conduct an interrogation, especially in the dark with no witnesses."

"I have a witness. We can talk upstairs in the lamplight."

He called into his lapel mike. A woman emerged from the car and crossed over to us.

"There's nothing to talk about," I said. "If you want to question me, I'll come to the station with you, after I've let my lawyer know we're having a formal conversation."

He pulled a piece of paper from a vest pocket. "I have a warrant to search the apartment. I showed it to Ms. Perec, but I wanted to wait until you got back to execute it."

So someone had been keeping an eye on the place, and had called the cops when I got back. I didn't like this, not one little bit.

"You got a warrant because I told my landlady I thought someone had broken into the apartment?" I said. "How can you search for missing items if you don't know what was there to begin with?"

"We're not—" he began, then cut himself short. "Take us up to the apartment, Warshawski. Hawks are up by three. I want to get done here in time to watch the finish."

I led them in silence up the stairs built onto the side of the garage. I unlocked the door and laid my arm out flat along the wall to fumble with the room switch. I looked around but didn't think anything had been disturbed since I'd left.

When we were all inside the room, I recognized the junior cop as the young woman who'd been smart enough to call Uber when we'd found Sabrina. Officer Rockwell, her name badge told me.

"Place doesn't look like it was tossed," Everard said.

"It wasn't. Little things were out of place."

In my own apartment in Chicago, where I live in chronic disarray, I might not have been able to tell. It was only here, where I'd barely settled in, that the room was tidy enough to see that a suitcase had been moved.

With Everard right behind me, I walked around the dividing wall to the bed alcove and pulled my suitcase out, slowly. Before leaving with my bags, I'd tucked two hairs into the frame, one of Peppy's next to the lock, one of mine by the back hinge. Both were still in place.

The cops put on the requisite blue gloves and began searching. It didn't take long in the small space. Officer Rockwell found the garbage bin upside-down in the tub.

"What was that about?" Everard demanded.

"Bad smell," I said.

I sniffed the bin, gingerly. A reassuring scent of bleach. It was still wet inside so I put it back top-down in the bathtub.

When they'd inspected everything, including the inside of my suitcase, and the clothes I'd hung in the freestanding wardrobe, Everard frowned, looking around.

"What were you looking for, Sergeant?" I asked. "And who told you to come hunting whatever it is?"

"Those are two good questions. I can't answer them."

"Can't or won't?" I said.

He shook his head.

"Okay, I don't know what you were looking for, but I'm betting the helpful informant was the same upright citizen who told you that Trig Garrity and Gertrude Perec were at the Dundee house the night someone hid Clarina Coffin's body there."

He gave a reluctant nod. "I'm betting the same thing. I don't really believe you came down to Kansas on a murder-kidnap spree, but when the information is so specific, I have to follow up on it. Where were you between when you went out through the Perec garden and when you got back?"

"Murder-kidnap spree?" I said. "What—is Coffin's death connected to Sabrina's situation?"

"They were both found in the same space. I thought you were a detective—doesn't that suggest a connection to you?"

"Of course. But is there any evidence that Sabrina and Coffin knew each other?" I thought of my earlier conversation with Faye Mitchell. "When Sabrina was healthy, she traveled the world playing matches. Could she and Clarina Coffin have met some-where? Maybe Coffin in her real identity was a scout for women's pro teams."

Officer Rockwell gave a snort of laughter, which quickly turned into coughing. I smiled at her. "You're right—unbelievable along ev-ery vector, including the idea that women's soccer pays well enough to hire undercover scouts."

"All very funny," Deke said drily. "Now that you've sidestepped the question long enough to come up with a good lie, where were you between six-thirty or so, when you disappeared into the Perec garden, and when I met you out front."

"I was hungry. I needed to eat. I found a place downtown that was mercifully free of basketball fans." I gave Everard the name.

I'd also doubled back to the park for the bag of food I'd aban-doned. Lawrence had a food pantry close to the park; I'd walked over to it and left my contribution outside the door. That information I kept to myself: it detracts from a good deed to brag about it to the police.

I turned to Officer Rockwell. "We met the night I found Sabrina out at the Dundee house. Did you get a statement on record from the Uber driver who took her out there?"

Rockwell looked at Everard, who nodded; she could answer. They didn't have a formal statement, she said, but Rockwell had re-corded the call.

"I want the Uber driver formally on the record before the federal guy who's creeping after me like Captain Hook's alligator, or even your own DA, persuades them to change their story."

"But Uber has a record of the ride," Rockwell said.

"File scrubbing is a wonderful hobby these days. I would love to know that testimony is safe."

Deke sighed heavily, but gestured at Officer Rockwell. "Find the driver, take a formal statement. Tomorrow."

"Yes, boss."

"Thank you," I said, voice dry. "Another thing I'd like to know is who is pulling all these strings that make the LKPD dance to my side on a night when every officer has to be on duty downtown. Maybe as an outsider I'm a convenient fall gal, but if it were my investigation, I'd be searching for a puppet master."

Deke's eyes narrowed. He was a good enough cop to resent being told his job, but he was also a good enough cop to know I was right.

The silence built, until he finally said, "Warshawski, if you've been lying to me, the consequences will be serious."

I looked at him steadily. "Sergeant, I have not told you a single lie tonight. Officer Rockwell has her recording. You can consult it if your anonymous caller gives you any more tips about me."

I had withheld information, I had implied false information, but that is not the same as lying.

He seemed ready to leave, when he said casually—the kicker that cops like—"What was in the garbage bag you took out of Gertrude's bushes?"

I blinked but didn't blurt out, *what garbage bag, what bush.* Gertrude must have watched me from the kitchen window.

"I threw out all the food I'd bought yesterday. I didn't want to eat anything the intruders might have touched."

Loud roars rose in the distance. The game must be over. Deke glanced at his phone, but said, "And where is that food?"

"Outside one of your food pantries." I looked at my phone and gave him the address.

He frowned some more, weighing my story. It was too easy to check, though, unless someone had already been to the pantry and taken the bag.

"Okay, Rockwell, you and me are on our way to our favorite part of policing, breaking up bar fights. The Hawks won by nine, the town is exploding, like it's the first time it happened."

When they left, I did what everyone does these days instead of resting or looking for something to read. I checked my messages. Still nothing from Peter in Spain. A bitter ache in my chest, maybe near the heart.

I would not, could not, sink into fulmination or self-pity. I would think, and act. Someone had been keeping an eye on my comings and had called the cops when they saw I was home. A window in the apartment overlooked Ohio Street. I lifted an edge of one of the blind slats. Rockwell was just taking off, her roof lights spinning, but Deke was sitting in his car.

The neighbors immediately across from Gertrude had a few small bushes around the edges of their lawn, but you couldn't conceal yourself behind any of them. A bit farther south, though, a house had a wrought iron fence lining the sidewalk, with a thick evergreen hedge between the fence and the house. Perfect cover. As I watched, a glint of light appeared. A cell phone screen turning on. Someone else was keeping track of Deke in his unmarked car, or was it of me at my window?

I turned out the lights in the big room, left on a table lamp in the alcove by the bed, and slipped out the door. I went down the stairs on my butt so that my shape wasn't silhouetted by the streetlamps. Pressing myself against the side of the house, I walked away from the street until I reached the neighbor's yard, where a large bush shielded me. I crossed the street and made a wide loop to come on the neighbor's house from the side.

The cell phone light was still on. I moved slowly, looking for an opening in the bushes that would get me close to the peeper. A floodlight came on and a loud voice demanded to know what the hell we were doing in his front yard.

"You have ten seconds to leave before I shoot," he thundered.

The peeper sprinted along the edge of the shrubbery. I followed, almost up with him, when I tripped on a root and fell hard on my chest. Got up in time to see him head down Seventh Street. I followed. And ran into a crowd of celebrating Jayhawk fans.

My guy bulldozed through the crowd. I had my elbows out, following. Cut through the mob and saw him disappear around the side of the Lion's Heart.

The Jayhawk fans had filled the street, dancing, shouting, spraying unwary passersby with beer. I pushed my way through the crowd to the sidewalk and moved cautiously around the building. The Lion's Heart back door opened onto a municipal parking lot, as full of people as the streets. It would be impossible to figure out where my peeper had disappeared.

Cars were cruising New Hampshire Street, honking in celebration. A Carrera was in the mix, with a couple of guys leaning out the windows yelling, "Rock Chalk!" High on life? Or on China Girl or whatever the Jayhawk street name was for fentanyl.

I stood with my hands on my thighs, catching my breath while the cold air froze the sweat around my neck. Tomorrow I would definitely start running again.

I straightened up. And came face-to-face with Deke Everard.

24

PERIODIC TABLE OF THE BODY

WHY DIDN'T YOU phone or text me when you realized someone was watching your place?" Everard demanded.

We'd walked to the Perec house, a short seven blocks. I was shivering, rubbing my arms, slapping my chest. I'd come out wearing a hoodie, no coat, so I could move faster, but cold air and fatigue had depleted me.

"I don't know if someone from the Bureau or the DA's office is spying on me, but someone is feeding you information about everything I'm doing, almost before I do it. Punk lurking in the bushes, maybe videoing me—could have been a setup by you to see what I'd do when your back was turned. And that is what you did, right? You parked around the corner and saw the whole story unfold."

He stared at me, his face angry under the lamplight, but he didn't speak.

"The peeper disappeared around the corner from the Lion's Heart, into the crowd in that parking lot. My Omicron Delta Beta pals in the Carrera were joining in."

"Were you stupid enough to confront them?" Deke demanded.

"Neither stupid enough nor strong enough."

"Then stay the hell away from them. We have a drugs unit. They are conducting an undercover investigation into who's supplying the downtown bars. If you screw that up, I will be the person cuffing you and I will be happy doing it."

"You told me you couldn't do anything about the frat boys be-cause they come under campus jurisdiction," I objected. "Now you conveniently have an undercover operation you can warn me away from?"

"It's on the QT. The DA brought in a team from Kansas City, in the hopes no one will recognize them. Chief told me this morning so I could keep you from derailing our work."

"Good to know, Sergeant. Outsiders can frame me, but I can't step on their delicate little toes. If Millay's driving around town, one thing is sure: oxy and meth and whatever will be flowing like lava from Mauna Loa. I best not keep you from keeping the peace."

He stared at me, hands on hips, a long menacing cop stare. "All right. Go up, go to bed. Stay there."

He waited until I'd started up the stairs to the apartment before turning around the corner to his car.

My head felt like a balloon, its string barely keeping it attached to my neck. My legs were lead. My body was like a periodic table, helium head, lead legs. The balloon bounced dizzyingly each time I dragged my leg up a step.

I had the key out, ready to work the lock, when someone grabbed my arm. My head crash-landed on my shoulders. Instinct, whirl, twist the arm around close to my body, dislocate the shoulder.

"Vic, don't!" she shrieked. "It's me, Zoë!"

I released her, fortunately before I'd hurt her.

"Why'd you do that?" she was aggrieved, rubbing her shoulder.

"You jumped me. When I'm investigating a murder I don't stop to ask for a business card." I unlocked the outer door, turned on the light and paused on the threshold to scan the room. It seemed free of intruders, except for Zoë, who followed me in.

Peppy greeted me with whimpers of joy, weaving around my legs. I knelt to fondle her.

Zoë gasped when she saw my face under the apartment lights. "What happened? Did someone attack you? Is that why you're so fierce right now?"

I moved to the bathroom and stared at myself in the mirror. I had mud on my face from where I'd tripped going after the peeper. I had a scratch on my right cheek, and a tear in the forearm of my hoodie.

I bathed my face, with Zoë standing in the doorway behind Peppy. I went to the kitchenette and filled the dishpan with hot water, set it by one of the straight-backed chairs, and took off my shoes so I could soak my sore, swollen feet.

"Who attacked you?" Zoë demanded.

"No one. I tripped and fell chasing a Peeping Tom. What are you doing here? You're not spending the night, you know, or even more than the next ten minutes."

"I saw on my scanner that cops were at the Perec place. I was covering a shooting in Eudora, and by the time I got back to Lawrence the cops were gone. Ms. Perec treated me like something she'd stepped in. Cady wasn't home. What was going on? I saw Deke was with you. Have you found Clarina's killer?"

"Not even close," I said.

Zoë had her phone out. When I realized she was taking pictures of my battle scars, I snatched the phone and deleted the shots. She protested hotly, but I stuck her phone into my back pocket.

"I can't be a sideshow for your paper, not at this point in the investigation. Someone is following me, someone is trying to frame Trig, or Gertrude, or me, or all of us. I need them to keep guessing on how much I know, and how much damage I've absorbed."

"I need my phone to record your comments. I promise not to take any more pictures."

"Zoë, please don't run a story about today's events. Take all the notes you want, but putting too much information out could help keep the bad guys ten steps ahead of me. Right now, it's only five or six."

She bunched up her mouth, thinking it over, but finally gave a reluctant nod. "If you give me back my phone so I can record what you say, I promise I won't use it until you've found the killer. Or for a week, whichever comes first."

"Fair enough. If I'm still floundering after a week, I'll probably risk the Douglas County DA's wrath and go home."

"Is that why Deke was here? Because someone was following you?"

"Deke was here because someone told him I had something on the premises that the cops would like to see."

The sparkle returned to Zoë's eyes. "Don't tell me I can't print this! What was it?"

"I don't know. If Deke does, he didn't share the news."

"You're hiding something. I know you are," Zoë protested.

"I'm trying to hide my eyes behind their lids, and you're in the way." I put a hand on her shoulder and marched her to the door. I just remembered to lock it before falling into bed.

25

THE LONG VIEW

I **SLEPT, BUT RESTLESSLY,** my dreams filled with chaotic images, mostly of Trevor the frat boy breaking into the apartment and brandishing a wrench over my head. I ran from him and ended up in the playground of my old grammar school. Peter was there, roaring with laughter. "I'm not fat-shaming you, Warshawski, I'm crime-shaming you. Get it?"

I woke at five, my sleep shirt wet with sweat. I took a hot shower and lay back down, hoping for more sleep, but the dream had unearthed old memories. Neighborhood kids used to circle me chanting "Christ Killer" because of my Jewish mother. They thought it hysterically funny that I would fight even when they outnumbered me five to one or so. My parents tried to stop me, my mother because my torn clothes and bruises distressed her, my father because I was distressing my mother.

"And because fighting is the least helpful solution to any problem, Victoria," he added. "What are you learning from your battles?"

"That I need to get stronger," I'd replied.

"No, *carissima*, you need to get smarter," my mother said.

Days like today, I didn't think I'd accomplished either.

I sat up and looked at my social media. Trevor the frat boy had reported my return to Lawrence. *Cops are all over Warshawski. We're waiting for the arrest report.* A dozen or so responses—"hotshots from Chicago get what's coming to them" was the most repeatable.

I wrote to Peter, a stone thrown into an empty well, trying to explain what was going on. The FBI's Stamoran or even the LKPD could be reading my mail, so I had to phrase everything carefully. *What's going on in Spain?* I concluded.

What was I going to do about the wrench? The longer it stayed by the boatshed, the more likely the evidence would deteriorate. Animals could crawl into the bag, attracted by blood—if there was blood on it. Maybe someone had been messing with me. Why would they have hung on to the murder weapon, anyway?

I decided the best way to get it to the cops was to have it turn up near the Dundee house. But what if it wasn't the murder weapon? Someone could have planted a wrench with animal blood on it to distract me, and the cops, from what was really going on. Maybe it was my short night and a feverish brain, but before I risked life and limb putting it on the Dundee place, I would find out if it had been used in an assault on a person. On Clarina, for instance.

I leashed up Peppy and took her to the park near the library. She nosed around in the bushes while I did a full complement of stretches and squats. The advantage of bad sleep—it wasn't quite seven-thirty when I finished.

We walked to the side street where I'd left the Camry. I put Peppy inside and went for a slow run along the streets, checking every few blocks for pursuers on foot or car, or even bicycle. When I was pretty sure I was clean, I went into the post office. Bought an express mailer.

Now came the trickiest part. Resumed my run, headed down to the river path and the boathouse where I'd parked the trash bag last night. The bag seemed intact. I slid it between the folded leaves of the box in my pack. Walked back to the post office and addressed it to my account manager at Cheviot, the private forensics lab I use. The post office wouldn't mail it without a name and return address, so I chose a bland name, Susan Hall, and used the street address for the Lawrence police. If it was returned, they'd have it.

Eight-fifteen now. I left my phone at the Perec apartment, where its signal wouldn't betray my movements. Changed into business clothes so I'd be ready to meet with Faye and the DA. Drove to the Buy-Smart on the west end of town for a couple of burner phones, paying cash.

If Cheviot reported blood on the wrench, I wanted to leave it at the Dundee house so the police would know it was connected to Coffin's death. But I had to believe there were cameras somewhere around the house—otherwise, how had they photographed Gertrude and Trig the night before I found Clarina? Someone had devices that operated remotely so they could be turned off when the party animals wanted privacy. I needed to locate those.

Assuming that the DA would keep me only a few hours, I could go out there this afternoon. Unless I was in jail, of course.

I used one of the burners to call Lou and Ed, to see if they could babysit Peppy.

"The DA wants to depose me this morning. I can't leave her cooped up in the car all morning, especially if he decides to arrest me. Cady might look after her if I left her in the apartment, but I'd feel more comfortable if I knew she was with friends."

"Tricky, Warshawski, can't have her in the yard, too much sharp metal. But we'll figure something out. You have time to drive out with her now?"

"I'm meeting my lawyer at the Hippo, supposedly at nine but I'll let her know I'm going to be late."

When we'd driven the ten miles to the hilltop farm, the men were in their work coveralls, getting ready to head to the yard. Peppy was ecstatic, jumping on them and racing in circles across the open land.

"She definitely needs to be in the country," Ed said, bending to fondle her ears. "What were you thinking, trying to coop her up in a bitty garage apartment, or worse yet, this old Camry?"

"You're right," I said. "You have a 747 I can borrow?"

The day was cold, with a biting wind sweeping across the hilltop, but the air was clear. I could see the silhouette of the tallest campus buildings on their own hilltop, but they were so remote they looked like a mirage, a mythical castle. Closer in, the river wound its way north of the town and made a loop before winding west. I watched toy trucks and cars move along the thin line of the interstate. A power plant belched a few puffs of gray-white smoke.

"The city uses coal power?" I asked.

"Yep," Ed said, but when he saw what I was looking at, he added, "Not that plant. That one—it was for Wakarusa. Hardly any-one lives out there anymore, and the ones that do buy their power from Lawrence. Thought that old dinosaur was going into mothballs. Owners had a different thought."

He and Lou exchanged glances, tight, annoyed.

"So what do you need to do that you can't risk the princess here?" Lou asked.

I shook my head. "I can't tell you, not without making you accessories, which would be a mean-spirited way of thanking you for your support."

"How about that?" Lou said. "She knows we like to accessorize. Most people see us in our work clothes and imagine that's how we always dress. She pictures us in earrings and what-do, but she thinks we'll tell all to Five-O."

I squatted next to Peppy. "Why are two Black men willing to risk prison or worse for lying under oath? They must know I'm in mud up to my eyeballs. Why do they want to join me there?"

Ed tried to squat on Peppy's other side, but his knees gave out and he landed on his butt. He clicked his fingers, and she turned to look at him. "Tell Ms. Know-It-All that we figured out a long time ago that we're Black men who run a junkyard, and therefore barely have the brains to tie our shoes."

Peppy licked his face, then turned and licked mine. I guess that made Ed and me spit siblings.

I told them about the pipe wrench, and Deke showing up uncomfortably quickly. "If the game hadn't drawn those big downtown crowds, he could have caught me red-handed."

"Someone doesn't like you," Ed said.

"Someone sees me as expendable. I don't think it's personal. I've sent the wrench to a lab I use outside Chicago, but if their analysis shows that it does have blood on it, I want to get the wrench onto the Dundee place.

"I need to scout the landscape first. From the time I found Sabrina Granev out on Yancy, I've been puzzled by how the cops got there so fast. They said a neighbor called in a disturbance to 911. And then, there's the photo of Gertrude Perec and Trig Garrity meeting on the Dundee kitchen doorstep—thanks, again, to a supposedly nosy neighbor. Yet there are no neighbors closer than a quarter mile.

"I don't know why it didn't occur to me earlier, but there must be cameras set up along the perimeter. I'm not dropping anything anywhere until I find out about the surveillance."

"You need help shinnying up a tree to look for them?" Lou asked.

"I figure I can park in the field I used before and come at the house from the back, but in case I run into trouble, I don't want Peppy with me."

Lou looked at me in disgust. "You are a moron, and that's a polite term for it. We'll keep the dog and you'll sashay around the property and then climb back in the car—which *we* are responsible for—and collect your dog?"

"She's crude, insensitive, but not a moron," Ed said. "That's harsh. She trusts us to babysit the princess, who is way more important than her, so it doesn't hurt that she won't ask us to drop her off and pick her up."

My face turned hot, but after arguing the point I was glad to concede. I would call them when I finished with Frank Karas, and they would collect me downtown.

26

LAW AND JUSTICE

THE DEPOSITION HAD its entertaining moments, especially because my attorney had been in law school with Frank Karas, the DA.

"Small communities," she said when we met over coffee. "We all rub up against each other. Frank has big ambitions, governor of Kansas, maybe, White House, maybe. Getting a Chicago felon behind bars would look good on his campaign literature. You have a reputation for mouthing off. Don't get cocky and we'll be okay."

"Right." I grimaced. "I always told my PD clients the two most dangerous emotions are anger and arrogance. Maybe you can mutter 'AA' if I'm getting off track."

"You'll be fine." She clapped me on the shoulder. "You know what you're doing."

We walked over to the Judicial and Law Enforcement Center. Inside the building, I put on a mask. None of the guards were wearing them and only a handful of the people putting their belongings on the security conveyor belts had them on. Mitchell nodded approvingly, putting one on herself.

She knew two of the guards by name and joked with them while we waited our turn to go through the body scanner. "You trying to disguise yourself, Faye, with that mask?" one of them joked. "People'll see those boots and know you in a second."

Like me, she'd dressed professionally for the meeting, but she was

still wearing yesterday's high-heeled cowboy boots, black suede fes-
tooned with giant silver stars and crescent moons.

I let Faye handle all of the logistics, checking in with a clerk, what
room we were in, how to find it. We were outside the door at 9:59,
but Karas kept us waiting until almost eleven, to make sure I knew he
was in charge of my life.

When he finally strode down the corridor, frowning, flanked by
a clerk and the FBI's Cornell Stamoran, the sight of Faye and me in
our masks drew him up short.

"Hey, Faye, no mask mandate in Douglas County, unless the libs
in Topeka put one in place overnight."

"No worries, Frankie," she said. "My client. She's got medical
sensitivities and can't be in a small room unless everyone is masked."

"It's Frank, and you don't set the rules in this courthouse," Karas
said.

"I know I don't, Frankie. Frank, I mean. And I don't want to inconvenience you at all. We can do this by Zoom. Just let us get back
to an open space—"

"Remote is not a good option," Karas said.

"Of course not, Frankie. Frank, sorry! But if that's the quickest
way to get this over, let's do it."

Stamoran tried to insert himself into the argument, but Karas
was smart enough to know he wasn't going to win this fight. The
clerk on his team went downstairs to find masks. While she was gone,
Faye commented chirpily on the weather. Karas ignored her, scrolling
through his phone.

When we finally settled around the table, the mood at the prosecution end was not cordial. We went through the usual preliminaries,
me spelling my full name—including "Iphigenia"—and various other
demographics.

Over our morning coffee, Faye and I had worked out the best
way to answer the predictable questions, about why I was in Kansas,
and how I'd come to be involved in Sabrina Granev's disappearance.
Keep it short, no long explanations about Angela's basketball career
or Bernie's pleading.

Karas probed into my career, into occasions where I might have been considered reckless. Why had I insisted on confronting Earl Smeissen or George Dornick or Robert Baladine?

"I acted in a way to protect the lives of the people around me, as well as my own." We went through about a dozen of my cases, including one where Mr. Contreras had taken a bullet. I curbed my impatience. They wanted to goad me into a misstep, and I could not misstep.

We finally got to the events of February 14–15 of this year.

Karas's main focus was on how I discovered the Dundee house, and how I'd persuaded Sabrina to go there.

"I don't understand the question, Mr. Karas," I said.

"It's simple: How did you persuade Sabrina Granev to accompany you to the Dundee house?"

"I still don't understand."

We went back and forth, until he finally broke it down into when did I talk to Sabrina?

When I found her in the Dundee house at midnight Monday night.

When had I talked to her previously?

I had said hello to her at dinner Sunday night.

What else?

Only hello.

Did you talk her into going to the Dundee house?

No.

Did you drive her or hire someone to drive her to the Dundee house?

No.

He wanted to ask about my drug use, and we went through a similar rigmarole where he finally had to break the query down into small pieces.

"Trevor Millay says he saw you ingest drugs at the Omicron Delta Beta garage."

He is mistaken.

We went through that three or four times, until Faye interrupted. "My client passed a drug test. Her car has been inspected, her home in Chicago has been inspected—"

I thought of the chaos I'd come home to last week, but I kept a tight clamp on my anger.

"No drugs have been found in her possession. Get over it, Frankie, I mean, Frank."

We were about an hour into the interrogation when a white man came into the conference room. He was wearing the kind of suit Armani cuts for you on Via Monte Napoleone out of a fabric that is never seen in retail stores. The Armani man looked vaguely familiar, but I couldn't place him. I looked at Faye, but she shook her head slightly.

Stamoran scribbled something on his yellow pad and Karas nodded. When we got to the end of questions on the Dundee house—how had I known where it was, how had I known Sabrina was there, hadn't I really been searching for drugs?—the stranger shook his head, not happy with the proceedings. He beckoned to Agent Stamoran, and the two of them left the conference room.

Frank announced a short break and followed the others out to the hall. His clerk stayed behind to make sure we didn't read any of the prosecution papers.

Faye cocked an eyebrow at me. We went into the hall, where the DA was huddled with the Armani man and Agent Stamoran. They stopped speaking when they saw us. Armani man clapped Frank on the shoulder, said he'd call him later, and headed for the elevators.

Faye muttered at me to stay put and went over to speak to Karas. I began a series of wall push-ups, my back to the trio. I heard her murmuring with Stamoran and Karas, but I focused on my workout. I'd reached thirty-seven when Faye tapped my shoulder.

"Looks like the wall's in good shape, Warshawski—you haven't even made a dent in it. We're done here, right, Frankie? Sorry, Frank."

I turned around. Stamoran was on his way to the elevator. Karas said he guessed they had all they needed today, but he reserved the right to call me back if more questions arose.

"You do that, Frankie," Faye said. "The truth is a beautiful thing and we're happy to show you enough examples of it to make you realize when you're looking at the stupefying ugliness of your buddies' lies."

27

POWER RANGER

FAYE DIDN'T KNOW who the Armani man was. Since we'd had to leave our phones in a lockbox during the deposition, neither of us had been able to photograph him.

"Frank is not happy; he's going to be looking for you to violate laws and ordinances. Please do not go one mile over the speed limit while you're in Douglas County," she urged me.

"Absolutely," I promised fervently, even though I was already planning my next infraction, trespassing on the land behind the Dundee house.

I phoned the scrapyard. Lou said Ed was tied up, but he would meet me behind the public library in an hour.

I wandered downtown. The streets were still full of the detritus of the night before—beer cans, whisky bottles, Styrofoam. A couple of homeless people were picking through the remains, sucking the last mouthfuls from cans and bottles. Someone had abandoned a full head mask of the ever-present Jayhawk on a bench. It looked tawdry next to the cigarette butts and half-eaten meals.

I started visiting souvenir shops. The third place I came to had a head mask. When Lou and Peppy picked me up, I was sporting a Jayhawk hoodie. I waited until we were on the road south before putting on the headdress.

"You know how stupid that makes you look?" Lou said.

"It also makes me look anonymous. Just one more idiot trying to recover from last night's victory dance."

He dropped me at a crossroads half a mile from the Dundee house. "You find yourself up the proverbial creek, signal us ASAP," Lou said.

I typed "Help" into a text box, ready to send if need be. Lou said he would circle back every half hour or so. To avoid possible cameras, he wouldn't stop at the Dundee place, but would wait five minutes by the nearest crossroads.

I left the road and walked up the hill to a stand of trees that separated a plowed field from the underbrush surrounding the house. I walked in their shadow until I was about two hundred yards behind the house, then headed into the thicker shrubs and trees that I'd encountered ten days ago.

The trees were bare of leaves, which meant I couldn't get too close to the house without being seen if someone was inside. I paused behind a brake of thorny bushes. The back of the house looked sullen, hostile, as if it resented any human approach. I skirted the property, crouching behind the undergrowth. I spotted a camera over the kitchen door, angled to photograph faces at the door. Another was mounted high in a tree at the mouth of the driveway, two more facing the house, attached to trees at the edge of the woods I'd just walked through.

Someone, somewhere, watched activity at the Dundee place on their screens. It wouldn't be Brett Santich. He was out and about in the world, without the leisure to monitor activity at a drug house—assuming he was as involved in the operation as Trig insisted. I liked to think it was the Omicron boys, laughing in their frat house over how clever they were to frame me, or Trig, but I didn't see them doing grunt work—they were in this for kicks. They'd graduate and move on to hedge funds, legally sanctioned larceny.

Santich or whoever was running the Dundee house parties was probably using local muscle. I wondered if that included the man with the gun who'd threatened me on top of Yancy. The construction site up there would be a convenient place to house surveillance monitors. Santich had been in a heated conversation with the gunman. Maybe he'd been using the Dundee place without Santich's knowledge.

I'd seen all I needed. Time to slide away. If Cheviot labs confirmed human blood and/or hair on the wrench, it shouldn't be too hard to place it near the house.

As I started to retrace my steps, a dusty SUV pulled into the drive and a man got out. With my bright red-and-blue Jayhawk head I was easy to spot inside the stand of trees. I dropped to the ground, pulled the headdress off, and tucked it under me. Lay completely still, heart pounding thick in my throat. Had I overlooked a camera? Had someone spotted me on a computer and come to tackle me? The dead leaves tickled my sinuses. Don't sneeze, you mustn't sneeze.

I turned my head slowly, just enough to see what the man was doing. He was turned away from me, watching the drive, so I couldn't see his face, but he was obviously looking at his wrist, checking the time. He pulled a phone from his hip pocket, stared at it, put it away again.

He turned his head in my direction. Brett Santich. I listened as hard as I could, worrying whether the hard hat from the construction site was coming down behind me, but Santich turned back, watching the road.

The ground was cold and I was getting a cramp in my left thigh. No you don't, I warned my body. Everyone behaves well right now, including you, tight muscles.

Perhaps ten minutes passed. Santich took his phone out again, but put it away when a black Range Rover roared up the drive, potholes negligible to a beast designed to cross the Serengeti.

A white man climbed out. I was so astonished I almost cried out: it was the Armani man from this morning's deposition. He'd shed his suit for outdoor clothes, buckskin jacket, jeans, cowboy boots, but they, too, had been cut for him by hand. He strode over to Santich and began a heated exchange.

I inched my phone from my hip pocket up to my face, careful not to lift face or arm. Took pictures that I hoped included the stranger, since I couldn't afford to peer at the viewfinder.

The pair argued for some minutes, then went inside. I didn't risk getting up even then—if they looked out the back windows I'd be too visible. When I was so frozen I thought I'd risk sliding backward into the woods, they came out. Santich took off at once with a great roaring of engine: he'd been chewed out and was taking it out on his machine.

The stranger climbed into his Range Rover, where he sat with the engine running for several more minutes. The tinted windows made it impossible to tell what he was doing.

My phone had been dinging. I cautiously moved my arm down and looked at the screen, keeping my head flat to the ground. Lou, wanting to know where I was. I phoned, since I could keep my head down while I spoke. I explained that I'd been pinned behind the house.

"I thought that was Santich scooting past in his dirty Kia," Lou said. "When the other dude leaves, call me—we'll come for you."

I warned him about the cameras, then lay still for another long while. Finally, the Armani man kicked his Rover in the ribs and galloped down the rocky drive.

I sat up, massaging my thighs until enough blood was flowing that I could get to my feet. I stuffed the Jayhawk head into my jacket pocket and hobbled through the woods on the fringe of the property to the road. Lou was waiting near the mouth of the drive, away from the camera.

I stumbled trying to gain a foothold on the running board. Peppy was in the front seat. She grudgingly moved enough to let me in, but rested her head on Lou's lap.

"You are one fickle dog," I told her. "I'm the one who's been out in the cold and could use a warm puppy."

Lou grunted. "You look a mess, Warshawski. Even so, I prefer the leaves and mud and so on to that fright you had on your head going in."

"It's a Jayhawk," I said. "You're local; you must know they are sacred to the town of Lawrence. Come to think of it, I haven't seen one at your place, either the yard or the house. You and Ed must have to pay some kind of steep fine."

He flashed one of his rare smiles. "It's why we live so far outside of town. What'd you learn, besides where the cameras are?"

"More questions than answers." I described Brett's and the Armani man's interaction. "I'll have to look up the sale of the land to the consortium that's building the resort. Maybe Brett held the house back for sentimental reasons, or because he was making a bundle from his cut of the drug parties."

"You say it looked as though Armani was chewing out Santich," Lou reminded me. "Might have something to do with that pipe wrench. Maybe the Range Rover was the brains behind putting you in the frame, except you slithered out.

"Could be nothing to do with the Coffin woman's death at all, some fight over land or business that has nothing to do with her. You can't rely on Trig's version—dude chases so many shadows he can't tell what's real anymore.

"Santich, for instance. Trig calls him a billionaire, but Ed and I, we deal with him strictly on a cash up-front basis. Too many bills he's ducked out on. Santich hasn't been smart about his land. That's how he lost it to this resort company. He works part-time for an insurance agency in the town, and it's not because he loves the work."

I digested that. "It's a strange site for a resort. When I went to look at it, they'd poured foundation for some smallish structures, so it's hard to know what the end product would look like."

"They let you onto the property? They act like it's so secret their left hands don't know what the left fingers are doing."

"They didn't let me on. I was exploring the area, wondering if the hilltop might house a drug lab or something. A guy with a big weapon chased me away—making sure I saw the weapon. Santich was in the middle of an argument with him when I arrived. That seems to be my cue in this play—Santich fighting with someone and I stumble on the fracas but can't figure out what's going on. I saw him at the field house my first night here, you know, fighting with Cady, with one of the basketball moms and then with Trig."

Lou laughed, but said, "There's so much money in drugs, I wonder if the resort is a cover for building an opioid factory."

"They've put up one pylon and were building the tower for a second," I said. "It didn't register with me at the time, but a resort wouldn't need a grid, just the usual utility poles. How much power does it take to run a fentanyl factory?"

"So that's it," Lou said slowly. "That's who wants that old power plant back online. The one you asked about this morning. That Range

Rover that you'd been waiting on, I know it, at least, saw it one time before it sprayed me with gravel just now."

He drummed his fingers on the steering wheel. "No reason not to tell you, I guess. Just that it still rankles."

He paused again.

"Ed and me, we've got plenty of contacts in the valley, we've been in business thirty-plus years, so we heard when the old Wakarusa power company decided to mothball the plant. Made an appointment with the manager, Clete Rotherhaite, to look it over, see what salvage we could handle.

"We arrived on time, but your Range Rover drove up before we'd done more than shake hands with Clete. Another SUV pulls in behind him—big old Lexus. Suit gets out of the Lexus, Power Ranger steps out of the Rover, cowboy boots, takes off a Stetson and puts on a hard hat, new, YANCY HILL on it in black. The Ranger asks what we're doing. 'After you,' Ed says. 'We're talking to Clete here.'

"Clete says we operate a scrap metal yard, but doesn't say who the Power Ranger is. Before we can ask, the Ranger says, 'Boys, don't go taking apart the turbines. There's life in this old girl.' Suit laughs, like he's the chorus."

Lou's hands on the steering wheel were steady, but his throat worked. "'Boys.' He saw our truck and talked to us like—well, we've swallowed worse. He wouldn't give his name, although we asked. Just said, 'Meeting's over, boys.'

"Clete didn't say shit. Stood there looking like a scarecrow in a minefield. We'd been knowing him a lot of years, so we called when we got back to the yard. We wanted to know what in sweet fanny's name was going on. He didn't answer, didn't call back. We tried the next day, and the same nonanswer. We were getting to be spitting mad, wondered if we should talk to a lawyer—that plant had been promised to us, but not in writing, so we decided to let it lay."

He shook his head. "His wife called us maybe a week after that. She said something in Clete's meeting with the Ranger upset him, made him feel he couldn't work the plant anymore. That same day we'd gone out there, he called her to tell her he was resigning, that he'd explain it all when he got home. Only he never got home. Went for a walk along the river to cool off, she reckoned, and fell down dead."

"That must have been a shock," I said.

"Doc told her his heart must've given up on him, anger and stress and so on."

"A heart attack? Was she surprised?"

"What are you?" Lou said, irritated. "A damned ghoul? Not everyone who dies in Kansas has been murdered."

"No, of course not," I agreed. "It just seems like such a convenient coincidence."

We'd reached town while we'd been talking. When Lou pulled the truck up in front of the Perec garage, I took out my phone and opened it to the photos I'd taken earlier.

"Yeah," Lou said. "That's the guy, the Ranger. You can kind of hear him. Turn up the sound."

I'd been shooting blind and had hit the video button. The mike had better ears than me. We got words, interspersed with bird calls and rustling leaves.

The Ranger was angry. "Goddamn idiot! . . . now cops . . . Dad . . ."

Santich, also angry ". . . your sister . . . she wanted . . ."

Ranger. "always resent . . . told Dad . . . bitch the whole deal . . ."

A minute where I couldn't make out any words, then Santich, fed up, "to investigate my house?"

Ranger laughs. ". . . freezing my nuts off."

That was when they went inside.

Lou and I listened to it several times, but that was the best we could make out. "Ranger has a sister who could bitch the whole deal, whatever the whole deal is" was his best guess.

"And a dad who's still in the picture. I don't suppose the suit in the Lexus could have been Dad?"

Lou shook his head. "About the same age as the Ranger. . . . About your other matter. Now you've seen the cameras, how are you going to get your, uh, accessory onto the Dundee place? Wouldn't it be easier to drop it at the cop shop?"

"Only if I want to be arrested. Besides, I want the cops to tie it to the crime scene. There are two camera problems—the ones the town has strewn around checking on traffic, and the ones at the Dundee house. If I could find a boat, canoe, something to get me across the river to the north side, then I could go upriver—it winds around Yancy Hill. I could go from there cross-country—"

"That Jayhawk helmet boiled your brain, Warshawski. The Kaw may look mild but it has a strong current. You some kind of wilderness genius?"

"I have rowed a boat," I said with dignity.

"In the dark on a strange river going to a strange place? Get a grip."

I climbed down from the cab and persuaded Peppy to join me. "Unless you'd rather stay in Kansas, roam those wide-open spaces?" I said to her.

"She's a smart girl," Lou said, when the dog finally jumped down. "Be better for her than some city apartment." He gave two quick beeps on his horn and drove off.

I was starting to build a long to-do list, but the first thing on it was a bath and a nap. I was cautious going up the stairs to the apartment, but no one was waiting for us. Whatever the Ranger and Santich had agreed on this morning hadn't led to any attacks that I could see. Nothing was hidden in the kitchen garbage or under the bed.

I leaned back in Gertrude's tub. It was small, to fit into the small nook created for the bathroom, but I still soaked for a good twenty minutes, drifting, ignoring my phone dinging to tell me people were texting.

When I got out of the tub, I called Deke Everard.

"What is it, Warshawski?" He was brusque.

"Something puzzling, Sergeant. I was out at the Dundee house today—"

"Doing what?" he snapped. "That is a crime scene—"

"Which I respected. I was curious about the cameras out there." I paused, to give him a chance to say, oh, we know all about them. When he didn't, I explained my theory, cameras that someone operated remotely.

"I found them placed in trees around the property. Great blackmail opportunity for someone hard up for money, as we know Brett Santich is."

"*We* does not include me. Get to your point, if you have one."

"Brett was there. He didn't see me, but he did see a guy in a Range Rover, dressed like a cowboy-wannabe, who was chewing him out. Same Range Rover showed up at the Wakarusa Coal Plant the day Clete Rotherhaite died."

Deke was breathing heavily. "Now you're going to tell me some guy who can afford a Range Rover killed Clete."

"Just questioning why the same rich-looking man is interested in the coal plant and the drug house."

"You keep wondering, but don't bother me. Unlike a private detective, I can't waste my time investigating imaginary crimes."

He hung up. I'd been going to share my scratchy video of the two men, but he'd forfeited that opportunity. Anyway, maybe he was right. Maybe Armani man meeting with Santich had nothing to do with Clarina's murder.

28

ILLUMINATORS AND BOOKBINDERS

ZOË CALLED. SHE told me my pals at Omicron were insinuating that I was committing murders and dealing drugs all over Douglas County. Did I have a comment?

"I wonder if that's what Trevor Millay's mother thought when she first saw his entitled screaming face: I hope my baby grows up to be the biggest troll under the bridge," I mused. "I don't have anything to say about the frat brat's libel. But one question I'm wondering about: it looks like this resort is going to be a mega-power user. They're putting up huge pylons, and they may be getting ready to bring the old Wakarusa coal plant back on stream. The plant foreman, Clete Rotherhaite, died a few weeks ago, supposedly of a heart attack. Can you sniff around that?"

"You think he was murdered?" Unlike Lou or Deke, she was excited by the suggestion. More big stories.

"Stranger things have happened."

"What will you be doing?" she said, suddenly suspicious. "Something more exciting that you're hogging?"

"This afternoon, I will be working for my Chicago clients, the ones who pay me," I said with as much emphasis as possible. "Tomorrow I am driving to Topeka, to visit the Kansas Origins Museum and Library. I want to see what light they can shed on the three photos I found in Clarina's trailer. Does either of those rouse your journalist curiosity to a fever pitch?"

She laughed and hung up. I actually did buckle down to some paying work, and finished two projects for my real clients. I went to bed in a glow of virtue.

In the morning, I drove to the Origins Museum, a Romanesque monster with a glass extension tacked awkwardly onto the back. A helpful guard directed me to Abby Langford, a tall brisk woman, perhaps in her fifties, who was working the reference desk.

I explained that I was trying to identify some pictures but I knew nothing about where or when they'd been taken. "I'm a private investigator, and I feel it's akin to someone asking me to find a missing person whose name or age they don't know."

"Let's see them. I'm betting they're a little more revelatory than you think," Langford said.

I'd stopped at an office supply store for some file folders. I opened these on the counter for Langford's inspection. When she saw the scene at the railway station, her eyes widened.

"Where did you get these?" she demanded.

I told her how I'd found them in Clarina Coffin's trailer. "I was third in line, behind the cops and whoever tore her home apart. Coffin was murdered—"

"I know." Langford cut me off. "I read about it. I knew her, and so the news—"

"You knew her?" I interrupted in turn. "Do you know her real name, then, or what she was doing in Lawrence?"

"So it wasn't her real name," Langford said. "I wondered about it, but she had a state ID; she had a right to use the collection. That's where these two photos come from."

She tapped the two reproductions. "Clarina said she was writing a history of the Lawrence area during the years immediately after the Civil War, and I helped her find contemporary newspapers from that era. This one"—the railway station scene—"was a fight between some Black families who were leaving Lawrence and white townspeople."

I wondered if she remembered all her patrons so clearly.

She made a face. "I'm afraid Clarina was the kind of person that we took turns avoiding. She was like the Ancient Mariner, telling you more than you ever hoped to know about what she was working on. She claimed she was going to rewrite Kansas history to refute the story of Free State heroism."

"She supported slavery?" I was astonished.

"Not at all. She was zealous about racial justice. She boasted she was going to show up the Kansas elites who didn't share her insights. I shouldn't be speaking of her this way, now that she's been killed, poor soul, but when I read about her murder, I wondered if she'd pushed too hard on a descendant of one of Lawrence's revered founders."

I thought again of Gertrude Perec and her annoyance with Clarina. Gertrude's story about the night before I found Clarina's body sounded bogus—she'd gone to the Dundee house in response to what she thought was an SOS from a friend. Maybe she'd gone there to confront Clarina in secret and had bonked her with a wrench—one lecture too many on the evils the abolitionists had committed.

According to Deke Everard, his mother and Gertrude were tight. Gertrude saw she'd killed Clarina and called Pat Everard. The two dragged Clarina down the stairs to the basement. Possible but improbable.

I asked the librarian if she could find the original news story where the railway fight occurred. She explained that librarians were honor-bound to protect the privacy of their patrons. "This means we don't keep a record of what anyone looks at. I know I can find the story, but it'll take me a little bit to track it down."

She took my phone number; she would text me when she had an answer. I set up shop in the reading room with my laptop and worked on my own caseload. I kept checking my messages, hoping against hope that Peter would get back to me, but only Zoë, Cady, and Murray wanted me. I let them ride.

I'd brought Peppy with me, since I was uneasy about leaving her alone in the Perec garage, with skilled B & E people planting weapons on me. Around eleven, I took Peppy for a walk around the museum.

Abby Langford texted me as I was putting Peppy back in the car. With a look of justifiable triumph, when I returned to her station she handed me a printout of a newspaper story about the fight at the station.

"I couldn't trace the burned building. In the 1850s and '60s, the Missouri scallywags, as they were called, often came into Kansas, especially to Lawrence, to burn and murder, so it would be hard to pinpoint exactly when this building was torched or what it had been originally."

She hesitated. "The photo of the woman, the one that's an original, would you be willing to entrust it to me for a day or two? I want to see if our conservator can bring up the detail more clearly."

"Is there something in it?"

Langford smiled. "I don't know; the print is too faded to be sure of anything. But the conservators work miracles."

"You must have seen something," I urged.

She shook her head. "It's a shadow. I'm not going to build a picture out of a shadow."

Maybe there'd be a faded message from the picture's subject, telling her name and her connection to the abolitionists of Kansas. A ghost message, directed at her unborn great-great-granddaughter, telling her to head to Lawrence.

"Did Clarina ever say anything to you about where she was from?" I asked. "Someone in Lawrence who met her a few times said she came from a town whose name was used to fat-shame her."

"The town's name was used? What does that mean?" Langford said. "The town was called Fat City and she belonged there because she was fat?"

"I don't know," I said. "I was hoping she'd dropped a more useful hint in something she said to you."

Langford shook her head. "She was full of what she knew and what she could do, including this story"—she pointed at the printout she'd given me. "But she never talked to me about her own life."

Maybe Coffin had been a fugitive from justice. She was far too young to be a 1960s radical on the run, and I couldn't see her as a January 6 insurrectionist, not with her insistence on teaching race history. Perhaps she was in a witness protection program, but that didn't make sense, either: federal marshals would have descended on Lawrence as soon as her murder was publicized.

"I hope your conservator can work quickly. The longer we go without a lead on her identity, the harder it will be to find her killers."

On my way out of the building, I passed a wall filled with tribute plaques, listing the people who had supported the library financially.

They were divided into categories based on size of donation, with fanciful titles from the medieval manuscript tradition.

Top donors, who gave north of a quarter million, were Illuminators, followed by Scribes, Calligraphers, and Bookbinders. There were three Illuminators, Matthew, Robert, and Pauline Tulloh, another six Calligraphers, who'd given a hundred thousand or more. As the donations got smaller the numbers of donors increased. There were a lot of them; this was a well-loved museum.

29

AMONG THE DEAD BONES

From the *Kanwaka Courier*, June 21, 1867

While we join with Rev. Hamer in offering prayers and condolences to Amelia Grellier, we deplore the recklessness that led inexorably to the death of her husband, Frederic. Many in our community spoke to him of the unwisdom in running a school for members of the Negro race. They are savages, unable to benefit from the kind of learning Mr. Grellier sought to instill in them. He even taught them to speak his native French language, which made them hold themselves above the white people in town, as if speaking the language of an effete and debauched nation could do anything other than increase debauchery among the savages!

Now we see the result of all this imprudence, to use the tamest word. His school has burned to the ground, taking his life with it. His widow grieving, his daughter—we will not further harrow the mother's feelings by referencing the daughter!

And the remaining Negroes who rose above their station by going to that school showed their true nature last night, in scenes of the vilest destruction at the train depot. They fought with officers of the law who were escorting them to the train, assaulted the respectable of the town who came to make sure they departed, and even smashed their own furniture in their efforts to use tables and chairs as weapons against the custodians of law and order.

We hear that Mrs. Grellier is returning to her people in Skaneateles in New York State and hope she can persuade her daughter to accompany her. Sophia Grellier living on her own is an
affront to every decent family.

THE ARTICLE INCLUDED the photo of the train station I'd found in
Clarina's trailer.

I read the story at the table in the Perec apartment. The language was like a thin icing over a cake made of worms and fecal matter. I had to sit with it for a long time before I started thinking about
the questions it raised.

The first was the easiest: the Grellier name. If Clarina had searched
out this article, maybe she was related to Frederic Grellier. I found a
number of Groellers and a handful of Grelliers, but none of them
matched Clarina's age or sex. None lived in Kansas.

I tried to dig into the Grellier history in Lawrence, but aside
from the newspaper account of the school's burning, the only other
mention I found was of baby Charles. An 1886 history of the town
mentioned his having been the first burial in the new town. He'd died
in 1855, aged three days, as his family was traveling from Kansas City
to Lawrence, part of a convoy of antislavery emigrants.

Perec was Gertrude's married name, but it was French. I called
Cady and asked if she could come up for a few minutes.

I took her over to the table and handed her the printout. "I found
this going through some of Clarina's things. I know she was harassing
you about the history you wanted to teach—did she show you this
article?"

Cady took it reluctantly, looked at it, and nodded. "She was showing this to a lot of people, even to Gram at the women's breakfast she
bullied her way into. What does it have to do with her death?"

"What do you know about the Grellier family?" I asked.

"Nothing! I never heard of them until Clarina tried to stuff this
article down my throat."

"Your grandmother is descended from the original settlers, isn't
she? Since 'Perec' is a French name, I thought perhaps she knows the
history of other French abolitionists who came out in the 1850s."

"Her ever-so-greats did come before the Civil War, at least some of them," Cady agreed. "But her husband was the Perec. Gram's family were English to the core on both sides and proud of it. She thought she was a rebel marrying a Frenchman. Although he wasn't French, of course, by the time they got married."

"And she never talked about his family?"

"Not much," Cady clipped off the words as if they were toenails.

"Your grandmother's so proud of her ancestry, she surely told you family lore," I persisted.

"Meaning what?"

"Meaning big events, fires like this, or fights at the train station, they get handed down with the story of what the ancestor was doing at the time. The day Germany invaded Poland, my grandmother's father was trying to get his cow out of the neighbor's pumpkin patch. He stopped with his hand on her horn. My grandmother said he repeated the story a thousand times.

"I'm sure your granny told you a thousand stories about Lawrence history and what your family was doing at key moments."

Cady stood motionless for a moment, her eyes big in her pale strained face. "Whatever Gram's people did, or didn't do, that was a long time ago," she finally said.

She turned on her heel and fled the room.

When I heard her reach the bottom of the stairs I leashed Peppy up again. "We're going grave hunting, girl. I bet there are rabbits."

The dog grinned: "rabbit" is one of the human words she responds to. She scampered down the outside stairs and ran in circles around me while I looked up the cemetery location. The oldest cemetery in town, historic, was on the east edge, entrance on Fifteenth Street. The same route I'd followed to Eudora to beard Trig at the recycling plant.

Clouds were moving in when I found the Grellier plot. The thin stone grave markers were so weathered the names were hard to read, but I rubbed dirt away with my fingers and saw a heart-breaking array, six children, the youngest the three-day-old Charles, the oldest only nine. Placed behind them, like a sentinel, a bas relief of the Liberty Bell dedicated to Frederic. Born in Chambon-sur-ligon France,

July 17, 1820, died Lawrence, Kansas, June 13, 1867, followed by the Liberty Bell motto: *Proclaim liberty throughout the land and unto all the inhabitants thereof.*

Amelia had returned to her home in New York state. Sophia, the daughter whose life was an insult to the decent people of Lawrence, wasn't buried with her siblings. Maybe she had followed the urgings of the *Kanwaka Courier* and joined her mother in New York.

Peppy had been running around among the graves, hunting rabbits, chipmunks, squirrels, but fortunately coming up empty. I called her to heel and drove back into town.

I had neglected the issue of who owned the Dundee house. The county building was open for another half hour. I found the recorder of deeds office and presented the Dundee address.

I apologized for not knowing the plat identifiers, but the clerk shook her head. "You're about the fourth person checking on that place. I can find that volume in the dark."

She brought out the large plat volume and opened it to the Dundee house. The adjacent lands on Yancy Hill were on the neighboring pages. The first registered title to the land had been in 1870 to a Theodore Wheelock. He claimed the land that the house sat on, and the wooded land behind it leading up to the top of Yancy Hill. The houses in the woods weren't mentioned. Maybe they'd already collapsed before Wheelock claimed the land.

Over the next three decades, Wheelock sold off chunks of the property to other people. These days the only part of the land still in Wheelock hands was one of the fields near the house. The house and one adjacent quarter-section between the woods and E. 1450 Road were owned by Brett Santich. The rest of the land going up the hill were now owned by a trust managed out of the Pioneer State Bank and Trust.

The entries were written in a flowing copperplate on parchment, which moved stiffly. I carefully turned the pages back to the beginning of the book. The first entries were in 1861, after Kansas achieved statehood. They were for houses and businesses in the part of town where Gertrude Perec lived.

The pages seemed to have been cut by hand. The first page, in particular, had a rough jagged top, as if the original clerk hadn't been able to hold the scissors steady.

I returned to the Yancy lands. Theodore Wheelock sold off sections of them to other people. I traced the history forward as best I could. In the 1870s, after Wheelock made his claim, he sold or gave parcels of land to other owners, including the Everards. The Everards still had a little land there, but the Wheelock fortunes had sunk in the 1930s, during the Great Depression.

That was when the Santich family acquired the hilltop and several thousand acres along the sides of the hill. The Santiches had prospered for a time, but fell in turn. I read a history of mortgages, sales, refinancing, and, finally, six years ago the selling of the top of the hill to a hedge fund managed by Pioneer State Bank and Trust in Topeka.

The clerk came over to the table I was using to tell me she was closing the office for the day. If I needed to consult the book further, they opened at nine in the morning.

I thanked her and got up to go. "One thing that puzzles me. The Dundee house—you probably saw it on the news—I guess that was built after Theodore Wheelock bought the land, but there are the remains of three or maybe four houses in the woods behind the house."

I showed her the plat and the woods where I'd found the remains of the chimneys. "The title starts with Wheelock, but it looks as if someone was building there before him. The drug house out there is called the Dundee place, but I don't see a Dundee anywhere in the title holders."

The clerk laughed. "This was the wild west back then. People built on land they didn't legally own. Dundee could have been one of those—he left, but the name stayed. There were a lot of land disputes in the early days of the town. Some people think my job is boring, but when I look at some of the title fights that went on, it's every bit as exciting as CSI. If I could write, I'd do a murder mystery out of these files."

I thanked her and headed into the night. It was almost five-thirty, not late, but dark. This time of year, waiting for spring, the early hours when night closes in drag down the spirits.

The library stayed open until eight. I left Peppy in the Camry while I did some deeper digging through local history and genealogy files. These were housed in the basement, in the Osma Room. I hunted through their catalog, looking for more on the fire that claimed Frederic Grellier's life. I couldn't find anything. I looked for the Wheelocks and found a number of small stories. They'd been early immigrants, coming from Auburn, a town in western New York State. When Theodore Wheelock died in 1897, the paper gave him a long obituary, with a list of his contributions to Lawrence, and the names of his numerous children and grandchildren.

The funeral had been held at Riverside Congregational Church, newly built on a bluff overlooking the river. The original church (oldest in Lawrence, the paper announced) had sat right on the river and been destroyed in a flood. Theodore had been one of the most important donors to the new building. The writer dwelt on his bravery in leaving a comfortable home in western New York State to serve the cause of those in bondage, especially because his family claimed descent from the earliest English immigrants to Massachusetts Bay.

The obituary also praised Theodore for beginning the "civilization and cultivation of Yancy Hill, which had, until his leadership, been a lawless wound on the body politic, home to Indians, coloreds, and every variety of sin and debauchery."

I thought of the remnants of the chimneys I'd seen in my first daylight trip to Yancy. Maybe they'd belonged to people committing sin and debauchery. Had he driven them away and destroyed their buildings? Or had they been so thoroughly debauched that they burned their own houses down around themselves?

I looked up the Everards, Deke's family. They were early immigrants as well, from Lynn, a town near Boston. Like the Wheelocks, their stature as early arrivals meant the papers covered their weddings and funerals, and even Deke Everard's graduation from the police academy eleven years ago.

What would it feel like to be so rooted in a place that everyone knew your family and your family's family, going back 175 years? I had no idea what the Warshawskis were doing in 1856, or even if they'd been doing it in Słonim, the town my grandparents had emigrated from. And the Sestieris, my mother's family? Had they been harmlessly minding their own business in Pitigliano, until the locals decided that Jews were purveyors of every variety of sin and de-bauchery, and needed to be eliminated? I felt a knife twist of grief for my ancestors and the turbulent lives history had forced them to lead.

30

ARMAGNAC TO THE RESCUE

RESTOCKED MY PANTRY after leaving the library but couldn't face cooking in the tiny kitchen. Even after I scrubbed the pots, I still could feel the intruder's hands on them.

I went back to the gastropub I'd found on the east side of town. I kept Peppy with me, along with my laptop. Trig had said that the construction on top of Yancy Hill had been approved by the county planning commission. I searched Zoë's paper. There was a brief comment under the heading, *Your Government at Work*.

The county planning commission approved the application for commercial construction on Yancy Hill. The project will include a resort, condos, and small retail shops. We're all curious about what kind of retail shops will be interested in a hilltop location outside of town, but the lawyer making the presentation said the shops would support resort activities.

I thought again of the pylons I'd seen under construction. Perhaps generating power was the development's real business, with a resort and shops as a way to sidestep environmental and construction permits. If the investors were expecting the Wakarusa coal plant to be their moneymaker, they could produce a lot more power than they needed, and sell it throughout the region. But why coal, with the push we all knew we had to make for greener energy?

Zoë texted. She'd had a painful interview with Clete Rother-haite's wife; could she see me in person? I sent her the restaurant name.

I was drinking Armagnac tonight—its rougher edges brace me when I'm feeling rocky. I was on my second when Zoë arrived. She ordered a local brew, as befit a young local professional.

She gulped down half the beer, then told me about her visit to Rita Rotherhaite. "He died only three weeks ago, so she's still pretty much in shock. You know, they kissed goodbye and he went off to work and then he called her to say he was resigning, but he didn't come home. She thought maybe he'd done something stupid like gone off to get drunk, even though he wasn't usually a drinker. See, his dead body wasn't found for two days, when some runners came on it. So she had forty-eight hours of worry and fear and then disaster."

Her vivid face was filled with anguish. "I wish you'd been with me. It was so terrible and I didn't know what to say. You know, two days by the river—animals—" She took my Armagnac glass and emptied it.

I was glad I hadn't had to face Clete's wife. Not another horror on top of all my own horrors, but I took Zoë's hand and pressed it.

"They must have done an autopsy," I said after a time.

Zoë made a face. "He'd been a heavy smoker, he worked in a coal plant, so his lungs were shot. Mrs. Rotherhaite begged them not to cut her husband open, not after all the other damage he'd suffered on the river path. So they did a CT scan, but not a full autopsy. Deke let me see the police report. The pathologist said there wasn't much reason to say it was anything but a heart attack. Deke said he showed it to me because you were peddling conspiracy theories. He said he wanted to make sure I, at least, had my head screwed on straight."

"Yes, keep your head screwed on," I agreed. "Don't be like me, unscrewing it at the least provocation and leaving it lying around in drug houses or places like that."

Zoë stared at me. "Vic—don't—I didn't mean—"

"You're right. That was mean-spirited. I'm getting so much unpleasant feedback these days that I'm becoming unpleasant myself.

"Clete Rotherhaite. Working around coal doesn't do your lungs a lot of good. A heart attack is sad but likely. Was his wife surprised that he resigned?"

"Yes and no. He'd been overseeing the plant shutdown. He figured his job would end by the end of the summer, so she was surprised that he quit on the spot. He said he'd explain why when he got home. All he told her was that the plant had a new owner who he didn't see eye-to-eye with. They wanted to bring the plant back on stream. Clete said he was past wanting to manage an active plant, and why hang on to be miserable when they could do like they'd always wanted, buy an RV and drive around the country."

Zoë's face crumpled with grief. "I don't know why this hits me so hard. I talk to a lot of people who've lost their loved ones."

I signaled to the waitperson for two more Armagnacs. Zoë protested that she didn't want more, but when they came, she drank hers, again too quickly.

She put on a determined smile and asked what I'd been doing. I told her about the cameras I'd found around the Dundee house. "They could be operated from anywhere, not necessarily from the Dundee house. I didn't see a control room either of the times I was inside. Whoever is controlling the feed can turn them off if they don't want their pictures showing up in a file someplace. But where are the controls?"

"Maybe up at the construction site?" she echoed my earlier thought. "You saw Brett up at the worksite. Maybe they gave him a deal when they started construction. Gosh, if that's true, Trig will have a nuclear explosion."

"It's a possibility," I conceded. "Santich has to know about the drug deals, but he seems like such an ordinary harassed man, taking his daughter to basketball games, selling insurance to support his family—if he was making a bundle from drugs why would he do that? People who know him tell me he doesn't like the insurance work."

I found a cash receipt in my bag and wrote down names on the back. Sabrina. Valerie. Power Ranger. Brett Santich. Trig. Clarina. Gertrude Perec. Cady. The Wakarusa plant. The Yancy project. The Omicron boys. The Dundee House.

"You can't believe Cady or her grandmother killed Clarina!" Zoë cried when she'd read the names.

"They have a connection to her, for sure, but how does Clarina tie into the Dundee house? For that matter, I have no earthly why Gertrude went out to the Dundee house the night Clarina's body was found. It feels as though there's a puppet master at work here, who didn't like the slow pace things were moving and decided to speed them up."

Zoë shook her head. "I wanted this to be my big breakthrough, but it's such a mess I don't know if we can figure it out before you have to go back to Chicago."

"I can't go back to Chicago until I clear up Clarina's death, so don't lose hope. And any day now, the local DA may arrest me, so you'll have a super-big scoop."

She smiled reluctantly. "I know you said you're second-guessing yourself, but you always seem to know the right thing to do. What will you do next?"

"I'm wondering how the Wakarusa plant connects to Yancy. I think I need to visit it myself, see if the guys will talk to me. A rich-looking cowboy was at the Dundee house today, fighting with Santich, and apparently this same cowboy was at Wakarusa the day Clete died."

Zoë interrupted, excited again. How did I know? When I told her I had a confidential source she tried to force me to reveal the name.

I wouldn't budge but showed her the video I'd shot. It was fuzzy and the angle was bad, since I'd been on the ground, shooting sur-reptitiously, but Zoë studied them under the flashlight from her own phone. In the end, she shook her head.

"If he was a power player from around here, I think I'd know him, but I don't."

I asked if she could find out whether the same people applied for a permit to restart Wakarusa as had applied for the permits to build on Yancy.

"I know the Yancy project came before the board two years ago, but do you have any notes on who presented the project?"

Zoë drooped. "There are so many meetings, so many committees. With me as the only reporter in the county, I can't keep on top of all the things that go on. It was right after I joined the paper, anyway, so I was still trying to figure out what meetings to go to."

"Really? Did your editor go? Your paper printed a couple of lines about the commission approving the construction. How did you know?"

"My editor?" Her mouth twisted in contempt. "His idea of journalism is checking Google News twice a day. No, I got it from Pat Everard and Gertrude Perec. Pat was chair of the planning commission that year. I asked them for a report."

"They didn't tell you who had applied for the permit?"

She shook her head. "I asked, but they said the application was handled by the Topeka office of a big national law firm, and that the commission thought the numbers were good and the paperwork showed the applicants had checked the right boxes for environmental quality, with a permit from the state EPA. Maybe I should have checked with the EPA myself, but—" She flung up her hands, despair, drowning, some signal of distress.

"Like you said, it was just two lines in the paper, but Trig saw it and went completely bonkers. He wrote a gazillion letters, claiming Santich had taken bribes to fast-track the application so he could get rid of his land at a profit, and that it would be an environmental disaster. I asked Trig how he knew, when he hadn't seen the plans, and he said, destroying the natural springs on Yancy, for one thing, and that anyway, if Brett Santich was involved it would by definition be a disaster. We ran two of his letters, but the rest were so libelous we couldn't risk printing them. And then he attacked me for being a chicken-shit. His words."

I finished my brandy and signaled for the check.

"This is hard, trying to work on this investigation and cover all the other stuff that's happening in the county," Zoë burst out. "Readers love disaster stories, like big car wrecks, and they also want to know about weddings and funerals. No one really cares about the library board or the county planning commission. I feel like I must miss big stories all the time because I'm covering the little stuff."

"You're wrong there. Local people covering local events is a big and dangerous hole in today's journalism. All these book bans, for instance, they happen at the local level, but all the small-town papers and radio stations have been swallowed by the big sharks, so people don't have any way of finding out what's happening in their own backyards. You're not missing the big stories; you cover a lot of ground. Your only problem is that you're doing it on your own."

Kind of like me, trying to run this investigation. At least I had Zoë helping out. And she had me. We were both understaffed.

31

LADIES WHO BREAKFAST

'D GROWN UP in the shadow of Chicago's steel mills, when the U.S. steel industry was booming and the plants ran three shifts a day. I'd helped my mother wash the windows and windowsills every morning, but by night they always had a thin layer of soot over them. I was lucky that my dad was a cop, working in a district far from the mills. Fathers of my girlfriends hacked and wheezed into handkerchiefs they covered with blood and tarry mucus. That's what Clete Rotherhaite's lungs had probably looked like.

No one wanted to cause his widow additional grief by performing a thorough autopsy. It was only me, wondering what the animal bites had covered up.

In the morning, I called Deke Everard to ask him again about Rotherhaite's death.

"No you don't, Warshawski. Little Zoë was already in my face about it yesterday. Rotherhaite's death was sad but natural. There is no cover-up going on."

"I didn't say there was. Just wondered what the guys at the plant had to say about it."

"The guys at the plant were like people everywhere—some were upset, some were cynical, some were resigned. Rotherhaite wasn't loved or hated, he was just a guy doing his job. You want to stir things up at the plant, see if you can create a conspiracy where nothing existed before, don't come crying to me if you find a thousand hornets stinging your ass."

"Copy that, Sergeant."

I hung up without mentioning my plan to talk to the guys at the plant, after I spoke with the gals at the Riverside Congregational Church—this was the day a group of them met for breakfast.

At eight, I saw Gertrude Perec come out of her house. She was bundled against the cold in a puffy jacket, but she had on dressy slacks and well-polished ankle boots. Her head was bare, so I could see that her faded blond hair was pulled into a chignon, and she'd put on a dusting of makeup. I wasn't going to match her for elegance, but with clean jeans, a knit top in my favorite rose, and a wool blazer, I looked respectable.

It was an easy walk from the Perec house to the church, but I drove so that I could leave Peppy in the car. Gertrude had been early, I guess, because knots of women were coming up the walk as I arrived. I followed them to the community building on the church's south side. A woman at the door smiled in welcome and introduced herself, Lucy Porter.

"Are you new in town?"

"Just visiting," I said. "I'm staying in Gertrude Perec's garage apartment."

"Oh! The detective." She eyed me avidly.

I agreed that I was the detective.

"Are you investigating our women's group?" Porter said.

"Just investigating breakfast, and a chance to talk to Gertrude. She's so busy . . ." I let the thought trail off.

"Yes," Porter said drily. "She is very busy with a great many things. I'm surprised she thought she needed a detective, she's so assiduous herself in conducting investigations."

"I understand she works with Pat Everard on a lot of committees?" I said.

"Oh, yes," Porter said, even more drily.

We'd reached the room where the breakfast was held. I asked Porter to point Everard out to me.

"Next to Gertrude, by the coffee urn. There's a goodwill offering—five dollars." She turned away, putting an arm around another woman in another warm greeting. I followed the crowd to the food table.

Pat Everard, with her head of graying curls, wasn't as elegantly groomed as Gertrude, but she possessed a similar authoritative air. When Gertrude saw me, she didn't seem to be filled with the charity one associates with church gatherings.

"What are you doing here?" she demanded.

I fished in my wallet for a five. "I want to talk to you and Ms. Everard. This seemed like a good place to do it."

"This is a church women's breakfast. It's unbearable that you think you can attack me here."

"Attack?" I poured a cup of coffee. It was thin and smelled bitter. Too long in the urn. "I want information that the two of you possess. I don't think asking for it is an attack."

"What is it you want to know?" Everard demanded.

"The planning meeting that gave approval to the project on Yancy Hill. When you reported on it to Zoë Cruickshank, you told her the application had been for a resort, with some condos and small shops."

"That was at least two years ago." Everard looked at Gertrude, who nodded. "I don't remember exactly what we said."

"This seems to be an enormous project. Since you chaired the planning committee, I hoped you might remember more details. How much did the applicant's lawyer spell out about the resort's power needs?"

"I just said, the meeting was years ago. I couldn't possibly remember details like that on short notice." Everard's dark brows rose in hauteur.

"Do you remember the firm the lawyer was with? It's not in the online minutes."

"The questions you're asking have nothing to do with Clarina Coffin's death," Gertrude said. "And even if they did, Ms. Everard's son is fully capable of following up on them."

"Has Deke talked to you again about what you were doing at the Dundee house?"

"*Sergeant* Everard knows everything about that unfortunate incident," Gertrude said.

Conversation in the room had died down. We were putting on a show, and everyone wanted to hear the dialogue.

I smiled so the audience could see I was the cool, relaxed member of the trio. "The whole project is so interesting," I said. "Have you been up the hill to look at the construction site?"

"Of course not," Gertrude said brusquely. "If this is your idea of an investigation—"

"But the Everard family owned land there, for generations," I said, eyes widening in astonishment. "I'd think at least Ms. Everard here would have some curiosity about what's happening to it. And then there was the sad death of Clete Rotherhaite. Not on Yancy land, at least I don't think it is. But on the river path right by the coal plant."

Gertrude and Pat exchanged glances—worried? Angry? I couldn't tell. They'd been friends a long time; an outsider couldn't read their cues.

"That was a natural death. It was unfortunate that it happened where it did, so that the poor man's body wasn't discovered for several days, but his death is not a police matter," Pat said. "I know Chicago is awash in unsolved murders, so that may have made you think all police forces are incompetent, but even before my son joined the force, the Lawrence police were able to solve local crimes without a hotshot private eye's help."

Gertrude nodded and brushed past me to face the room, smiling, holding out her hands. "I'm so sorry for the delay. A mix-up with the woman who's been staying in my garage apartment. Pastor Tracy, could I prevail on you to lead us in a blessing?"

Behind me, Pat Everard murmured, "Well done, Gertrude," and found a place at one of the tables.

The youngest woman in the room got to her feet to offer thanks for the thin bitter coffee and the sweet rolls, with a special thanks to Ashley and Judith, who'd done the baking this week. I'd paid my five dollars, so I took a muffin and some fruit and found a seat at the same table as the woman who'd accompanied me into the room.

"She's the detective," Porter said, when the rest of the women turned to stare at me.

There was a mixed flow of greetings—*Do you work with Pat's son?*

We think he does such a wonderful job; we heard Gertrude had a detective living with her. Her life isn't in danger, is it? But Gertrude cut the flow off with a reading of the minutes, the agenda, the good works the group was doing with Bring Lawrence Home, the book they were discussing at tomorrow night's book club meeting, a fictionalized account of Henry Wadsworth Longfellow's love affair with a woman named Fanny Appleton.

Gertrude smiled. "You know I feel a connection there—one of my great-great-grandfathers was a cousin to the Appleton family, so of course I was enthralled by the story, but I'll look forward to everyone else's reaction."

"As long as we don't spend too long on our important family connections," one of the women at my table muttered.

A woman at another table raised her hand to say she thought the group should invite me to speak—it wasn't often they had a chance to meet a real investigator—but Gertrude shut that down with a firm hand. She assured the room I wouldn't be staying in town much longer.

"But two murders!" the woman said. "We'd all like to know if our lives are in danger when we walk along the river path."

There was an assenting buzz, which Pat interrupted. "This is how fake news takes hold. The man who died on the river path was not murdered; he had a heart attack. But if people want to hear from detectives who actually know what they're doing, I'll talk to Deke and see if he can send an officer over next week to speak to us. They have some bright young women on the force these days."

The meeting ended soon after, but several women came over to me, asking if I knew who'd killed Clarina. One bold soul brought up the trolling Trevor Millay was conducting. She wanted to know if it was true that I'd been to a drug party at the old Dundee house.

"I went to the Dundee house to rescue a student who'd taken an overdose," I said. "As Pat Everard just pointed out, it's so easy for facts to get garbled these days, but you can definitely check that one with Deke Everard. Or if you know Brett Santich? I understand he owns that house. Maybe he can shed some light on what's been going on there. As far as walking the riverfront—it's always good to let a friend know where you're going to be if you're out alone."

Everyone bused their own plates and flatware, while two other women packed up the leftover muffins and fruit. These were destined for a homeless shelter, someone told me.

I strolled over to Pat and Gertrude, who were trying to end a conversation with Pastor Tracy. "Pastor, I'm sorry to interrupt. I have a few more questions to ask Ms. Everard and Ms. Perec while they're together."

"Of course." The pastor looked at me curiously, but moved away from the pair to speak to someone else.

"There's nothing to discuss," Gertrude said.

"Just one last thing." I kept smiling—the only way to keep from shouting at her. "Yesterday I read an obituary in the *Kanwaka Courier* about a guy named Theodore Wheelock, who staked the first claim to the land. The paper praised him for—"

I unlocked my phone and found the photograph I'd taken of the story. "Yes. Until Theodore began plowing and planting on Yancy, it had been 'home to Indians, coloreds, and every variety of sin and debauchery.' Clarina read that and came to see you about it, didn't she? And that's what she wanted Cady to include in her Kansas history curriculum. That must have seemed like a terrible assault to the sense you both have of being descended from Lawrence's founders."

Gertrude stood frozen, like one of those plastic ice cubes with an insect inside. Pat put an arm around her.

"That's enough. You can't come into a church, pretending to be a detective, and hurl accusations like that. I'm calling my son to see what action we can take to make you leave town."

"The tried and true tar and feathering? I don't think the LKPD would countenance that."

"You need to be out of my house by the end of the day today." Gertrude choked out the words. "Pat, can you drive me? The shock—I need to sit down."

"If Ms. Perec suffers from your words, I will hold you accountable," Pat Everard spat over her shoulder as she tenderly escorted Gertrude from the room.

Pastor Tracy hurried to their side and took Gertrude's other arm.

"What was that about?" Lucy Porter asked me.

I was staring after them. "Genealogy," I finally said. "Their roots in this town are very important to them."

What was it Cady had said when I'd asked about French settlers in Lawrence? *Gram's family were English to the core.*

I'd bet my meager IRA that Gertrude's birth name had been Wheelock.

32

URBAN COWBOY

I T WAS EARLY afternoon when Peppy and I drove across the bridge to the path on the north side of the Kaw. I should have been hunting for housing, after Gertrude's ultimatum, but I had an urge to see if I could stir up the thousand hornets Deke had threatened might come for me if I went to the coal plant. The day was gray, chilly, with a threat of drizzle in the low-hanging clouds.

The south side of the river, where we usually ran, was parkland, with a well-kept trail surrounded by trees and benches. The north side also had a trail, but heading west it was surrounded by industry. Dump trucks and semis rocked the roads. A train with sixty or so coal-filled hopper cars ran near us, its horn sounding like a cow in anguish.

We passed a salt mountain, a yard filled with school buses, a couple of cement plants, some motels, a light industry park, and then suddenly we were in open country. The Wakarusa power plant stood out in the near distance, its main stack a rusting orange sentinel keeping watch over farmland.

The state had created a two-hundred-mile-long trail on this side of the river. The trick was finding a way from the road down to the Kaw. The roads had been laid out by someone with a mania for squares. Every time I thought I was getting close, the road made a ninety-degree turn and led me deeper into farmland.

I finally came to the plant's access road, the one Lou and Ed must have taken the day they thought they were going to bid on the plant's scrap. A blinking red light in the distance marked the gates and guard station.

I didn't try to drive to the guard station but returned to the main road and pulled over to one side. There was no shoulder; the Camry was uncomfortably close to the drainage ditch between road and field. We were about a quarter mile from the river, on the edge of a field plowed for the winter. I let Peppy out, and we crossed the field. That makes it sound simple. Washington crossing the Delaware, yes, piece of cake in a small boat on a tidal river that bucked and heaved under him. V.I. and Peppy crossing the field. Piece of cake on foot over large clumps of dirt mixed with straw.

Peppy wasn't bothered—she ran in hunting mode, crisscrossing the field as if it were smooth grass, periodically returning to me with a big grin. Yellow-breasted birds skimmed the furrows, whistling to each other as they found insects in the earth. I was the creature who was out of place, stumbling my way through the heavy clods.

When we reached the river, my thighs and knees reminded me that I hadn't done any squats for months. Something else for my to-do list. I shared a peanut butter sandwich and part of a water bottle with the dog while I caught my breath.

Peppy was eager for a swim after her run, but the water surface here was oily and iridescent with coal dust. I leashed her up. "You'd come out a black lab if you went in," I told her, "and you'd have enough carcinogens in your system to poison a city block."

Now that we were close to the plant, I could see that the stack was periodically belching clouds of gray smoke, like an elderly smoker trying to blow rings.

The river made a number of tight bends here, so that while the plant was close, it was maddeningly hard to reach. We could hear machinery, which also sounded elderly, going *ka-thunk,* and then pausing to wheeze as it worked its way to the next *ka-thunk.*

As we followed the trail around the river's tight loops, I realized that apart from the plant noises, the nearby undergrowth was quiet. The whistling birds who'd flown around us while we crossed the field were keeping away from the dirty water and contaminated bushes.

Around one loop, we came to a place where the bushes and grasses were flattened by tire tracks from all-terrain vehicles. I guessed this was where the cops and ambulance team had driven to reach Clete Rotherhaite's body.

Runners had come on him lying on the side of the trail, but that had been three weeks ago. I couldn't see any remnants of his death, but Peppy sniffed uneasily around the spot.

"Anything in the undergrowth, girl? A pipe wrench? A rock with skin on it?"

The two of us hunted but didn't find any possible weapon. Of course if he had been murdered, the river was right there to take care of the evidence.

The plant appeared suddenly around the next bend. It was enormous, covering an area that might hold a couple of football fields. Despite its age and the crust of grime covering the buildings, the complex held an air of menace: I dare you to try to get rid of me.

A fence surrounded the plant, but it, too, was old. Especially down here by the river, sections of it were so rusted that the prongs had come away from the metal posts. We were standing at the back, so I couldn't tell how many people might be at work, but we were at the end where the coal came in. A half-dozen hopper cars stood on the siding.

The noise had been growing as we'd gotten nearer. This close in, it was ferocious. Peppy whined, pawed the ground, looked pleadingly at me. I hated to torment her further, but I pushed away one of the rusted sections of fence and crossed into the yard.

Someone was overseeing the hopper cars, but his back was to me. He didn't see the dog and me as we passed. When we walked across the tracks a thundering noise shook the ground. One of the cars had released its load into an underground shed. The train engine blew its horn and begin inching forward, moving another hopper into position over the shed. I took out my phone to photograph the scene.

With Peppy clinging to my legs, I circled the plant and reached the entrance. A trio of men in hard hats and safety vests was sitting at a card table inside the plant's open doors, eating doughnuts and drinking coffee. Two of them were smoking. They all had phones out. Every now and then, one would lean across the table to shout something at his friends, but in that racket you couldn't carry on a conversation.

I walked up to them, smiling happily, Little Miss Sunshine, bringing joy to the jobsite. I tried to say, "Hi, guys," but the machinery swallowed my words.

The men looked up at me, taken aback by my arrival.

One of them stood so he could bellow in my face, "Who are you, and how in hell did you get into the yard?"

I put a couple of my cards on the table. "I'm an investigator; I walked up the river trail with my dog, looking for the place where Clete Rotherhaite was found."

The two men sitting looked at my card, looked at the standing man, waiting for his reaction. The last of the hopper cars must have dumped its load because the noise dropped enough that we could hear each other.

"You investigating Clete's death?" the standing man said. "That was a hard way to die. Hard on Rita, for sure, but, hell, we'd worked together going on twenty-five years. Hard on all of us. We'd just as soon let him rest in peace."

"I hear you," I said. "Insurance, you know, companies have all the sensitivity of a blast furnace."

"What?" the man was indignant. "They threatening not to pay his life insurance?"

"Workers' comp," I said. "They'll pay out if he was still employed when he died. That's the problem. Some suit in Chicago said he'd quit, that he wasn't on the Wakarusa payroll when he died."

The man spat, aiming about an inch from my foot. "You working for the company?"

I didn't flinch or move my foot. "Neither the insurer nor the coal plant. I'm independent, trying to get the facts so that Rita Rotherhaite can at least get the indemnity payment she's entitled to."

The three men looked at each other again, nodded infinitesimally. The ringleader took us inside, past giant boilers and pipes, conveyor belts and heavy fans. A scene from Walter Mitty. *Pocketa-pocketa.*

We crossed the floor and went into a room in a far corner that was sort of soundproofed. Peppy remained glued to my legs, whining at the noise, the heat, the smell of sulfur.

"That whole day was fucked, if you'll pardon my French," the spokesman said. "Clete, he was like a cat on hot bricks from the moment he walked in the door. Then Lou Arata and Ed Lyndes came by. They thought the place was being mothballed, they were going to bid on some of the pipes, things easy to dismantle that a two-man crew could handle. Arata and Lyndes, they were in this room here with Clete.

"I'm the day shift foreman so I'm down in the yard, when this dude drives up in some hundred-thousand-dollar ride. You can tell he's a suit even though he's wearing boots, jeans, the whole western look, all brand-new, like he opened the boxes this morning. Right behind him another suit drives up in a white Lexus, this one with a jacket and tie, carrying a briefcase.

"'Good news, fellas,' the cowboy says, like he can make us think he's one of the boys. 'Your jobs are safe for another few decades. This plant is a good cat with nine lives, she's got a whole bunch more in front of her.'

"The cowboy wants to look around. Suit works for him, so he has to follow him into the plant floor with his leather shoes. Would have been funny except they weren't a funny pair. Suit is tapping his wrist, time's a-wasting, cowboy draws out the tour just to be ornery, asking questions about the boiler, the pressure, whatever.

"Finally he gives us a wink, he's had enough fun with his flunky, and asks to see Clete. I point to this room but say Clete is meeting with a couple of guys interested in buying scrap. The cowboy just barges on in, suit at his heels, like your dog here.

"About ten minutes later out come Lou and Ed. They're usually an easygoing pair, take life in stride, but they were mad enough to fire up engine number two." The foreman pointed toward one of the boilers.

"I went in to see what the hey was going on, and I hear Clete yelling at the suits. 'How much do you know about coal? Yeah, you got all those papers, Tulloh, you're the owner now, but how much do you know about coal, how it works, what it does? You showing me these papers means you know jackshit.'"

"Tulloh?" I interrupted. "Like Tulloh Industries?"

"I suppose," the foreman said. "Heck, maybe they bought the plant, although why anyone that rich wants something this old beats me. I guess that was Clete's point, too.

"Cowboy was grinning all over his face, like he's pulled a fast one the rest of us are too slow to notice. Anyway, the sidekick says to Clete, 'He owns the joint, he can do what he wants.' And Clete says, 'Of course you can do what you want. Just not with me. I'm out of here.'"

"He left there and then?" I asked.

The men shook their heads, almost in unison. "He stayed to take care of the payroll and stuff. The cowboy and the suit took off, leaving it up to Clete to notify the crew that everything was about to change.

"You know, we got just a skeleton in place waiting to see what management was going to do about the plant. Now it looks like we're coming back on stream, starting to bring in new coal, but that's been since Clete died. After the cowboy left, Clete called everyone out into the yard, about twenty of us, explained there were new owners, they'd have to talk to the union about seniority, job security, so on, but that he, Clete, wasn't going to be back."

"And he went off for a walk along the river?" I said.

The foreman eyed me narrowly. "He worked his full day, and anyone who says otherwise is a goddam liar. He drove off at four when the shift ended."

"Did he do that a lot?" I asked. "I mean, walk by the river when he needed to think things through?"

One of the other men laughed. "Clete? His idea of thinking things through was a beer and a football game. Told him he should have got a job in Oklahoma, where the teams win more than they lose, but he was Jayhawks and Chiefs through thick and thin, and with the Jayhawks, that's a lot of thin."

"Him and Rita, they liked to garden," the foreman said, "but I wouldn't say he wasn't big on nature."

"So he didn't say anything to any of you, like I'm going to miss this sad old plant so I'm going to walk down by the river and take some pictures?"

They stared at me. "Are you trying to say he was trespassing, and Rita can't collect?" the foreman said.

"Oh, no," I said. "Just trying to make sense of it. He worked the full day, the full shift, he died essentially on the premises, so he was on the payroll and at work. That's what I'll tell the workers' comp board, anyway. I wouldn't want to confuse their tiny brains with all this talk of coming and going."

"Tiny brains, that's a good one." The foreman spat again, this time aiming away from my foot. We were buddies, I guess. "Let's not confuse those tiny brains."

They saw me to the exit. Yep, that proved we were pals.

Peppy refused to go back the way we'd come. The earth quaking as the hopper released its load had unnerved her. I led her away from the plant toward the gate with the blinking red light. She broke into a flat-out run. My shoes were too heavy with mud to keep pace with her, but I found her on the far side of the gate, sides heaving. We walked at a sober pace to the car.

33

OUT OF THE MOUTHS OF BABES

I HAD MUD INSIDE my socks as well as clumped to my shoes. Next to high heels, my running shoes were the worst choice for hiking through farmland. Peppy was panting, thirsty from running, and from the fear she'd felt at the plant.

When we reached the shops near the bridge, I pulled into the lot behind the Boat Yard and walked down to the river's edge. Close up, I could see the strong current Lou and Ed had talked about. I let Peppy go in swimming, but kept her leash attached in case she got into trouble. I took off my own shoes and socks and stuck my feet into the current. Big mistake. In seconds my bones were aching from the cold.

I rinsed the worst of the mud from my shoes and put them back on. Horrible. Clammy wet rubber on bare feet. Fortunately, the strip mall where I kept buying clean clothes was behind the Boat Yard. I'd stop for socks on my way out.

Claiming to be a workers' comp investigator had gotten me a nice amount of information about Clete Rotherhaite's last day at the plant. His last day alive, probably.

If Tulloh Industries had bought the old Wakarusa plant, they must believe there was a fortune to be made on Yancy, doing something that required a power grid. Maybe they'd found valuable minerals, lithium or something, that would take a lot of power to dig up and refine.

Clarina had trespassed. The Yancy foreman had referred to Trig's "harassment brigade," coming onto the jobsite. She'd stuck her nose in many places where no one wanted to see it—the Congregational women, the Yancy jobsite. Maybe she'd visited the coal plant, too. She'd discovered something about the Yancy project that Tulloh needed to keep secret. He got Santich, or perhaps the gun-toting project manager, to kill her.

I could call Deke and tell him I'd solved the case: one of the Tulloh family had killed Clarina because she was trying to shut down the resort. She was the one Santich and Tulloh complained "would bitch the whole deal." It would be very nearly worth all my pain and trouble to listen to him erupt.

How does coal work? You set it on fire, you bring water in those big boilers to steam temperature, the pressure drives some turbines that somehow connect to a power grid and make it run. Presumably the owners knew that same minimum amount, so what did Clete Rotherhaite think the Urban Cowboy didn't know? And why did that mean Rotherhaite had to die?

A small boy with a shock of dark hair falling over his eyes wandered down from the Boat Yard parking lot. "Your dog is a good swimmer."

"Yes, she is."

Peppy came out to see who was accosting me and sprayed water over the child, who shrieked with laughter at the shower.

"Does she bite?"

"Nope. She's a mellow girl." I showed him how Peppy could take a treat from my mouth without biting me, which made him shriek again.

"Does your mom or dad know you're down here?" I asked.

He made a vague gesture. "Mom and Auntie Holly are talking, talking, talking."

"Then let's go see what they're talking, talking, talking about."

I stuffed my filthy socks into one of the bags I use for the dog and squelched up the hill, Peppy in tow.

Holly, the waitress who'd told me about the Dundee House, was in agitated conversation with a redheaded woman. Holly had a cigarette in one hand, which she was waving so furiously I thought she might stab the redhead with it.

I'd seen the other woman before. She'd been emptying the recycling bin at the University Press building. And Trig had her picture on his screen saver, bending over the boy with the dark hair.

"Are you Ivy?" I said. "I'm V.I. Warshawski. I was sitting down by the water with my dog when your kid came down."

"The dog can swim real good," the boy told his mother. "And she took food from the lady's mouth. She didn't bite."

"Ivy, you take Timmy on home. I need to go in and start my shift," Holly said.

"Before you take Timmy on home, can we talk for a minute?" I said. "I saw you at the University Press building. And your picture on Trig's computer."

Both women froze, but Timmy said, "Trig, he took me to the zoo."

"He sounds like a good friend," I said. "A super good friend who wants to make sure your mommy doesn't get hurt. He even went to a haunted house in the middle of the night to make sure your mommy didn't find any ghosts or zombies."

I smiled at Timmy while I spoke, to make sure we both knew a haunted house and ghosts weren't real. He tugged on his mother's jacket, wanting to know if she saw a ghost, if Trig killed a ghost.

"Who are you?" Ivy demanded. "What do you want?"

"I'm a detective, private, who found Sabrina Granev in the Dundee house. A day later, I found Clarina Coffin's dead body there." I spoke softly, directly into her ear, hoping Timmy couldn't hear me.

"Trig and I are leading suspects in Coffin's murder. I'm trying like mad to find her actual killer before the DA gets tired of waiting and charges me. Or him."

Ivy looked at her son, who was staring anxiously at us. I'd brought trouble to his mother, but I had a cool dog. Hard to figure out whether I was good or bad.

"Timmy, I need to talk to this lady for five minutes. Auntie Holly will let you play with my phone, okay?" She handed her device to her sister, who took Timmy to one side—out of earshot but close enough to leap on me if I threatened her sister.

"Trig knows you clean up after those parties," I said, "so he came out to the Dundee House when he saw cop activity there on his scanner. He didn't want you walking into the arms of the law."

"How do you know Trig?" she demanded.

"I met him because of this mess," I said. "How do you know him?"

"You think he's Timmy's father?"

I shook my head. "I think he wants to be Timmy's father. The birth father isn't in the picture?"

She gave a shout of laughter, raw, harsh, humorless. "He's in the picture, he got me the job cleaning the damned house."

"Not the Omicron brat—kid—Millay?"

"You're half smart, half clueless," she said.

"Santich?" I was even more incredulous.

"Brett Santich. The usual stupid story. Married man lonely and hurting, cruising without his ring. Used to come in here Friday nights. I worked here then, like Holly. Then I'm pregnant, and he reveals all. Wife, kid, mortgage, no money for another kid. So what does he do for me? Gets me odd jobs, like cleaning that old house. It is haunted. You go in there, you feel the spirit of all those drug ODs, but it's an extra hundred bucks once or twice a week. What a good daddy!"

"So that's why Trig hates Santich so much," I said slowly. "How did he find out?"

"He overheard me shouting at Brett about a year ago, out at the Dundee place. Timmy was starting school, he needs stuff. He needs a dentist, he wants the toys the other kids have. I need money, Brett doesn't have any. I told him to sell another damned acre of land. Two thousand would take care of the kid for a year. He's whining what would he tell his wife, when Trig pops out of the darkness—he was there to post one of his stupid signs on the house."

She stopped, panting. "I swore him to secrecy, but he likes to help out, takes the kid to the zoo, gets him presents for his birthday. You're right—he'd like to be Timmy's daddy, but Trig! He's so—creepy! It's like walking on broken glass, being grateful for what he does for us but not so grateful that he thinks he can, you know—"

I nodded sympathetically. "When did Brett start using the house for the drug parties?"

"What difference does that make?"

"Brett needs money, so he's letting people use the house, no questions asked. Meanwhile, he had to sell the family land on top of

Yancy. I'm wondering if the people running that project also get a cut of what he does with the house, and how it connects to the Omicron boys."

She hunched a shoulder. "I don't know. The deal for the land went through when Timmy was born. I thought Brett would have cash to burn, there'd be money for Timmy, but it turns out he had a triple mortgage to pay off and so he's *still* in debt. Asshole. I really know how to pick them. As for the Omicron boys—they're creeps but they're not in charge. They do it for kicks, I guess, to see how much they can get away with."

She paused, dialing back her bitterness for a moment while she thought. "The parties were something Brett worked out privately, during the lockdown, I guess. The Omicron boys got wind of them and pushed in, but someone else must be involved. On account of the cameras. They only went in about six months ago, and Brett, he's super careful about them. I have to go clean up exactly when he says because he can turn the cameras off, but he doesn't always have access to the master switch."

"I don't suppose you know where that is?"

She shook her head. "Along with everything else. I must have been born stupid. Holly's the smart one."

"Timmy's a lively kid," I said. "I know you're on a hard road, but you're doing a good job, or he wouldn't be so confident and outgoing."

"You think so?" She brightened a little and straightened her shoulders as she walked back into the bar.

34

ON TOP OF OLD YANCY

THE ROTHERHAITES LIVED in Lecompton, a few miles up the road from the Wakarusa coal plant. I hated to bother Rita Rother-haite, especially after Zoë had already been there, but I wanted to see if her husband had said anything to her that would clarify what he meant when he said the Power Ranger didn't know anything about coal.

The visit was as painful as I'd feared. The couple had been married for thirty-four years; Rita didn't know how she would sleep through the night without Clete snoring next to her.

"The men at the plant were surprised that he'd gone walking by the river," I said.

"It never would have come into my head," she said. "First when he didn't come home, I thought maybe he'd gone out to get drunk. He only ever did that one time before, when our boy Milo died in Afghanistan, but then when two days went by—I thought if I called the sheriff Clete would never forgive me for making a fuss—but while I was still making up my mind, up came one of the deputies with the news."

"When your husband called, did he say why he was resigning?"

"The new boss said Clete should be happy they were reviving the Wakarusa plant because he'd get to keep his job. Clete, he said he explained the Wakarusa was so old it couldn't produce power safely. They had three accidents last year, which is too many, especially when you know the plant is only at quarter capacity. That's what they fought about. Clete, it was safety first with him. I'm not risking any more of my men's lives, that's what he said he told the boss. And of course he was right."

"Did he mention the new boss's name?" I asked. "Was it Tulloh?"

She shook her head slowly, tears shining on her face. "You'd think I could remember every word of my last conversation with my own man, but I can't. You don't know it's going to be the last time, and you don't do more than stand there while you've got the vacuum in one hand, thinking, maybe make him pork chops for dinner. Pork chops, and him about to go off and die."

I waited while she went through that terrible litany we all recite, regrets and remorse, things undone or unsaid, the things we wished undone or unsaid. When she was calmer, I apologized again for disturbing her, and offered the conventional hope that she had family or friends to help her through this hard time. She brightened; her girl Tara was coming to visit with the baby. Maybe she'd go back to Independence with her for the summer, help with the older kids.

The sun was setting when I got back to the Perec house. I sent a text to Cady: Haven't had time to hunt for new quarters. One last night here and I promise I'll be out in the morning. She wrote back with an apology for her grandmother's harshness and said morning would be fine.

When I'd looked up the Tullohs earlier, I'd only read some articles in the business press. Now I called up images. They weren't a family that relished being photographed, but I found Matthew, the patriarch, with Emmaline, at a reception for their fiftieth wedding anniversary seven years ago. They did not spend their billions on high fashion. He wore a suit that had been through many meetings; she had on a flower-print dress that could have come off the rack at Target or JCPenneys.

In contrast, their daughter, Pauline, was shown laughing with the senior senator from Kansas. She had on a navy cocktail dress that looked like couture work, while the sons were dressed in the modern version of evening wear—collarless shirts hanging over the trouser waistband, and box-cut jackets.

I even found a YouTube clip, a segment with Matthew Tulloh's mother, filmed by someone who called her "Auntie." Mrs. Tulloh had been 103, sharp-featured, her voice quavery with age but perfectly clear, and surprisingly vindictive.

"Everyone said Emmaline Wilton married beneath her when she said 'I do' to my boy," Mrs. Tulloh chortled. "She had those three grain elevators, and he had a pocketful of dirt. Look at the Wiltons now, all of them charity cases Matthew puts up with for Emmaline's sake."

The videographer panned the room and settled on a cluster in a remote corner, a weedy morose man perhaps in his sixties, and two younger men in ill-fitting sports jackets and khaki pants. "Yep, that's Emmaline's brother's boy and his sons. He squandered the elevators their pa left him. He didn't think my Matthew knew how to count to five, so he wouldn't listen to Matthew's advice, and look at him now." Mrs. Tulloh laughed again.

The party had been seven years ago. Matthew's mother died not long after the event, a happy woman, I guess.

An article in *Kansas Business Today* had a reporter at the party who wrote, "There are reports of feuding between the two Tulloh sons, as well as between the cousins, but all we saw at the party was a family that supports each other and the Salina community that they call home."

I didn't know if the brothers were feuding or supporting each other in Lawrence, but they were definitely playing a role here. I'd seen them both. The older, Jacob, had been standing next to Agent Stamoran in the press conference the LKPD chief had held after I found Sabrina. The younger, Robert, was the man I'd seen arguing with Brett Santich outside the Dundee house yesterday morning.

Robert was the urban cowboy Lou and Ed had run into at the Wakarusa power plant. The man who'd laughed off his foreman's concerns about the plant's safety and forced his subordinate to tour the plant in a business suit and loafers. A man who loved using his position and his money to humiliate others.

True, that, but it was secondary to the question about what was going up on top of old Yancy. If Tulloh Industries was reviving a dying coal plant, it wasn't because they were building a resort. I see pylons that size when I drive the route into Chicago past the area's nuclear reactors: they are feeding megawatts into the Chicago grid. What on earth was Tulloh building that had the power needs of a city?

I went back to the corporate website and read it with greater attention. Tulloh Industries had nine major subsidiaries, some of them doing things I couldn't understand even when I read the descriptions a half dozen times. The dropdown menu of countries where they had factories, mines, or cloud services included most of the globe.

They were ruthless in putting down strikes by workers in Africa and South America. Famous for exacting tax concessions from governments both foreign and domestic. Funders of various petroleum industry think tanks aimed at combatting climate change information.

I thought of Sherlock Holmes's description of Moriarty as a spider in the center of a web with a thousand strands. Moriarty knew what every strand connected to. I wondered if the patriarch, Matthew Tulloh, kept similar watch over his thousands of subsidiaries and factories. Not that Tulloh was a criminal enterprise, at least not in the narrowest definition of the word, but definitely not an outfit to tangle with.

Matthew Tulloh had brought the FBI in to oversee the investigation into Sabrina Granev's disappearance. His son Jacob had been right next to Agent Stamoran at the Lawrence police chief's press conference two days later. If the FBI jumped when Tulloh snapped his fingers, a county's judicial system might turn somersaults.

I felt sweat beading on my neck. If Frank Karas, the DA, told the LKPD to arrest me, that would be easier to deal with than if the urban cowboy and his daddy decided my body should join Clarina's and Rotherhaite's in some remote corner of the county.

I tried phoning Valerie Granev, but again my call went to voicemail. I left a message asking after Sabrina's health, telling her that I was on the trail of whoever ran the drug parties at the Dundee house. I finished by asking, *Do you know what the company is building on Yancy? Are you under orders not to talk to me?*

I texted Deke Everard. No hornets buzzing around me yet, but that may happen soon. The new Wakarusa owners have a lot of muscle in their power plays, both in the physical plant and in the county's planning board. You told me I was making your job hard because you didn't know what I was doing. Shoe fits both feet. I don't know what pressure the Tulloh family is exerting on your team, but it's making me nervous.

Murray called as I was staring at a plate of risotto, trying to talk myself into eating it. "Guess where I am, Warshawski."

I wasn't in the mood, but I played along, anyway. "The second moon of Jupiter?"

"Albuquerque. You owe me a plane ticket and a night in a hotel."

"Is there some reason I should be—" I cut myself short. "You went down to talk to Sabrina's father."

"Valerie is such a strong presence we were forgetting that the girl—strike that," he said hastily. "Young woman has two parents. I figured Ramir Granev might not talk to the fourth estate, but he opened up to a worried dad who wondered if Ramir's wilderness camping would be a good thing for his daughter. I caught up with him at the outdoor store where you told me he worked."

"Murray, I hate to stroke your already outsize ego, but that was genius," I said. "What issues is your daughter facing?"

"What so many entitled kids are dealing with these days—opioids. My ex-wife and I agree on hardly anything, but our girl's health scare brought us back together. We got LiliBeth into a good rehab pro-gram, but, dang, she's sixteen, going back into school is like sending her into a drug factory. Ramir shared his grief over his own girl. He and his wife didn't even know she was addicted until she went down to Kansas and some crazy woman lured her to a drug house."

He paused, but I declined the bait.

"Sabrina's in Florida," I said. "Is Valerie down there with her?"

"Valerie had to go back to work. Ramir spent the weekend with Sabrina, but both parents are scared for her future. 'Don't make your child's success your happiness,' he warned me. Made me feel a heel for inventing LiliBeth, but not such a heel that I stopped asking ques-tions. The monsters you said Sabrina was seeing—I asked if she was strong enough to look at a photo lineup. That was a major blunder—why was a worried dad worrying about some other kid looking at a photo array?

"I said, sorry, the cops were hounding LiliBeth to try to ID her dealer and I wondered about his kid and her dealers. He said every time he or Valerie tried to mention that, she got hysterical again.

"I congratulated him on getting the funding for his wilderness camp. He said basically the same thing we saw on the news—it had been a goal for many years but was hard to enjoy with his daughter so ill.

"I asked if he thought his coworkers had clubbed together out of sympathy for Sabrina. He said his coworkers didn't have that kind of money. He wondered if that billionaire woman who makes mysterious gifts had heard about him on the news and decided to fund his program. Or maybe Valerie's coworkers—they had more money than the people he worked with."

"Most likely it's Valerie's bosses." I told him about IDing Robert Tulloh as the man who'd taken over the Wakarusa power plant. "Sabrina gets into an expensive rehab center, Ram gets his wilderness camp, all the parents have to do is tell me they don't want me investigating."

"It's that kind of story?" Murray sucked in a breath. "You think the pressure on that Bureau guy—what's his name?—Stamoran? You think Tulloh is pushing on Stamoran to arrest you?"

"No, just to get me to back off. But this coal plant—the foreman who thought firing it back up was a safety risk was conveniently found dead on the river path. Local LEOs assure me it was a heart attack, but you know the saying—if it quacks like a killing.

"The plans they filed with the county were for a resort and some ancillary shops, but the day I went up to the construction site, I saw pylons, big things that would be good for bringing power from this coal plant to something needing more watts than a resort. A resort on an out-of-the-way Kansas hilltop."

"What are they building?" Murray asked.

"Today's top question," I said drily. "Kirmek, the construction firm working on the Yancy site, also needs some attention. The foreman is armed, although who isn't, these days? My second day here I climbed Yancy Hill and saw Brett Santich in a heated discussion with the guy."

"I'll shake a few trees, see if they're connected," Murray said, meaning Mob ties, "but this definitely means you're paying my air-fare."

"To Albuquerque, but not for your hotel. I know you didn't stay at Motel 6."

In the years he'd worked for Global Entertainment, Murray chafed at the company's slipshod journalism but had enjoyed their lavish travel allowances. That was one of the reasons it took him so long to go freelance. That and the fact that no one is earning a living doing real journalism these days.

When we finished dickering, I'd agreed to cover a coach ticket, not the first-class he'd shelled out for ("I'm six-two, Warshawski, you can't expect me to fold up like a piece of laundry in one of those tiny seats." I was unmoved).

When we hung up, I caught up with Lotty, Sal, and, of course, Mr. Contreras. Angela and Bernie had brought him up to the North-western campus yesterday. Angela had an afternoon game, Bernie a nighttime hockey match. He'd watched both matches, probably the loudest voice in the bleachers, then taken them out for pizza.

Everyone was happy, except he missed me and Peppy and he was sure the dog walker wasn't giving Mitch enough exercise.

35

PANTS ON FIRE

ZOË CALLED AS I was getting ready for bed. She'd gone to the Lion's Heart this evening with some of her besties as cover. She'd stumbled into the kitchen, pretending she thought it was the bathroom, and saw the dishwasher dealing out the back door.

She'd taken a surreptitious picture, wondering if he was the guy who'd been spying on me from the bushes Sunday night. I shook my head—I'd never gotten a look at the peeper's face.

"But here's the interesting thing, Vic," Zoë added. "The bar almost went under during the pandemic. One of my girlfriends, she works for Pioneer State Bank and Trust, where the Lion's Heart owner banks. He's a guy named Don Wilton, he lost a lot of money during the pandemic. He couldn't get a PPP loan, he couldn't pay his mortgage on the bar, and he was having a going-out-of-business sale, like, all you can drink for twenty dollars or something, when suddenly he was back in business."

"So he found an angel. Interesting," I said. "Your friend say who?"

Zoë laughed. "She went all Banking Act on me, even though she'd broken a million regulations telling me as much as she had. So I think she doesn't know."

I told her what I'd learned out at the Wakarusa plant, and from Rita Rotherhaite. "If you have time, can you check the EPA filing the Yancy project made when they applied for planning permission? Gertrude and Pat claimed not to remember when I bearded them at the church breakfast yesterday. The plant foreman said Rotherhaite was worried that the new owners plan to run the plant either above its capacity, or without making the repairs and upgrades and so on that it needs."

"Lois Lane is all over it, Wonder Woman. What will you be doing?"

"Finding a new place to stay. Gertrude gave me the boot."

Over my second cortado the next morning, I tried to sort out my housing options. I should never have roomed in the Perec home to begin with, so getting the boot wasn't a bad thing, just a time-eating inconvenience. I found a website where people advertised for room-mates, but none of the furnished places would let me bring a dog.

We were inside the Hippo, where the barista brought Peppy a small dish of milk. Even if it had been selfish to bring Peppy to Kansas with me, she was making friends.

I ran through my short list of local acquaintances. I could camp out in the Dundee house, I supposed, seat of the action. Peppy would have the woods to roam in and we could play hide-and-seek with Brett Santich and the Yancy man he'd been arguing with.

That sardonic thought reminded me of Clarina's trashed trailer. I finished the egg sandwich I'd ordered and headed west, toward Yancy, toward the Prairie View Mobile Home Park. Mignon Travers was still in her padded desk chair, still focused on her device.

"Yes?" She didn't look up.

"I'm looking for a week's rental furnished," I said.

"Month minimum," she said to her screen.

"I just need a base for a week, two tops, to sort out Clarina Coffin's murder. Is her place available?"

Travers turned her attention to me reluctantly. "Oh. The private cop. The Coffin woman's place is still a mess. Unless you want to spend a fortune on a new stove and everything, you don't want to live there. The park owners are fighting with the police over who's responsible for cleanup, so it may never be fixed. You want a week? Just you?"

"And my dog. She can catch both mice and cockroaches, so I wouldn't need to shoot them." Not that I'd seen her do either, but

Peppy comes from a long line of hunting dogs. Not one that stretched back to the Pilgrims in 1620, but respectable, nonetheless.

Mignon snorted: my joke was not very funny. "I guess. Long as she doesn't pee or crap inside. She does that, out you go, but you pay to replace the carpeting. Got someone who's coming back from Florida in ten days. They'd be glad of the extra rent. Three hundred for the week. Includes electric, but butane for the heater is fifty extra. You provide your own linens."

She ran my credit card, told me she'd get Al to bring over a bottle of butane when he came this afternoon, then reached above the desk for the key. Peppy and I walked down the gravel lanes to 1422 Bluestem. The unit was a double wide with an electric cooktop, a refrigerator under the counter, a modest shower, and a big bed. It was cold, with a musty smell from being shut up all winter, but it was clean; it would do.

I drove back to the Perec house to pack. I put the towels and bedding into Gertrude's washing machine, but yesterday's coal-laden clothes I stuck in a garbage bag to take to a Laundromat. I had been tempted to run them through Gertrude's machine, to leave black grime caking the inside, but that pettiness was adolescent, unbecoming an adult detective.

As I packed, I inspected each garment, each toilet article and piece of paper, for any signs of Friday's intruders, but didn't spot drugs or trackers or bloodstained tools.

Peppy was yawning anxiously, uncertain because I'd put her food and bed and toys into a box. I took her down the stairs with her box and put both into the Camry.

I finished carting everything to the car, then rang Gertrude's front doorbell to return her key. Deke Everard came to the door.

I was preparing to tell him about Clete Rotherhaite and the unnatural exercise he'd been taking before he died, but Deke forestalled me.

"My mother says you came to the church women's group and accused Gertrude Perec of murdering Clarina Coffin."

"I'm sure your mother is too honorable a person to lie, especially about so serious a matter. What did she really say?"

His face was stern. "Maybe the Chicago PD has the resources to let you waste their time, but we're thirty percent understaffed here. You don't get to spin me around. Tell me why you made this accusation, and I will decide whether to ask the DA to file charges against you."

"Is your mother here now, comforting Ms. Perec? Let's go in and talk together, so you're not playing telephone tree, delivering messages that get garbled in transmission."

I didn't wait for his reply but brushed past him into the house. Gertrude and Pat were sitting together on a sofa. Cady was standing near a window, running the cord to the drapes through her fingers.

Gertrude straightened her shoulders when she saw me. "Have you moved out?"

"Yes, ma'am." I put the key on an end table near her. "I put my used linens in the garage washer. I can stay to dry them if you want."

"I'll take care of that." Cady's voice was low, affectless.

When none of the women said anything else, Deke said, "Mother, you called me here to lodge a complaint against V.I. Warshawski. Can you repeat it, please?"

"I said you accused Gertrude—Ms. Perec—of murdering Clarina Coffin."

I pulled up a straight-backed chair so that I could sit facing the two women. "Ms. Everard, could you please repeat my exact words?"

"I don't remember the exact words, but you implied—" Pat Everard glanced at her son. Whatever she read in his face made her stop talking.

"Let me help." I turned the chair so I could see Deke as well as the women. "All the events I've been involved in, from Sabrina Granev's disappearance through Clarina Coffin's death, have centered on Yancy Hill. Sabrina and Clarina were both found at the Dundee house on Yancy land. Gertrude Perec and Trig Garrity were caught on camera at the Dundee house the night Clarina's dead body was discovered."

"You were at the house that day as well," Deke said, a pulse throbbing in his neck.

I stared him down. "Yes, indeed I was. When I found Sabrina

Granev, Clarina Coffin was probably in the basement, dying if not dead. If I had known her life was in the balance, I would have alerted your emergency crew and told them to go down there. I am paying a heavy price for saving Sabrina Granev's life."

"Yes, all right," Deke muttered.

I was angry, but I made myself put my bitterness to one side. I shut my eyes, slowed my breathing, until I could speak levelly.

"About six years ago, Brett Santich sold land on Yancy to an anonymous developer. Trig blames Santich for all the troubles around the land, the school, and so on, but word on the street is that Brett sold because he's overleveraged, not because he's sinking money into a development on the hilltop. Someone told me he had three mortgages. I guess when you're a homeboy, the banks give you extra leeway, but it probably wasn't a good thing, because the sale supposedly didn't help him with the third mortgage.

"Monday I did a title search. The first registered claim was to a man named Wheelock, in 1870. A little later, Henry Everard claimed land out there as well. Clarina did this same search. Like me, she came on Theodore Wheelock's obituary. His contemporaries praised him for getting rid of Indians and what the newspaper called 'coloreds' that were making Yancy an undesirable place on the outskirts of this highly respectable town.

"I asked Ms. Perec whether Clarina had shown her these documents. She had. I said Ms. Perec must have felt this was a terrible assault on her family's good name. She told me to get out of her garage by the end of the day. Which was a good idea. I shouldn't have been living there, anyway, given how hostile Ms. Perec is to my involvement in the investigation."

"She's not the only one," Deke said. "The LKPD has enough qualified officers to solve crimes without your help."

"Not five minutes ago you told me the force was thirty percent understaffed. I won't say you need my help, but my help means I'm focused on this one situation, not the dozen or twenty new ones that crop up every day."

"That's not the point," Deke said. "You may think you're doing good, but you don't file reports, we have no idea what you're doing, you could recklessly destroy months of surveillance, the way you did by confronting the Omicron House guys."

"Is there someone at the LKPD I can put on speed-dial to check who I can and can't talk to?" I said, voice low and mean. "I am tired of being blamed for everything that is wrong in this county. That house in the woods was being used for drug parties before Sabrina Granev and I came to Kansas. If I had the time and interest to take on those frat rats, I would bet one or all of them have parents who are major donors to the university, and so the investigation proceeded slowly, hoping the boys would graduate before they had to be confronted."

I knew I was being reckless, speaking without counsel present, but I was too angry to care. "And you know *damned* well that I am no more responsible for killing Clarina Coffin than your mother is. On top of that, Clete Rotherhaite's death. I was out by the Wakarusa coal plant this morning—"

"You have a hell of a nerve! I told you yesterday not to come to me with imaginary crimes. Not content to screwing up one murder investigation, you think you can turn every unusual death in the county into a murder? And then investigate it on your lonesome to show up me and my force, with no other resource than a dog who couldn't find a steak in a butcher shop?"

I squeezed my eyes shut, took a steadying breath. "When you stoop to attacking my dog, it shows how far in over your head you are. Honestly. Go after me all you want, but I assure you, if Peppy were left in a butcher shop for three minutes, there wouldn't be a bone left."

I got up. "Ms. Perec, going back to the actual murder the sergeant is investigating, your reaction to Theodore Wheelock's obituary was so intense, it makes me wonder if he was your ancestor."

Gertrude stood as well. "I am proud of my family and with good reason. We helped build this town. My ancestors left a comfortable home in Skaneateles to make sure this state came free into the Union. We drained swampland and turned it into productive farmland. We helped write laws that have kept this town and this county safe for almost two centuries."

I stood still in the middle of the room. "Where did your family come from? Skinny Atlas?"

"Why do you care? Do you want to go there and harass any of my relations still living there?" Gertrude spat. "My mother fought against segregated housing both here in Lawrence and at the university. My family resigned their memberships in the private clubs that excluded Black people. None of that meant anything to Clarina. She wanted to turn us into cartoon figures who talked and acted like rednecks. Yes, she got under my skin, but I wouldn't murder to stop her making her pathetic woke videos. Now you may leave."

"Videos? Did the LKPD find these?" I asked Deke.

"She put them up on Instagram and TikTok," Cady spoke in the same listless voice. "The Yancy school board watched those videos the night they voted to fire me. At least that's what I've heard. Clarina had footage of herself with Trig picketing the school, but she also secretly videoed me when she was trying to argue me into letting her put what she called true Kansas history into my syllabus."

"She tried to video us at the breakfast she came to," Pat Everard said. "She wanted to push us into saying something she could make a fuss about in the social media world."

She smiled, a tight triumphant twitch of the mouth. "We got our friends to sing a hymn, and so she finally put her wretched phone away."

Cady followed me to the door, her face a study in unhappiness. "I'm sorry, Vic, sorry I invited you to stay here. Sorry I tried to get you to help look out for Gram."

"Murder investigations take a toll on everyone. Me included, so it's better that I stay someplace more private. One last thing, though—the town your grandmother said your family came from. She called it 'Skinny Atlas'?" I spelled out what I thought I'd heard.

Cady gave a tired smile. "It's one of those trick words, like 'Ptolemy,' that don't sound like they're spelled." She spelled it out for me: Skaneateles. "You're not really going to go there to bother any Wheelocks still living there, are you? Gram took me to visit once when I was twelve so I could feel connected to my roots, but we didn't know any of the Wheelocks or Entwistles who still lived there.

And they wouldn't know anything about land deals in Lawrence from a hundred fifty years ago."

"I'm not going to bother the Wheelocks of Skaneateles," I said. "But if you were a creep who thought your town's name gave you license to bully a chubby girl, maybe you'd think it was funny that your town was called Skinny something."

36

THE AGONY COLUMN

S I WAS getting into the Camry, Deke stood inside the car's door so I couldn't close it. "What is it you think you found out about Rotherhaite?"

"He quit after a heated argument with the new owners at the Wakarusa coal plant. Rotherhaite said he wasn't going to work for someone who knew nothing about coal."

"So now you're going to get local industry involved in your crap. You don't know anything about coal, either, do you?"

"My crap? A drug house I discovered is now my crap? A dead body I found is now my crap? Was it my arrival that caused Clete Rotherhaite to quit his job in fury with his new management?"

He knew he was wrong, and so he sensibly kept quiet. I wasn't quite so sensible. "Clete Rotherhaite supposedly went for a walk to cool his head after he resigned. He was someone whose idea of exercise was lifting a beer can."

"Just leave Rotherhaite and the plant alone. If you can't, I will lock you up for obstruction."

"Yes, you do hold the power cards here. If you could kindly move your law-enforcing body away from the door, I will get out of your auntie Gertrude's line of sight and thus prevent another heart attack in the making. And if you would release my Mustang, and me, then I'd be glad to abandon all my crap and go back to Chicago."

He moved away from the door but came back as I was pulling it shut. "I need to know where you're going from here."

"To the library. What else have I done that you should know about? I told you about Brett meeting some heavy outside the Dundee house, right? Is that on Everard land?"

"Don't push me, Warshawski. Everards don't own anything out there anymore. I don't know what the Wheelocks own, if anything. I need to know where you're staying."

I gave a tight smile. "In case Karas finally signs an arrest warrant? I usually start the day at the Decadent Hippo. Or you can look at your tracking data—you must be following my phone these days, or those CCTV cameras that are perched on top of so many of your town's streetlights."

He put his hands together, parody of a prayer. "Could you, as a personal favor, make my job a tiny bit easier and tell me if you've found a place to crash?"

He was a good cop, and not usually this confrontational. It dawned on me that he was attacking me because he was caught between what he thought was right and what his chief and the DA said he should be doing. And on top of that, I'd attacked his mother. I told him where I was staying.

"What? You think you can solve Coffin's murder by being right on the spot there?"

"And you think I should cooperate with you when you challenge or criticize every step I take?"

I slammed the door. That's what you get when you cooperate with law enforcement.

I made a face as I gunned the engine. I sounded like Trig Garrity: they're all pigs whether they're public or private. Thinking of Trig made me remember the wrench. I hoped it had arrived at Cheviot. I hoped it held some conclusive evidence of Clarina's murder. I felt as though my head might split into pieces, like the jagged veins of a pomegranate, my brains spilling out in little red seeds.

A truck convoy from Kirmek Construction was bouncing along Sixth Street, spewing gray exhaust over my windshield. They were hard at work up on Yancy. I pulled off the road until the trucks belched past.

I'd landed in a strip mall, which reminded me that I needed to supply my own linens at the trailer. At the Buy-Smart outlet, I bought cheap bedding and towels.

When I got to the trailer, Al, whoever he was, hadn't been around yet with the butane, but I was too tired to mind the cold. I was too tired to mind anything. I made up the bed but crawled in without undressing, beyond shoes and blazer. Peppy curled up next to me, as exhausted as I was.

A warning bark from Peppy woke me a few hours later. It took a minute for me to remember where I was, but I heard banging on the side of the trailer and stumbled to the door.

A heavy-set man in a lumberman's checked shirt was attaching a cannister of butane to a nozzle. "You're just about set here, miss. I've switched on the electricity, too. Turning on the heater is pretty straightforward, but if you have any problems, talk to my mom and she'll give me a call."

I switched on the heat. The butane ignited, and the trailer's baseboard heaters came to life. I heated up some canned lentil soup on the two-burner cooktop and set up my computer. The trailer park boasted Wi-Fi, but I thought it prudent to use my personal router. I sent messages to both lawyers—Freeman in Chicago and Faye Mitchell in Kansas City—along with Murray and Zoë to let them know I'd moved.

I called Lou and Ed to tell them where I'd landed, and also to report on my visit to the Wakarusa power plant. "They were unloading a half dozen hopper cars of coal. The day shift foreman and two of his buddies were pretty cooperative; they just don't know much. But what they told me has left me with a lot of unanswerable questions about how Rotherhaite really died."

I told them what I'd found out. "He seemed to think the plant would need a lot of upgrading before it could be fully operational again."

"He was right about that," Ed said. "Place is inefficient, and it doesn't have any computer controls. Should be sold for scrap. I'd think the Power Ranger outbid us for the scrap, except they wouldn't be bringing in new coal if they were going to scuttle the plant."

"What does it take in coal and human power for a plant that size to be running full capacity?"

"Depends," Lou said. "Maybe a hundred, hundred-fifty people spread over three shifts if they were going twenty-four-seven. If you didn't see a lot of activity, sounds like they're just doing a maintenance level of firing."

"Except six hoppers?" Ed said. "Sounds like they're gearing up for more action."

"I wondered if the resort was a side hustle, with the power plant being the main action," I said. "If they bought it cheap, maybe they figure they can turn a big profit on selling excess energy."

"Be careful around that plant," Lou put in. "People don't like you snooping, they could put a world of hurt on you that you'd never recover from."

"Mr. Sunshine," Ed said. "Don't try to scare her off. Number one, she's doing righteous work. And number two, you should know by now, lady don't scare easy."

That was comforting, even if not accurate. When we hung up, I called Zoë. She was predictably cross that I hadn't taken her with me to look at the coal plant, especially when I told her that Rotherhaite's body had been found nearby.

"Thank goodness you came down here to investigate. Otherwise, no one would know anything. How can I get to the place where they found his body?"

"You need to be on the river path. That's easiest to reach if you get on it in Lawrence, by the bridge. Otherwise it's a mess going across country from the road. If you bike along the path, you'll see where the grasses and bushes are all beaten down by the emergency response crews, but you'd have to go soon. Any more rain or snow will obliterate the traces."

"You want to go out there with me tomorrow morning?"

"It's time I talked to Mr. Brett Santich," I said.

Zoë knew the name and address of the insurance company where he worked part-time. Once again, she bartered local knowledge for a seat at the interview table. I assured her she had a big career ahead of her—as a Mob enforcer.

My conversation with Cady, Gertrude, and Deke had been so fraught this morning that I'd overlooked one crucial point. If Clarina had come from Skaneateles, someone there would know her real name. When Sherlock Holmes was trying to find someone, he'd post an ad in the Agony Column of the *Times*. I guess Facebook and Instagram are today's equivalent. I drafted an ad, using the clearest of the pictures of Clarina that Zoë had taken for the *Herald*'s story about the Yancy school picket.

> Skaneateles, NY Natives: Do you know this woman? She was using the alias "Clarina Coffin" when she was murdered in Lawrence, Kansas, ten days ago. If you know her, or know anything about her, please get in touch with private investigator V.I. Warshawski @viwarshawski-investigates.com.

I found Skaneateles on a map. Syracuse was the closest big city, but Skaneateles was also near Auburn, where Harriet Tubman had lived, and Seneca Falls, home of the first women's rights convention. Just the place to produce committed abolitionists, or today's woke equivalent.

I paid to target the ad for all those places, then took Peppy for a long run, all the way to Yancy Hill and back. For the first time in months, the first time since Taylor's killing, despite my disturbed sleep, I was moving freely through space. I had a plan, I was making connections out of all the data I'd been uncovering. My investigative skills were reviving.

37

FISHING WITHOUT A LINE

THE GREAT PLAINS Agency was in a new building in a strip mall on the west side of town, not far from the trailer park. I'd looked at their website before driving downtown to pick Zoë up at the *County Herald*'s office. The five agents on staff had posted their photos with short bios. Santich said he was a fifth-generation member of the Douglas County community, committed to its economic well-being. He could assist with farm and farm implement coverage in addition to regular personal lines.

I'd only ever seen him looking angry. In his online photograph his tanned, square-jawed face looked reassuring, like the old Marlboro man: *You can trust me, ma'am, to take care of you and the little ones.* It wasn't impossible to think he could attract someone like Ivy.

A woman in her forties was staffing the front counter when Zoë and I arrived. She smiled hopefully—new business walking in the door. Her name was Patsy, she was here to help.

We asked for Brett. He was in but busy. Did Zoë and I have an appointment? We said we were happy to wait: he had been recommended as the best agent for our unique needs.

Patsy phoned him, then apologized. "He has an appointment offsite that he's just about to leave for. Any of our other agents would be glad to assist you gals, at least to take your information until Brett can get back to you."

Zoë started to say we had questions only Brett could answer, but I shook my head at her and said, "Tell him he's been recommended as someone who understands special coverage, especially when older, more rural property is involved. We're looking at a location that had been a drug house and we're wondering what we need to do to make it insurable. Ask Brett who else in the agency could handle this."

Patsy looked puzzled, but insurers bend over backward to win clients, so she relayed the message. After a brief chat, Patsy asked for our names. An even briefer chat and she told me Brett would be out to get us right away.

"That was cool, Vic," Zoë said when we'd backed away from the counter. "Now I know why you're the star."

I was expecting an instant eruption, but a good five minutes passed before the door behind Patsy's counter opened and Brett came out. He looked as he had on my other sightings: face set in harsh lines. The Marlboro man was going to drive me out of Dodge.

When he saw Zoë holding out her phone, ready to record, he snapped, "Zoë, put your damned phone away. I have nothing to say to the media, or to whoever your sidekick is, about drug houses. No reputable agency would insure them."

I put on my most professional smile. "Mr. Santich, I'm sorry we're intruding. I'm V.I. Warshawski. Not exactly a sidekick, more like a private investigator looking into Clarina Coffin's murder. You and a buddy went into the Dundee house yesterday. The security cameras were turned off, so I had to assume you were the owner, or at least knew who operated—"

Santich cut me off hastily, with a nervous look at Patsy, who was practically levitating in her eagerness to eavesdrop. "We'll continue this conversation in the parking lot. Patsy, I'm on my way to the Schapens, to talk about covering their new spreader."

He tried yanking the outer door open, but the hydraulic arm didn't allow for violent gestures. Zoë and I followed him into the parking strip.

"I'll give you five minutes, but, Zoë, if you try to record this conversation I will smash your phone."

"That's a little excessive, and even pointless," I said. "Two of us here are witness to everything you say. What I'd really like to know is what you and Robert Tulloh needed to talk about that was secret and urgent enough to be at the Dundee house yesterday morning."

"What makes you think I was at that place?" Santich demanded.

"It's strewn with cameras. There's a record."

He curled his lip. "No record of my presence that I know about."

"So you are in charge of the surveillance," I said. "However, you didn't shut off my own camera."

I pulled up the video I'd shot while lying behind the trees. The resolution wasn't great, but Santich was recognizable.

Beads of sweat glistened at his hairline. "You were trespassing," Santich hissed, "which means you have a hell of a nerve trying to ask me questions about people I talk to."

"Why was Tulloh so angry? Was it about the drugs, or about the murder? Or about a connection between your house and the Wakarusa coal plant? He's been seen at both places."

"We were having a private conversation. That is my house, on my land, and the people I talk to are none of your business."

"It is your house," I agreed. "It's also where significant crimes have been committed—murder being the most serious, but America is suffering from such a horrific opioid epidemic, I can't believe you could host drug parties and take them lightly."

I paused, but he didn't speak. "When I saw you on the Yancy jobsite, in another argument, I thought maybe the construction crew had been using the house without your knowledge. I imagined you might be a hero, taking them to task, but after seeing you yesterday with Tulloh, it's clear you're involved with all the key players. Did you cut someone out of their share of your drug sales? Does Tulloh have some hold over you?"

Santich's Adam's apple worked, but he prudently kept quiet. I saw Zoë had surreptitiously pressed the record button on her phone.

"Going back to the surveillance cameras nailed to the trees and the back door and so on, I've been trying to figure out where the controls are. Surely not here at the agency, where Patsy is listening to every word you speak. I suppose you could do them from home. The lazy criminal often takes the easiest route, but you've got a wife and daughter who could find their way into the computer controls at any time. You wouldn't want them to see what happens at the Dundee place. Of course, you're not quite so finicky about what Ivy or Timmy might stumble onto."

A pasty pallor appeared beneath his tan, making him look like a painting where the colors were running. He was rocking on the balls of his feet, and he gave off a sweet, sickly odor. I wondered if he might faint. If he cracked his head on the asphalt, that wouldn't help Ivy, his wife, or either of his children—or the investigation.

"You need to sit down." I looked around for a bench, but this wasn't a scenic spot; no one wanted to sit watching the traffic on Route 59.

He ignored the suggestion. "What do you want?"

"So many things," I said. "Justice, mercy, peace for starters, but from you, mostly I want knowledge. I want to know what they're building on top of Yancy."

"A resort," he said thickly. "Everyone knows you were harassing Gertrude Perec and Pat Everard about the planning permits, but they were legitimate permits, and what they specify is a resort and shops."

"There's a particle accelerator west of Chicago," I said. "They have a ring a kilometer around with magnets that whip particles into racing almost at the speed of light. That accelerator needs the kind of power they're getting ready to bring onto Yancy. Tell me what kind of resort needs that much energy."

"How should I know?" he muttered. "Maybe they're building a physics lab."

"What a great idea," I said. "That will be a nice surprise, a present from Tulloh Industries to the University of Kansas. Why call it a resort, though, unless old Mr. Tulloh likes giving people fancy surprises. Is that why Clarina Coffin was murdered? She was going to spoil the surprise?"

The pasty pallor was fading, but he was still sweating in the cold February air. "Just because your ass is in a sling over the Sabrina girl's OD and the Coffin woman's murder, you think that's on the top of everyone's mind. You're fishing and you don't have a line."

He was trying to speak contemptuously, but it didn't quite come off.

"I'd think crimes of that magnitude in your house would be at the top of your mind, too," I said. "Let's see what knowledge I've been able to fish up even without a line. Two nights ago, someone broke into the apartment where I was staying—someone with sophisticated lock-picking skills who could get in without leaving a mark on the lock plate. Maybe they were looking for something they thought I had, maybe they were trying to plant something on me. I think it was the plant, because they called the cops, and told them I had something hot and juicy for the law to find.

"However, nothing showed up, despite a diligent search, which must have annoyed the would-be planters. If your buddy Robert Tulloh was calling that shot, he must have been furious. I'm picturing the text or voicemail: *Meet me at the Dundee house.*

"When you got there, he screamed and yelled. *Why were you holding drug parties there,* I imagine him bellowing. *We don't want attention paid to Yancy because we're building this secret physics project or whatever it is, and drug parties and dead history buffs bring all kinds of attention.* Did he add, *Can't you do anything right?* Is that the insult you've been hearing your whole life?"

Santich was plucking at his throat, but he didn't speak.

I turned to Zoë. "What did the planning commission tell you about the environmental impact statement?"

Zoë said promptly, "The commission chair said the lawyers who filed the plans had submitted an environmental impact report that showed they'd had the site inspected and approved for the use on the application, namely a resort and an unspecified number of stores."

"So if the builders are doing something else, something naughty on that site, they'd want to keep it on the down-low, wouldn't they?"

"For sure," Zoë said vigorously.

"I can guess that the Tullohs, or whoever the investors are, would be seriously annoyed about drug parties near the hilltop. They don't want anyone nosing around until it's too late to backpedal on what they're actually doing. By the way, a present to the physics department, that was inspired thinking."

Santich's jaw worked. He was still off-color, and my praise didn't seem to boost his spirits.

"Was Clarina killed because she was poking around the physics resort and threatening to go to Douglas County's de facto bosses, Gertrude Perec and Pat Everard, with what she was seeing?"

At that Santich gave me a contemptuous smile. "You don't actually know anything. You think you have some fancy skills that will get me to tell you secrets I don't know so you can look important back in Chicago."

It was a good shot, but I ignored it. "What about Trig? Is he as big a nuisance as Clarina? Is his life in danger now?"

"Garrity?" Santich said. "He was born useless. No one takes him seriously."

"Then why did he have to be lured out to the Dundee house along with Gertrude Perec the night that Clarina died?"

"What I heard, he showed up, wanting to break in. Who knows why he went in the first place, unless he thought there'd still be drugs on the premises and he could help himself."

"That's a good storyline," I said. "Not as good as the physics lab, but still credible. Wouldn't you agree, Zoë?"

"I would if I didn't know Trig doesn't touch drugs," she said. "He's been arrested a gazillion times, and they've done a bunch of drug tests, but he's always clean."

I turned back to Santich. "I know you have to get out to the Schapens to talk about their—shredder, was it? No, spreader. I won't keep you. Just one more question. The construction on top of Yancy, when they made their application to the planning commission—what was the name on the project?"

"I wasn't involved in the application. It would have been a conflict of interest." His words came out slowly—his throat was dry, his voice constricted.

Zoë spoke up again. "I went into the planning committee minutes for that date before I came over here. The applicant was Yancy Project LLC. Yancy Project LLC took me to Pioneer State Bank and Trust in Topeka. They're the trustees. Right now the only name on file for whom to call with questions is Pioneer's trust department, so I called them, and they referred me to their lawyer, who wouldn't answer questions."

"It's looking like all those layers of secrecy are shielding the Tullohs," I said. "Are the Tullohs in turn shielding you? Is that why Frank Karas is looking at me and Trig instead of you for Clarina's murder?"

"No one wants to arrest me because they know I haven't broken any laws."

"The drug parties?"

"The fraternity asked my permission to use the house so they could hold barbecues out there. They paid me rent, they kept the house clean, I didn't have any reason to check up on them. Of course, now we won't be renting it out to them anymore."

"You have an amazingly fertile imagination, Mr. Santich. I understand Marvel is always looking for talent. Gift-wrapped particle accelerators, frat boys holding barbecues, Ivy cleaning up after those s'mores—they do leave a gooey trail everywhere they go, don't they?"

Santich shifted his weight from foot to foot. "You don't live here. So nothing that gets done here is any of your business. And you are not part of my life, so nothing I do is any of your business." He turned away.

"But I live here, Mr. Santich," Zoë said. "And I'm responsible for getting news to the hundred twenty thousand people in the county. A big construction project is big news. It could mean jobs, after all, which is always good news. It could also mean water and air pollution, which is always bad news. Whether it's good news or bad, I'll dig it out and report it."

Santich looked at her, then me, hands clenched into fists as they had been yesterday morning. And as they had been yesterday, hanging at his side, longing to punch someone but knowing he couldn't, at least not in full view of his office.

"You do that," he said thickly. "You report it. As for you—" He looked at me, jerked his head toward the parked cars.

I followed him to his SUV, the old, dusty Kia he'd been driving the night I'd first seen him at the field house. "What do you know about Ivy and Timmy?"

"Only what she's told me. I wondered why she would take on as scutty a job as cleaning up after one of those parties. It's a kind of hard way for her to get child support, isn't it?"

"How'd you even find her?"

"I'm an investigator," I said. "I investigate."

"Don't go investigating Ivy. You won't find the clear-cut victim story she wants you to believe."

He stumbled over to the Kia. I rejoined Zoë, but as we got into the Camry, Brett still hadn't started the engine. Before turning out of the lot, I looked back at the agency. Patsy was standing at the window, watching the end of the drama.

38

MARLIN FISHING

O F COURSE, ZOË wanted to know who Ivy and Timmy were.

"Ivy is someone who may have loved Brett too well, but not wisely. I can't tell you anything about her—I don't even know her last name. I met her by chance. She cleans, or used to clean the Dundee house after their parties."

Zoë digested that. "And Timmy?"

"I said she may not have loved wisely."

"Oh. She had a kid. Brett's married with a kid. He really is deep in quicksand, isn't he. Mortgages, dead bodies, angry investors, a second family."

"I still don't understand why local LEOs aren't paying close attention to him," I said.

"Maybe they are and they're playing it close to the chest. You'll figure it out though; I'm counting on you to make this a complete story."

"Get in line," I said harshly. "I feel as though a thousand people are counting on me. I'm tired of it."

My dad, talking to me earnestly after my mother's death, when I ran wild through South Chicago and his pals in the Fourth District picked me up and brought me home, instead of booking me. *I'm counting on you to honor your mother's memory by acting in a way that would make her proud.* Bernie counted on me. Clients counted on me. Peter's student Taylor had counted on me, and they were dead. And who could I count on? Not Peter, who wasn't even returning my texts.

"I'm sorry, Vic," Zoë said in a small voice. "You seem so cool and knowledgeable, like you can figure out anything, but I didn't mean to make you mad."

I forced a smile. "You didn't make me mad, I did that to myself. The words you used, they're a trigger for me these days. You can't count on me to make this a complete story—it's more responsibility than I can handle."

She didn't speak again until we reached the newspaper offices, then said, "Can I ask advice when I'm stuck? Will you keep sharing your discoveries with me?"

I nodded. "We have to keep working together. We're all each other has right now. You know those photos of people fishing, where it's some giant marlin or shark that pulls them off the boat into the water? Tulloh Industries, Clarina's murder, the drugs, the Yancy construction, Clete Rotherhaite—they're a giant fish that's trying to drown me. If I go under, you save yourself."

"No, Vic. If you go under, I'll win a Pulitzer writing it up."

I couldn't help laughing. "That's the spirit. You do that."

I dropped her at the newspaper office and drove on across the river. I was on the far side of the bridge from the Boat Yard and the strip mall where I kept replenishing my wardrobe. On this side, there were sandbars and rocky shallows. I walked down to the edge and let Peppy splash around while I sat, trying to collect myself. Deep breaths, singers' breaths that Gabriella had tried to instill in me. I found myself weeping, as if my mother's death had happened three days, not three decades, ago.

After a time, the light on the water changed from brown to silver to black. I got stiffly to my feet, called Peppy to heel. On my way to the trailer park, I stopped at a wine shop, where I found a bottle of Terre Nere, a Sicilian red I've recently come to love. It's hard to find; maybe it was a sign that my luck would change.

Back at the trailer, I lay down. Peppy lay beside me, licking sweat from my neck.

"We're okay, girl," I said. "We'll make it through. Not clear how or when, but we will."

I forced myself to think about my open investigations in Chicago. First, though, I checked on the ads I'd placed this morning on social media. Five people recognized Clarina under five different names. When I wrote back, asking for particulars, it turned out only one of the five was missing, and I found her readily through a voter registration database. She'd moved to Arizona eighteen years ago and had cut herself off from her family.

Maybe my luck wasn't turning after all. However, I settled down to work. With the butane heater turned on, the trailer was warm enough, but it felt like a cold and lonely place. I was grateful for my dog's presence. I kept a hand on her neck, her warm soft fur a comfort as I verified details on the résumés one of my clients had sent me: both candidates looked too good to be true, including one who claimed to have been a navy SEAL. Maybe not the most common lie in the English language, but a recurring cliché on today's pumped-up résumés. I was tempted to dismiss him out of hand, but I sent a request to the Navy.

I resisted the impulse to drive into town for dinner in a clean well-lighted place. I had my bottle of Terre Nere. I stirred up a mushroom risotto from the supplies I'd bought and made myself eat a large serving. Back in the saddle, V.I., back in the saddle. Client work, regular meals, regular workouts, soon I'd be ready to join the SEALs myself, or at least be able to pay my bills.

At eleven, when I got ready for bed, I studied my reflection in the bathroom mirror. Not so many ribs showing, but what I focused on was a gold pendant Peter had given me, made to his specs in his Institute's Conservation lab. Inanna, goddess of life and death, childbirth, and war, brushed my breasts.

"Your avatar, V.I.," he'd said when he placed it around my neck a year ago.

Inanna was a warrior goddess, he'd explained. When she went into the Underworld to be a goddess to the dead as well as to the living, her shepherd-husband cavorted around on her throne. She made him take her place in the Underworld so that she could return to the land of the living.

"Can you do that?" I asked the small amulet. "Can you return me to the land of the living?"

I sent Peter a text. I never thought of you as the kind of person who would ghost me instead of telling me directly that you were through with our relationship. My words for you: conscientious, wryly humorous, razor intellect, responsible. But that was before Taylor's father shot you. Maybe the shooting, the anguish over your student, reconfigured your character. It did mine. I'm easily depressed, second-guessing myself in ways I never did before. But I am still wearing Inanna. Xxxx V.I.

Right before I turned out the light, I got pinged by the U.S. Navy. My candidate had, in fact, been a SEAL; he'd lost a leg in combat and was transitioning to civilian life. It pays to do your best work even when you think there's no point. What a bundle of wholesome self-advice I was producing. Maybe that would be my new career—creating those little front-of-the-store books that tell you how you, too, could be perfect with a minimal amount of work.

I rechecked responses to my social media ads for Clarina Coffin and again had harvested a handful of duds. I was drifting off to sleep when my phone rang. A handful of friends are allowed to breach my silencing settings. My heart beat faster, imagining Peter, responding to my text. I couldn't find the light switch in the strange room, but I picked up my phone.

Not Peter. Angela Creedy. A stab of disappointment, but Angela wouldn't call at eleven-forty-five on a whim.

"Vic, I know this is a strange time to be calling, and a strange thing to be calling about, but do you have another phone? Can you call me back?"

She hung up before I could answer. I found the light switch and sat up, bewildered, even frightened, fearing she or Bernie must be in trouble.

Another phone. I found a burner in my backpack and called.

"This is crazy and even creepy, Vic, but—but Sabrina's mother is here. She wants to talk to you but she's afraid her calls are being monitored. Bernie's in a match in Ann Arbor, that's why it's me calling."

She handed the phone off to Valerie Granev.

"Ms. Warshawski? I have the engineering skill to tell that someone has planted spyware on my phones. I have three, and they are all contaminated. I need to be quick, before someone figures I'm using this phone and starts monitoring it.

"I'm in Chicago to collect my daughter's belongings. Sabrina is—

she is recovering, I think, I hope, but slowly. She won't be back in school, or anyway, not this school, not for a long while, if ever."

Her voice quavered, holding back tears. She stopped for a beat; I heard Angela urge her to drink something.

"Sabrina is in the best institution in the country for dealing with addiction and brain impairment. We—Ram and I—we couldn't have gotten her in on our own, at least not so quickly, and we couldn't afford to keep her there without help. I—I was asked—told—not to communicate with you, to fire you—after you agreed to help me—us. I told the FBI you had not kidnapped my daughter, that you saved her life, so I hope they're not charging you with a crime.

"Angela told me you have to stay in Kansas because they suspect you of a murder in that same house where you found Sabrina. I'm sorry, sorry my daughter's troubles brought all this grief to you, sorry I can't talk to you directly, but for me, Sabrina comes first."

"Of course your daughter comes first for you, but I also know the Tullohs made a handsome gift to your husband when you fired me. I'm cleaning up a giant mess involving drugs and at least one, maybe two, murders as the thank-you gift I got for saving your daughter's life. I want you to show some gratitude."

"I can't—Sabrina—"

I cut her off. "Tell me what the Tullohs are building on Yancy."

"I don't know. Honestly I don't know. It's nothing to do with avionics, so I'm not on the distribution list. All I can tell you is that the brothers are arguing over it. No one knows what Matthew thinks. Sometimes he talks to Pauline instead of the sons."

She hung up abruptly.

I called back, and spent some time talking to Angela, who was understandably worried by Valerie's behavior. The whole time we were speaking, I could hear Valerie in the background, urging her to hang up before someone traced her to the house.

I turned off the lights, but it was a long time before I went back to sleep.

39

FERMENTED CABBAGE

SOMETIMES MATTHEW TULLOH talked to his daughter instead of his sons, Valerie had said.

The sons both lived in a gated community with their father near the company's Salina headquarters. Of course, being billionaires, they had plenty of other homes. New York and London to be close to financial centers. Palm Springs for golf, Mont Blanc for winter sports, Sardinia for peaceful getaways.

Pauline's main residence was in Mission Hills, a wealthy enclave in Kansas City. Pauline had been married and divorced some years ago. There wasn't any mention of children, while the brothers both had three each. She'd separated herself geographically, at least a little; maybe she'd separated herself enough emotionally that she'd confide in a female PI.

"What should I do?" I asked Peppy. "Cold-call on the phone, at the front door, or a text?"

Peppy pawed at my knee.

"Try her in person, right you are."

It was possible that she was in the family enclave in Palm Springs or the one in Sardinia, but Peppy and I set off for Kansas City in a hopeful spirit. The sky was an eggshell blue, a color that made me feel young and optimistic: spring would be here soon; I would solve Clarina's murder; I'd hear from Peter; I'd figure out if I wanted to end my life as an investigator and take up something new and amazing.

Pauline's mansion was set well back from the road, surrounded by a high iron fence with movable spikes along the top. The road itself was a discreet ribbon in the middle of a large parkway, barely noticeable for the creek that ran alongside it. I let Peppy splash in the creek and chase rabbits across the parkway before shutting her back in the car.

I left the Camry on a nearby cross street and walked back to the Tulloh place. When I buzzed an intercom set into one of the gateposts, a man answered. I explained I was a detective working on the crimes around the Tulloh family's Yancy project and hoped to speak to Pauline.

The man who spoke to me was waiting at the top of the walk. He escorted me around the side of the house to a glassed-in porch overlooking a garden with a pond and ornamental fountain. Pauline Tulloh was inside, sitting cross-legged in a white wicker chaise longue. She was in leggings and an oversize shirt, and her toes in her braided leather flip-flops had been groomed and painted turquoise. The sun picked out a range of colors in her hair, from a dull gold to a glossy brown. It was so expertly painted that it ended up looking fake.

When the man, whose name I learned was Mellon, ushered me inside, Pauline didn't get up, but waved me to a wicker basket chair. Mellon left me at the doorway, but returned almost immediately with a tall glass holding a greenish liquid, which he put on a round table next to Pauline's left hand.

"It's my ten A.M. pick-me-up. Do you want one? Grass, lemon, a little fermented cabbage as an immune booster."

It sounded revolting. "My body would collapse under so much health," I said.

"You're a private detective. Does that mean you want bourbon or rye?"

Mellon's expression remained bland, but he murmured that they also had Sardinian fizzy water or coffee. I was eager to try a billionaire's coffee.

When Pauline lifted her immune boost to drink, I saw a ring, gold, covered with small red stones, on the traditional wedding ring finger.

She saw me staring and laughed. "Such a beautiful ring. When my husband and I parted, I saw no reason to resize it for another finger."

She drank some more fermented cabbage. "What's the Yancy project?"

"I was hoping you could tell me," I said. "Yancy is a hill outside the northwest border of Lawrence. The Kaw makes a loop there and creates a kind of embrace around the hill. A hedge fund owns a big chunk of the hill. Two years ago they got planning permission to build a resort and some shops, but they are putting in an eye-popping power grid. I'd like to know what they're actually building."

Pauline looked into her glass. "I see, yes, I see a power grid, I see trucks. I don't see the Tulloh name."

"Tilt the glass," I said. "Look a bit farther north, to the Kaw and the old Wakarusa Power Plant. It now belongs to your brother Robert."

She held the glass out. Mellon materialized to take it away, returning a moment later with coffee in a small porcelain pot, a porcelain mug, and a little pitcher of cream. I drank some coffee, black. Mellon or whoever staffed the kitchen did a nice job. It wasn't any better than the Hippo's, but the porcelain elevated it to something special.

"And is Robert also in charge of the construction on this hilltop?" Pauline asked.

"I don't know," I said. "He keeps popping up in the area. The FBI was having me deposed for my involvement in saving the life of a young woman whose mother works for your family's company. Your brother showed up in the conference room and ended the interrogation. It was an interesting display of power, a private citizen derailing a federal interrogation.

"Two days ago, your brother Robert showed up outside an old house at the bottom of Yancy, a house that still belongs to one of the original owners of the hill. Robert was chewing out the owner, a man named Brett Santich."

"You think that proves that my brother is the secret owner of the hedge fund?" Pauline asked. Her husky voice was languid, almost mocking.

Being rich means you can ridicule the people around you to derail a conversation you don't like. Being a detective means staying serious and straightforward.

"Your other brother is also interested in some aspect of the Yancy project. Two days after I found Sabrina Granev close to death in that house at the base of Yancy, Jacob seemed to be coaching the Lawrence police chief during a press conference on Granev's health."

"Jake and Robert do like to boss people around," Pauline said. "Mellon, what's Jake's connection to the Lawrence police chief?"

Mellon had been hovering just inside the door. "Jake and Chief McDowell were fraternity brothers at Wichita State thirty-three years ago."

Pauline nodded. "So it's not surprising the chief would welcome Jake's support at a press conference."

"When your brother Robert was arguing with Brett Santich, I overheard part of the conversation. I confess that I only caught a few words, so I may be filling in the blanks wrong, but he thought somebody's sister might 'bitch the whole deal.'"

"Real-life detectives actually do go listening at keyholes." The mockery was more pronounced.

"We're like everyone else—electronic keyholes, and mine wasn't very sophisticated. My recording suggested you resented your brothers and that might lead you to kill the deal."

"Resent? I try not to think about them that much. Daddy didn't want me working in the company. Mother was never involved; she let Daddy make all the decisions, turning her grain elevators into Tulloh gold. He thought that was a good model for me to follow.

"I married one of his rising executives so I could play the good daughter/wife role, but when my husband saw that no outsider would ever have a top job at Tulloh, he left for a start-up. And he left me. And then Daddy bought the start-up and shut it down.

"Since then, I try to pay no attention to anything any of them are doing, but sometimes Daddy still comes around whining because Robert is impetuous and stupid, and Jake is too cautious and also stupid." Her voice hadn't changed pitch or cadence; she might have been talking about what a nuisance it was to clean the birdfeeders that dotted the garden outside the sunroom.

"And has he come around whining about Robert and the Yancy project?"

Pauline studied her fingernails, which, like her toes, were perfectly manicured. "In a general way, he wants the boys to know how important it is to clear the ground of obstacles before you start building. He might have meant there were unexpected problems with the building site, but it could have been metaphoric, of course."

"You know a woman was murdered and left to die in that house on Yancy land."

She gave a sardonic smile. "You think that she might have been an obstacle to the building site? Robert killed her to show Daddy he could remove obstacles?"

"If she was in the way of the project, I expect he would have had someone do it for him."

At that she laughed. "That would be Jake. Robert loves getting his hands dirty."

"Murdering a woman would leave a lot of dirt on your hands. Not all the perfumes of Tulloh Industries could sweeten them. If you could bitch the Yancy project, would you?"

"I don't know what I could do to derail it, assuming it is a Tulloh Industries thing."

"If your father confides in you, I expect you could tell him your brothers are making serious mistakes over in Lawrence."

"Such as?" Her voice hadn't changed, but her face looked alert, cautious.

"The planning commission approved plans for a resort and some shops. But it looks as though they're installing a big power grid, which is perhaps why they bought a coal plant. It would be a resort on the scale of the country of Monaco to require that much power."

"I expect Daddy knows about that," she said. "He likes old coal plants. Coal makes him feel connected to the ground, and the ground is where his fortune comes from—coal, gas, but wheat and sorghum are where he started. He's suspicious of financial instruments that are separate from the land."

"But he must have a huge investment portfolio," I objected.

"Of course. He has a whole building full of portfolio managers. But he likes them grounded in reality. No crypto for him."

"Does your mother have a role in his business decisions? I gather he started with her grain elevators."

"Daddy turned her into a billionaire, while her brothers lost all their land and the elevators their father left them. Why would she regret it?"

"That's definitely what your grandmother Tulloh believed, isn't it?" I said. "Someone recorded her at your parents' fiftieth anniversary party. She was quite gleeful about how badly your mother's family had fared."

"Mother doesn't like conflict. She let Grandmother Tulloh say a lot of things that were hard to listen to. She won't fight with Daddy either, so she sometimes asks me to support—charities—he might not like."

Her hesitation before "charities" made me ask, "Is Brett Santich one of your mother's charities?"

"Santich? Oh, the man you saw Robert arguing with. If Mother knows him, she hasn't shared that knowledge with me. No, there are other people in Lawrence she cares about, but not him. Mellon."

She didn't raise her voice; he appeared at once.

"The detective and I are done here. Can you make sure she leaves the premises, maybe get Johnno to escort her out of the village?"

I got to my feet. "You don't have any role in the company?"

Her smile reappeared, but it was brittle. "I do have a role. I cash dividend checks and admire the boys."

40

"A" STUDENT

COLLECTED PEPPY AND walked with her along the creek bed, trying to decipher Pauline's comments. She had been strangely revealing of her family's dynamics, all delivered in a cool tone that made it sound as though she didn't care. Was I supposed to think we'd been intimate, and so I wouldn't question anything she or her family did?

Then there were comments about her brothers and their different ways of dealing with obstacles. Did she know that Robert had killed Clarina, or was she saying he was capable of doing so? And what about her statement that she gave money to her mother's—charities?

The dog and I had walked as far as a small commercial strip. While I waited in line at a coffee bar, I looked up Mellon on my phone. Geoffrey Mellon, forty-seven years old, had studied social psychology and homeland security at Wichita State University, had worked for a private security firm, then joined Tulloh Industries nine years ago. Doing what was impossible to discover, but he'd clearly proved himself worthy of bringing Pauline her fermented cabbage.

I shared a bagel with the dog as we walked back to the car, but I poured out the coffee. Three dollars and undrinkable. At least I could expense it.

We were just getting into the car when a text came through from Abby Langford, the archivist at the Kansas Origins Museum and Library. The museum's conservator had finished studying the photo I'd found in Clarina's trailer. He wanted to deliver his report in person; could I come in this afternoon?

The museum was seventy-five miles away, but those were Kansas miles, not Chicago. I was in the museum parking lot a little over an hour later.

Abby Langford greeted me at the reference desk with a worried frown. Before we met the conservator, she needed to talk to me about something truly serious that she'd learned only after her earlier message.

"I asked one of my coworkers if there were other materials Clarina looked at which might show what she was working on. I know I told you we protect our readers' anonymity, but in this case I decided to bend that rule.

"We have diaries belonging to dozens of early settlers; Clarina went through many of them during the fifteen months she used our collection. All of us in reference agreed she seemed most interested in one of the last collections she came on. These were the diaries of a Lawrence woman, a Mrs. Florence Wheelock. We were fortunate that the family gifted us with the diaries because Florence wrote in them for close to sixty years."

I made enthusiastic noises. "Fabulous. The Wheelocks were the first people, at least the first European settlers, to claim land on a place just outside Lawrence called Yancy Hill. Yancy is where Clarina's body was found. A current-day Wheelock descendant was at a drug house on Yancy the night Clarina's body was found there. Maybe the diaries can give some background on the Wheelocks' relationship to Yancy. I'd love to see them."

"We'd love to see the diaries, too." Langford's smile was thin-lipped, tight. "There are seventeen volumes altogether, starting in 1858, when Florence was thirteen, and ending in 1919, when she was seventy-four. The three volumes covering 1864, when she married, to 1877, are missing. We believe Clarina Coffin smuggled them out of the library. You didn't see anything in her home that could have been these diaries, did you?"

My heart sank. "If she had them, whoever tore her place apart found them and took them. What do they look like?"

Langford called to a young man sorting books in an area behind the reference counter. He disappeared into the stacks and returned with a trolley holding a collection of old books.

Langford took a box from the trolley and removed a cardboard binder tied shut with string. She opened it to show me a stack of paper, pieces of all different sizes, some with type set on them, some flimsy pages torn from mail-order catalogs. She let me look closely at one of the pages, as long as I didn't touch it. The immature handwriting was full of spelling mistakes.

"When Florence started her diaries, the family had no money, so she wrote on whatever she could find—bills of sale that she picked up on the town streets, things like that. She explains where she's getting the paper, and the paper itself is historically interesting. This carton represents 1859 and 1860, and it's fascinating for what she shows us of daily life while the border wars over slavery and statehood were in full sway.

"Then Florence began making a little money sewing for people in the town, and she bought journals. The first ones were accounting ledgers. I suppose that was what she could find, or what was cheap. She was passionately invested in her own education. She did odd jobs for a local schoolteacher in exchange for personal tutoring in the man's home at night. A lot of her entries from those years are school exercises, practicing her handwriting, composing little essays on U.S. history."

Langford opened one of a trio of large books to show me the accounting headers. The pages were marked off in squares for easy computation. Wheelock had written over the lines, but the ink was faded now, and the squares made it look as though her words were behind bars.

"When she married, and married a man of wealth, she started buying Italian leather-bound books. It's three of these that are missing."

She patted a row of books bound in a soft red leather. The skin had cracked with age. Langford explained that the family hadn't kept them in a controlled environment. She seemed almost as upset by that as by the disappearance of three of the volumes.

Langford wouldn't let me handle them, but she did measure them and let me photograph the fronts, with my flash turned off. The books were about six by eight inches, and perhaps an inch thick. Wheelock hadn't written every day, and as time passed, her entries grew shorter, but it was still an impressive record.

"You think Clarina stole the missing volumes?" I asked.

"She's the only person who's used them in the last five years."

"Could they be mis-shelved?"

Langford clicked her tongue impatiently. "Of course we thought of that, and we've done a thorough search, since my colleague told me they were missing. I'm hoping you can look at the Coffin woman's personal effects. Perhaps she took the covers off to make it easier to smuggle them out."

"In that case, you'd have found the covers here, surely?"

"She could have taken the covers to the women's washroom and put them in the trash there."

"I went through her trailer a week after her death, and the only things I found of interest were the pictures I brought in. As I said, whoever searched her trailer when she died got to them long before I showed up. It's possible the Lawrence police have them—they wouldn't share evidence with me, but they'd talk to you if you called and described what's missing."

Langford nodded and made a note.

I prodded the conversation away from the diaries. "You said your conservator had found something interesting?"

"Of course. And it is interesting. The loss of these journals has me rattled; sorry." She made a phone call, and a few minutes later a short, round man trotted in, carrying a cardboard folder fastened with a string around a button.

"Is this the detective? V.I. Warshawski? Have I pronounced that correctly? I'm Tommy Gellman. Your photograph is unique in my experience, I would say. It's a great pity it wasn't properly preserved, a very great pity." He looked at me sternly.

"It's a great pity that the woman who owned it was murdered," I said. "Thugs who trashed her home are responsible for the damage."

"That is sad. I was hoping you could give me more of a prove-nance. When you looked at it, what did you notice that was unusual?"

I felt I was back in Ms. Ruttan's high school English class, try-ing to cover up the fact that I hadn't read *Return of the Native*. "I did wonder about the flowers in her hair. She looks as though she's in mourning, so the wreath seemed odd. But I don't know anything about fashion history. Were flowers a part of Victorian mourning?"

He beamed. I might get an A after all. "When Queen Victoria ordered her court to mourn Albert's death with her, she decreed that jet was the only jewel that could be worn in court. After that, the demand for jet boomed not just in Britain, but in the States as well. Victoria spawned an industry for mourning jewelry in both countries. Another mourning token that people loved was jewelry made from the beloved's hair. People wore hair rings and brooches as a sign of love, not merely mourning, of course, as you must know if you've read your Austen—" He looked at me severely, and I nodded, pretending I had read my Austen.

"But what Abby thought she saw I've been able to verify. The wreath this woman is wearing is made of hair entwined with artificial flowers. But the hair is from a person of African heritage. A white woman sporting a Black person's hair—likely a man, since you can see the signs of a pregnancy in her waist and in her face—that is extraordinary." His face shone with excitement.

He showed me a magnified segment of the wreath, made as clear as his technology would allow.

I had to take his word for it. I couldn't distinguish the threads of hair from the faded stems of dried flowers.

"You don't have any way of identifying where the picture was taken?" I asked.

He shook his head regretfully. "I'm guessing it was taken by an amateur, a family member, someone like that. Professional photographers usually had their names somewhere on the print, and there's no trace of that.

"The dress looks to be from the 1870s, when the fashion was for hoopskirts to be flattened in front, as this dress is. That's what makes it possible to see the outline of her pregnancy." He used a paintbrush to trace a barely visible bump in the front of the frock. "Any middle-class woman of that era would have owned a dress like this for special occasions, so it's possible she isn't in mourning. Women of ordinary means wouldn't have owned a great many dresses, so this could have been what she wore to any special event, even church services. In those days, getting photographed was a special event."

Abby Langford had mentioned that Florence Wheelock had done sewing to make money. I asked if the picture could be of Wheelock.

Langford said, "We don't have a record of any photographs. Perhaps Coffin found it inside one of the diaries and didn't let us know."

"In which case it's the museum's property," Gellman said.

"We don't know anything about Clarina Coffin," I said. "She hid her identity amazingly in this age of constant surveillance. This could be a picture of one of her own ancestors. It's not mine to gift to you. Until we find out who Coffin is, what brought her to Lawrence, and who this woman is, no one can lay a claim to it. I want it back now so that I can show it to people in Lawrence who may recognize the woman in the picture. I'm also going to put it out on social media."

"Let me keep the original for safety's sake," Gellman pleaded. "I'll give you a high-res copy that you can show around without harming this. My lab can also restore the damage where that little tear is in the print."

I gave a reluctant agreement, demanding a written signed receipt, with the proviso that if I found someone with a legitimate legal claim to the print, the museum had to get their permission to keep the picture. Gellman took me to his office, where he produced the receipt. He also gave me three prints of the woman with the wreath in her hair. He clearly had already planned to keep the original.

Before I left, I asked Abby Langford if Gertrude Perec had used the collection recently. "She's a descendant of Florence Wheelock. If there was something scandalous in the books, perhaps even a reference to who this pregnant woman was—an ancestor whose misstep would sully the good Wheelock name—Ms. Perec might want to hide it."

Langford shook her head. "I double-checked that to be certain. Clarina Coffin was the only person to request these diaries in the last five years."

On my way out, I stopped to look at the donor wall. Gertrude's name was there among the Bookbinders, people who'd given the museum between one and ten thousand. She was listed as Gertrude Wheelock Perec.

41

GERTRUDE AND CADY

SMOKE BUT NO FIRE?

NOW DO YOU understand why it was a mistake to involve that Chicago detective in our affairs?" Gertrude said.

"But, Gram—Frank Karas told her she had to stay in Lawrence."

"He didn't tell you to invite her to live with us. Even though she's moved out, she seems to think she has some kind of special right to barge into this house." Gertrude's lips had almost disappeared, the line of bitterness was so pronounced.

"Because she came around with that picture?" Cady said. "Do you know who it was, Gram? Was that Florence Wheelock?"

Gertrude massaged the sides of her face. Tension had her clenching her jaw so hard that it was painful to move it.

"I don't know who it was. And neither does Pat Everard."

The detective had gone to the Perec house first. Gertrude had told Cady not to answer the door, or at least to tell the detective they had nothing left to say, no more patience for any insults the woman might spew out. Instead, Cady had spoken to her on the doorstep, and then invited her into the foyer.

Cady thought the photograph was exciting. A white abolitionist ancestor six generations back who perhaps had had a relationship with a Black man was remote enough to be romantic, not problematic.

"You know I have several photographs and even a daguerreotype of Great-grandmother Florence. I've shown them to you. This picture the detective is waving around doesn't look the least bit like her," Gertrude said fiercely, after she'd finally forced Warshawski to leave.

"Do you know the diaries Vic was talking about?" Cady asked. "They sound interesting, something we should try to publish."

"My mother gave them to the Origins Museum while I was away at college," Gertrude said. "One of the professors in the history department at the university here had been reading in them for some book he was working on. He persuaded Mother that they were falling apart because we couldn't keep them dry and cool or moist enough or whatever it was. So she gave them to the museum.

"There were many better ways to do it—a loan, for instance. Even if it helped preserve Florence's diaries, Mother lost control over an important part of our family's history by letting that historian into our lives. Once they're inside your house, your life, outsiders think they have a license to control it.

"And sure enough, this Chicago detective came trampling right through our privacy. She dared to ask if I'd gone back to Topeka to take charge of the diaries, if they mattered so much to me. A polite way of asking if I'd stolen them."

"Do you know what ever-so-Great-grandmother Wheelock wrote in the volumes that are missing?" Cady asked.

"Unfortunately, I wasn't interested when I was a teenager. Over the years I've gone to Topeka sometimes to read in them, especially around important celebrations in our town's history. The diaries aren't of universal interest, unless you are wondering how people celebrated marriages or did their housework."

The words were innocuous, but her look was so fierce that Cady didn't ask any more questions.

Pat Everard had come over to commiserate: the detective had gone to her house after she left Gertrude. "Did Ms. Chicago ask you why the Coffin woman would have stolen the books?"

"Oh, yes." Gertrude sighed. "I told her I thought as little as possible about Clarina Coffin when she was alive and wouldn't think of her now if people like this Warshawski didn't keep rubbing my face in her affairs. Anyway, I asked her what those diaries had to do with Clarina's death. She said until she read them she had no idea, but she was checking to see if Clarina came from Skaneateles. She wondered if I was still in touch with relatives there—after almost two centuries!"

"She asked me the same—and she knew my people came from Lynn," Pat said. "It reinforces the argument that what she's doing is simply harassment, not investigation. In fact, after she left my house, I called Deke and told him that he needed to get Frank Karas to either charge her or send her home. He said I made it sound like training a dog: *Go home, Warshawski!*"

Cady suppressed a giggle.

"Then he asked if I could imagine the outcry if he tried to force her or anyone to leave town for the crime of asking two older women questions about their families."

"But he could make it unpleasant for her to stay here," Gertrude argued. "You know, routine traffic stops, searching her car, checking her insurance. Tickets every time she goes a mile over the speed limit."

"Gram! You can't be serious," Cady cried. "Those are all the things we protested the police doing to African-American and Indigenous drivers after Michael Brown and George Floyd! You were one of the strongest voices in that struggle. And, anyway, like Aunt Pat said, Vic didn't ask to stay here. The cops told her to. Or the DA did, at any rate."

Gertrude bit her lips and turned her head.

After a pause, Pat said, "Deke did suggest we get an order of protection. That would force her to stop harassing us. I'm talking to our lawyer in the morning about filing for one. You should, too, Gertrude. And you, Cady."

After Pat left, Cady said, "Gram, I know Clarina talked about those diaries with you and Aunt Pat the morning she came to the women's group breakfast. I was there that morning, remember?"

"Of course I remember," Gertrude said. "She'd been reading a number of different diaries. The Fremantle women kept them, the Entwistles, even Arnie Schapen's great-grandmother, not just Florence Wheelock. The Coffin creature wanted to show me some photocopied pages, but I was too angry with her for inciting the board to fire you to pay attention. I very much doubt if my responding to her inuendoes that morning would have kept her from being murdered. She liked to hint and wink her way around scandal, but it was all smoke if you pressed her."

Cady agreed with Gram—Clarina had shown her photocopies of some diary entries when she was trying to butt in on Cady's syllabus. Not Great-grandmother Wheelock's, but one of the other pioneers, Augusta Fremantle, who wrote contemptuously about Amelia and Sophia Grellier for not keeping their linen freshly washed and ironed. Maybe worth killing over in 1856, but not today.

More troubling was what neither Gram nor Aunt Pat had said this afternoon, either to each other or to Deke, let alone V.I. Warshawski. Aunt Pat had come over the Saturday before Clarina's death, an event so commonplace that Cady didn't linger downstairs after letting Pat into the house. She'd forgotten her phone, though. When she walked back down to the kitchen, Aunt Pat was exclaiming, "She didn't!" and Gram was saying, "I assure you, she did. I told her no one would pay attention to such a ludicrous claim. She said, 'Everyone loves a juicy story, especially one about people who think—'"

Gram paused, then said, "There's no nice way to repeat this. She said people like me who think their shit is clean enough to eat."

Cady's lips had pursed in a silent whistle.

"She said she knew how you and I looked down on her, but by the time our history was splashed all over the internet, we wouldn't be so high and mighty."

And then, three days later, Clarina was dead. And Gram had been at the Dundee House when it happened.

42

AUNTIE KALINA'S TREASURE

BEFORE MAKING DINNER, I checked my ad again. I had another four responses, but again, when I looked up the names, I found the missing people relatively easily. Depressing.

Back in the trailer, I looked into Gertrude's claim that her family had fought for civil rights in Lawrence. Her mother, Maris Clover Wheelock, seemed to have been as involved a citizen as Gertrude. Among other activities, Maris's name appeared in the 1950s and 1960s newspapers for taking part in discussions of segregated housing and public facilities.

Gertrude's own name began popping up in the late 1960s, when the county and university were in the same throes over civil rights, abortion access, and the Vietnam War as the rest of the country. I saw a picture of Gertrude and Maris dedicating the Clover-Wheelock Women's Health Clinic in old East Lawrence.

After her mother's death, Gertrude created a foundation in Maris's memory, which chiefly supported the Clover-Wheelock Health Center. Gertrude gave the town sweat equity by helping run a food pantry, an after-school program for low-income girls interested in STEM, and the town arts council, along with service in elected offices, like the county planning commission.

Gertrude and Pat had received every conceivable civic award available in the county, and many state ones as well. I couldn't imagine any revelations from a nineteenth-century diary that would make them want to kill Clarina Coffin.

But what had brought Gertrude to the Dundee house the night Clarina died there? I couldn't begin to figure that one out, so I went back to my ad. Eleven new responses had come in. Ten were false alarms, but I had a feeling the eleventh was the right one. Lucia Bednarek wrote that she hadn't seen or heard from her sister for almost two years.

"You say she was found dead. If you think there's a reward for finding her, there isn't, but if it's her, I guess I need to make arrangements for her funeral, unless she got married or had a kid, which means she has a closer relative than me."

She'd attached a snapshot of a stocky woman with dark curly hair who stared aggressively at the camera. It was clearer than Zoë's shots in the *County Herald*. Although the woman in the Dundee house cellar had been pale, drained of life, I was pretty sure Clarina was Lucia Bednarek's sister.

I wrote that to Lucia, adding, "I'm not expecting a reward, I'm just trying to establish her identity." I included references, people who could vouch for my not being a scammer, including Deke Everard. "It would be good if we could have a phone conversation, but if you're more comfortable talking to the police, here's the main switchboard number for the Lawrence Department."

I attached a link to the stories Zoë had run about Clarina's death. After a few minutes, Bednarek agreed to a phone call. She was at work; she'd phone in the morning.

I spent a restless afternoon, trying to stay focused on Chicago client reports and not on the clock. I wanted to share Clarina's identity with Murray and Zoë, but I couldn't let that genie out of the bottle until I had complete certainty from Lucia.

I finally took Peppy for a long walk, down to the river, passing the boathouse where I'd hidden the wrench. Why couldn't Lucia Bednarek talk tonight? I fumed, spinning rocks into the river.

Of course, she could be doing the prudent thing, checking my credentials. I walked back to the trailer, stopping for sushi at one of the little carryout places that dotted Sixth Street. I ate it while I watched Mike Shepherd use amazing intuitive leaps to solve crimes in

Brokenwood, New Zealand. He was like so many other modern detectives who solved crimes in an hour or so without a lot of evidence. I wondered if they went to a special detective school where I could take a refresher course: the Zen of detection, something like that.

At ten, as I was getting ready for bed, Lucia called.

"I'm at the Kansas City airport. I thought maybe I should come out in person to see Rickey, or see if it's Rickey, but I don't know where you are or how to get to you."

I was going to suggest a rental car, or perhaps a bus service, but she sounded dejected, maybe scared. I told her I'd pick her up, but to wait in the terminal, since I was fifty miles away.

She called again as I pulled onto the interstate, wanting to know where I was, and yet again fifteen minutes after that. Clarina had annoyed everyone she met; I wondered if that was a genetic trait.

Lucia Bednarek was pacing the sidewalk in front of the terminal when I pulled up. She was a thickset fair woman, very like the snapshot of her sister except for her lighter coloring.

"Finally!" she greeted me. "I've been waiting so long I thought you'd gotten lost."

She was carrying a large suitcase and wearing a puffy coat that doubled her circumference. It took some doing to get her and the coat into the front seat. Peppy, eager to help greet her, didn't make it easier, but Lucia said she didn't mind dogs, she had a dachshund at home.

"My neighbor, she's agreed to come over and feed Jippy and walk him while I'm away. How long do you think I need to stay here?"

"I expect not more than two days. Where did you book a room?"

"I've never traveled like this before," Lucia said. "Not on the spur of the moment, just getting on a plane, like I was in a movie or something. But if Rickey was murdered—I didn't think they'd have gangs in a place like Lawrence. When I read about the town, it didn't sound like a violent place."

"Her death is strange for anyplace," I said. "She wasn't shot, though. Someone hit her on the head."

"She must have made them mad. She was always getting our dad totally pissed off. She made everyone around her mad at her, me included, but especially our dad. She wanted him to change his name, can you believe that? She said 'Bednarek' made people tease her more at school than they already did. They'd yell 'Who wants to take a fat girl like you to bed' and instead of fighting back she'd come home bawling that it was all Daddy's fault, and he should change our last name. Of course he wouldn't, but she changed her first name. Not that I blame her for that. They called her Ulricke, for Pete's sake, after our grandma. She changed it to Rickey."

"Did kids at school make fun of her because your town was called Skaneateles?" I asked.

"Yeah, that, too. She was always kind of stocky, not fat, built pretty much like me. No one ever bothered me like they did her, but in seventh grade, God, makes you glad you only have to be a teenager once! This gang of girls started telling her she should move to Fatty-atlas!

"So then she started telling people she was adopted, and her real family was named Bradshaw and came over on the *Mayflower*. It was embarrassing. She always had a different story about who she was and who her real family was. Sometimes they came over on the *Mayflower*, sometimes they were British aristocrats who had to go into hiding after the Revolution, and so they hid out in the hills around Skaneateles.

"The worst was the time she claimed she was Black, that we had adopted her and wouldn't tell her. See, she was kind of dark-complected and the rest of us Bednareks are blondies. She made a fool of herself at one of the Black historical society meetings. I wished she really had been adopted, it was excruciating.

"Not that I wished her dead, but I didn't miss her when she took off. She'd done it before, been gone once for three years, and then came back because she couldn't keep a job."

"What about the rest of your family?" I asked. "Didn't anyone miss her?"

"It was just the two of us. Daddy's family are mostly in Michigan, and Mother, she only had her own mom and our auntie Kalina. Mother and Daddy are both dead. And no one was friends with Rickey, she was just so weird. Every now and then someone at church asks about her, but no one really noticed she was gone. Or if they did, it was a relief not to listen to her conspiracies about the way Mother and Daddy lied to her about her true identity."

I could feel how embarrassing it must have been to see her sister make a spectacle of herself. Even so, I felt sympathy for Rickey, who felt so different from the people around her that she kept trying to create an alternate version of her life.

"Did she ever claim to be a navy SEAL?" I asked, thinking of the job candidate I'd been vetting.

"What? Why would she do that? She wasn't interested in the navy or physical fitness or any of that stuff."

"What about social justice?" I asked. "The one person in Lawrence who she connected to is a guy who leads protests over environmental issues. He joined her in picketing a school where a teacher was fired for having too woke a curriculum."

"That would be Rickey all right." Lucia sighed heavily. "That summer George Floyd was murdered, it was like Rickey invented Black Lives Matter. She took part in every march, and she filled the living room with posters and literature. Then she started worshipping at this Black church in Auburn."

"Do—did—the two of you live together?" I asked.

"I still live in my folks' house. Whenever Rickey was in Skaneateles, she'd stay there."

We had reached the Lawrence exit of the turnpike. I asked Lucia again where she was staying.

"I didn't know where I was going, I didn't know how to find a hotel. All I was trying to do was figure out how to get to Kansas. And then I had to pay a fortune for traveling at the last minute. I thought they had compassion fares for bereaved people, but can you believe? The airline wanted to see Rickey's death certificate. How could I show them a death certificate when I didn't even know if she was dead? Can't you put me up?"

"I don't live here," I said. "I'm renting a trailer with one bed and no spare sheets. There are a dozen motels in the area; we'll find one with good rates."

"Just for tonight? If there's a couch or something?" Her voice trailed off plaintively. "You're the person who told me my sister is dead. Probably is dead, I think you could give me a little support."

You'd think a private eye with a reputation for toughness and recklessness could put her foot down, but I thought of the journey she'd made. Seeing the dead body of a sibling, even an unloved one, was going to be a shock.

"Just one night. Tomorrow we'll book you into a motel."

When we got to the trailer I asked Lucia if she needed to eat. I half expected her to demand a meal, but she said she'd found food at the Chicago airport where she changed planes. "They had this huge food court. Chinese and Mexican and everything."

She dropped her coat on the couch next to her suitcase. She tossed underwear and a sweater onto the floor, found some pajamas decorated with owls and penguins, and a toiletry bag. She didn't bother to pick up her clothes, just demanded the bathroom.

"I'm on New York time. Beddy-bye for me."

I had left my papers out on the kitchen table and was pulling them together when Lucia put a hand on my arm. "There. That proves it's Rickey."

She was looking at the photo of the woman wearing the floral-hair wreath.

"You know her? Is she one of your ancestors?"

Lucia gave a derisive bark. "In Rickey's dreams. That's what started her most recent outburst. When Auntie Kalina died, Rickey, she thought she'd go through all the papers in the attic to see if there was anything valuable. She found a box of letters and diaries and photos going back to eighteen-hundred-something. Rickey said they were letters and newspaper stories and so on about abolition and slavery. This picture was one of them. So, of course, Rickey got it in her head that we must be related to these abolitionists."

Lucia was gesticulating wildly, slapping her forehead for emphasis. Her pajamas and toothbrush fell to the floor.

"I tried to tell her that our family was still in Kielce, in Poland, during the American Civil War. Auntie Kalina moved into that Skaneateles house when her and Uncle Jarvis came to live in Ska-neateles, and all those papers were probably in the attic when she moved in, but once Rickey made up her mind to some fairy-tale story, nothing could change it."

"I don't suppose you brought any of those papers with you, did you?" I tried to sound casual, not like Peppy with a rabbit in view.

"Rickey took them all when she left. She showed them to me when she first found them, but when I wouldn't believe they belonged to our family, she said she was going to take them someplace where she could prove she was descended from the women in the letters."

Lucia's lips tightened with remembered anger. "She said since I couldn't see the papers for what they were, I'd lost any right to read them. She grabbed them away from me and left the house. I thought she was taking them back to Aunt Kalina's place, but when I didn't see her for a week or so and went over there, the house was locked up.

"Some real estate company in Syracuse was putting the house on the market for this distant cousin who Auntie Kalina left it to. I got the agent to let me in to see if Rickey had left a message or anything, but she hadn't. And all the old papers were gone, too."

"What about the distant cousin—did you ask them if they knew anything about your sister?"

"Please. This is some guy in Arizona who we never heard of. I guess Auntie Kalina looked at how crazy Rickey was and decided to leave the house to someone as far away as possible. She knew I didn't need another house, since I already own the one that belonged to our parents."

Something in her voice made me think Lucia was pretending to take the high road. She may have thought Auntie Kalina should have left the house to her.

I prodded Lucia back to the papers Rickey had found in the attic, to see if she remembered anything from her brief chance to study them.

"The writing was so faded you could hardly make it out, but some woman named Carruthers had been murdered at a school along with the man who ran the school. Whoever was writing the letter said the murders upset her mother so much that the mother was going back to Skaneateles.

"Why Rickey thought that proved anything about our family tree beats me. I'm kind of surprised she didn't call herself 'Carruthers,' since that was the dramatic part of the story. Rickey always wanted the most dramatic role. But Coffin was her favorite pretend great-great-grandmother."

"Why Coffin?" I said.

"There was this woman, Martha Coffin, who lived in our area back during the Civil War, and Rickey was obsessed with her, her and her sister Lucretia. They both had a million children, so Rickey pretended she was descended from them. 'They knew how sisters were supposed to act,' Rickey would say, like it was my fault we couldn't get along." Lucia's face turned red, then she remembered her sister was dead.

"I don't know where this Clarina name came from, unless Rickey stumbled on some other Coffin sister who was called that."

"I think Clarina was a Kansas suffragist and abolitionist." I picked up Lucia's pj's and toothbrush and steered her toward the bathroom.

While she was noisily brushing her teeth, and then showering, I stuffed her sweater and underwear back into the suitcase. I saw she'd packed a black dress and heels, anticipating a funeral.

I opened the couch into a bed. I'd only bought one set of sheets and I wasn't in the mood to share, but I did bring a blanket out for her.

When Lucia saw the sofa bed she was dismayed. She wanted a pillow, sheets, a better mattress.

I gave her my Death Eaters smile. "All those things are available at any of the motels in the area. I'll be glad to drive you to one of them right now, or in the morning as soon as we've been to the morgue."

"Oh, all right," she grumbled.

When I went into the bathroom, I had to remind myself to be thankful that Lucia had answered my ad. She hadn't closed the shower door tightly, and there was a quarter inch of water on the floor.

When I emerged, carrying towels heavy with water to the kitchen sink so they could drain overnight, Lucia said, "It's freezing in here. Can't you turn up the heat?"

"It's as high as it will go. Socks will help. And your coat."

43

THE SERGEANT'S SOFTER SIDE

DESPITE HER COMPLAINTS about the couch, Lucia slept heavily, and loudly. I shut the door between the bedroom and the living area, but the walls were thin, and Lucia's snoring kept jerking me awake. The first time, around one in the morning, I sent a text to Deke Everard.

> I've found someone who thinks she can identify Clarina Coffin.
> Is Coffin's body in the Kansas City Medical Exam facility? Do you
> want to ride over with us in the morning?

I switched my phone off; Deke would call as soon as he read the message and I wanted as much sleep as Lucia's saw blades allowed.

In fact, Deke, or actually Peppy, woke me at eight. He was pounding on the trailer, which sent her into a frenzy of barking. I pulled on a pair of jeans under my sleep shirt and staggered to the door, Peppy at my heels, keeping up her warning.

Lucia was sitting up on the couch. "Can't you shut up that dog? I'm trying to sleep."

"You'll have a better time tonight when you're in your motel bed." I opened the door and let in the sergeant.

He was wearing the frown that had become his permanent greeting to me. "This had better be on the level, Warshawski."

"Good morning, Sergeant. I'm glad to see you, too. Come in and meet Lucia Bednarek, who thinks Clarina may be her sister."

I stepped aside to let him enter. Peppy, uncomfortable with the tension in the room, was growling softly, hackles raised. I kept a hand on her head. "Easy, girl. He can't help himself, but he isn't going to hurt us."

"You can't let a man in here," Lucia screeched. "I'm not dressed."

Deke walked over to the couch. He crouched next to Lucia and spoke in a soft warm voice that I'd never heard.

"My apologies, Ms. Bednarek. I'm Deke Everard. I'm a sergeant with the Lawrence police. Warshawski here texted me that she'd found you, but she wasn't answering her phone. I didn't know I'd have the pleasure of meeting you first thing this morning. If Clarina Coffin was your sister, I'm sorry for your loss. I'm sorry, too, that we have to ask you to identify her body."

Lucia blossomed under his tender manner. "That's okay, officer. I'll just be glad to have some closure with my sister. And I'm grateful to this other detective tracking me down. Like I told her, my sister was always making up stories about herself and using fake names, but her real name was Ulricke Bednarek, except she changed it to Rickey."

"Of course until you see her, we won't know for sure the dead woman is your sister," Deke said. "Why don't you put on some clothes so we can drive over to Kansas City and get this ordeal out of the way. Warshawski, you come outside with me. We'll chat in the car while Ms. Bednarek is dressing."

"Sure, Sergeant." I produced a Little Miss Sunshine smile. I was carefree and openhearted, not frowny and mean like Deke. "I just need shoes and socks."

And to brush my teeth and wash my face. I did all these things at a leisurely pace. Deke's frown deepened and Lucia cried out to hurry it up, she needed to get into the bathroom.

When I finally went outside, Peppy came with me, sticking close to my legs. A fine freezing mist was blowing. Deke's unmarked car had a grille between the front and back seats, which didn't allow room for the dog to get in with me. I insisted on staying outside with her, which didn't improve the sergeant's temper.

"How did you get on to this woman, what is her name? Bednarek?"

"It was an inspired guess." I told him what Trig had told me, about Clarina's having been bullied over her weight and her town name. "There was a newspaper article Clarina had studied, dating back to the 1860s, about one of the abolitionists coming from Skaneateles, but until I heard your aunt Gertrude say the name out loud, and say that her own family had come from there, I didn't know how to pronounce it. I ran an ad on social media; Lucia Bednarek responded. She decided to fly out on the spur of the moment yesterday evening."

"And you couldn't tell me you'd made this Skaneateles connection?"

"I figured you knew all these things, since you grew up hearing these stories from your mom and Aunt Gertrude. As for the guess to try Skaneateles, I could see you roll your eyes if I asked you to believe something Trig said."

He bit his lip and looked away.

"I was pretty sure she was Clarina's sister," I added, "but I wasn't going to notify you until I was convinced. I didn't want another lecture on hotdogging or wasting police resources."

"I'll bite: What made you believe her?"

"When she came into the trailer last night, I had a photo on the table that she recognized."

"Photo of Clarina?"

"No. It was one that Clarina had found in a great-aunt's attic, supposedly with a cache of documents that dated to the Civil War. The sisters had argued over their provenance—Clarina thought they were papers from her family, Lucia says they belonged to whoever originally owned the house.

"When Clarina took off for Lawrence, she seems to have brought all those papers and photos with her—she kept making veiled hints to Cady and to your mother and Gertrude about evidence she had of Lawrence's history. Anyway, I found the photo in the trailer where Clarina had been living."

Deke slammed his right fist into his palm. "Why am I only hearing about this photo and the attic and crap for the first time? What did you do with all the papers you found? Concealing evidence in a murder investigation is a crime!"

Peppy gave a warning bark: *Don't slug V.I.* I thought uneasily of the wrench I'd sent to the Cheviot lab in Chicago. My excuse to myself was that I wasn't sure the wrench was evidence of a crime. Plus Deke had impounded my car, as if he thought I really was a criminal. I stayed confrontational.

"It's okay, girl. He's frustrated that I figured out something he couldn't. Sergeant, I was third in line at Clarina's trailer. Someone had searched it with a violent hand. Then your crew went in. And then me. This photo, which was an original, not a copy, was there, along with blurry printouts of newspaper photos dating to the 1860s. These were the scraps you and the intruders left behind."

I paused, still smiling, to give him a chance to acknowledge his crew had been sloppy. He didn't say anything.

"Either your crew or the first intruders had taken all the other documents. I had only those three pictures, so that's where I started. At the Origins Museum and Library in Topeka, they dug up the newspaper article for me, the one Clarina had found. They couldn't identify the photo, but they gave me some provenance for it. I showed it to your mother and to Ms. Perec yesterday—didn't your mom tell you about it?"

"I do not consult with my mother on active investigations."

"You just show up when the water is getting a little hot? Your mother and Ms. Perec are sitting on a secret. Do you know what that is?"

"A figment of your imagination," he said grimly. "You're harassing them because you can't justify—" He cut himself short, remembering in the nick of time that I had probably identified Clarina Coffin. "My mother wants to file an order of protection against you."

"Right. That will help protect her and Ms. Perec from me consulting with them as I uncover more information about Clarina's death. Rickey, I should remember to call her."

We were both getting wet. And cold. The dog was, too, but she didn't seem to mind. Deke wasn't going to show any weakness, such as admitting that standing in freezing rain is not pleasant, so I suggested he might like to look at the photo.

"Hopefully Lucia is dressed by now, but you can wait on the step if you're worried."

He followed me in without saying anything, but once we were inside, his professional manner returned. He smiled at Lucia, said they'd stop for something to eat on their way to Kansas City.

I handed Deke the print that I'd left on the table. "Does she look familiar to you?"

"She's old, Warshawski, not someone I would have met before."

"In a family photo album, I'm thinking."

"Unthink it. I have not seen this picture before. Tell me about it, Ms. Bednarek. This was among your sister's possessions, right?"

Lucia started the same saga I'd heard last night. Peppy followed me into the bedroom where I changed out of my wet clothes.

Lucia had used the bedroom to dress. Her penguin pajamas were on the floor, along with the socks she'd slept in. I kicked them to the door. I'm not much of a housekeeper, but it annoyed me that Lucia thought her role as chief mourner entitled her to fill up my space.

I hung my own damp clothes over the baseboard where the heat came into the room and put on dry ones before checking my phone: it had been dinging with incoming texts while I'd been outside with Deke.

Leo Knaub, my account manager at the Cheviot forensic lab, had left five messages, demanding that I call ASAP. I have company, I wrote back. Give me ten minutes.

When I went back to the main room, Lucia had gotten as far as Great-aunt Kalina and the papers in her attic, and why Rickey thought she had a right to stuff that belonged to them equally.

Deke was saying, "You said no one in your town liked her much. Would someone have followed her out here to kill her?"

"After she'd been gone two years?" I said. "I suppose it could have taken that long to track her down. She seems to have been quite skillful at avoiding surveillance."

"She rubbed people the wrong way with all her make-believe," Lucia said. "People didn't want her around, but it's not like she threatened them. At least, I don't think she did. . . ."

Her voice trailed off uncertainly. "Do you think she was maybe blackmailing someone? And she ran away under a fake name to keep them from killing her?"

"Before we worry about killers from Skaneateles, why don't we drive to the morgue and make sure that Clarina really is Rickey Bednarek," I said.

"*We* aren't driving to the morgue. I'm taking Ms. Bednarek. And I don't want to see you in my rearview mirror. If Ms. Bednarek wants to tell you about it when I bring her back, that's her business."

"I'm sure Lucia is going to want to give media interviews," I said. "And she's going to want to be someplace more comfortable than this trailer, with its one bathroom, and a shower that floods the floor if you don't close the door just so."

I stuffed Lucia's pajamas and socks into her suitcase, found the ziplock bag for her toiletries, and put her toothpaste and makeup into it, and forced the case to close.

Lucia watched me, squawking. "Those are my things! Now my pajamas are going to get all wet. And my funeral outfit!"

"Sergeant Everard will help you check into a motel when you get back from Kansas City. It will be so much easier if you already have your case with you."

I took her picture and forwarded it to Zoë. Lucia Bednarek from Skaneateles. Probably Clarina's sis.

Zoë replied instantly. Is she with you? I'm coming straight over.

I wrote back, Deke's here, about to take her to KC to see the body. I'm disinvited.

Even before they were out the door, Deke's phone rang. He looked at the screen, then back at me. "You sicced Zoë on me? Do you need to win every confrontation you're in?"

"Only when my expertise is disrespected."

44

WRENCHING PROBLEMS

THE TRAILER FELT more depressing than ever. Between my damp clothes and the towels Lucia had soaked, the place smelled like a wet sheep. I took everything to a Laundromat and left them to wash while I went on to the Hippo.

I sat in my favorite spot, on a stool in the window, and drank my first coffee while staring at nothing. My shoulders relaxed; at my feet, Peppy curled up around her empty milk bowl and fell asleep. We'd both been too stressed lately.

When I'd ordered a second cortado, I called Leo back.

He got straight to the point. "There's a DNA match between blood traces and hair on that wrench, and a DNA request filed two weeks ago by the Lawrence Kansas police. If this wrench is evidence of a crime, our lab can't hold on to it. It needs to be with the police or the FBI ASAP. In addition to the hair, we found microscopic traces of scalp tissue. If you're not going to take care of reporting these items, Cheviot will."

"Did you find fingerprints on the wrench?" I asked.

"Nothing usable. The surface doesn't hold prints well, and too many hands had been touching it, some in gloves."

"Leo, I found this wrench underneath a garbage can in the apartment I was renting. It had been put there in the hopes that the cops would find it and arrest me for Clarina Coffin's murder. I was hoping it was a red herring, but sent it to you to find out one way or another."

"Now you know. And that means you act now. If not, Cheviot will terminate our relationship with you."

"Do you want to send it directly to the Lawrence police?" I asked. "I have the address here."

"Of course—" he started, then stopped, imagining the legal headaches if they sent this out of the blue to the LKPD. Cheviot investigators spend half their lives in court, testifying on forensic evidence. It wouldn't do their own reputation a lot of good to explain why they'd had the wrench in their possession for the better part of a week without notifying the cops. They could blame it on me, but that would not only add to their days in front of a judge, trying to exculpate themselves, but it would also end my relationship with them. Other, more important clients would hesitate to send them confidential projects when word leaked out through my connections that they'd screwed with me.

"You are a piece of work, Warshawski," he finally said. "Do I send this to you or your lawyer?"

"I'm in Kansas, Leo. Give me five minutes to get an address for you."

I called Lou. "You know how you told me you and Ed like to accessorize?" I asked, after a hurried catch-up. "I'm ordering accessories online. Could I have them delivered to you?"

"What are we talking about?"

"Mmm. Something like punk metal jewelry."

"That's what I like to hear. Me and Ed, we've been eating our hearts out, longing for that heavy-metal look, and we're the guys who can carry it off. Send it to the yard; we're there in business hours more than we're home."

When I called Leo back with the scrapyard address, he told me I'd have the wrench Monday morning. "If we don't see a report that it's in law enforcement hands by Monday night, you and I will be having a very serious conversation."

"Copy that," I said. Forty-eight hours, roughly, until I needed the wrench in the LKPD's hands, with proof I could share with Leo. Piece o' cake.

I was gritty-eyed from my short night's sleep, but too restless to go back to the trailer to try for more. Although the sky was still overcast, the drizzle had ended. I walked with Peppy back to the Laundromat to put my linens in a dryer.

Before turning to my Chicago clients, I remembered another distraction: I had to let Murray know I'd discovered Clarina's identity—he wouldn't forgive me if he learned it from the wires first.

Murray was impressed by my investigative skill, but asked if knowing Clarina had been born as Ulricke Bednarek gave me a reason for her murder.

"I suppose it's possible," I said. "If her sister can be believed, everyone in Skaneateles despised Clarina. I'm focusing more on Lawrence. Do you want to go to New York and track down whoever she'd most annoyed?"

"If you'll pay first-class airfare," Murray said.

"I'm not paying any airfare at all. This case has already put me several grand in the hole just for legal fees."

I told him about my meeting with Pauline Tulloh. "She discussed her family's dynamics in a cool impersonal way. I wondered if that was a deliberate distraction—you know, show the audience how the billionaires bicker, keep their attention away from the important acts on the other side of the stage."

"Those being?"

"Whether her brother engineered Clarina's, or Rickey's, death. The most genuine thing she said was that her mother asks Pauline to support charities that she knows her husband won't approve of. It sounded as though charities might mean indigent friends and relations."

"You know, Warshawski, you should hire yourself out to a pest management company. People want to know if they have rats or roaches or whatever, and you just stand in the middle of their living room. Pretty soon, every vermin within a mile will come charging out to get you. No one in Lawrence cared about that hill or that house or even the drug sales until you came along."

I wasn't sure if that was a compliment or the most unpleasant criticism I'd ever endured, but when we hung up, I finally buckled down and cleared up the skimming that one of the partners was doing to the accounts at a law firm I work with. Put the report and a bill in an email. I entered my time sheet against the four thousand dollars Valerie Granev had paid me. I was about sixteen hundred down.

Zoë called as I was on my way back to the Camry to collect Peppy. She had made it to the morgue in Kansas City in time to intercept Deke and Lucia in the lobby.

"Clarina is Lucia's sister, all right. They look amazingly alike, even though Clarina was dark and Lucia is so blond, but it's not just that, it's that they have the same whiny-aggressive attitude."

She hesitated, then said in a rush, "I know you feel too many people are counting on you, but you are amazing. You figured out Clarina must have come from Skaneateles. And, guess what, Ben Pike, my two-fisted tightwad of an editor, agrees that the story will sell, so he's paying to send me to New York to get background on Clarina. Ulricke. I don't know if I'll ever get used to calling her that. Anyway, if I were in the room with you, you'd get the biggest hug you ever got in your life."

I laughed. So much better to hear than being called a pest magnet. "When do you leave?"

"First flight to Syracuse tomorrow morning, by way of Chicago. Want me to stop and say hi to any of your friends during the layover?"

"Call them all and tell them that thanks to me, you're the next Martha Gellhorn."

The dog and I walked down a side street to my favorite sandwich shop. I was going to take lunch to a park so I could eat outside with her.

The air was cold but not unbearable; I had my heavier coat over a hoodie, and Peppy was wearing fur. As we crossed Massachusetts Street, a Porsche revved its engine and turned in front of us, rubber squealing, missing us by a hair. I pulled Peppy against my legs and watched the Porsche go down Seventh Street, past the Lion's Heart, then turn the corner toward the municipal parking lot.

Peppy and I followed. The Porsche was in the lot, close to the Lion's Heart back door. The engine was running with that deep thrumming good sports cars make when they're idling. I put the sandwich down so I could use my phone to take his picture. The weedy-looking kid whom Zoë had photographed dealing out the back door emerged. He looked furtively around, didn't see any cops, and handed over an envelope. Trevor gave him one in return.

I walked over as he was getting into the car. "Trevor!" I cried in a hearty voice. "Good to see you again."

He looked up, startled. He'd posted my photo on his trolling messages, but he was the kind of jerk who didn't actually register women's faces, probably not women his own age, let alone someone old enough to be his mother.

"We keep meeting in parking lots," I said. "First at your fraternity, and now down here. I have a nice video of you and your buddy at the Lion's Heart. I'll be sharing it with Sergeant Everard at the LKPD."

He took a step toward me, fists balled, expression ugly, but a cluster of shoppers passed us on their way to their cars. He climbed into his ride, slamming the door hard, made a great show of gunning the engine.

I pulled Peppy away as he roared out of the lot and saw she had her nose in my lunch bag. I yanked her head out of it.

"Is this your payback for taking you far from home? Stealing food?" I asked.

She wagged her tail doubtfully.

"Yep. My bad, leaving it on the ground."

I walked back around the corner, past the bar again, on my way to get another meal. It was the lunch hour, and more people were starting to show up for noon-day drinks. I was crossing the street to keep the dog away from the crowd when someone else I recognized went into the Lion's Heart. Brett Santich. I was tempted to tell him he'd missed young Trevor, but decided it would be more interesting to see if he was meeting someone. I trotted back to the library so I could leave Peppy in the car while I checked out the bar.

The room was full enough when I got there that no one paid special attention to me. My prey was at a corner table near the kitchen where he could see the room. He seemed to focus on each newcomer for a few seconds, deciding on friend, foe, or neutral, so I didn't stare but wandered to the bar to order a drink. I don't much care for beer, but it seemed the easiest way to blend in. I ordered a Free State, since that was the local brew Zoë had drunk, and took it to a corner where I could stand looking at my guy without seeming to.

Don Wilton, the Lion's Heart owner, came out from the kitchen and sat down with Santich. The two men didn't seem to be talking as much as waiting—every time the front door opened, they'd look over and then shrug. After ten minutes or so, their party arrived: they both sat up straighter, and Wilton gave a half wave.

They were joined by a tall tanned man in pressed jeans and cow-boy boots, wearing a Stetson and a fringed leather jacket over a sweat-shirt that advertised Wichita State University basketball. Not Robert Tulloh. The other brother, Jacob.

Jacob Tulloh with Don Wilton. I felt like one of those cartoon characters whose hair stands on end after an electric shock. The Wilton family, those losers who lost their share of the family grain elevators while Matthew Tulloh turned his wife's into a massive fortune. Grandmother Tulloh cackling over the losers at Emmaline and Matthew's fiftieth anniversary.

The Wiltons were the charity Pauline Tulloh supported for her mother, her hapless siblings and nephews. An angel bailed out the Lion's Heart in the depths of the pandemic. Grandma Tulloh would have forbidden any money going to the Wiltons, but Pauline helped her mother help her cousins.

Jacob Tulloh and Lawrence police chief Rowland McDowell were old pals going back to their college days. If Santich was useful to the Tullohs in their Yancy dealings, Jacob would see that he wasn't harassed by the local law.

The trio headed for a narrow staircase rising behind the kitchen door. I hadn't noticed it before and went over to look.

The barman appeared at my side. "What are you doing here?"

I smiled. "Admiring the architecture."

"You've admired it long enough. Pay for your beer, which you haven't drunk, and get out."

I paid for my beer and left, the bartender close behind me. I closed the door slowly so that I could check the lock mechanism. Unlike the upper floor, Wilton used a standard keypad lock, easy to bypass. The bar had an alarm system. Harder to bypass, but not impossible.

45

ROOKIE MISTAKES

I TEXTED DEKE THE videos I'd made of Trevor with my peeper at the Lion's Heart. "Not saying they were dealing drugs. Just envelopes, maybe love letters. Hope you had a meaningful trip to the morgue with Lucia."

I was whistling a little under my breath as I reached the Camry, feeling smug. My finger was on the key's unlock button when I was jumped. Arm around my neck, chokehold. Reflexes: stomp on the foot behind me. Hit steel-toed boots. Drop arms and head. Elbow into rib cage behind me, teeth into arm, snarl of "fucking bitch," and a sharp pain, back of the head, on my hands and knees, unable to resist the thick arms lifting me, slinging me into an SUV.

I never completely lost consciousness, but by the time I recovered enough to know what was happening, we were on the interstate, moving fast. My wrists were crossed in cuffs underneath the seat belt. I smelled of sick, a dribble down the front of my hoodie. I hadn't eaten lunch, not much to throw up.

Two figures were in the front, separated from me by a plexi panel. The high headrests meant I couldn't make out their shapes.

Peppy. My dog, locked in the Camry, she would be so scared. I had abandoned her, I'd brought her to Kansas with me, and she would die in the car while I died on a remote river path. Helpless tears trickled into my nose and made me sneeze.

"She's awake."

I knew the voice, struggled to put a name to it. The driver grunted. "You hit her too hard."

"Bitch had her teeth in my arm."

"Tell Mr. T that when he can't get sense out of her."

Geoffrey Mellon. Pauline Tulloh's perfect Jeeves, doubling as a hitman. The car hit a pothole, jolting me; the figurine of Inanna bounced with me, hitting my breastbone inside my clothes.

Warrior goddess, life, death in her hands. No sniveling. Use the weapons you have, the strength you have. Do not die without a fight. I slid my cuffed hands to my left and unlocked the seat belt. Slowly. The driver could see me in the rearview mirror. Quick and sudden moves would catch his eye.

I leaned back in the seat, eyes shut to slits, moaning softly. Caught his gaze in the mirror. He watched my head lolling with the car's motion, a satisfied nod, back to watching the road.

My phone was in my hip pocket. I slid my hands around to the right side. Edged it out. Text to Lou and Ed. *Dog at library. Kidnapped.*

The driver stood on the brakes with a great screeching. I was flung forward, managed to turn sideways, got my knees to take the hit.

"Bitch has her phone. You worthless moron, why didn't you search her?"

"You're the one who shoved her in the car, said we had to get going," Mellon said.

The driver came around and wrenched the door open. I put every muscle I had into my kick, getting him square in the belly. He wanted my phone, he was not going to have my phone. He leaned over me and I jerked my cuffed hands up under his chin. His head whipped back. I kicked again. Mellon came at me from the other side, grabbed my phone.

A car stopped behind us, a woman's voice worried: Was anything the matter? Should she call for help?

The doors slammed shut on my outcry.

"Sick dog, getting her to the vet, she's pretty wild," Mellon said. "She got herself tangled in her collar back here but we're okay now."

We took off again. The driver was furious about his neck; he was going to be in a brace for a week, for sure. The bitch, meaning me, was going to pay for sure. "And we're behind schedule as it is with all this crap going on. Jacob is having fits, wants to pull the plug."

"Robert will keep it going," Mellon said. "Jacob is so cautious he won't cross the street on a green light. Pauline is twice the man he is, but the old man won't see she's the one who should be on the board."

Bitch was going to pay, all the crap going on. I recognized that voice. He was behind schedule. When he bent over me, I'd seen the .358 in his belt. The crew chief I'd encountered on top of Yancy.

I shut my eyes, rocked with the rocking of the car, tried not to focus on my throbbing head, my longing for water, tried not to worry about Peppy. Someone would see her in the car, someone would trace the car to Lou and Ed, she'd be okay. Would a runner find my bones while they could still be identified? Would Peter be grief-stricken when he heard about it?

We rocked and rolled for more than an hour before the car came to a gentle stop. I braced myself for battle again. The driver opened the window.

"You have a permit for this lot?" a woman asked, sticking her head in, and then, "Oh, Mellon, didn't know it was you."

Mellon exchanged a few good-natured words with the woman. She released a barrier and we passed a sign saying we were entering the private parking lot for Tulloh senior staff, permit required. The sun was setting, glinting an orange light from the building directly in front of us. It felt like fire to my aching eyes.

Mellon seized my right arm, yanked me out of the backseat, undid my cuffs and refastened them behind my back. The driver came over to face me, hand turned flat. I pulled my chin to my chest a nanosecond before he delivered an upward chop. He hit my nose. Blood spurted out on his hand and jacket. He swore, swung his arm to hit me again. I went rubber legged and he chopped the air.

"Enough, Chet," Mellon said. "The old man is waiting, and you look a mess now, covered in blood."

Chet swore, called me a list of tired insults, grabbed my left arm and propelled me forward at a pace close to a run. I pounded along next to him. Each footfall felt as though my head were being hit again.

We jogged past the Tulloh campus, rows of long low buildings fanning in a semicircle around the main structure, the glass building that was sending out orange sparks in the setting sun.

We landed inside, stopping at a lobby counter whose curves mirrored the lines of the front of the building. The woman sitting there greeted Mellon by name.

"This is the woman Mr. T wants to talk to?" she said. "What happened to her?"

"Chet got a little carried away," Mellon said. "He may have broken her nose."

"Fucking bitch tried to break my neck," Chet said. "And now she's bled all over me."

"They're expecting you on the bridge," the woman said. "Chet Bezory, you should clean the blood off before you go up. Mr. T doesn't like his employees to look scruffy."

"Scruffy is okay for me?" I asked her.

She looked at me for the first time. Her lips curved in a sneer. "You'll do just fine."

"The bridge?" I said to Mellon. "As in on top of the warship overlooking the expanse of empire?"

Mellon grunted and urged me forward with a hand between my shoulder blades. Only James Bond starts a successful fight in the heart of enemy quarters. I let him get away with it. "You'd do the same, right?" I said to Inanna.

"I'd do the same what?" Mellon demanded.

I'd spoken out loud. Careful, Warshawski. You cannot lose your wits, not when you're about to meet Mr. T.

"As Pauline," I said. "You'd help your mother, save her from your father, right? Help her fund one of her loser cousin's bars? Did you report that little subterfuge to Mr. T? Does Pauline know you don't respect her privacy?"

"You talk too much."

We'd reached an elevator. He swiped the control panel with a card from his back pocket. There were two possible destinations, G and 4. We were going to 4.

The bridge covered the front third of the building, as nearly as I could tell. An amber glass box set against the back wall was apparently

Tulloh's lair. Mellon shoved me onto a straight-back chair and went into the box.

The floor in front of me held open-plan cubicles. Even though it was a Saturday afternoon, most of the desks were taken. I wandered over to see what people were working at so hard.

The cubicles didn't have ceilings, but the walls blocked noise from other parts of the floor. I peered into one filled with monitors that showed security prices from Shanghai to Rio. Pride of place went to the Chicago Board of Trade. That wasn't surprising, since Tulloh's chief business was in commodities. It made me homesick, though, to see the CBOT logo on the screen.

Another cube held a squad of young people doing something intense at computers. Along one wall, a bank of monitors showed the premises, flashing pictures from the different outbuildings, including the cafeteria and the chapel.

After staring at the screens for several minutes, I realized I wasn't looking only at the Salina headquarters, but at Tulloh operations around the world. I saw a couple of men taking a cigarette break in what the monitor identified as west Texas. A loudspeaker adjured them to get back inside and back to work. A couple in Riga were caught embracing. It was sickening, terrifying. Did employees not know they were under constant surveillance?

Coworkers spoke in low murmurs if they spoke at all. No music was piped in, but most employees sported earbuds. I wondered if that let them listen to their own music, or if it was to make them constantly available for phone calls.

I found a woman's toilet tucked in behind Mr. T's amber box. It was a difficult business, pulling my jeans down with my hands behind my back. A woman came in as I was struggling to hoist them back up.

"They're looking for you!" she cried. "What are you doing in here?"

"Peeing," I said. "I didn't think they'd appreciate it if I squatted on the office floor."

"Don't you know how big a mistake it is to keep Mr. T waiting? Get out of here now."

"I know you're nervous, but it would be such a good deed if you'd get my pants up for me before I scurry in to face the terrifying Mr. T."

She made a face, wrapped her hands in paper towels, and nervously yanked my jeans into place and did up the zipper. She tried to hustle me out of the room, but she didn't have Mellon's upper body strength. I stopped to look at myself in the mirror over the sink.

My face was shocking. Blood from my nose had splashed up onto my cheeks and into my hair from the speed walk I'd been forced to do. I'd been hit on the back of the head; it had bled into my hoodie. Real blood. Taylor's blood, Clarina's blood, blood everywhere. I swayed, room swooping black.

You will not faint, you will not be weak in front of these monsters.

Yes, warrior queen. Upright into battle, battle until the end.

46

THE WANT BONE

MATTHEW TULLOH WAS sitting behind an old-fashioned wooden desk, the kind with two sides and lots of drawers and pigeonholes. He was dressed for the range in cowboy boots, an open-necked shirt, and jeans. His face was sunburned, except for the top inch or so of his forehead, which looked almost white in contrast. Presumably he wore a cap in the sun, but it was disconcerting to look at him, as though he'd started to put on clown makeup and stopped partway through.

He stared at me. "Don't like to see blood on a woman's face. Unfeminine. You been fighting my men, huh? Not feminine at all."

"I got my period on the drive over," I said. "Nothing more feminine than menstrual blood."

His mouth twisted in disgust. "Potty-mouthed, too. Hate that in a woman."

"Bullying," I said. "I hate that in everyone, including you and your vassals."

"You're not in a position to hate anything about me, missy. You're here by my orders, you'll leave if I say you can and when I say you can. You talk to me respectful, or Mellon here will make sure you do."

Old-fashioned wicker chairs were grouped around a table to one side. I moved over and sat in one of them.

"Didn't say you could sit, either," Tulloh snapped.

I didn't try to respond. My arms were aching from having my

hands cuffed behind me. My head was aching, I was seeing double. I couldn't waste energy sparring with Tulloh.

He brooded for a few minutes, then said, "You've been looking into that Coffin woman's death, right? Except her name wasn't Coffin."

I didn't say anything.

"So what have you found out?"

"She was hit on the head. She died."

"You've been at it for two weeks. I know you've found more than that."

"I'm sure you know everything I do and more besides, Mr. Tulloh. Her birth name was Ulricke Bednarek. She was a history buff and a gadfly. She died in circumstances stranger than her name, in the cellar of an abandoned house at the bottom of Yancy Hill."

"Come, come, Ms. Warshawski, don't pretend to be stupid or naïve. You discovered her name when the Lawrence police were stymied."

"News travels quickly," I said.

"Small towns, everyone knows everything quicker than you can say Google," he said. "What's your interest in her death?"

"With news traveling so quickly, I'd think you could answer that already."

"I'm hearing a lot from Lawrence these days. You've riled up some leading ladies in the town, suggesting they're hiding secrets about the project on top of that hill. What's it called?"

Mellon supplied the name.

"Right. Yancy. The police say you're snooping around a mothballed coal plant, and asking about that project on top of Yancy. I know those things, but no one can tell me why you're poking so many rattlesnakes."

"You told me not to be naïve, Mr. Tulloh. Don't you act like a senile fool when we both know you're not."

Behind me I heard Mellon's quick breath—I was poking the king of all rattlesnakes.

"You keep track of everything happening in Lawrence. You have a pet FBI agent who tells you what's happening on the justice side, and your son Jacob's buddy, the Lawrence police chief, fills you in on the law side, on how the investigation is going. No one knows why

Clarina-Ulricke was murdered. She claimed she knew things about the land your company is building on. She claimed she knew things about the families that used to own the land. If the police have found any evidence that backs up those claims, I'm sure they've told you. They haven't told me."

"But what have *you* found?"

"Your wife's nephew is dealing drugs out of his bar," I said. "He maybe helped supply the drug parties out on Yancy land."

He breathed faster, his face contorted in angry lines. "Pauline propped up that loser, thought she was doing her ma a favor. Well, Emmaline knows what a bunch of blood-sucking leeches her brothers and their spawn are. She tried talking sense into Pauline, but Pauline keeps bailing them out because she knows it raises my blood pressure. Same reason she went to that pinko school in Lawrence instead of Wichita State like her brothers and most decent people. And she wonders why I don't want her hands on the company controls!"

I looked at Mellon. "So whatever Pauline does, you report back to Daddy. I'm sorry I fought against coming out here: this is fascinating. A company doing business in a hundred and four countries, worth hundreds of billions of dollars, and the owner still is crawling around in the details of his daughter's life."

"Of course I am." Matthew was contemptuous. "You never had children yourself. One marriage you couldn't handle, and a bunch of lovers you can't commit to, a woman like you can't begin to understand the importance of family."

My mother, fierce, protective of me after losing most of her own family to the death camps. My father's love spread around me like a warm cloak. My cousin Boom-Boom and I, going to the wall for each other. I wasn't going to sully my family's memory by saying all this to Tulloh.

"The Coffin creature bragged she had some documents," Tulloh said. "She told everyone who listened, but no one knows what happened to them. Do you?"

"She had a great imagination," I said. "I expect she invented them to make herself interesting."

"She brought family papers with her to Kansas. They disappeared. If you know where they are, I want them."

"You want them because you share her interest in Kansas history?" I asked.

"If I want them, that's all you need to know." His eyes almost disappeared into the white stripe of his face. It had been a long time since anyone questioned his appetites, his wants.

Mellon and Bezory, they were the ones who'd searched Clarina's trailer before the cops got there. They'd searched the apartment over the Perec garage. They'd planted the wrench, but they'd also been hunting. They'd engineered a search of my home and my office in Chicago.

I'd learned about these papers last night. Deke had learned this morning. I could not—would not—believe Deke was one of Tulloh's secret reporters. But he'd have mentioned the papers Clarina supposedly took from the house in Skaneateles in his report about the trip to the morgue. Besides, Lucia was telling everyone about them. She probably told Zoë when they met at the morgue this morning. The story might already be on the *Douglas County Herald*'s website.

"Where are the papers?" Tulloh insisted.

"I don't know," I said. "I've never seen them."

"That dead gal, what I'm hearing is she was claiming she could shut down the Yancy project. What have you found out about that?"

"Nothing. She gave a lot of people a nod and a wink about secrets but none of them has surfaced."

"You've been detecting all this time and you've detected nothing? Your reputation and all, I find that hard to believe."

I leaned forward and spoke earnestly. "I've learned the best espresso in Lawrence is at the Hippo. Brett Santich's little girl is a basketball fan. Your daughter is hurt that she isn't part of your operation. Lawrence wine stores carry some sophisticated Italian reds. Clete Rotherhaite questioned your son Robert's judgment about the safety of the Wakarusa plant. He's dead. I wouldn't call that nothing after a mere ten days in the town."

"Rotherhaite was the kind of hard worker America needs. His death, that was a great pity."

You could take that to mean Tulloh had chewed out his son Robert for killing the plant manager. Or maybe the rattler really thought it was a pity Rotherhaite had died. Unlikely but not impossible.

"Why is that Yancy project so important?" I asked. "Your hundreds of billions of dollars and thousands of plants and what-do, why do you need that plant on Yancy."

"Because I want it!" he snapped.

"I guess if that reason has worked well for you all these years, there's no need to abandon it now."

"I think you know where those papers are," Tulloh said, "or you know who knows. You hand them over to Mellon, you could get back to Chicago and leave all this Kansas trouble behind you."

"A dream come true, in fact," I said.

I didn't say what we both knew: if I found the papers, I'd be dead in the first ditch we came to. As it was, I could hardly believe I was leaving the building alive, but he told Mellon to drive me back to Lawrence.

When we got to the SUV, Mellon locked me in the back with the cuffs still on. Chet Bezory didn't join us.

When we pulled into the library garage, he undid the cuffs and let me out.

"Mr. T wants those papers. He figures you're the person who can find them, but if you do find them and try to hide them, Mr. T will know. You watch your step."

"Always," I said. "Watching my steps is the core of my fitness regimen."

He took my phone from his pocket and tossed it at my feet.

47

CRASHING

I **SAT ON THE** garage floor cuddling my dog. She was frenzied after all her time alone in the car. She'd raced around the garage, zooming past me, until she'd worn herself out, and finally collapsed in my arms. This could not go on. Tomorrow I'd see if Lou and Ed could take her until I was ready to go home. If not, I'd drive her back to Chicago myself.

Peppy started licking my face, working at the crusted blood.

"Not your job, girl, not your job." My arms were stiff and swollen, but I pushed myself standing.

It was only twenty before six, I saw when I looked at my phone. I felt as though I'd been in Oz and back, but it was only five hours ago that I'd been carelessly whistling, thinking about Don Wilton's ties to the Tulloh family. The unsent text to Ed and Lou was on the screen. I erased it, stuffed the phone into my hip pocket, took Peppy to the park behind the library.

It was hard to coax her back into the car. As we were driving toward the trailer, I remembered that my towels and sheets were still at the Laundromat. I collected them, went back to Bluestem Lane.

I stood under the shower, washing the blood from my face and my clothes. That was another outfit going into the dumpster, another shopping trip behind the Boat Yard on the horizon. They should start giving me discounts.

I ate some cold risotto while I checked my voicemail and texts. Lucia Bednarek had left a long rambling message.

"That was poor Rickey, all right, lying there dead. Even though she could be a pain sometimes, she was my sister, she was my only living relative, and now she's gone. I want to take her home and have a proper funeral, but that policeman, the nice one with the beautiful manners, he said they keep the body until they find the killer. Can you believe that? What if they never find the killer, I asked, but he says they always do. I was hoping to stay with you again tonight, but when the nice sergeant drove me out here the place was locked up and no sign of you, no answer to your phone, so he took me to a motel."

I hadn't thought I could be grateful to Mellon and Mr. T for this afternoon's abominations, but at least they'd spared me another night with Lucia.

I had a message from Deke, telling me I'd better not have left the jurisdiction without checking in. He also said he'd looked at the pictures I'd sent him of the Omicron kid dealing with someone at the Lion's Heart back door.

"Do not think you are the cowgirl who can gallop in and solve Lawrence's drug problems. You will be in way over your head, and you will upend months of careful investigation here."

Zoë wanted a confab before she left for New York. Lou and Ed were double-checking Monday morning's accessory delivery. I sent them a quick thumbs-up. I was too exhausted to reply to anyone else, certainly too beat to talk to anyone.

All I wanted was my bed and eight hours of solid sleep. Which meant making sure Mellon, Chet, or any of their pals didn't jump me.

"What are we going to do, girl? They've put trackers on my phone, for sure, and probably the car as well."

I thought it through as carefully as I could for the blanket of fatigue that enveloped me. Finally, I tucked my phone into a paper bag, in case Mellon had put in malware that videoed me, and left it on a counter. I collected some basic supplies—hoodie, dark wool cap, some of Peppy's food and bowls—into my backpack, rummaged in the trailer's drawers, where I found a palette knife and some WD-40, because you never know, and drove back into town. Left my smart-phone at the trailer where it could tell everyone I was in the trailer.

Seven on a Saturday night, the main downtown streets were packed, despite the cold weather. The Lion's Heart had a line at the back door. I drove a few blocks farther east and seemed to be in a different town and a different era. Small houses with crooked roofs lined the brick-paved walks and streets. I picked a parking spot at random and set out with Peppy, circling the block to make sure no one was with us.

It took us twenty minutes to get to Trig's apartment on Vermont Street. Seeing Peppy and me flustered him. He was appalled at the thought of giving us a place to sleep.

"Trig, you know all those protests you've tried outside the coal plant, and the development on Yancy, and so on? There is a real, genuine billionaire who bought the coal plant: Robert Tulloh. I think he also owns the Yancy project. You see my face? The crew chief up on Yancy did that to me this afternoon, while he was driving me out to talk to Robert's daddy."

Trig stared at me. "Robert Tulloh? He did this?"

"One of the people who works for him and his father, Chet Bezory. Clarina apparently told them she had a document that could upend the project. They want that paper, they think I have it. They let me leave the Tulloh headquarters alive because they're hoping I'll lead them to it."

"What, you've come here so they can follow you and beat me up, too?" He tried to shut the door, but I moved inside with Peppy.

"I walked here. I made sure I didn't have company. I left my phone behind because they probably installed trackers in it while they were threatening me. No one knows I'm here. I'm on your side on this, Trig, the side trying to stop whatever is happening out at Yancy, the side trying to find Clarina's killers. They beat me badly today, as you can see. I need to sleep. Help me, tonight only. I'll crash somewhere else tomorrow."

"Do you have the paper they want?"

"Nope. I'm not even sure it exists. Or did she show it to you?"

He shook his head, slowly, nervously looking around. "She never showed me anything, just kept hinting that she had dynamite. I got tired of hearing her brag about what she would do when she never did anything."

"She might have bragged too many times to the wrong person," I said. "You know I found out her real name. Her sister says Clarina, or Rickey, I guess we should call her, she always was living some fantasy life."

He nodded. "I read Zoë's story. So now you're a hero."

"You led me to it, telling me that kids had fat-shamed her with her town's name."

He couldn't help preening a little.

"Here's your chance to show you're willing to back up your talk with a little walk, a short walk. I'm a sitting duck out in Clarina's trailer park if the guys get trigger happy."

He'd spent so many years carrying signs and ranting in the editorial pages that he was startled at the thought of real action, even an act as passive as giving me a place to sleep. He glanced around, saw his computer with Timmy and Ivy on the screen saver.

"I met him a few days ago," I said quietly. "His mom was visiting the Boat Yard the same time I was. He's a bright, active kid—I know you're making a difference in his life."

Oh, V.I., low blow—do this for Timmy. However, it tipped the balance. He had a small side room, a glorified closet, really, with an inflatable bed that he'd bought for Timmy. I could crash there.

He dug a cleanish sheet from a drawer and draped it over the inflated mattress, showed me the bathroom, which was surprisingly immaculate, watched me fill Peppy's water dish, and shut the closet door on us. It was just after seven-thirty when I collapsed onto the mattress, Peppy wedged alongside.

It was a little after three when I woke. My nose was sore and swollen and my shoulders ached from having my arms cuffed behind me, but I had slept for eight restful hours, with no dreams of blood or guns despite my broken nose.

"Peppy, I'm going to leave you here with Trig. You'll be safe. Either I'll be back or Lou and Ed will come to get you."

I moved silently into Trig's front-room-cum-office. He was asleep in a room beyond, or at least someone was snoring loudly there. I took one of his pieces of poster paper and wrote a note: *Off to try to get evidence about Santich's involvement in this mess. If I'm not back by 8 a.m., call this number and explain to the man who answers why you have my dog. He'll come to collect her.*

48

SECOND-STORY WOMAN

THE LION'S HEART door was locked when I got there, but there was still a light showing in the second-story window. I walked on for another block, came at the bar from the back, where the municipal parking lot lay, and sat on a concrete slab behind some bushes. I could see the square of light projected onto the ground even though I couldn't see the window itself.

As I waited, I began hearing the sounds of the night. Even in town, small animals rustle about. The wind blew papers across the parking lot. Near me, someone was groaning in their sleep. As my eyes adjusted to the dark, I realized that I had invaded a communal bedroom. I saw three people sleeping on the ground near me, including the groaner, but one man was sitting up, watching me.

"You a cop?" he asked.

"Nope. I'm a robber."

"You're in the wrong place if you want to rob anyone. No one here has the price of a night's sleep, or we'd be in a bed somewhere. I could use a drink, though, and a smoke."

"When I've finished my robbery, I'll come back and help you out," I promised. "As long as you don't call the cops on me."

He made a sound that might have been a laugh. In the dark, as I waited for the second-story light to go out, he ended up telling me his story, three tours in Afghanistan, too much anger when he got home, couldn't hold a job, his wife left him, taking their child with her. "Randy's eleven now. Every now and then I get myself shaved and bathed, go see him for a few hours."

It was past four when Don Wilton came out the back door and drove off. I waited another ten minutes, waited out a patrol car making a sweep of the parking lot, and then walked to the east side of the building.

Underneath the bottom of the fire escape, I took the time to ground myself. The bottom rung was almost three feet above my head. When I stretched my arms up, a stream of pain ran through my triceps.

V.I., the Candace Parker of the detective team, moves through traffic, squats, times her jump, leaps above the guards, whacks her hand on metal but can't grasp it. This time my traps screamed at me.

"Tough it out," I muttered. "You want this body to go back to Chicago alive, you play through the pain."

Flex the hands, squat, jump, hold on to a bar. Yes. Biceps trembling, hoisting the weight up, getting a second rung, swinging the feet, finding the wall, bracing myself, scooting crablike up the wall until my arms found the fourth rung and there was room for my feet on the ladder.

Sweat was running down my neck. My thighs were quivering along with my arms when I was finally next to the window, but I was there. A triumph.

I sprayed the palette knife with WD-40, slid it between the upper and lower frames, moved it slowly until I could push the knife handle partway through the gap. Sprayed the area with more WD-40, slid a finger in behind the knife and pushed at the catch until the paint and grime gave way and it moved. Pushed up the bottom sash, hooked a leg over the sill.

"Spiderwoman!"

The hoarse voice beneath me startled me so much that I let the sash come down on my butt.

"Could have used you climbing up from the irrigation trenches in Kandahar," he called.

My vet friend. It was oddly comforting to have his ghostly voice keep me company. I made a circle with my gloved left thumb and forefinger to let him know I'd heard him. Pushed the sash back up, slid into the upper room.

The window I'd come through didn't have shades or a curtain, but I needed to risk turning on a light. My flashlight would provide only a slow and uncertain way of exploring the room. Anyway, a bobbing pinprick of light might arouse more cop suspicions than a block of light from the window. After all, Wilton himself had been here late. People would be used to it. I hoped.

When I switched on a table lamp, I found myself in a Jayhawk memorabilia store with modern office equipment scattered around it. The KU flag hung on the windowless north wall, with the U.S. flag next to it. Jayhawk posters, trophies, framed laminated team pictures and newsclips were on the other walls and shelves.

A couple of computers faced the flags, sitting on a metal worktop that ran the length of the south wall. Papers taped above them looked as though they might be work schedules, or possibly delivery schedules. They could be innocuous—an active bar requires a lot of deliveries.

They could also be schedules for drug deliveries. After all, Trevor Millay was still dealing at the bar's back door. The relationship between drugs and the Lion's Heart could go deeper than one frat boy looking for thrills. Don Wilton had a heavy clout: the wife of the state's biggest billionaire was underwriting his bar. Santich was an associate, supplying the Dundee house for drug parties. Maybe that wasn't his only location—perhaps Santich was augmenting his child support by running a chain of drug houses around the county.

I hit a key on the keyboards for both machines. One brought up a screen needing a password, but the other came to life with surveillance footage. These weren't as sophisticated as the surveillance videos I'd seen in Tulloh's headquarters, but the shots included the bar underneath me—the cash register, front and back doors, the corners where waitstaff might be pocketing money from the table or doing their own deals.

However, when I tried to look at archival footage, the machine demanded a password.

I wished I were a DA who could subpoena the records from the computer. I wished I'd had the forethought to bring a thumb drive with me, because when I looked closely at the keyboards, I saw that Wilton had been careless with his passwords: they were taped to the countertop next to the keyboards. The password for both was Go-Hawks!

49

THE KINDNESS OF STRANGERS

I KEPT MY GLOVES on, which made typing cumbersome, but I was able to log in to the computer that was playing the surveillance images. I was looking for the Dundee house history. After a tedious half hour, with half my attention on any sounds of anyone entering the bar, I realized Wilton was a sloppy record keeper. He didn't keep separate archives for photos from the bar versus the Dundee house. He didn't label anything, so that when I finally found a folder, it contained pictures of the bar, porn movies, and the occasional snapshots from Yancy.

I had to open each file to see what it covered, but I finally found the Sunday night where Sabrina went missing. The cameras had been on early, showing first Trevor with a group of guys who I assumed were his Omicron brothers carrying cartons of supplies into the house. The motion detectors were sensitive; as the night darkened, the occasional fox or raccoon triggered a shot.

Around nine-thirty, guests started arriving at the house. They were young, for the most part, perhaps college students, perhaps people from the small towns that dotted the county. The faces weren't in great focus, but good enough that a cop or a blackmailer might make use of them.

A little after 11:00 P.M., Sabrina Granev arrived, a ghostly, skeletal figure, stumbling up the kitchen steps. At eleven-thirty, lights in the house flashed off and on and the partygoers suddenly burst outside, moving so fast that several tripped and fell down the kitchen steps. They picked themselves up and streamed quickly to their cars.

The cameras went black. This had to be when the killers were carrying Clarina into the house. Don Wilton was here at the Lion's Heart, looking after his bar and turning cameras on and off in response to orders from Robert? Santich? Maybe Mellon as Robert's lieutenant?

The cameras stayed black until after I arrived. They were switched on in time to photograph me with Sabrina. They showed the first responders and stayed on until three, when they recorded Gertrude Perec's and Trig's separate arrivals. These were the photos that had made their way to the LKPD's doorway.

At that point, the cameras went dark again, which meant they missed my finding Clarina the following day and calling for the cops.

All that confirmed what I already assumed, but it was frustrating that I couldn't find footage of the killers arriving with Clarina's body. They'd ferried her in during the interval between the end of the party and my own arrival, since I'd stumbled on the blanket she'd been wrapped in. I guessed they'd come through the woods, not by the road, because of Sabrina's screaming about monsters, but I couldn't find any pictures to prove that.

I opened the second computer, which held more files. They were as disorganized as the surveillance footage, but they seemed to contain Wilton's financial records. Receivables, payables, more porn, emails to liquor distributors showing proof that the bar could meet its obligations.

I could hear seconds ticking away in my head. I needed to find something more concrete while I was here. Proof of what was really underway on Yancy, proof of where Clarina died, better still, proof of why she died.

And then, by luck and not skill, I stumbled on some audio files. The most recent was from yesterday, when Wilton was meeting with Jake Tulloh and Brett Santich.

"I spoke to McDowell. The Coffin woman's sister has no idea what evidence the Coffin broad claimed she had hold of. We didn't find a trace of secret papers in her trailer, or at the Dundee house. We know she went up to the Dundee place a few times, we got her on camera, but she apparently just liked to be lonely in the woods.

"Daddy's going to talk to the Chicago dick, dickette I guess"—Wilton and Santich snickered obediently—"this afternoon. I know you went through her things when she was at the Perec place, Chet, but you go to her trailer and give it another once-over. Mellon will take care of searching her car and looking through her phone."

My stomach churned. I'd been right, they'd been pawing through my private space. I'd have to get a new phone, new malware, new everything, and even then I'd feel the slime of those slugs on me.

"So are you going ahead with the installation?" Santich asked.

"I don't know. Daddy hates to give up; we've put in upward of a hundred million, what with the plant and all the equipment we've already bought, and of course Robert is ready to go torpedoes and full steam ahead. I'm not so sure myself. We'll see at the end of the day.

"But, Santich, your fucking head is on the block if this goes under. If you hadn't been trying to make a few bucks on the side with your asshole drug sales, no one would have paid any attention to the Yancy project until it was up and running."

"If your father wasn't the richest man in Kansas, you'd be selling insurance or shoes to make ends meet," Santich said. "You don't have any vision. At least Robert does, even if he likes to jump off the high dive."

"What's that supposed to mean?" Jacob's voice was ugly.

"It means if this whole business comes crashing down, it won't be because of the Dundee house, it'll be because you thought you could skate around the environmental impact statement. You think your money is some kind of force field that protects you from stuff ordinary people have to face. I warned your lawyer, when he made the presentation to the county that you can't hide a project this big by pretending it's a resort—"

There was a sound of glass crashing. Jacob must have thrown something, or swept the table clean. I looked from the computer to the floor. Chunks of glass still lay under the far counter, as if Don had brushed them out of the way.

"Clete Rotherhaite thought he knew better than us, too," Jacob said.

Below me, I heard my vet's hoarse voice calling, "Spiderwoman."

"In a minute," I called back, intent on the audio.

My vet called "Spiderwoman" again, and then another man spoke, the same twang I'd just heard on the recording.

"What are you doing here, dirtbag?"

"Hey, man, you don't own the sidewalk."

"I own the building and you're turning it into an eyesore."

There was the ugly sound of someone being kicked, someone crying out, and then footsteps going around to the back of the building.

I closed the file, went to the window. Slid out as I'd slid in, closed the sash, climbed down the fire escape, and jumped from the bottom rung. Pain ran up and down my body like voltage through the Yancy pylons.

My vet was on his side, knees drawn up to his chin, rocking in pain. I crawled over to him. I was holding his hand when a squad car pulled up and shone a spotlight on us.

"What are you two doing?" The officer spoke on the bullhorn instead of getting out of the car.

"Resting," I called.

Wilton heard the bullhorn and hustled around the side of the building, looking from us to the squad. He beetled over to the car, yelling that we were breaking in. While he blocked the cop's view, I casually stuffed my palette knife and WD-40 into a crack between the foundation and the ground.

Wilton came over to us with the cop. "They were breaking into the bar," he huffed. "I caught them in the act."

"Oh, please, Don," I said. "You caught my friend here resting against the side of the building. You kicked him so hard he's having trouble getting to his feet. I was walking by. I heard you."

"Who are you?" Wilton demanded.

"One of your less-satisfied customers," I said. "The one who found Sabrina Granev dying of an overdose out at the Dundee house."

"You!" Wilton swore. "You goddam cunt, I'm going to—" He remembered the cop before he issued the whole threat.

"Going to what?" I asked.

Next to me, the vet started to laugh but was overcome by a coughing fit.

The cop demanded an ID. I dug my driver's license out of a zip pocket in the hoodie.

"Oh, the Chicago detective," she said, making "Chicago detective" sound like "pizza-peddling pedophile." "What were you doing here?"

"As I said, I was walking by. Don here was kicking an Afghan vet." I was careful not to say I'd seen him.

"Every damned homeless freak in this town claims they were vets," Don said. "You use it as an excuse to guilt students into giving you money for drugs."

"Which you conveniently stock," I said.

"It's five in the morning," the cop said. "All three of you, knock it off, unless you want me to take you to the station and book you. And you, Chicago detective, how did you happen to be just walking around?"

"Sorry, officer," I said, contrite. "As you pointed out, I'm from Chicago. I don't know all the local ordinances in Lawrence. If you're not supposed to take walks early in the morning, I won't do it again."

My vet coughed again, covering another laugh.

The woman debated making more of an issue of it, but Wilton was insisting that I'd been breaking into the bar, that a light on the second floor was on, which proved it.

"You forgot to turn it off yourself, man," my vet croaked. "Watched you leave, saw the light was still on, figured you're rich, it don't matter to you if you burn electricity twenty-four-seven."

Wilton said that was a lie, but the cop was tired, her shift was close to ending. She told the vet and me not to move, that she was going to check for signs of forced entry.

Although it was clear that none of the doors had been tampered with, and that the alarm hadn't gone off, she gave in to Wilton's demand that she search me for my lock picking or alarm bypassing tools. When she found only my flashlight and my phone, she told all of us to go home to bed.

Wilton grumbled that he was going to file a complaint, but she was smart enough to ignore that. She got back in her squad, watching to make sure we didn't hang around.

Wilton went into the bar. I squatted next to the vet.

"Let's find a place where you can bathe and get some sleep. Can you walk a few blocks?"

He pushed himself upright, clutching my arm to keep his balance. "I'm not going to a shelter."

"I won't take you to a shelter. If you'd like, I'll pay for a room at a motel for you. I owe you that and a lot more for saving my butt just now."

He was limping, and we stopped several times on the four-block walk to the car while he caught his breath. When we got to the Camry, he sank into the passenger seat, exhausted.

"You said you were a robber, not a cop," he said. "But that cop back there said you were a Chicago detective."

"I'm a private eye, not a member of any government force. I live in Chicago, but I'm down here helping out a friend. Right now, I'm not sure which side of the law I'm on. I'm going to collect my dog, and then take you to a clean bed. You rest here; I'll be back in twenty minutes."

At Trig's place, I used my picks to let myself in. Trig was still asleep, which was a mercy. I'd worried that Peppy might bark out her indignation at my abandoning her yet again.

When we got back to the car, she sensed the vet's troubles. She leaned over from the backseat and laid her muzzle along his neck.

I drove him to the motel where I'd hoped to park Clarina's sister Friday night, clean, but spartan and therefore affordable. Gave him a couple of twenties.

"You need to see a doctor," I said.

"You're a good-hearted Spiderwoman, but what do you know about life on the street? Where am I going to find me a doctor?"

I took a moment to open a search engine on my phone. "There's a VA clinic here in town." I wrote the address on the pad of paper by the motel bed. "If you still have your dog tags, they'll see you for nothing."

"Maybe." He bent down to say goodbye to Peppy. "Been a long time since a beautiful lady gave me a kiss. Take care of Spiderwoman."

50

COVER STORY

MY MUSCLES WERE screaming at me to get to bed. I drove on west of town, past the turnoff to Yancy, and found another anonymous motel, like the one where I'd taken the vet, bare bones but clean.

A sign by the front door told me dogs weren't allowed. The dawn was plastering its rosy fingerprints on the night sky as I smuggled Peppy in through the rear entrance.

No toothbrush, no nightshirt, but a shower, a clean bed. I just remembered to hang the DO NOT DISTURB sign on the door. I was asleep by the time I'd pulled the covers up to my chin.

It was past one Sunday afternoon when Peppy woke me, urging me to let her outside. I got out of bed, legs stiff and swollen from my long day yesterday. Weight work, which used to be a regular part of my workout, was another thing I'd let slide lately.

I stumbled outside with Peppy. A man collecting used bedding from one of the rooms saw me with the forbidden dog but shrugged and looked away.

The motel backed onto a field ploughed for winter. I let Peppy run free and did a standing workout, twenty minutes of lunges, squats, nerve glides, taking it slowly, until my arms and legs felt less like swollen sausages attached to my torso and more like usable limbs.

As I stretched I could see the tops to the grimy orange smoke-stacks of the Wakarusa power plant. We weren't far here from the river walk where Clete Rotherhaite had died.

The audio file I'd stumbled on held staggering revelations. The Tullohs went into the Yancy project using a proposed resort as a cover for something that required power on a massive scale.

Clarina had tried to stop them, using her tried-and-true method of pretending, maybe even believing, she knew secrets about local history that would derail the project.

In a way, Clarina-Ulricke had died from an overdose of make-believe. But just as she'd tried in Skaneateles to claim that she was Black, or descended from *Mayflower* Pilgrims, she had no proof. She had only the desire to make herself seem important, and she'd chosen the wrong theater for that particular drama.

There were plenty of questions about Clarina-Ulricke's murder—where and why had she met her killers, besides who had struck the fatal blow—and even what she had said that made them strike her. But even if she'd stolen diaries from the Origins Museum and Library, she apparently hadn't given Tulloh's team any believable proof that she could derail the project.

The wrench would arrive tomorrow. I'd get it to Deke Everard. If it proved to be Clarina's murder weapon, he'd take care of hunting out the killer. Or Chief McDowell would oblige Matthew Tulloh by burying the wrench under a pylon. Perhaps they would bury me next to it.

I wished I could go home as soon as I offloaded the wrench to the LKPD, but that wouldn't get rid of the bullseye Matthew Tulloh had painted on my head. Maybe I could make some use of the recording I'd heard in Wilton's office, if I could copy it before he erased it.

I called Peppy to heel. I found the man who was collecting sheets and towels from the rooms and gave him a five. I drove to the trailer to change clothes and pick up messages.

On Wilton's audio, Jake Tulloh had mentioned his crew were searching my trailer and the Camry while I was with Matthew. Putting on clothes those vermin had touched made me squirm, but I couldn't keep going to the Laundromat, let alone buying new outfits every other day. I packed clean underwear and toiletries in my back-pack, inspecting them for signs of trackers. I went through the Camry and found an Apple tracker in the spare tire well. I left it in place—I'd remove it when I needed to get someplace I couldn't afford to be seen.

I had to get Peppy out to Lou and Ed. If I put her in harm's way, I would not be able to live with myself. I also needed to find an anonymous place to spend the night myself. I couldn't jeopardize Trig's safety by crashing in on him a second time. I'd been lucky they hadn't followed the Camry to the motel where I'd spent the rest of the night.

Knowing that Tulloh's grasping fingers had been invading my phone made it hard for me to touch it, but I needed to read my messages. I drove to the Buy-Smart on Sixth Street and bought two more burner phones. Over coffee at the Hippo, I manually entered phone numbers for the people I most needed to be in touch with, including my clients for whom I had active projects.

I sent out messages to them from the burner, telling them my main number was compromised and to use this one until further notice. I listened to the messages on my smartphone, sickened again by knowing other ears had heard them first.

Mr. Contreras had called, as had Lotty, Sal, and Bernie. Deke Everard wanted to hear from me ASAP. Cady Perec had seen the news about Clarina's identity and wanted to talk to me.

Her message made me search my news feed. And there was young Zoë Cruickshank's byline, picked up by Reuters and the AP, reprinted all over the world. She was in Skaneateles, New York, she'd interviewed people who'd known Ulricke "Rickey" Bednarek as a child, people who had no use for her, people who knew she was a brilliant woman who just needed to find her niche, people who told how her father had beaten her, people who said she'd driven her mother to an early grave with her carryings-on.

"Those two girls never got on," one neighbor said. "The father favored the older one, the mother liked Ulricke better, and when they got to be grown-ups, it was like they channeled those parents: Lucia, the older responsible one, Ulricke like her mother, whining, not able to face life with an adult attitude."

Zoë had looked up the property records for the house their aunt
Kalina had lived in. She learned it had been built for Elias Entwistle in
1830, and passed from him to his daughter, Amelia Entwistle Grellier
at his death. It had been inherited by Sophia Grellier Carruthers, and
passed down through that family until 1993, when Louise Grellier
Carruthers sold it to Kalina Bednarek.

> The papers that Rickey Bednarek found in the attic when her
> aunt died may connect the family to the Grelliers who went to
> Kansas as abolitionists in the 1850s. Until we locate those papers
> we'll never know the full history of what Clarina-Rickey was
> doing in Kansas.

Zoë included a link to the story I'd seen in the 1867 *Kanwaka
Courier,* about Amelia Grellier returning to Skaneateles after her husband's death, and concluded her first dispatch by writing,

> Did Frederic Grellier's death in a terrorist attack in 1867 cause
> Rickey Bednarek, aka Clarina Coffin's, death a hundred fifty-seven
> years later? We have a private investigator looking into the details
> in Lawrence, Kansas, while I'm exploring them in western New
> York. The *Douglas County Herald* has a hotline for anyone with
> information about those papers that Rickey took away with her.
> And, of course, if you have information about Rickey Bednarek's
> murder, we will pass it on to the Lawrence police for you if you
> wish to remain anonymous.

The hotline was Zoë's cell phone. Very enterprising of her. As
was making it sound as though the *Douglas County Herald* had the
funds to hire me as their investigator. I sent her a congratulatory text
and called Lou and Ed. They were delighted to take on dog sitting
"the princess." I promised to be at their farm by six—"unless I've been
kidnapped or arrested or knocked out."

"You could *say* all those things happened, and they're good ex-
cuses, but how could you prove it?" Lou said.

When I'd hung up I sat back and thought again about the Yancy
project. The resort was a cover for—what?

I put Peppy into the Camry and drove to the library, to use their computers. Looked up revived coal plants, and found they were a pet project of people building bitcoin mining companies. I couldn't follow all the technical specs, but cryptocurrency requires tens of thousands of high-speed computers, and they in turn required thousands of megawatts of power. I read about one bitcoin facility in Kentucky that was operating with four coal-fired power plants.

I couldn't make my poor dog spend more time locked in the car. I walked down to the river with her and sat on a bench while she explored the underbrush and dabbled her feet in the shallows.

If the Tulloh brothers were putting up a crypto mining operation on top of Yancy, the Wakarusa coal plant was ready-made to generate the power. Pat Everard and Gertrude Perec would never have approved a bitcoin mine, but they'd given a pass to a resort. But what about Matthew? Was he on board with bitcoin mining?

I called Pauline Tulloh. I was prepared to leave a message on her voicemail, but she surprised me by answering herself.

"I met your father yesterday," I said. "He had Mellon and Chet Bezory beat me up a little and drive me to the headquarters in Salina."

"Oh?" It was her usual cool drawl.

"I wondered whose idea it was."

"Not mine," she said.

"Not just the kidnaping, and the threats—your father will have me killed as soon as I lead him to a crucial piece of evidence he wants. I wondered if he placed Mellon with you to spy on you for him, or if you and Matthew agreed Mellon was on loan to you, but his primary allegiance was to Matthew."

She didn't speak for a beat, then said in the same cool voice, "Everyone connected to Tulloh owes Matthew their primary allegiance. What evidence is he looking for?"

"Whatever Clarina Coffin claimed to have found that would derail the Yancy project. You said your father hates crypto, but I think that's what your brothers are building on top of Yancy. A data-mining facility."

"Daddy doesn't want any of us speculating in crypto, but if the money the boys make from it comes from coal power he'd be glad to take part. Coal comes from the ground, that's what he thinks is reliable. What evidence is Daddy looking for?"

"My private opinion, it doesn't exist. My public opinion? I'm hunting for it like mad in the hopes I'll live long enough to keep him from killing me."

Another short silence, and then she said, "I see," and hung up.

51
TROUBLED IN MIND

DEKE TEXTED ME as I finished talking to Pauline. Warshawski, this is my 4th message. We need to talk. Don't make me put out an APB.

I called him and said he could meet me at the library if he wanted to see me. I went out to the car to give Peppy some attention until I saw his unmarked car pull up.

He was wound too tight for ordinary niceties. "What were you doing at the Lion's Heart at five this morning?" he demanded.

"Protecting a homeless veteran. Don Wilton had kicked him pretty hard for using his building as a backrest."

"Don't fuck with me, Warshawski. Officer Helios reported that you claimed to be going out for a walk. Randomly, outside the same bar where your Chicago college students were drinking two weeks ago."

I backed away to calm myself. The person who loses their temper loses the battle. "Yesterday, after you took Lucia off to view her sister's body, I wandered downtown. First, I saw young Trevor Millay dealing at the Lion's Heart's back door. I sent you the photos."

"And I'm repeating my response. Leave the local drug scene to us," Deke said. "Besides which, I wouldn't arrest Vladimir Putin based on those pix. It is not a crime for two people to hand each other envelopes in broad daylight in a public parking lot."

"I did think they were amazingly brazen. Almost as if they had protection." I eyed him steadily.

"Do not slander this department. I will not stand for it!" he cried so loudly that everyone in the lobby stared at us.

"Your chief and Jake Tulloh are frat brothers. They share their secrets, so presumably the LKPD knows that Don Wilton is Jake and Robert Tulloh's cousin. Their sister, Pauline Tulloh, bailed out the Lion's Heart during lockdown, so you can bet Wilton is ready to do whatever the Tullohs want, including handling the computer feed for the cameras out at the Dundee house."

Deke sank back in his chair, his eyes squeezed shut. He was trying to make sense of things he knew and things he didn't want to know.

"That still doesn't explain why you were at the Lion's Heart at five this morning," he growled, eyes still shut.

"I was like Bluebeard's wife," I said. "I wanted to see what was behind the steel door that leads from the bar to his office. I hoped Wilton left things unlocked so I could take a look."

"And had he?" He sat up, frowning fiercely, daring me to lie.

"Let's just say I was able to look inside without breaking his door locks or security codes," I said.

He stared at me for a long moment. "The window. Son of a bitch. I went and looked the place over after I read Helios's report. You went up the fire escape. He doesn't have an alarm on the window, I take it."

"Climb up and check it out. I can't confirm."

"Or deny. Right. When I talked to Helios, she remembered that the drunk you were helping called you Spiderwoman. When you looked inside Don's office, what did you see?"

"If I had access to the criminal justice system's legal machinery, I'd get a warrant," I said. "If I had access, I'd wonder if drug supply routes and schedules were taped next to the computer monitors. I'd look at the footage from the cameras spread around the Dundee place, because I'd wonder if Don was the person who controlled those cameras."

"So now you're not only Spiderwoman but Wonder Woman," Deke jeered.

I smiled. "Wondering woman, more accurately. Because I'd also wonder what conversations Don secretly recorded."

"You'd have to have grounds for a warrant, and the speculations of a wall-climbing private eye don't constitute grounds."

I bowed my head, acknowledgment. "You're right. One thing that actually happened, I'll share with you for nothing. Matthew Tulloh's daughter Pauline has a bodyguard–cum-butler, man named Geoffrey Mellon. He's really on Matthew's payroll.

"Yesterday, Mellon jumped me, together with the crew chief from the Yancy project. They stunned me and carted me off to Tulloh's HQ in Salina. Matthew Tulloh is a scary guy. He and his sons think that Clarina really did find a document that would derail Yancy. He's keeping me alive until I lead him to it.

"On another topic, Cady Perec is worried about your mother and her grandmother. You remember those diaries that disappeared from the state Origins Museum? Cady thinks Gertrude may have stolen them and given them to your mother to hide."

"Is she infecting your brain or you hers? Those two women work hard and do nothing but good for this town. And you think they're capable of theft of some ancient history books? And killing that strange woman over them?"

"If there is an explosive document, I'm betting it is connected to those ancient history books. I don't know what your team found in Clarina's trailer, but we know she had a photograph of a riot at the local train station over some Black settlers leaving town in the 1860s, along with a mourning photo from that same era."

"If I was killed tomorrow, you'd find Patrick Mahomes's photo in my bedroom," he said. "That wouldn't mean my death was connected to the Chiefs."

"I don't know—a jealous fan from Chicago might resent all those Super Bowl trophies and take it out on you."

He couldn't quite hold back a smile, but said, "Clarina was obsessed with Kansas history from the 1860s. I had an earful from Lucia all the way to KC and back. I know Matthew Tulloh is a billionaire and I'm just a sergeant getting by on my paycheck, but I think he's wrong about there being any evidence. Clarina *wanted* to find a document that would make her famous, but it doesn't exist."

He got to his feet. "I guess I should thank you for IDing the Coffin woman. Not that it helps ID her killer or a motive."

"I'm pleased you feel grateful. That will keep me going in the dark watches of the night. You are a good and dedicated cop, but you have a chief who is close to the Tulloh family. I am not making up what I heard on a recording in Don Wilton's office: Chief McDowell is reporting on what you and your team discover to his old fraternity brother, Jake Tulloh. You don't want to believe this, but you need me here."

"The LKPD does not need you—"

"Not me specifically," I said, "but someone outside the chain of command who can keep a secret and also keep asking uncomfortable questions."

He stared back at me, his expression bleak. After a long moment, he turned on his heel.

52

JUGGLING CHAIN SAWS

T WAS A relief to reach Lou and Ed's hilltop retreat, a relief to sit with a drink around their fire pit and tell them everything that had happened in the last few days, including climbing into Don Wilton's office.

"When I was a boy, my dad took me to a fair they were holding outside Topeka," Ed said. "Little thing, suitable for a colored neighborhood, rides that could've fallen apart if they went too fast, a sad pony carrying us around a circle. There was a man who juggled chain saws. That's what really stuck with me. Chain saws.

"That's you, Warshawski. Those are going to come crashing down on you. You want to cut off your head, your choice, but the princess here doesn't have a vote. You leave her here with us until you get this business done."

Lou nodded. I didn't argue. It helped to know I didn't have to worry about Peppy's safety, although I warned them that my chain saws included the probable bugging of the Camry. "I found an Apple tracker in the spare tire well, which I left in the library parking lot, but they may have put other devices in harder places to find. In which case the mad billionaire may send his vassals to call on you."

"You are a lot of fun to know," Ed said. "Good thing you've got a cute dog. And where are you spending the night?"

"Crashing at Zoë's while she's living it up in western New York,"

I said. "I'll meet you at the yard tomorrow when my accessories come in."

I drove back into Lawrence and parked in the visitors' lot at the new police station, leaving my infected phone in the trunk so that Tulloh would know where to find me. If someone decided to blow up the Camry, the police would surely investigate it there. I rode the free bus back downtown. It let me out near the library. I crossed the street and sat on a curb, watching people getting off and on the buses that pulled in there.

When I was reasonably sure no one was waiting for me, I walked down to the *Douglas County Herald* building near the river. Zoë had told me she was the only person who regularly spent time there.

I could hear the river nearby while I worked the lock, heard the murmur of voices from the homeless camp underneath the bridge, metal plates on the bridge surface clanking as they bounced under the passing cars.

I was working in the dark, but it was an old lock that needed touch, not sight. In a few minutes I'd jiggered the tumblers into place.

I switched on my flashlight and saw a cadre of gray tails slither under doors as I walked along. How good to know I wouldn't be alone in the cold damp building.

In one of the disused offices, I found an array of mismatched furniture, including a couch. It was dusty, but the cushions were reasonably firm. A quilted tarp was draped over a pallet mover. It was dusty, too, but it was heavy. I lay on the couch, fully dressed except for my shoes, the tarp pulled up to my chin. I sneezed for a while, but my sinuses adjusted and I drifted into sleep.

I was warm enough under the tarp, but I woke often, wondering about the rats, about Peppy, about whether I'd left Lou and Ed exposed to danger, and how good the surveillance on me was. At six, I got up for good. There were toilets at one end of the hall. The women's room was reasonably clean—no doubt Zoë's work—and even had warm water for my dusty face and heavy eyes. I brushed my teeth, combed my hair, and looked like a woman who hadn't slept much but who at least had a clean face.

I walked across the river to the Boat Yard, which was already open, doing a brisk business with truckers and work crews heading to the industrial sites along the river's north bank. There were a couple of Kirmek trucks in the mix, one laden with more phone pole–size logs. Women with kids in tow were crowded at a front table.

At first I kept looking around nervously, wondering if some Tulloh hireling had followed me to the paper's offices and then to here, but no one was paying attention to another exhausted, ill-kempt customer. I sat at the counter, building up my strength over corned beef hash with an egg, reading Zoë's latest dispatch from Skaneateles.

The yard where Lou and Ed brought new life to old metal was another half mile up the river from the café. They hadn't arrived yet; the gates to the yard were still locked. I found an old car seat lying outside the fence and lay in it drowsing, watching the eagles pass overhead.

A sharp wind was blowing from the north, from home, but I was too tired and achy from my poor sleep to do jumping jacks or anything that might keep me warm. I was glad when the FedEx truck pulled up to the yard gates. I hoisted myself out of the seat and lumbered over to meet the driver.

Lou and Ed pulled in while I was signing for the box. Cheviot wanted to see my signature on the form, so it was good that I'd shown up in person.

Lou unlocked the gate. "You want to look at your accessories in the shop, come on in," he said.

I shook my head. "Anything that gets on them will be analyzed and can be traced back to the metal or dust in your shop. I'm going to take them to the library and use one of their sound rooms; they're not sterile, but they're pretty clean."

The box wasn't heavy, but it was cumbersome. The men looked at each other as I started out of the yard.

"Someone sees you walking across the river with that, even if they shoot you first, they're going to figure we know you. Get in the truck, Warshawski."

I got in the truck. Peppy was there; they weren't going to leave her alone on the farm. She greeted me with a polite thump of the tail but I was not forgiven for leaving her alone in the car too many times the last few days.

At the library, no one questioned me when I signed up for one of their sound studios. I opened the box and found the wrench, wrapped in a clear plastic evidence bag, labeled with the chain of custody, from me to Cheviot and back to me to deliver to Deke.

I had not thought this through. I cursed myself, but repacked the box. In the Osma local history room, I tucked it carefully behind some outsize atlases.

I rode the free bus out Sixth Street to the Buy-Smart outlet where I bought latex gloves, a box cutter, and some two-gallon clear plastic bags.

Back in the library I made sure I had on gloves, opened the box again, and removed the wrench in its evidence bag. I couldn't remove the chain of custody label from the evidence bag. I cut open the bag. Careful not to touch the wrench, I dropped it into one of my two-gallon bags.

As it lay there, I noticed again the embossed *K* in its circle. I'd been looking at that *K* every day for the past two weeks. Kirmek Construction. I wanted to scrawl on the bag in red ink, "Look at Chet Bezory's tool box, see if his fourteen-inch pipe wrench is missing," but that would not be smart.

I put the bag with the wrench in it inside a second two-gallon bag and wrapped that into a ten-gallon black garbage bag.

Now the scary part. I found a bus that took me within half a mile of the Dundee house. I walked up 1450 Road until I was close to the house, then cut across the field on the Dundee house's north side. Crouching down to make use of what cover I could, I went into the woods behind the house. I wished I'd felt safe going back to the trailer—my boots would have been a boon on this rough terrain. Two consecutive nights' sleep would have been welcome. A companion. A message from Peter.

My mother had hidden alone in the hills near Livorno, waiting for a signal that a dilapidated fishing boat was waiting to take her to Lisbon. Her father had just been arrested. Italy was no longer safe for her. She was eighteen. She had hiked the 160 miles to the coast at nights, carrying her cardboard suitcase with her grandmother's red Venetian wineglasses wrapped in her few clothes.

How much sleep had Gabriella had in those eight nights? How had she found help in Lisbon, where she knew no one and didn't speak the language? And then she'd ended up in Chicago, imagining her glorious voice would find her a paying job in one of the rough bars on Milwaukee Avenue.

Gabriella, help me find some of your courage, your indomitable spirit. I began singing one of her favorite Mozart arias, my voice rusty and scratchy. Along with my triceps, I'd abandoned my vocal exercises these last five months. When I returned to Chicago all would be different.

"Porgi, amor" brought me to the fringe of bushes on the perimeter of the Dundee house. Pale green buds were emerging along the branches, but it would be some weeks before they provided cover between the woods and the house. I pushed the bags deep into one of the densest clumps of undergrowth, estimated it was in a direct line about seventy-five yards from the far edge of the house.

I was starting back the way I'd come when a black Jeep Cherokee bounced up the Dundee house drive. Chet Bezory, the Yancy project foreman, jumped out without taking time to turn off his engine and headed toward me.

My throat pulses choked me. Had he seen me from the hilltop? Or despite my care, had I shown up on the Lion's Heart camera feed?

I crouched low and started to run up the hill, where the tree cover was thickest. I'd gone about thirty yards when a bullet whined near my head. I dropped to the ground and began crawling at speed.

"Whoever you are, come out or eat lead," the voice boomed through a megaphone.

I couldn't suppress a nervous giggle. *Eat lead,* language from an old cowboy movie.

Another shot whined overhead, hitting a thick tree branch. It cracked and fell, briefly blocking the route behind me, giving me maybe a fifteen-second edge. I reached the remains of the trail I'd followed three weeks ago and picked up speed. The ground had been muddy a week earlier, but it was cold enough now that the soil was packed; I wasn't leaving footprints.

Just as I reached the first ruined house, it started to snow. Now I would leave a trail. I looked around wildly for cover and squeezed myself through a gap into the remains of the chimney. And made myself a sitting target. V.I! You used to have good instincts, what happened to them?

I squatted, patting the ground, seeking anything that could be a weapon, and felt—empty air. I risked a quick look with my flashlight. A hole, partly filled from years of leaves and branches, but bricks jutting from the inner wall offered a makeshift ladder.

Hand over hand, feet flailing, losing my grip and sliding the last six feet to the bottom. Tree roots and bricks cut into my jacket. I chanced another quick light.

I was in an old root cellar. A light shone above me. I stuffed the flashlight into my pocket. Backed into the cellar against one dirt wall and looked upward. A hand had come through the gap I'd used, then a head. The light played along the old chimney wall, pointed at the branches and leaves along the outer wall, missed the opening down to the cellar.

The hand and head withdrew. Dimly I heard two voices, men, impossible to tell whose. More faintly still, renewed crashing through bushes and branches. And then quiet, sudden, enveloping, as if the air were a velvet blanket folding around me.

I collapsed on the ground, muscles weak from relief, sweat soaking my hoodie. After some time listening until I was sure my pursuers had disappeared, I shone the flash again to look at the cellar. And sat still, dumbfounded. A small table, a chair, a metal chest placed on a trestle. Best of all, a battery-operated lantern. I switched it on.

The dirt walls held shelves that must date back to the house's origins. Hand-printed labels were still stuck to some cans, with lettering so faded that it couldn't be read. Some of the cans had exploded, but so long ago that the contents had dried past identification.

The chest had a padlock, but the chest itself was made of a light metal. Using a stick as a lever, I pried the top open. The padlock held, but the metal around it peeled back.

I brought the lantern over to inspect the contents. Most of what lay inside was paper. The top document was a notebook with the University of Kansas logo on it. Inside the front cover, Clarina Coffin's name was printed, with the address of the Prairie View Trailer Park. "Reward if found and returned," she'd written.

The notebook seemed to be Clarina's journal, which included an autobiography called "Following in My Family's Footsteps," along with notes she'd made about documents she'd read in various libraries. She'd also felt free to help herself to some original material. Tucked between two pages in her notebook was a yellowed piece of newsprint, so fragile pieces fell from it when I tried to lift it. I could see the header: YANCY LEDGER, KANSAS OLDEST NEGRO NEWSPAPER, June 28 1867.

A binder held more original documents, including telegrams and letters from members of the Grellier family and people named Entwistle. Zoë had mentioned that name in her first report from Skaneateles. Elias Entwistle had built the house where Clarina found the old letters and papers that prompted her move to Kansas.

Beneath the binder were three books bound in red leather, which had faded with time. I opened one to the elegant script I'd seen last week in Topeka. Abby Langford and Tommy Gellman, librarian and conservator at the Kansas Origins Museum, would be horrified to see Florence Wheelock's precious journals down in this damp cellar.

An additional journal, in a different hand, bound more simply in mildewing cardboard, lay at the bottom of the chest, next to some packages of dried fruit and yogurt chips.

I barely had feeling in my hands. The latex gloves I'd worn to keep from leaving prints on my evidence bag were no protection from the cold.

I thought about leaving everything in situ, but I was afraid Tulloh's team would come back to the chimney when they didn't find me in the woods. If they really started searching, it wouldn't take long to uncover this hideout.

I needed to save the journals. If my pursuers found them, they'd either destroy them outright or leave the paper here to disintegrate.

Florence's three volumes fit into my daypack, although I couldn't zip it completely shut. Clarina's notebook I tucked into the waistband of the jeans I'd been wearing since yesterday morning. The cardboard-bound journal was too big, its contents too fragile, to risk wearing it. I carried it in my left hand over to the brick ladder.

My shoulders and arms were still throbbing from the battering they'd taken on Saturday. Those same battered muscles needed to hoist me up the chimney stack, one-handed to protect the binder. Inching up, leaning into the brick stack so it took my weight, fumbling for each handhold, pushing up with my quads.

When I reached the top, I stuck my head cautiously around the chimney stack. My sweat froze in the harsh wind.

The snow had stopped, leaving only a thin cover on the ground, but enough to show that my pursuit had gone back to the Dundee house. I would also be leaving prints, but that couldn't be helped. At least I knew which way not to go.

I moved as quickly as I could, ordering my body to ignore the cold, ignore my swollen legs and trembling arms, repeating my old basketball coach's mantras. *It's not the size of the dog in the fight, it's the size of the fight in the dog. Quitters never win; winners never quit.* That was before St. Cecelia beat us 98 to 40, but we never quit.

I'd planned on walking in the road when I got there, easier terrain in my running shoes. A few yards from the edge I tripped on a root. I was clutching the cardboard journal and so I fell awkwardly, hitting my right shoulder hard. I lay still, catching my breath. A black Jeep Cherokee cruised by, slowly, Don Wilton in the backseat peering out the open window into the woods.

When it passed, I counted the seconds until it reappeared. About three minutes, and then five more as it made a return trip. I could lie here until the weather warmed up, when flowers and bushes would grow high enough to mark my grave. Or I could get back in motion.

Crawling, latex gloves in tatters, fingers bleeding, shoulder pounding. Lying flat every time I heard tires on gravel.

And then a crashing through the undergrowth, a short sharp bark, a man's grunt. "Got her."

53

BEAUTY TREATMENT

PEPPY WAS LICKING my face, whining. Lou scooped me up. Compared to a car door, I apparently didn't weigh much. Ed had the engine idling. Lou dumped Peppy and me into the backseat; the truck was in motion before Ed shut the door.

"What in the name of anything holy are you trying to prove, Warshawski?" Ed said. "You're a dog person, not a cat, you don't have nine lives to squander. When I said there were corpses better-looking than you, I didn't mean you should go for it as a beauty treatment."

"Ease up, man," Lou said. "You got her started with your chain saw juggling. She figured she had to do something better than that to keep your attention."

Waves of fatigue were carrying me away. I struggled awake. "How come you two were on that road just now?"

"Remember, Warshawski? Back when you told us about your accessories, you said you needed to have them on Dundee land so Five-O would connect them to the Coffin woman's murder. You went silent for so long we thought we'd better take a look. Princess here, she was all for letting you rot in the woods so she could stay with us, but Ed had a moment of softheartedness, he insisted we come out.

"Not much we could do without jamming ourselves up, but we saw the Yancy project foreman driving up and down in that Cherokee, so we knew he was probably hunting you. I dropped off the princess and Lou. What were you doing there?"

"I found Clarina's hideout. I have her papers. Here with me."

I must have fallen asleep midsentence, because the next thing I knew, Lou was slapping my face; we were at the mountaintop house. I was in a point beyond exhaustion, but I had to get a message to Deke about the bag of evidence. My smartphone, with his mobile number, was in the Camry trunk near the library, but Lou said he wasn't going to risk his license by driving a corpse around downtown Lawrence.

"Give me the keys. Give me your phone passcode so I can look up the number. I'll text him from this doodah. And then it will go into the compacter."

It's hard to text from a burner keypad, so I kept the message short: CC murder weapon in bush 75 yards east Dundee house.

54
LIBRARY PRIVILEGES

A LONG BATH, A long nap, a vegan dinner Ed created from the produce in his and Lou's greenhouse, and I was more or less ready to face whatever had built up during the day. They drove me to the trailer so that I could pick up my smartphone. I opened it to a truckload of messages.

Deke had phoned and texted, six messages that escalated in fury, ending with, You are not leaving the jurisdiction until you explain that wrench to me.

Murray wondered why I'd gone dark. Mr. Contreras wanted me to come home. My erstwhile client, Valerie, wanted to talk to me. Zoë had sent an urgent text, Call, I've found the original owner of that house.

I wrote down my messages; I'd answer them from a different phone when I was outside both the trailer and the Camry. An exhausting way to spend time but essential until I got back to my Chicago computer experts, who could clean my phone for me.

"You going to sleep here, or you want to hunker down with the rats again?" Lou asked. We'd gone outside to talk.

I made a face. "Tulloh is keeping track of me, I'm sure, either through his contact at the LKPD or through whatever tracers they have on my phone and the Camry, but so far they don't seem to know I've found anything. I should be safe for another night, anyway."

Ed moved the door back and forth. "Door's okay. Be hard to re-move. But this lock isn't worth the price of the key."

Lou nodded. "Got an ABUS padlock at the shop. Length of 100 chain. Even if they have the right bolt cutters, the noise will wake you long before they get in. Back in thirty. Anyone comes looking for you, hide under the couch."

"That's a hell of a way to leave the princess's ma. I'll stay here and tell her my life story while you collect the hardware."

Lou grinned. "Thought you'd man up. Be sure to tell her all the different ways chain saws have figured in your life."

Ed grunted and made a flicking motion. When Lou had left, we inspected the furniture and the bathroom fittings for booby traps. Ed disconnected the cooktop electrics and made sure they hadn't been wired to electrocute me.

When Lou returned with the chain and padlock, we moved the bed so that if someone threw something through the window, say a Molotov cocktail, I wouldn't be under it, and would have a clear path to the door. They made sure their numbers were on my speed-dial.

I walked back outside with them.

"You're carrying a load of dynamite on you. You going to keep it here?" Ed asked.

We'd packed all the journals into the lining of one of Lou's old jackets. It was oiled leather, and heavy, but it had a lining buttoned into it where I could pack my documents. I moved with the lumber-ing gait of a woman close to her due date, but on a dark February evening I hoped no watcher would be suspicious.

"They searched this place on Saturday. They searched me, they searched the car. I think the papers and I will be safe here for one night." I spoke with more confidence than I felt, but these documents had cost me too much trouble to want to separate myself from them.

I dreaded being alone in the trailer, but I kept up a bright face while the men packed Peppy back into the truck and took off. When they'd disappeared, I walked over to the building the trailer park advertised as a common room and gym. This was a double-wide unit with an old treadmill and some arcade games for children. No one was there, so I sat on a stationary bike to call Zoë.

Her eager voice vibrated the phone's speakers so loudly that my ears were hurting. I slid the volume bar down and still could hear her over the wind banging on the door.

"Vic, you're not going to believe this, but I found the family that used to own the house, you know, the one where Clarina or Rickey found all those papers? Their name is Carruthers. They were a prominent Black family in Skaneateles, but in the nineties—1990s, I mean—there was only one immediate family member left, and she got a job in the Clinton administration, something in the State Department, then she stayed on in DC, teaching at one of the universities there."

"She sold the house to Elise and Clarina's aunt when she moved?"

"That's right. Well, here's the creepy part. I mean, I tracked her down, it wasn't hard—Louisa Carruthers, her name is, but Rickey also tracked her down. Professor Carruthers—she's eighty-something now, she's retired from teaching but heads a foundation.

"Anyway, Professor Carruthers said this strange woman wrote her, claiming her name was Martha Carruthers, that she'd been adopted at birth by a Polish family, but that she was a cousin to Professor Carruthers, only she needed the professor to give a DNA sample so she could prove it. Of course, the professor refused. She had her secretary write back to say she did not respond to such letters, from white people who imagined there was glamour in being Black and not to bother the professor again. Only, guess what?"

"Martha Carruthers was a name Clarina-Rickey was using?" I asked.

"Yes!" Zoë cried, triumphant. "I talked to the neighbors who knew Clarina and they said she kept claiming she was Black and descended from this family who were important in the civil rights movement. I guess when Clarina-Rickey heard back from the professor, she retreated and decided to be descended from white abolitionists."

"That's great work, Zoë," I said. "Did the Carruthers family have a Kansas connection?"

"The professor didn't want to talk much about her own family, but she said her people had originally gone from the Auburn area out to Lawrence, and then come back to Skaneateles after the Civil War. 'It was not a hospitable climate' was how she put it."

"So at least we know now what made Clarina come out here," I said. "This is great. When do you publish?"

"Someone from the *Washington Post* showed up in Skaneateles today, so if I'm going to scoop, I have to publish in time for the morning cable feeds. Ben Pike is even giving me more money to stay on." She hung up, beside herself with excitement.

The Camry was still in the police parking lot. I decided to leave it there one more night and rode the free bus downtown to get some dinner, the journals weighing down the coat, giving me practice in rebuilding my muscles.

My skin prickled all the way through supper and on the bus back, not knowing if anyone was watching me, or where they were watching from. Life in a surveillance state must feel like this, constant exposure, constant vigilance over what you said and who you said it to.

55

PRANKING THE SERGEANT

BACK IN THE trailer, I checked the windows and the perimeter a half dozen times before settling down with my trove. I started with Clarina's notebook.

Her handwriting was big and sloppy, hard to decipher. I'd gotten as far as following the footsteps of "my Grellier ancestors" from Skaneateles to Kansas Territory in 1855 when a car pulled up outside the trailer's door.

My heart went cold. I stuck the notebook back behind the lining of Lou's coat. I switched off the living room light and pressed myself against the wall next to the door.

A pounding on the door, and then Deke Everard said, "I know you're in there, Warshawski. Open up before I get a bar and pry the door apart."

I called out that the door would be open in two minutes. Police—especially angry frustrated police—don't wait long before busting down doors. I got the lights on, picked up the key from the kitchen countertop, and got the padlock undone.

I went outside, pulling the door shut behind me—standard advice every defense lawyer gives their clients. Only let them in if they have a warrant. Invite them in and they can make themselves at home.

"I've been trying to reach you since one this afternoon. Where have you been? What's the meaning of your text about finding evidence of Clarina's murder in the woods behind the Dundee house?"

Every nerve in my body was on high alert. Lou and Ed told me they'd put the phone through their compacter. If Deke had had a warrant to search the yard, they would have told me. I was grateful for the dark, which hid any nervous twitches I might be making.

"My text, Sergeant?" My voice came out light, steady, annoyed. "Was someone pranking you, sending you on a wild goose chase after evidence? Or were they pranking me, claiming I was texting you?"

"Don't push me, Warshawski, because you'll be pushing yourself into a holding cell. We have a photograph of you at the Dundee place yesterday."

"Do you, now," I said. "Sent to you by the same helpful people who provided you with photos of Trig and Gertrude there the night Clarina's body was found?"

"Do you deny you were there?"

"I wasn't at the house," I said. "Interesting that you got a picture of me there. Must have been photoshopped. Maybe that's what happened with Gertrude and Trig?"

"Not at the house, in the woods behind it."

If he hadn't been a grown man and a police officer, I would have said he sounded sullen.

"Yes, I was in the woods. I wanted another look at Yancy, at the woods, and the remains of those old houses behind the Dundee place. I was hoping for some hint about what connected Clarina to that property."

I spoke to him earnestly, innocent, not knowing why he was so agitated.

"You're in the woods at 9:03 A.M. and at 1:16 P.M. I get an anonymous text telling me there's evidence of Clarina's murder in those woods. And then a SOC team finds the wrench—where you stashed it."

"Wrench?" I said blankly.

"You're not a good enough actor to go on Broadway," he snapped. "You know about the damned wrench."

"Even if I knew what you were talking about, I wasn't hanging around in the woods for four hours waiting to text you."

"No, but you were there dropping off a plastic garbage bag that contained evidence of a murder."

"It's time for Faye Mitchell to join this conversation. You are making wild accusations and I am not listening to more of them without my lawyer present."

I hit her speed-dial icon but got her voicemail. "Deke Everard is with me at the Prairie View Trailer Park. He claims he found evidence of a murder in the woods behind the Dundee house and is blaming me for it. If we move to the police station, I'll let you know."

Deke walked around in a circle, venting steam, came back to face me. "I'm not booking you, not yet, but one fingerprint on that bag, on that wrench, and you will be in a cell so fast your feet won't have time to hit the ground."

He turned to go.

I said, "By the way, Sergeant, someone shot at me, more than once, in those woods, and I ran. Does the photo include that?"

"You're making that up!"

"Not for one second. You should find evidence of where I landed flat on the underbrush. And a branch fell on the trail when the shooter hit a tree instead of me."

He stared at me for another long minute, face tight with emotion. Not anger, I thought, but frustration. He turned on his heel and got into his car, leaving with a great spinning of gravel. I went back inside. Collapsed onto a chair, muscles too weak from stress to hold me up. He was almost certainly recording me. If he'd asked me directly about the evidence bag, I could not have lied on the record.

56

FAMILY STORIES

AFTER DEKE LEFT, I sat up in bed reading through Clarina's spiral notebook. It was a jumble of details from her archival research, her fantasy history, and her grievances, first against her sister and then, as she spent more time in Lawrence, against the Perecs and Pat Everard for not paying appropriate attention to Clarina's knowledge of Kansas history.

She'd done impressive research in the Lawrence and Topeka libraries. At first I jotted down notes about the Wheelock, Entwistle, and Everard families as she recounted some of their history, but she tangled together nineteenth-century history with twenty-first-century slights. It became impossible to figure out which century she was writing about. Her list of grievances expanded to include staff at the University Press.

> You'd think a press in the same spot where John Brown led freedom fighters into battle against slavery would be eager to publish books set back then. I showed them a proposal, and even made the mistake of letting them see one of Sophia's letters. That won't happen again! They wanted the letters but not my historical writing.

Her proposal wasn't in the notebook. Maybe I'd overlooked it when I was nervously cleaning out her trunk, but she might have handed Kayla Huang a handwritten paragraph torn from this note-book.

Elsewhere in the notebook, Clarina wrote about Cady Perec's course, how Cady "didn't have the spine God gave a goldfish." Clarina said she'd fought for Cady's rights at Yancy school and Cady repaid her with disrespect.

I flipped through the pages, hoping for something more substantive. If this was what Matthew Tulloh thought could derail the Yancy project, he was spending time and money chasing a chimera, and chasing me in the bargain.

The last entry in the book returned to her grievance with the University Press. She'd found something that would let her tell the truth about Yancy to the world. "I can't wait to see Queen Gertrude's face when I tell her. And the snobs at the Kansas press! They're wrong if they think I'll let them publish my work. I'll go to a real university, like Harvard. They'll make these Kansas people look like the hicks they really are."

This entry was dated February 7. Whatever she'd found out, she'd given some inkling to the Kansas hicks, because six days later she was dead.

57

LOVE STORY

BUT WHAT DID you find?" I demanded out loud, before remembering the trailer might be bugged. Clarina maddened everyone around her in life; I tried to curb my annoyance with her in death.

I put her notebook into its protective plastic bag. I slipped it behind the lining of Lou's coat and carefully extracted the cardboard-bound journal.

"Sophia Grellier, her book" was written on the inside cover, with "Carruthers" inserted sometime later.

The early pages dealt with the Civil War, the struggle Sophia had to look after the house while "Mother continues poorly after Baby's death and Papa is absorbed in his important educational work."

In an 1860 entry, I found a first mention of the Carruthers family. This was the family Zoë had located, whose only living descendant was the professor in Washington.

Sophia described the Carruthers as a free Black family who had come from Auburn, at the suggestion of Mrs. Tubman, to help establish a settlement for freed Black people on a hill outside town.

They are calling it Yancy Hill, for they tell me that in the Hausa language of Africa, Yancy means freedom. Miss Anna Carruthers, who was highly educated at Oberlin College in Ohio, assists Papa in the school, which he has renamed as Yancy School. Miss Anna's father is dead, but her brother Nathan looks after

house and farm with manly zeal. Three other families are joined
in this small settlement, all working for one another in the most
noble cooperative spirit.

In Anna I find the first true bosom friend I have met since we
first moved to Kansas territory.

In February 1863, Nathan joined the First Kansas Colored Infantry
Regiment. Sophia wrote about her and Anna's fears for his safety, about
the bandages they rolled, the uniforms they made and mended, and
the quotidian, responsibility for growing food while the men were all
away at war, christening presents for babies born despite war.

In 1865, Nathan returned to Yancy. After that, he appeared more
and more often in the diary, with Sophia uncovering more and more
instances of his remarkable gifts and sweet personality. Late in 1865,
he and Sophia were married by the local white Congregational church
minister, Louis Hamer.

In a ceremony only Papa and Anna Carruthers could attend, for
fear of the increasing violence in the town against Negro people.
We spent our wedding night secretly in the schoolhouse, where
Anna laid out for us a cold feast, including a cake, and spread
blankets and cushions on the floor.

Clarina had underlined this section in red, and written "SHAME
ON YOU, LAWRENCE!!!" in large red letters in the margin. "These
are my people, I'm sure of it, and the town treated you vilely."

Clarina must have written Professor Carruthers in Washington
after reading the journal. Clarina's need to be important, to be a
player in big historical events, felt painfully embarrassing.

Through the end of 1866 and into the following spring, Sophia
wrote of her and Nathan's longing to find a place they could move to
where they could live together openly as husband and wife without
the fear of mob violence. They were considering moving to a Black
settlement in Canada, or perhaps back to the Auburn district.

And then came the attack on the school and Frederic Grellier's and
Anna Carruthers's deaths. I'd seen the *Kanwaka Courier* story about
their murders when I was at the Origins Museum. The newspaper

article had been written in a cruel spirit, blaming Frederic's support of Black education for his murder.

The *Courier* hadn't mentioned Anna Carruthers's death in the conflagration. I suppose as a Black woman she was considered beneath their notice.

For Sophia, the murders created a trauma that must have been unendurable. In the days leading up to the murder, she recorded the ugly letters her father received, accusing him of sex, "consorting" with Anna. The letters ordered him to close the school or pay with his life. Sophia quoted one in her journal as saying, "We don't need n– here, and edicated n– is the worse."

2 July 1866

The day of the murders I was approaching the school with a supply of milk and bread so that the children could have a nuncheon, when I saw the cowardly demons throwing kerosene on the building and setting it ablaze. I screamed and ran, scattering milk and bread. The monsters fled, but by the time I reached the school it was a bonfire. Father and Anna were heroic, sacrificing themselves to move the children to safety. As the children emerged, I smothered their smoldering clothes in my skirts, which fell to rags around my legs by the time we were finished.

Nathan saw the blaze from where he was working on the riverfront and came running but by then the inferno blazed with such heat we could not enter the building. As soon as the flames had died near the entrance, we saw the bodies of our dear ones, charred and contorted from the fire, along with two children they had not been able to save.

Nathan took the surviving Negro children to their homes on Yancy. Kind Mr. Schapen appeared with his wagon and drove the white children to their parents.

I could not bear to leave Father or my sister Anna's bodies, although I knew I must find the strength to break the terrible news to Mother. If there is a God, I pray he reward Mr. Schapen for his support and friendship throughout that terrible day, for he went to Mother, came back with more men and a wagon to carry the bodies to the undertaker to be fitted with coffins, and then stayed with Mother until the worst of her overwrought nerves could be calmed.

My cherished Nathan's grief surpasses my own. The sister with whom he shared every hardship, every grief—my love cannot salve those wounds. He has gone to stay with his mother on Yancy Hill. We agreed that I must not attend his sister's funeral—a white woman at a Black person's funeral would incite the mob to greater violence. And if they learned that Rev. Hamer had married us! My only consolation is the small life growing inside me. I hadn't wanted to tell my beloved until I knew with more certainty, but I told him before he left my side, and it did, indeed, bring him some measure of relief. If it is a girl we will call her Anna in honor of our beautiful sister. A son we will name for Papa.

Once Papa's funeral was over, Mother announced her intention to return to New York state. She needs more support than I can provide, alas. It is a sad reversal of roles, her need to return to the Auburn district. Twelve years ago, she was alight with a different kind of fire, kindled with the desire to loose the bondsman's chains. It was I, eight years old, who cried bitter tears at leaving my grandparents, my friends, my little bedroom hung with white muslin curtains. But poor Mother—she lost one babe on the journey to Kansas, and five more little bodies are now joined by their Father in this prairie cemetery. She can take no more sorrow, no more hardship. Grandmother Entwistle may purse her lips up in displeasure, and cry that Mother has her reward for marrying a man with more ideals than common sense, but she and my aunt Hypatia will nurse Mother back to health.

I helped her pack her trunk, and saw her safe into the cars taking her east.

And then went to pay my respects to Mrs. Carruthers and to see my beloved, whose face, whose strong arms wrapped round me I sorely needed. But when I arrived in Yancy, I was greeted by new horrors.

In the place of the tidy houses in the woods were their charred remains. The only house still standing was Mrs. Carruthers', but when I went to the door, a strange white man, reeking of alcohol, and missing so many teeth I could barely make out his speech, cackled in a horrible way and said, "The n-'s had all made tracks, and a good thing, too. They'd a disappeared in the night afore we could burn them down. Got rid of that big black buck who we all seen eyeing the schoolteacher's girl. Good riddance to the teacher, traitor to his race, good riddance to the n-. And if the girl shows up, good riddance to her, too." He waved a shotgun in my face. I stumbled through the grass, and somehow made it home before I fainted.

I sat back in my chair. The woman in the mourning photo Clarina had brought with her from Skaneateles had been Sophia Grellier Carruthers.

Pogrom on pogrom, is there no end to the hate and violence we bestow on one another?

58

THE DUNDEE HOUSE GETS ITS NAME

READ THROUGH SOPHIA'S journal to her final entry in 1875. She finally moved to Skaneateles when her child—Nathan Frederic Grellier Carruthers—was five.

> I thought I could outmatch the Wheelocks and the Everards and the rest of them, and let my boy grow up where his father and I had been happy, but after they forced Rev. Hamer to retire I felt I had no friends left in this valley. Here in Skaneateles Mother and the Entwistle relatives are almost as cold and rude as Florence Wheelock, but I have the comfort of Mrs. Tubman and Mrs. Wright and their circle.

It was past three when I finished Sophia's journal. I hoped whatever secret Clarina had uncovered lay in Florence Wheelock's journals, but my eyes and shoulders ached from leaning over the faded script. I needed to lie down for a time.

I packed Sophia back inside Lou's coat. I made another circuit of the yard around the trailer and finally fell into a jumble of dreams, where the rioters fighting open housing in the Chicago of my childhood grinned, dancing around Clarina Coffin's murdered body. Sophia Grellier Carruthers watched from the sidelines, hands folded over her pregnant stomach. She was talking to Peter, saying you're right to keep your distance.

It was a relief when I came fully awake again a little after nine. I stood in the shower until the hot water ran out, trying to wash the dreams and turbulent thoughts out of my head.

I couldn't face more time alone in the trailer. I took Florence Wheelock down to the library to read.

Wheelock, Gertrude Perec's ancestor, had performed an Eliza Doolittle transformation on herself, from illiterate child of a poor farmer to wife of one of the town's top citizens. Somehow her own experience of poverty, and being an envious outsider to the lives white middle-class girls were leading, hadn't made her sympathetic to other outsiders, such as the town's Black or poor white populations.

Instead, she looked scornfully at them, even her own sisters. She often wrote witheringly about them doing the back-breaking farmwork she'd escaped, enduring multiple pregnancies. She wrote that they could have followed her example, but they preferred "to remain in the mud."

The three volumes Clarina had filched covered the years 1865 to 1872. As was true with Sophia Grellier's journal, Clarina had defaced Florence's writing with her own comments. I started by looking for those.

She and Theodore Wheelock belonged to the Riverside Congregational Church. He was one of the church elders, a group that seemed to make up the church's management committee. He and some of his pals disliked the minister, the Reverend Louis Hamer, who kept trying to ram sermons on racial equality and justice down their throats. When people learned that Hamer had married Sophia and Nathan, Florence wrote so angrily that sparks leaped from the paper.

In the margin, Clarina had written in red ink, "Queen Gertrude's racist supercilious heritage on full display!!"

Finally in 1869, Wheelock controlled a majority of the elders, and they forced Hamer to retire. It was then that Sophia left Lawrence for New York State.

An 1870 entry explained how the Dundee house got its name.

November 18, 1870

Mr. Wheelock was finally able to lay claim to the rich farmland on Yancy Hill. Rev. Hamer had his supporters in the congregation

as well as his detractors, and one such has always been Simon
Booth, who used his position as county recorder to oppose
Mr. Wheelock's claim. But with the November election behind
us, and Henry Everard now installed as the county recorder,
Mr. Wheelock had smooth sailing.

Nine years ago, when the school burned down,
Mr. Wheelock installed a Cyrus Dundee in the Carruthers house,
the only house in the colored settlement still standing. Dundee
has a slattern of a wife and five or perhaps six raggedy children,
but he has a shotgun. Over the years he has shot at any coloreds
trying to sneak back onto the property.

At least now I knew why the drug house was called the Dundee
place. It seemed heartbreaking, the house that Nathan Carruthers
had built with his mother and sister first handed over to an illiterate
drunkard, and then made the site of Brett Santich's drug parties. Perhaps some shaman or priest could perform a purification ritual.

I turned back to Florence's journal. And in the next paragraph
found the hand grenade Clarina had tried to lob at the Yancy project.

Mr. and Mrs. Everard joined us tonight to celebrate the liberation
of Yancy. Mrs. Everard and I suggested changing the name
Yancy to something more Christian, since the word is a heathen
one, bestowed by the riffraff who used to camp there, but
Mr. Wheelock advised against it.

He has given me the old, illegitimate record for safekeeping,
and what safer place than here, where only my own eyes look.

I read the entry a half dozen times, trying to take in the meaning.
Theodore Wheelock had finally been able to claim the rich farmland
on Yancy. He had given Florence the old illegitimate record, and
she had kept it in her journal, where only her own eyes looked. The
illegitimate record. Wheelock had laid claim to the land, he'd been
turned down by the county recorder, but with a new man in office,
he'd been able to push his claim.

Wheelock had claimed land that belonged to the Carruthers
family. This meant that all the subsequent sales of the land—to the

Everards in the 1870s, to the Santiches in the 1930s, and the Santich sale to the Yancy project two years ago—were invalid. Assuming the original title still existed. And that it was valid.

I imagined Clarina hinting to Gertrude, to Brett Santich, to anyone in her radius, that she had proof that the title to Yancy land belonged to the Carruthers family, in fact to Professor Louisa Carruthers in Washington.

Gertrude would have hated the world to know her ancestors had stolen the land, but the legal implications were explosive.

Fifty years ago, even ten years ago, courts would likely have ruled that Wheelocks, Everards, and so on had de facto rights to the Yancy property. Today's courts were starting to recognize the rights of African-Americans to property that had been forcibly seized from their ancestors.

I went back through the diary, trying to see what I might have missed. It was four o'clock, and my eyes were aching from the strain of a day reading words handwritten so long ago. I moved to a table with a magnifying lamp on it.

And saw, in the margin of the November 1870 entry where Wheelock was laying claim to land on Yancy, faint remnants of dried glue, a patch an inch or so wide, that extended to the bottom of the page.

I took out Clarina's scrapbook of photographs and newspaper articles, went through it page by page. I finally found it: a piece of parchment, roughly an inch wide by perhaps a foot long, torn around the edges where it had been removed from the recorder's book, folded in half to fit the size of Florence's journal. It had slipped down behind a plastic cover in Clarina's KU notebook. I pulled it out slowly, protecting the edges from further damage.

When I laid it on the page in Florence Wheelock's journal, patches of dried glue on the parchment strip exactly fit into the glue traces in Florence Wheelock's journal.

It was a record, created in March 1861 by the Douglas County Recorder of Deeds. Even though the ink was faded, the recorder had written carefully in a fine hand; it was easy to read the text.

The recorder had proclaimed: "Know All Men by These Presents" that land with plat numbers 1594-632 to 1594-660 on Yancy Hill was registered to Phyllida Carruthers and her son Nathan, that they owned the title free and clear of all encumbrance, that the property included five brick houses, a barn, a section of farmland and a section of timber that stretched to the top of the hill.

The recorder hadn't been able to refrain from exulting in the margin, "We are truly a state now with a freely elected government. Our first recorded deeds in Douglas County!"

59
PRESSING BUSINESS

─────────

I **NEEDED SOMEONE ELSE** to know what I knew. Someone who would act quickly, and who would make sure that the Carruthers family was recognized as the legitimate title holder to the land on Yancy.

I didn't want to keep carrying these diaries around with me and yet I was terrified of leaving them where they could be damaged or destroyed. I finally went back to the Osma Room, where I'd briefly stored the wrench.

Before I put my fragile hoard behind the outsize atlases where I'd left the wrench, I photographed the pages, moved them to a text, and sent them to Zoë. You know what to do next, I said.

I walked to Gertrude Perec's house and rang the bell. Gertrude came to the door and told me to go away, that we had nothing to discuss.

"But we do, Gertrude, either on the street or indoors—your choice. We can discuss what Clarina Coffin said that got you to go to the Dundee house in the middle of the night. Did she tell you she'd learned that your Wheelock ancestors stole the land on Yancy from the Carruthers family? Did she offer to show you the proof if you'd meet her at the Dundee house?"

Gertrude's jaw worked. "She claimed so many different things it was impossible to believe any of them."

"But you couldn't be sure. You wanted to see what she'd found."

"Gram!" Cady had appeared behind Gertrude in the foyer. "Is this true? Did you see her before she died?"

Gertrude swayed, looked as though she might fall. I pushed my way into the house and put an arm around her. Cady took her other arm and led her into the living room. Settled her in an armchair.

"Gram, what happened? You have to tell me the truth now. What did Clarina say to you?"

"She came up to me at church that Sunday," Gertrude whispered. "She said she wanted to see how I acted when I wasn't queen of Lawrence any longer. I asked what she was talking about and she wouldn't say, just smirked all over her nasty face and said 'wait and see.' I wasn't going to give her the satisfaction of watching me beg for information. I turned and left her standing there smirking."

"Of course you told Pat Everard," I said.

"Of course," she agreed. "Pat had watched her, anyway, and wanted to know what was going on. Then, Monday, I got a message to meet Clarina at the Dundee house at three in the morning and she'd show me proof."

"She phoned, or texted?" I asked.

Gertrude shook her head. "A typed letter through the mail slot. I went. I told Pat, she thought it was dangerous, so she followed me out there, and waited in the road. No one came except Trig. I thought Clarina had sent him, they worked together like a couple of deranged people, but he didn't seem to know anything about what Clarina knew. Finally I left."

"Did you keep the letter that was dropped through your mail slot?" I asked.

"I burned it. I wanted nothing to do with Clarina or her hints and insults. I want nothing to do with your hints and insults, either."

"Of course not," I agreed. "It's a pity you burned the letter. There's no way to prove whether Clarina wrote it."

"Of course she wrote it," Gertrude said.

"There's no 'of course' about anything in Clarina's life or death," I said. "I'd thought maybe the killers wrote it, trying to implicate as many people as possible in her death, but of course they thought her body would lie undiscovered in the Dundee house basement until it was a skeleton. They didn't know I'd find her."

"And what about Trig? Why would Clarina want to meet him in the middle of the night?" Cady asked. "They were such buddies, or at least, it seemed that way."

"He went there for a completely different reason," I said. "Nothing to do with Clarina. But where was she killed? Did she go up to Yancy Hill and taunt—"

I cut myself off. Of course. Her note about the snobs at the Kansas University press. She had tried to peddle her story there. I stood abruptly and headed for the door.

"But where are you going?" Cady asked. "You can't just run off like that in the middle—"

"Gertrude needs to confess everything to Deke. Get her to do that, and it will clean up one part of the investigation."

Cady called after me, frantic with questions, but I hurried back to the bus stop near the library. A freezing rain had started to fall. I was still wearing Lou's jacket, a couple of sizes too big for me, now that I wasn't carrying a load of books, but the oiled leather kept me dry until a number 10 bus arrived. I rode it out to Westbrooke Circle, to the University Press.

Kayla Huang was in the lobby, chatting with the receptionist. The pair stopped mid-laugh when they saw me. "You're the detective, right? I'm sorry I don't remember your name," Huang said.

"V.I. Warshawski. I have an awkward question, so I'll ask it bluntly. Yesterday I stumbled on a notebook Clarina Coffin was keeping—part journal, part fantasy autobiography."

The burner camera didn't offer the clarity of my iPhone, but it showed the text well enough. I scrolled through the pictures I'd taken of the diaries and of Clarina's notebook until I found her incensed comment about finding a real university to publish her book.

"You told me it had been a long time since you'd seen Clarina. She apparently found—or thought she found—startling new information about Yancy a week before her death. And it implies she showed it to someone at the press here."

Huang shook her head, puzzled. "Not to me. Graham?"

"I guess she could have come while I was on break," he said doubtfully. "She was so recognizable, I'm sure I would have noticed her even if she didn't stop at the counter here."

Out of the corner of my eye, I saw red hair and a blue smock come into the reception area and then scurry down the hall. I darted after her.

"Ivy!"

She broke into a run. I caught her as she was opening a rear door.

"Ivy, did Clarina talk to you here, the week before she died?"

"Mind your own damned business. Thanks to your interference, I have less money for Timmy than I did two weeks ago."

"You are not nearly as stupid as that remark makes you sound," I snapped. "Thanks to Brett and Don Wilton you got money to clean up after drug parties. You are incredibly lucky you were never arrested in a police raid. Were you here when Clarina came in the week before Valentine's Day?"

"You're not going to frame me for her murder."

I sighed. "Only if you committed it. Clarina came in, she was full of herself, you were the only person in the lobby and she couldn't help gloating over her find. What was it?"

"She didn't say, just that all the high-and-mighty people in Lawrence would be shown up for the bigots they've always been. She had something that would blow Yancy Hill sky high. She said she wanted Kayla Huang to know she could beg and plead to publish her but it wouldn't do her any good."

Huang and Graham had appeared behind me, but I signaled to them to stay back.

"Did you tell Kayla any of this?"

"Oh, please. Clarina was so full of herself. Everyone who hung anywhere near Trig knew that. I wasn't going to look as stupid as— whatever it was you said, that stupid—by telling Kayla or any of the other editors."

"But you told Brett," I said, tone conversational, taking it for granted.

She hunched a shoulder. "Maybe."

"And then—" I started to say. Stopped. The letter, that fragment I'd found in the woods behind the Dundee House.

"You and Brett had a laugh about it," I said. "She was pathetic. She thought she'd make Kayla crawl to her, now that she had identified Yancy's original owners, but poor Clarina! She wanted recognition more than anything, and Brett, or at least Robert Tulloh, understood that. Brett asked you to get him a piece of the Press's letterhead. Do you know what he did with it?"

Ivy's eyes were wide with fear. "He said, a practical joke."

"It was very practical." My voice, harsh with judgment that I couldn't suppress. "He invited her to come to the Press for lunch to discuss her findings with an eye to a book contract. And then I suppose he jumped her, or Chet, the Yancy crew foreman, yes, with his Kirmek pipe wrench, a good tap on the skull on a wintry day, no one notices her fall, into his arms and then into the back of his truck."

"Ivy!" Kayla Huang gasped. "You didn't—you couldn't!"

"Wait until you have a child to support before you say, oh, you couldn't!"

Before I could react, she bolted out the door and into a pickup. I was on foot with no way to follow.

"Is that right?" Graham said. "She really helped lure Clarina to her death?"

My shoulders sagged. "I expect she's right, I expect she didn't know why Brett asked for letterhead. And he probably didn't know, either—he was doing whatever the Tullohs asked of him so he could keep on trying to pay down his debts, look after his wife and daughter, throw the occasional bone to his girlfriend and son."

"You said Clarina found proof of who originally owned the land on Yancy," Kayla said. "What is it?"

"The title was originally filed by a Black family named Carruthers." And now Ivy was on her way to Brett, Brett would tell Tulloh and Chet that I'd seen the proof. I needed to get to the recorder's office. As soon as Tulloh understood that Clarina—and now I—had proof of the original title, he could destroy that first volume of Douglas County titles and deeds, and with it proof that the Carruthers title had been cut from the book.

It was four-thirty now; half an hour before the office closed.

60

BOOK REPORT

THE CLERK WAS tidying her papers for the day. She gave me a look that was half-humorous, half-exasperated. "You do know the office opens at nine in the morning, don't you? It isn't necessary to wait for fifteen minutes to closing to look at a record."

I apologized, but said, "I want to look at the very first deeds registered here, after statehood."

"Yancy doesn't figure in the records until 1870," she said.

"You said this place was like the wild west back when people were first filing claims. I want to see how wild the west was."

She cocked an eyebrow, her attention caught. I followed her into a side room where the older volumes were stored. She rolled a ladder over to the corner and pulled the first volume from the top shelf.

"All these have been digitized," she said, "but we're keeping the first volumes for historical reasons."

She laid it open on the big table in the front room and watched me, forgetting that she was eager to get out of the office.

We bent over the book together, looking at the first titles filed in Douglas County in the winter of 1861.

"When I came in here last week, I noticed that the top of this first page had been cut so that the first entries are lower than in the rest of the book. I thought perhaps the parchment had been cut by hand and they hadn't done it evenly. What really happened is that someone cut that first entry out of the book. The first title filed in Douglas County after Kansas became a state had been removed.

"No!" she cried. "That isn't possible. No one is allowed alone with these books."

"Not now, maybe, in the twenty-first century. In 1870, though, when Henry Everard was the recorder, and a close friend of Theodore Wheelock, he was happy to let Wheelock cut out the original title. Wheelock registered the Yancy land in his name in 1870 and shared some of it with Everard as a thank-you gift."

I turned to the 1870 registration I'd looked at on my first visit. The clerk read it, then returned to the first page.

"What was there originally, then?" she asked.

I had put the registry of the Carruthers' title into a plastic sleeve. I pulled this out of my daypack now and removed the title to the land on Yancy. The strip of paper exactly fit the gap on the page.

I had photographed the pages from Florence's journal where she boasted about getting the title registered and showed those to the clerk. The woman frowned over the page.

"This is—I don't even know the word. Staggering. Shocking. If it's true, it completely undoes all the titles to Yancy plats that flow from the 1870 registration. I—we have to get an expert to study this. Lawyers—what do we do if you're right and the Wheelocks and the Everards stole the land? Unless they didn't know they were stealing?"

"The diaries Florence Wheelock kept make it clear they knew exactly what they were doing. But even if they didn't know, these records don't show any transfer of the title from the Carrutherses to the Wheelocks—just that Theodore Wheelock staked a claim to the same plats deeded to the Carruthers family nine years earlier.

"I agree, it will be a huge legal mess. Particularly since Tulloh Industries is building on top of Yancy now, in the belief that they own the property."

An outfit like Tulloh has a legal department with thousands of attorneys. They could probably mount a successful defense for claiming the land, or at least tie up claims in litigation for so long that they'd build their crypto farm or whatever it was before the case was settled. They really hadn't needed to kill Clarina-Ulricke.

The clerk looked at me helplessly. "I need to talk to Amos—Amos Clapton—he's our recorder."

I put the fragment back into the plastic sleeve and returned it to my backpack.

The clerk said, "If that was cut from our deed book, then it belongs here."

"If we establish its authenticity, and prove that it was cut from this original volume, of course it stays here. But anyone could walk in and take it away with them while you were busy assisting someone else."

"No one could go into our book storage room without my knowing they'd been here," she said. "When I leave the office, even for five minutes, I lock the door. You really mustn't carry that title around with you—it's—what if you were mugged and someone stole your backpack?"

"You could be right," I said. "But I believe Clarina Coffin was murdered by someone who wanted this scrap of paper. It needs to be with the police or the FBI until it's authenticated, and the chain of ownership on Yancy has been established. I'm going to keep it safe until then—it goes into a bank first thing tomorrow."

She eyed my pack, as if debating whether she could wrest if from me, but finally picked up the 1861 deed book and took it back to her inner room. I was on my way out the door when the landline on the counter rang.

The clerk answered, and then said sharply, "Yes, she was here."

I left the door cracked open and pressed myself against the wall.

"The FBI? Oh, goodness, I wish I'd known. I should have guessed she was a criminal, she acted so wild. You should have called five minutes ago . . . She'll have to go out the east door, the rest of the building will be locked by now, but does she have a weapon? Am I safe? Yes, I can lock myself in my office. You'll call when you've picked her up?"

I skittered down the hall, looking wildly for an escape route. The west door had a chain and padlock across it. Stairs going down or up. I ran up. At the top of the second flight, I almost ran into a guard talking to a man in a suit. I slowed my pace, just a working person on her way to her office, not someone wanted by the Faux BI.

"Don't think they'll make it pass the Elite Eight," the guard was saying.

"Don't be a killjoy, Dree, I know they don't have last year's depth but my crystal ball says repeat."

The men's basketball team's chances in the NCAA tournament. No one cared what I was doing.

I walked to the far end of the hall and found Judge Bhagavatula's chambers. The door to the courtroom wasn't locked. I walked behind the bench and knocked hard on the door on my left.

"Judge Bhagavatula?" I called, not too loudly. No answer. This door opened as well. The judge's law books filled several shelves. I picked *Kansas Statutes, Courts to Domestic Relations*. I pulled the Carruthers title record from its plastic sleeve and placed it near the beginning.

When I moved back into the hall, the guard and the man in the suit had left. I peered over the railing. Mellon and Don Wilton were in the lower hall. Somehow they'd acquired vests that read FBI, and they were escorting the few people still in the building toward the east exit.

I shut my eyes briefly. Breathe, don't panic, don't abandon your training, find a secondary stairwell. Clinging to the wall to avoid being spotted, I skidded around a corner, found the fire EXIT sign I was looking for, moved down the stairs to the basement, found a door to the janitors' room, beyond it an exit to the parking lot. One step at a time, push the door open.

I was almost home free when my phone rang. I pressed the switch to silence it, but a hand came from above me. I kicked out furiously. A terrible pain along my skull and then darkness.

61

COAL DUST

I WAS COLD. I knew my mother was near, but when I tried to open my eyes to look for her my head felt as though it would splinter from pain. My throat was raw. I smelled vomit and something harsher. Steel mills.

I was sitting on something rough. The ground by the mills. What were we doing there? Had Gabriella gone to complain about the coal dust? *Cappotto. Aqua.* Coat, water, I begged her, but my throat was so raw I couldn't get the words out.

"Did the bitch say something?" a rough voice asked. English. This wasn't South Chicago.

I felt someone leaning over me. Kept my head bent down, breathed through my mouth, produced a half snore.

"She's still out. Why'd you hit her so hard? We need her conscious and talking. She stinks, by the way."

I knew that voice, thin baritone. It was agony to think, to concentrate. They'd hit me, too hard, and so my head hurt. I'd been running. Escaping. I had to move my mind to the other side of its mountain of pain, figure out where I was, who was with me.

I wanted to stand, to get away from the men, from the pain. My feet were tied together. There was a metal pole at my back. I was tied to that as well.

"What about the reporter, that nosy bitch hanging around the detective?" The first speaker, the rough voice.

"She's still in New York. No chance Warshawski handed it off to her. Anyway, the courthouse has been sealed off." The thin baritone, impatient with underlings.

"Maybe she ate it," a tenor suggested.

The rough voice laughed. "In that case, put a bullet through her and dump her by the river."

"No bullets," the baritone said. "Natural causes, just like Rotherhaite."

Rotherhaite. Coal. The smell that made me think of steel works. I was at the Wakarusa coal plant. The thin baritone, that was the urban cowboy who'd bought the plant. Robert Tulloh.

"Cops have the wrench," the tenor said. "Cunt here managed to hide it when Chet put it in her room. She planted it in my woods. Another dead woman with a head wound, not even Big Matthew's friends can make that go away."

Robert Tulloh laughed, ugly sound. "You're underestimating his powers, Santich. Like you underestimate everything, including your debt load. Bezory, you'd better do a more thorough job than you did with Rotherhaite, hide her deeper in the bushes."

I opened my eyes a slit. We were on the floor of the coal plant. What had they done with the afternoon shift workers?

"Wake her up," Tulloh said. "This is getting boring. We need to get going."

A bucket of water over the head. That did wake me up. Flushed the vomit from my jacket. Protective reflex, arms to face—except they wouldn't rise that high. They were bound to my sides at the elbows. Feet tied, arms bound, wits gone a-begging.

Tulloh pulled a chair up right above me and straddled it, chin resting on the back. "You've been a busy little cunt, haven't you? Snooping around in things that don't belong to you. Time to turn over that scrap of paper you found. It isn't yours."

I let my eyelids droop, through the veil of lashes saw his arm sweep toward me. Let my head fall. He hit the metal pole behind me hard, swore, stood, and kicked me in the stomach. No protection from that.

"You think you found something valuable, but you didn't. Any more than the stupid Coffin woman did. The girl at the recorder's office said you showed some bogus piece of paper, claiming some Black family a thousand years ago squatted on Yancy, but we own the land. We'll do what we want with it."

"Then why kill Clarina?" my voice came out in a croak.

"She was a pest, a nuisance, a cockroach. We don't tolerate vermin at Tulloh, and you're a bigger piece of it than she was."

"A lot of people know I found the Carruthers 1861 title to the land on Yancy. I sent a photo to the nosy reporter bitch. Editors at the University Press have seen the title. Your daddy will—"

He backhanded my face. He was wearing a ring. Blood on my lips, in my mouth.

"What did Clarina tell you she found? The title? Or the diary where the Wheelocks boasted about stealing the land?"

"She told that useless piece of shit Trig she'd found something that would blow Yancy sky-high. She didn't tell him what, but Trig told Ivy, trying to impress her, or warn her to stay away from loser Santich," Tulloh said. "We knew Coffin had something we needed to see."

"Loser Santich knew how to get her to come out to the Press," Santich snarled. "The real loser is your hulking Neanderthal who hit her too hard and killed her before we could get her to talk."

"Not a problem this time around." Tulloh grinned, showed perfectly capped teeth. "We're not letting him hit this one."

He ran his fingers around my jaw, a caress. I bit him, hard. He laughed, punched me again. "Hellcat. Good. We'll have more fun all the way around. But in the end, you will tell me what I want to know. Where is that title?"

I didn't speak. I had no clever remarks left in me, no questions I wanted answered, nothing to say, nothing to hear.

Tulloh told Santich to take off my shoes and socks. He lit a cigarette and knelt to hold it to my instep.

Bezory smacked his hand away, grabbed the cigarette, dropped it and stood on it. "Fucking moron! You don't light a fire in a coal plant."

"You don't call me names, Bezory, you work for me." Tulloh stabbed Bezory's chest with a finger, backing him away from the cigarette.

"I'm not one of your lapdogs like Santich here, or that creep of a houseboy Mellon. You want to blow up the plant, I'm out of here."

I put my left heel on the floor, wriggled the right foot out of the rope, then the left foot. Santich was watching the other two men. Ten seconds, roll as far as possible to my left, retrieve the cigarette, roll back. The cigarette was still glowing. I held it against the rope around my left wrist.

"Afraid of fire?" Tulloh jeered, flicking his lighter in Bezory's face.

Rope fraying, left hand burning, left hand free, pull the rope away from the pole, leap up. I ran across the floor toward the doors. Skidded on an oil slick. Tulloh was on me. Hands around my throat, he dropped the lighter into the oil.

In the nanosecond between the flame and the fire he lost his hold, bellowing with fury, fear. I slid away, ran out the door, to the river, into the blessed terrifying cold.

62
ROWING PRACTICE

LOU'S COAT FILLED with water and dragged me under. I wrestled myself free of it and stood, feet in the muddy shoal, choking out oily water. Onshore I heard Tulloh and Bezory shouting but not what they were saying.

I couldn't stay in the cold water, didn't have the strength to swim across the river. I grabbed at the bushes close to the shore and was pulling myself out when I heard voices on the river.

"Hey, guys, look at that! Fire coming out of the stacks!"

"Pull!" someone shouted. "This is practice, not a sightseeing trip!"

"Help!" I screamed, louder than Callas at La Scala.

I screamed again, and again, and the boat turned toward me. A racing boat, eight oars. I flopped into the boat, landing on someone's knees. Outcries: *what the fuck was I doing in the river on a winter night, mind your knees, I guess practice is over for tonight, huh? And look at those flames. The place is on fire.*

"Running from the fire," I gasped out the words.

"Anyone else there?"

"Don't know," I said.

One woman thought we should go ashore and check, but the person I'd landed on said I was wet and frozen and needed emergency care; best call the fire department.

An ambulance was waiting when we reached the boathouse. I stayed awake just long enough to give my rescuers Lou's phone number.

63

HOMEWARD BOUND

WE SAW THE fire shooting from the stacks up at the farm. Should've guessed it was you. How'd you make that happen, anyway?"

"My warm personality," I said.

Ed air-punched me.

I'd been moved from the ICU to a regular bed, but I was still fragile—broken ribs where Tulloh had kicked me, more damage to my nose and upper teeth. One or both men had been with me ever since they got the call from the rowing team.

"Tulloh is a mean rattlesnake even when he isn't cornered. You bested him in the plant, big-time, and he isn't likely to forgive and forget."

The fire had burned for over a day before the firefighters got it under control. They'd kept it from spreading to the underground coal storage, but there was enough coal dust in the air that it blew out the windows and melted joins in a number of the pipes. It would be a long time, if ever, before the Wakarusa plant could come back on stream. Which meant that even if Tulloh Industries made good on their claim to Yancy land, they wouldn't have a dedicated power supply for the crypto farm.

The first week after the fire, once the doctors discharged me, I spent at the Hilltop Farm. Lou and Ed were reluctant to allow any officers of the law on their land, so when Deke Everard wanted to interview me, we did it at my third favorite spot in Lawrence, behind the Hilltop Farm and the Hippo—the public library.

Faye Mitchell, my Lawrence lawyer, was with me, to enforce an agreement that the entire conversation was off the record and that I had immunity from any charges in connection with unauthorized entry into Don Wilton's office above the Lion's Heart.

I gave Deke the same story I'd told Faye. He took the information to Brett Santich, telling him they could get him dead to rights on running a drug house, on kidnapping me, and a bunch of other charges unless he was willing to cooperate. Santich was the weakest link among the coconspirators; he apparently revealed enough of the drug operation to get the LKPD to apply for a warrant to search Wilton's office and his computers.

Frankie Karas didn't want to issue one, but Deke's application coincided with a story Murray ran, showing evidence of unreported payouts by Tulloh Industries to Karas's campaign chest. Zoë and Murray had been working in tandem. Zoë had been reporting the history of Yancy, the role of the early Anglo settlers in killing the Black residents and seizing their property. Murray decided to go after the present-day power brokers.

Of course, the police chief should have made the decision about applying for a warrant, but Chief McDowell had announced a leave of absence. Zoë, inspired by Murray, had dug up evidence that the chief and his wife regularly took vacations on Matthew Tulloh's yacht, the *Prairie Schooner*. Zoë was using FOIA to apply for the chief's phone records, to see how often he'd called Jake Tulloh.

When the story of the payouts broke, Karas backed down and issued Deke the warrants he was requesting for the Lion's Heart computers. It's one thing for a billionaire to bankroll Supreme Court Justices, but a county DA has to face voters every few years. Revelations that Karas was giving Tulloh's subordinates favorable legal treatment in exchange for financial favors had a number of local lawyers ready to challenge him in the upcoming primary.

After Deke and I finished, I agreed to talk to Gertrude Perec. She wanted me to come to her home, but as with Deke, I insisted we talk in the library. Pat Everard and Cady came with her.

"My mother gave those Wheelock diaries to the Origins Museum when it first opened in 1960," Gertrude told me. "They made a big deal of it—daughter of one of Kansas's founding families donating family treasure. I was a sophomore out at Wellesley—Wheelocks had been sending their daughters to Wellesley since the college opened. In the 1870s Florence Wheelock made sure her daughters had the same education as their Massachusetts cousins. A hundred-forty-year tradition broken by little Missy here—" She patted Cady's knee.

"Kansas," Cady said. "My girlfriends and I all went to KU."

"I hadn't bothered with the diaries, growing up," Gertrude said. "The time or two I tried to read them, I couldn't decipher the handwriting. But I think my mother did. I think she gave them away after she read about how the Wheelocks took possession of Yancy. That was when she started agitating for civil rights and so on here in the town. Of course I thought it was noble: 1960, the sit-ins started that year, and then the Freedom Riders, Freedom Summer. I didn't have to go south like some of my college friends, I worked with my mother right here in Lawrence.

"But then Clarina showed up. First she was criticizing Lawrence history in general, saying we thought we were special, abolitionists and so on, but we had just as much blood on our hands as any southern town. She got on everyone's nerves, but she never had any proof.

"Then she started harassing Cady and the Yancy school about teaching woke Kansas history, and that made me angry."

Pat Everard nodded. "The day she showed up at Riverside, determined to lecture us on our history and on our duty, I asked her, 'Were you ever on the front line of getting a university to integrate its dorms? Did you ever make sure your town, whatever it was, offered Blacks and whites the same economic opportunities? Did you ever fight your local bank over punitive mortgage rates? Don't come lecturing to us until you show you took risks yourself.'"

"Clarina said, 'My whole existence is a risk, which you will never appreciate.' If Cady or her mother had ever said something like that to me, I would have smacked them," Gertrude put in.

"And then, about a week before she was killed, she started in on the 1860 Wheelocks, how they pretended to be for freeing the enslaved, but were just as bad as any southern lynch mob. She said she could prove we'd never had a right to Yancy land.

"The night you found that college student in the Dundee place, I had a call—I thought it was from Clarina. Ulricke. Saying she'd show me the proof if I'd come out to the Dundee house. I don't know why I lied and told you she'd put a letter through my mail slot. Anyway, I guess you know that part—how I showed up at the Dundee house and found Trig."

"Why did Trig go out there?" Cady asked. "Did the same person who tricked Gram tell him Cady was there?"

I shook my head. "He has a police scanner. He saw there was activity out there and he—well, he was trying to look after Ivy and her little boy, Timmy. He knew she cleaned out there after the drug parties, and he wanted to make sure she didn't walk straight into cop arms.

"Which she did anyway," I added sadly. "I don't know if they're going to prosecute her for her role in Clarina's death, but she did blindly do whatever Brett Santich asked. Including giving him some Press letterhead to entice Clarina to show up where it was easy to kidnap her. The building is in the middle of a kind of park, without much traffic unless people are going to the Press. It was easy for them to ambush Clarina."

Deke had been a silent member of my conversation with his mother and Gertrude. He followed me out to the street, where my Mustang was waiting—freshly detailed at the LKPD's expense.

"I hope you'll accept my apologies," he said. "I was getting tied in knots by too many different interests. I worried that my chief was not—let's just say upholding the law equally for everyone. I worried about Karas. The FBI creep was jerking my chain. And then you—you may be right a lot of the time, but you can be pretty hard to take, galloping in from the outside like you know stuff we hicks don't understand."

"That's not my intention at all," I protested. "I had a terrible fall and winter. I was questioning my judgment on things as simple as ordering dinner, let alone figuring out a series of crimes in a jurisdiction where I didn't know anyone or anything."

"Yeah, maybe. I'll just say every time you were proved right, it made my blood boil. I so wanted you to be wrong about something." He laughed self-consciously. "Including Clete Rotherhaite. By the time we finished listening to all Don Wilton's audio files, it was clear that Rotherhaite was murdered, by Mellon and Bezory—they did all the muscle work for the Tullohs. I don't think we'll ever get anything to stick to Matthew or Robert. They're shelling out big-time for legal counsel for Bezory and Mellon, so we may never get anything to stick to them, either."

"But why did they kill Rotherhaite?" I asked. "He didn't have any power to stop their data farm."

"He did, though. Tulloh was still in the room with him when he called the Kansas EPA about the plant being too old to handle the power demands Yancy was going to put on it if the data farm went up. And also that Tulloh's lawyers had lied about the purpose of the project in their filings with the planning commission. What you didn't hear was the next part of Wilton's private recordings: Tulloh called Rotherhaite back and said he'd thought things over, cooler heads prevailed, a walk by the river where they could be private, work it all out. Only it was Mellon waiting for him there."

He handed me the Mustang keys and walked me to the car. "Do me a favor, Warshawski. Even if your closest friend in the universe is playing the Jayhawks for the national title, watch her on TV, okay?"

I was glad to part from him on good terms. He was basically a good cop, just one in a bad spot.

As I got ready to return to Chicago, to friends and responsibilities, I kept wondering if, or maybe how, the Tullohs would exact their revenge on me. My last full day in Lawrence, a sleek Mercedes convertible came up the drive to the Hilltop Farm.

The men were at work. I walked out with the dog, every muscle braced. It was Pauline Tulloh who got out of the car.

I raised my eyebrows. "I can't offer you fermented cabbage, but there's coffee or tea."

"I won't be staying. Tulloh Industries is undergoing some structural changes, and I thought you should hear about them from me. Robert will be going to Lagos to oversee our African operations. Jake will be taking over as chief operating officer, and Daddy decided I should be a financial officer. He thought I showed good judgment, trying to warn him that Robert was dabbling in crypto, even if it was the computer end, not bitcoins."

Her voice was as calm and arrogant as it had been when I saw her in Mission Hills in February.

"He agreed that we shouldn't try to revive the Wakarusa plant. We'll sell it for scrap. He says in hindsight you showed good judgment and that he was too hasty in accepting Robert's interpretation of your actions. Mother agreed. She asked me to see that you got compensated for your time and trouble."

Perhaps a more moral person would have ripped up the check Pauline handed me. However, it seemed like the right amount, a hundred thousand for six weeks of travail and lost income, for the expenses of life on the road, for Faye Mitchell's fee. Mitchell wasn't running a charity, she said, and she billed accordingly.

I'd been cleared by the local doctors to drive, but they advised local trips only for another week or so. Ed and Lou said it had been years since they'd been in Chicago. Ed drove the Mustang. Peppy and I followed in the truck with Lou.

Mr. Contreras was beside himself with joy when we arrived. I'd warned him that the men were vegetarians, so out of his trio of specialties he served up spaghetti with the sauce he makes from his home-canned tomatoes. Because it was a festive occasion, he followed up with his home-distilled grappa.

After the fourth shot, Mr. Contreras began singing one of his grandmother's folksongs. Lou said he'd had a grandmother, too, and began belting out "Froggie went a-courtin'." Ed said he'd also had a grandmother who also sang. Around midnight, Mr. Sung from the second floor was at the door, almost weeping because we'd woken the baby.

Unfazed, Lou said, didn't he have a grandmother? And didn't he want to honor her memory? To my astonishment, after downing a steadying shot of grappa, Mr. Sung produced a song from his Korean childhood.

After that, I couldn't resist singing "Il fervido desiderio," my favorite of the Italian songs my mother used to sing for my father and me.

64

HAPPY EVER AFTER— OR AT LEAST FOR A FEW DAYS

MY BRUISES HEALED. A plastic surgeon got my nose more or less back to where it had been in January. I started working out, started eating, started spending more time with friends.

Was it my triumph over the billionaires that cured the anguish and self-doubts that had deviled me the last six months? Nothing is ever that simple. The murder of Peter's student would stay with me for the rest of my life, but recovering from my own injuries, seeing justice done to Clarina Coffin's memory, helped bring an end to my self-torment. I'd pushed myself, been pushed, almost past the limit of my endurance, and I had endured.

Mr. Contreras joined Bernie, Angela, and me when we went to Kansas in late April to celebrate Yancy Day. Louisa Carruthers, the George Washington University professor who was the last living descendant of Sophia Grellier and Nathan Carruthers, came out for the celebration.

The Dundee house, named for the illiterate white drunkard whom the Wheelocks and Everards had installed there, was renamed. Professor Carruthers chose to call it Yancy House, since her ancestors had named the hill Yancy, meaning "freedom" in the Hausa language.

Zoë had been working with Gertrude and Cady Perec to publish excerpts from the Wheelock diaries in the *Douglas County Her-*

ald. Professor Carruthers gave her permission to publish sections from Sophia Grellier Carruthers's diary as well. This history fired up public imagination. Zoë appeared on Colbert and all the other big shows, sometimes alone, sometimes with the professor. Books, streaming shows, movies, all were in the works by the time I returned to Lawrence.

Pauline Tulloh had made an unexpected investment in the *Herald,* with the proviso that Zoë stay on for a minimum of three years.

Valerie Granev came to Yancy Day, without her daughter or husband. She apologized again for abandoning me to the challenges I'd undergone.

"My daughter's health and safety had to come first," she said. "My husband says I could have figured out how to protect her and stand up publicly for you, but that's easy to say in hindsight."

Sabrina was finally showing signs of recovering from her own brain traumas, Valerie said, which made Valerie all the more certain she'd made the right choices.

I didn't say anything, let silence build, until Valerie said, "Can't you acknowledge my apology, and understand why I had to act as I did?"

I gave a half nod. "I saved your daughter's life and you hung me out for bears to eat, but I acknowledge your apology."

A week after we got home from Kansas, I returned late from the office. As I came up the walk to my building, a man got out of a car parked in front. He was thin and pale, and although he called to me, I didn't recognize him.

"Perhaps you think I don't deserve to be remembered," he said quietly.

"Peter?" I was too dumbfounded to say anything else.

He came up to me. "I have a short story and a long story. Will you let me tell them to you?"

We walked up the street, not speaking, until we found a bench. The sun was setting; the semidark made it easier to talk.

"When I left Chicago—when I left you—I knew you were suffering as much or more than I, but I didn't have the strength to give you the support you needed. I didn't have the strength to get myself through the day, let alone to help someone else. I fled to the place I've always gone when the world around me has been too much—I ran backward, into the past."

"Yes," I said, just to show I understood.

"As you know, ancient Sumer and Syria have made up my professional life. I'm a newcomer to the Phoenicians. I'm useful on a dig because I have decades of experience in examining potential sites. I know careful but efficient ways to approach them. I also have decades of important contacts among people who fund archaeological digs, and among government officials who decide whether we can dig, but I'm a junior member of the Mediterranean group.

"However, I was not a helpful member of the Malaga team. I was still recovering use of my shoulder. Spanish physical therapists have been most helpful in many aspects of my recovery. Especially a Syrian refugee, who was glad to work with someone who could speak her form of Arabic, but that came later." He lifted his arm and moved it in a wide arc; he was recovered, at least physically.

"Yes," I repeated, wondering if he was about to confess an affair, and how I might feel about that.

"I took to driving off down the coast by myself. Very much not a good team player, but the international group cut me a lot of slack. My reputation, you understand, and my years of being director of the Institute—many of them have known me a long time.

"Quite by chance, I found a place some ninety miles away from the main dig that seemed to have a strong Phoenician stamp in the place-names of the nearby hilltop settlements. I began some preliminary explorations on my own. I acted completely out of character, as if I were Lawrence of Arabia, whom I've never admired. But I hired some local people, and we began to dig in what seemed the most promising spot."

He stopped speaking. Sitting next to him in the dark I could smell his sweat, the sickly smell of someone who was afraid. I took his hand, held it gently.

"We found a children's burial site." He spoke in a rush, so quickly I had to strain to follow the words. "Hundreds of small bodies, all buried in a mass grave. There's controversy over the Phoenicians, whether they practiced child sacrifice. I don't know what those small bodies were evidence of, but—they merged with Taylor, with my student, sacrificed by their father. I couldn't face myself, the world, the horror of millennia of parents murdering their children.

"The past where I sought refuge seemed as if it had betrayed me. I fled. I was driving so wildly that I drove over the side of a cliff. My body was flung free, the car crashed to the bottom and was destroyed.

"People who witnessed the crash set up a rescue operation, but I had no identity. My phone and passport had been in the car. After a week or so in a coma, word trickled around about the injured American. My Spanish colleagues came to the hospital in Algeciras where I'd been taken and identified me.

"My recovery was slow, but the therapists, as I said, were splendid. I got a new phone, I saw your texts, I followed what you were doing in Kansas as best I could from your young journalist's reports, and from Murray's, but I felt so much shame I couldn't reach out to you."

"Shame?" I echoed.

"You had been as badly damaged by Taylor's death as I, but you kept on doing what you do well, doggedly looking for some measure of justice in an unjust world. I had fled, and then fled again. How could I face you?"

I thought back to all the months of self-doubt, self-torment, loss of weight, loss of acuity. "I have a long tale of my own, but I won't tell it tonight. I'll give you the short one, instead."

I undid the top three buttons of my shirt, and held out the little figure of Inanna, just visible under the streetlights. "My avatar did not desert me."

Interlude III

13 October 1935

Auburn, New York
To: Mrs. Eleanor Roosevelt
The White House

Dear Mrs. Roosevelt

I do not have enough words, or the right words, to thank you for appearing at the funeral of my mother, Sophia Grellier Carruthers, and for the words you spoke about her. Hers was a strong and dauntless spirit in the cause of Equality for all. Your recognition of her work and her gifts has been the greatest possible consolation to my wife and me.

Yours most truly
Frederic Nathan Carruthers

NOTES AND THANKS

CHICAGO HAS BEEN my home for more than five decades, but I grew up in Lawrence, Kansas, and have a strong attachment to the land of my youth. The land and its history keep speaking to me, drawing me into stories both real and imagined. *Pay Dirt* is the fourth of my novels to be set there.

My family moved to Kansas from upstate New York when I was four. We spent our first nights in the Eldridge Hotel, which had been the headquarters for the antislavery forces in their battles with the slavers who crossed the Kaw and burned down homes and buildings to try to terrorize the abolitionists into leaving the state.

I grew up proud of our antislavery heritage, proud that Kansas came free into the Union in 1861. I grew up ignorant of the fact that well into the twentieth century the town was segregated, that Black students couldn't live in student housing at the University of Kansas where my father taught, that the town had real estate covenants that dictated where Blacks, and Indigenous people, and Jews could own homes. Knowledge of injustices in my home state has come to me slowly.

Pay Dirt was inspired by two books which I read in 2021, *The Agitators,* by Dorothy Wickendon, and *This Is Not Dixie,* by Brent M S Campney. *The Agitators* recounts the friendship and solidarity among three women in the Auburn, New York, area: Harriet Tubman, Martha Coffin Wright, and Frances Seward. The two latter women were white, they were committed both to abolition and to racial equality, and they provided material support to Tubman, who settled in Auburn partly as a result of their support.

This Is Not Dixie tells a very different story, that of active and widespread anti-Black violence in Kansas in the decades after the Civil War, including rape, lynching, forcible seizure of property, and mob action in driving Black residents from various communities.

I had the germ of an idea involving the violent seizure of land from Black settlers in the 1860s and 1870s, and how that might play out in contemporary America. It took me a very long time to figure out the right narrative arc for this story. I started the novel by creating many pages of nineteenth-century diaries and letters among my fictional antislavery families. In the end, I didn't use most of them, which was a sadness, but the right decision for the shape of the book.

Along the way, I incurred many debts.

I have also taken liberties with the Lawrence landscape.

Contrary to popular belief Kansas is not flat. Eastern Kansas has the same rolling hills you see in Ohio or Missouri, and the University of Kansas is spread out across the top of a large high hill—people who work at the university are said to be On the Hill.

Yancy is a fictitious hill on the outskirts of Lawrence, just southeast of the Kaw River.

I have also taken liberties with Lawrence and Douglas County law enforcement.

Lawrence has an outstanding police department, with a true commitment to community and to building coalitions with community social service organizations. I am grateful to Chief Rich Lockhart and his team, Investigations Commander Major Trent McKinley and Deputy Chief Adam Heffley, for taking most of a day to step me through their operations. Thanks, too, to Laura McCabe for making all this happen.

Unfortunately, it is the nature of private eye novels for the PI to be at loggerheads with the police. Every officer mentioned in *Pay Dirt* is a complete fiction and bears no resemblance to anyone at the LKPD. Chief McDowell in particular might be more at home in Chicago than in Lawrence—perhaps that's where he'll appear next.

In practice, because Yancy is outside the Lawrence city limits, the Douglas County sheriff's department should have been investigating crimes there, but involving the sheriff would have meant bringing in another cast of characters; keeping track of them would have ground the story to a halt.

I have a loving connection to the Lawrence Public Library, where I learned to read and where my mother was children's librarian for many years. I'm proud of my hometown for its strong commitment to this library at a time when many public libraries are under attack. This is where V.I. Warshawski finds a home from home in *Pay Dirt*. Thanks to Kathleen Morgan and the library team for suggesting the Osma Room when V.I. needed a place to sequester some of her own documents. Mrs. Osma was the reference librarian when I was growing up. She had a formidable knowledge of the library's resources. She might pretend to consult a card catalog, but it was all in her head.

Angela Wilson gave essential advice on criminal law at the state level. Danielle Cassel spent an afternoon talking me through titles and deeds; I have an uneasy feeling that I may not have followed her advice carefully enough. In addition, the recorder's office in *Pay Dirt* is completely a creation of my own imagination.

Martha Swisher suggested "Il fervido desiderio," which V.I. sings when she and her friends are having a late-night semidrunken songfest.

Kathy Arata Lyndes and Louis Lyndes Arata kindly let me use their surnames for Lou and Ed. I admire the way Kathy and Louis changed their names when they married to entwine their lives with each other.

Tom Laclair helped identify the muscles V.I. injured during the perilous late chapters in the novel.

Federica Caneparo helped me learn the traditional songs Italian mothers, including Gabriella, sing to their children.

Many people provided support and advice during the long process of creating this novel, in particular Erin Mitchell, Jolynn Parker, Marzena Madej, Jonathan Paretsky, Barb Wieser, Jo Anne Willis, Eve Paretsky.

Above all, I owe an enormous debt to Lorraine Brochu. I wrote and discarded seven drafts before arriving at the storyline that makes up the book. Lorraine read them all, with care, with thoughtful comments, and without a complaint. I am most grateful.

Any mistakes in this novel—and there always are some—are down to me, not to the many people who gave so generously of their time and knowledge.

POSTSCRIPT

PAY DIRT IS the twenty-second novel I've written about my private detective, V.I. Warshawski. When she and I started, I didn't imagine such a long career for either of us. My goals with my first novel, *Indemnity Only*, were both simple and grandiose: I wanted to create a woman private eye, and I wanted to change the narrative about women in fiction.

When I began my writing career, U.S. cities were just beginning to admit women to their regular police forces. Up until the early 1980s, women had been on the margins as matrons in women's or juvenile prisons. We had our first U.S. Supreme Court justice the year before *Indemnity Only* came out. Our first women in senior cabinet offices were still in the future.

Crime fiction, indeed, much fiction and a lot of historical writing described women's characters basely on our sexual activity. Women with active sex lives were wicked, trying to get good boys to do bad things. They were properly punished for their efforts. If they were chaste, they were saccharinely virtuous, but so unable to act that they could barely tie their shoes without adult supervision. The exception were nuns, who had a luminous authority. Even Harriet Vane and the combined female intelligences of Shrewsbury College needed Peter Wimsey to rescue them.

The most common role for women in crime fiction was as victim of murder or sexual violence.

V.I. was neither vamp nor victim, but a woman like me and my friends, doing a job that hadn't existed for us when we were growing up. She was cocky, she was resilient, she became a PI because she was convinced she'd be good at the work, and she saw a need for her particular outlook and skills. She also had a sex life that didn't define her moral character: her moral compass was, and is, centered on questions of justice, of voice, of making sure that those whom the world seeks to silence get a hearing.

It took me eight years and a lot of false starts to create V.I. I have never had her self-assurance, even if we share the same sardonic sense of humor, and the same regrettable tendency to leap before we look.

Publishers were cautious: forty turned down that first book, one explaining that a novel set in Chicago had regional interest only, and not enough Midwesterners read to make it worthwhile to publish a book set here. But V.I. found a home at the Dial Press—thanks to Nancy van Itallie, and to Juris Jurjevics, whose passing I mourn.

V.I. also found a home with readers. I'm grateful to those who feel at ease with her particular brand of humor and of stubbornness. I'm grateful to the readers who wanted to read more of V.I.'s adventures.

In the years since that first book came out, the mystery has changed dramatically. Whereas it took a year to find a publisher willing to take a chance on a woman detective, especially one in Chicago, we now have so many novels by women, and novels with women heroes, that I can't keep up with them all. That's a luxury I didn't imagine when I started, when Marcia Muller, Sue Grafton, and Linda Barnes joined me in redefining women in fiction.

V.I. is tougher, braver, and cleverer than me, so much so that she even ages more slowly; she's about fifty to my seventysomething. Even so, the strange world we inhabit these days has taken a toll on her. She is more prone to self-doubt, less cocky. She needs some time off. While I work on a new venture, she'll be recharging, perhaps tracing her family roots in Poland and Italy, or hiking the Canadian Rockies with her dogs. She and I are grateful to all the readers who've followed her on her many adventures; we both promise she'll be back, ready to look danger in the eye and take it on.

ABOUT THE AUTHOR

Hailed by the *Washington Post* as "the definition of perfection in the genre," Sara Paretsky is the *New York Times* bestselling author of twenty-four novels, including the renowned V.I. Warshawski series. She is one of only four living writers to have received both the Grand Master Award from the Mystery Writers of America and the Cartier Diamond Dagger from the Crime Writers Association of Great Britain. She lives in Chicago.